Island in the Sun

by

Charles Carrin

with Dorothy Easley

ENDORSEMENT

"During the years Charles Carrin was my pastor in Atlanta and first shared with me the story, Island in the Sun, I knew immediately this was one of those rare, human dramas God had graciously preserved for all to know. It tells our generation something which it desperately needs to hear—and it tells it powerfully through the hearts and lives of people who lived nearly two centuries ago. These people were real. Their faith was real. The fire that burned through their homes and churches was real. Best of all, the triumph of their trust in a living God was real. I'm convinced the book, Island in the Sun, is a story that has come to stay."

Annie Pye Kurtz, wife of Wilbur G. Kurtz, historian and technical advisor for the movie, Gone with the Wind.

Dedication

I began writing this story many years ago after my grandmother shared with me the account of her father's tragic Civil War past in Florida. Through tears, she revealed a part of family history even my own mother did not know. My grandma explained her long silence. "My father was a Union solider during the Civil War. When I married, I discovered that my father-in-law had been a loyal Confederate. I quickly learned if I wanted peace in my home I had to close the door on that part of my family's past."

What she went on to tell, brought us both to tears. From that moment I began searching for every stream that flowed into Florida's river of historic truth. I visited battlefields, Indian mounds, fortresses, and historical sites. I interviewed families, searched for lost cemeteries, and at least once had a door slammed in my face when my question touched an old, unhealed wound. This story was borne from that compulsive quest.

I knew Grandma was not alone in her secret pain; there were many others whose testimonies paralleled her own. I wanted this book to be about more than my grandmother's family. To better represent Florida's past, I have deliberately fictionalized characters, obscured identities and locations, changed names and chronologies.

I dedicate this book to my grandmother, Dollie Dickinson Blanton, 1882-1977, and to all—white, Seminole, Miccosuki, black—whose ancestry lies buried in Florida's sun kissed soil.

Foreword

Trapped between the fires of the Seminole War and the Civil War were pioneer families whose chief aim was to spend their years in independence and peace in Florida. Their frontier philosophy was, "Give us our guns, and leave us alone." Tragically it was many of these same homesteaders whose blood provided the ink to sign documents of both wars. Their brief interlude between fighting red men in war paint and white men in blue uniforms was less than twenty years. This was a period unique in American history.

The story before you is about James and Dorothy Danbury and their five sons. Four were theirs by birth; the fifth was an adopted black child whom they loved and reared. How that child—unexpectedly and violently thrust into their home—radically changed their lives is told in the story before you. Their farm on the Bellamy Trail near Madison, Florida—their "Island in the Sun"—became a forfeit to the tomahawks and bayonets of war.

To the Seminoles the whites were unwelcome invaders, forcing new rules on the "red man's domain." That enforcement was often done through treachery and abuse. Even so the Florida tribes endured decades of harassment and deceit without open warfare. They genuinely hoped for peace with their opponents; but in the final test, the opponents were unwilling to make peace. In consequence all white settlers, the innocent as well as the despotic, were targeted for the "red man's revenge." The two contenders for the land temporarily parted like rogue waves, awaiting the inevitable moment that slammed them against each other with unspeakable violence.

The names of "Mad Tiger", "Alligator Chief," "Wild Cat," Tiger Tail," "Asi Yoholo," and an endless list of other Miccosuki Nobles would be charred forever into the minds of pioneer whites. Cabins would be burned, families massacred, and yards muddied with blood. Even so settlers poured into the Florida Territory. They came in farm wagons and ox-carts, on horseback or on foot; others grouped covered schooners together in wagon trains, a few arrived in boats. Some came preaching and praying, others came drinking and swearing. But they came. All brought with them a spirit of defiant independence; this self-sufficiency became the only way of life they knew.

The Seminole War began in 1835 and initiated a seven-year period of horrendous tragedy to red and white men alike. U. S. Soldiers quit the field in 1842, the War having never been won and the Seminoles having never surrendered. The Indians were paid two cents an acre for their land. Thousands of men and women wearing leg-irons and heavy chains were crowded into the Tampa Bay stockade and, like cattle, deported on ships to the West. Their crime was loving Florida and defending their homes. Those who escaped—some wives without husbands, some children without parents—fled to the Everglades to reestablish their Nation.

In the brief period of peace that followed, the pioneers found themselves as the unchallenged owners of good land. With that ownership came determination hard as steel. Never again dare anyone try to take Florida from their control. Theirs was a will not to be harassed. But harassment came. And with it the shattering blast of war returned in greater violence than before. The nation divided, North against South, family against family, church against church. In their panic the pioneers seized their muskets anew and leveled the sights on the same government that had earlier deeded them the land. Where Indians had burned farms, white soldiers burned cities. Settlers who had forced red men from their hunting grounds found their roles reversed with themselves now defending the same soil.

Caught like fish in an outgoing tide, many settlers did not know where to commit their allegiance. Some merely fled deeper into the interior and died of privations. Others frantically defended one side against the other and failed. There was but one way out. Only a few found it. These souls heard a "call from above." It was a call to a battle of a different kind, a call of the Spirit. It did not offer escape, but it did promise victory.

In the crossfire of men's frantic emotions, the Danbury's private kingdom became trampled under the bloody feet of invaders. Above the noise of that struggle, they heard "The Call". At the risk of losing each other, their home, and everything they owned, they threw their lives by faith into answering that summons. The tragic price they paid and the spiritual victory they won is before you.

With the Danburys, come back to Madison, their island in the sun.

Prologue

The red and yellow Spanish flag snapped in the wind against a bright Florida sky as it received a final, tearful salute. Governor Jose Callava, representing the Spanish Crown, exhaled nervously as he glanced at the somber crowd. Behind a line of elegantly dressed soldiers, half-a-dozen black-robed priests clutched rosaries and prayed quietly. Elderly ladies with black veils blowing in the wind dropped to their knees and made the Sign of the Cross. A shadow of sorrow fell across Callava's face as the banner slowly descended, then hung limply near the bottom of the pole.

On the other side of the mast flanked by a row of sun-tanned American soldiers, General Andrew Jackson gave the order to hoist the Stars and Stripes. It rose to the jubilant, brassy notes of the nation's new anthem, "The Star Spangled Banner," ringing from a military band and echoing across the palm-lined Pensacola Plaza. From the harbor the USS Hornet boomed a twenty-one cannon salute as a wild, drum-rolling cheer rose from the American troops.

At least one member of Jackson's troop fully comprehended the historic magic of the moment that July day in 1821. He was a lithe, twenty-two year old private, blue-eyed with honey-colored hair, from Massachusetts. He saw much more than soldiers and sea gulls. After others broke rank, he stood transfixed. He gazed at the pole's new flag smiling proudly. In that moment it seemed as if every inch of Florida's fifty-four thousand square miles was his own. Best of all, he had shared in the ceremony that pried it loose from a European power. America had given birth to a new child—Florida!

Someday he would tell his grandchildren about standing at the very spot where the state was born, about how close he was to its first Territorial Governor, General Jackson. He would never forget Jose Callava's face when the Spanish soldiers ceremoniously presented him the folded imperial flag. The memory of those elderly women weeping into their veils would be engraved forever in his mind.

Standing there, wind whipping his uniform, breathing the fresh sting of salt air, he was totally absorbed in anticipation. There was a new fragrance of freedom in the breeze, the smell of challenge and excitement. He closed his eyes. Somewhere under that blue Florida sky he envisioned a clearing with a log cabin, barns, a smoke house, pastures, and shade trees clustered about it. The soil was rich, the garden green. Best of all, he could see children and a wife playing in the yard. He heard music, laughter, sounds of happiness. That piece of Florida would be his own private island—his island in the sun. Somewhere deep inside, a Voice told him it would come to pass; it was as certain as the flag cracking in the wind overhead.

But unknown to the solider, dark clouds were already gathering. According to Spain's treaty with the United States, Native Americans in Florida were entitled to the same protection and benefits as white citizens. The soldier did not know that his government's refusal to honor that provision—like a storm hidden beyond the horizon—would strike his dream with terrifying violence. Nor did he know that four hundred miles away another violation was taking place that would add to his challenge. A young black man his same age was being goaded onto the auction block at the Charleston, South Carolina slave market. Dressed only with a rag tied around his waist, his body shining with sweat, he stared fearfully at the band of rough-looking buyers before him.

The soldier knew nothing of these two violations nor how each would demand retribution from his dream. Instead, standing there in the beauty of the Pensacola Plaza, he felt only a wonderful connection to earth, to Heaven, to all that was grand and holy. It was a moment of magnificence.

Someday, when his military duty was over, he would come back to Florida. He knew that. Someday! Someday!

Chapter One

A bolt of lightning flashed with a frying sound directly above the old man`s buggy. It shattered a tree on the creek bank in front of him. The explosion of orange light against the night was blinding. His horse, knee-deep in the stream, reared into the air, tottering as if she would fall sideways.

"Hold on! Drusilla!" he shouted. "Hold on!" Debris tangled about her legs as she fought for secure standing on the rocks. "Hold on!" he yelled again as another blast of fire rattled the darkness and shook the forest.

Bracing himself into a half-standing position, he gripped the reins with one hand and tried frantically with the other to protect a large leather-wrapped bundle on the seat beside him. At mid-stream the buggy shook violently and skidded sideways, sinking its right rear wheel into a crevice.

"Pull! Drusilla! We're gonna make it!" the man shouted as he slapped her with the reins. "By God's help, we've *got* to make it!

The horse strained against the surge, and with a desperate lunge, pulled the wheel free. A moment later they were on the bank.

"Thank You, Lord!" he wept aloud. "You got us through—now get us the rest of the way."

Ahead of him a path led off into a jungle of trees. Vines hung from oak limbs. Ferns and a tangle of thick underbrush covered the forest floor. The trail was a shortcut leading to a farmhouse a quarter mile away. The constant flash of electricity provided his only light until, finally, the yellow glow of a lamp shone through the forest. The horse quickened her pace toward the lighted window.

Stopping a short distance from the house, the old man sat unmoving. He seemed powerless to go further even though rain pounded in driving torrents. Ordinarily the scene of the giant live oak stretching over the home had a beauty that warmed his heart. Not so tonight. The worst part of the storm would erupt when he got inside. He closed his eyes as if trying to draw strength for what lay before him.

Pulling the buggy closer to the steps, he sprang to the ground. He splashed through the mud to the other side, carefully picking up the leather-wrapped bundle. He ran his hand inside the tarpaulin; it too was soaked.

"God help!" he groaned and bent over the form to protect it from the rain. "James!" he hollered, rushing toward the door. "James! Dorothy! Open up!"

A second later the door jerked wide. A tall, lean young man stood in the entrance staring bewilderedly. The old one darted into the cabin and dropped onto the hearth. Throwing back the leather tarp, he exposed the unconscious form of a small black boy.

"Jethro!" the couple exclaimed aloud. "That's Jethro! Brother Blanton, what happened? Where did you find him?"

"I've just walked through Hell!" he yelled sobbing. "Through Hell! There's been a massacre at the Hadley place. Jethro's all that's left! The Miccosukis killed everybody!"

"A massacre? At the Hadleys?"

"Yes! The Hadleys!" he yelled again, thrusting the child into Dorothy's arms and leaping to his feet. "All of them! Ain't nobody left!" He shook his fist, "Hell couldn't be worse!"

"God! No!" Dorothy cried. "God, No! Not the Hadleys! Not Isobel and Matt!"

"Every single one of them," Brother Blanton wailed. "Little Jimmy, Sandra Dee, every one of 'em, butchered in their own yard. Jethro's mama and papa are gone, carried off by the Seminoles— would've gotten him too if he hadn't hid in the chicken coop."

Paralyzing grief settled upon the cabin. Overhead three young faces, wide-eyed with fear appeared at the slats of the loft. Eight-year-old George was the same age as the child Dorothy held close to the fire. Edward was seven, and Franklin was only six. Two-year old Joseph, thankfully, was still asleep.

A moment later James rose from the hearth. He dropped a heavy log bolt against the door, closed the shutters, and took down his gun. There was nothing else to do. He had prayed, as had the Hadleys, for God to bring peace to the Florida wilderness. That had not happened. The drums of war were now beating as closely as the pounding inside his chest. James' heart was racing, calling on God for answers.

Matt Hadley had been a wonderful friend. James couldn't believe it! Not Matt! Not Isobel and their beautiful children!

Looking up to the loft, he spoke to the boys, "We're O.K. Don't worry about nothing. God will take care of us."

But his words mocked him; they were empty and unreal. He had no more assurance for his family than Matt had had for his. More than anything, he wanted his family to know they were protected. But how could they? Madison would never be the same! Nor would Blue Springs Church. Nothing would be the same. Nothing!

He let out a long, wrenching sob. Jethro's mama and papa loved their boy as much as he and Dorothy loved theirs. But where were they? Heaven only knew, and Heaven didn't seem to be doing anything about it. He turned toward the door and slammed both fists against it.

"God, where are you?" he wept. "Where are you?"

Brother Blanton gulped down a mouthful of coffee. He took off his wet clothes, wrapped himself in a blanket, and collapsed across a bed in the corner of the large, open room.

James went to the loft where George was sobbing. Dorothy could hear the child asking "But, why? Papa, why! The Hadleys ain't done *nothing* to make the Indians mad at them!"

There was louder sobbing, then wailing from all three children. James quit trying to explain and started praying.

Dorothy looked pityingly at Brother Blanton. That dear pastor! She knew he hadn't had food in days. Her guess was that Jethro had been without food even longer. Holding the child closer to the fire she pulled off his wet clothes and wrapped him in warm blankets. She tried to get sips of beef broth and liquor between his lips. Rocking back and forth she pressed him against her breast and wept. Every motherly instinct in her welled up for him, and every thought of Miccosukis filled her with unspeakable fear.

The child swallowed the broth only twice. Once his eyelids parted slightly then closed again. He was afraid to open them, afraid of what he would see, afraid that the massacre was still happening. The memory of what he had seen might never go away. But Dorothy would never turn loose of Jethro. Never! With God's help, she, James, their boys, would heal his wounds. They would do that for Jethro's parents, for Matt, and for Isobel. God had put this child in their arms; only God could ever take him away. She did not care how others might react to her and James rearing a black boy along with their own boys. That did not matter. Nothing would come between her, James, and God's plan for their family.

A moment later James came down from the loft holding Edward. He placed him on the bed opposite Brother Blanton. Twice more he made trips up the steps. Finally everyone was on the lower floor. Dorothy was glad they were together; somehow, she felt more secure. Outside the storm slammed against the house. There were noises she had never heard before, frightening sounds. Each of them flashed dark forms of Indians in war paint sneaking toward them. She prayed the storm would keep the Seminoles far to the south.

Brother Blanton's breathing was erratic and troubled with occasional low groans. His body was restless and tense. James lay across the end of their bed stroking the boys and speaking softly as they drifted back to sleep. George's body twitched with a tormenting dream. Finally everyone was quiet. Even the storm lessened.

Dorothy was thankful for the silence. In the quiet, the memory of a special Sunday at Blue Springs Church came to mind. It was the previous spring when the newcomers, Matt and Isobel Hadley, made their first trip from their home on the Fenholloway River. Jethro and his parents were with them. Matt was a naturalist identifying plants and making sketches for a university in Maryland. Isobel's father, a doctor in Charleston, had given them the black family before they left for Florida.

That day at Blue Springs, everyone shared dinners in the backs of their wagons. Over the meal, conversation centered on Major John Phagan, Federal Agent to the Seminoles, who had succeeded in getting a new agreement with the Indians. After dinner while the men continued the subject of the treaty at Payne's Landing on the Oklawaha River, the women found a private spot to talk about gardens, children, and quilting.

On that Sunday Brother Blanton baptized Gilbert and Odessa Mallory in the spring north of the church. Afterward everyone walked downstream to the confluence of the stream and the Oithlacoochee River. From there they returned to the pine log meeting house for an hour of singing. It was then Dorothy saw Jethro standing alone in the Hadley's wagon. He was a handsome child with a bright countenance she had not seen in a slave child before.

Now sitting with him on the hearth, cradled in her arms, that memory came rushing back. It was almost as if she had foreknown that God had a mission for his life—a mission that involved her and James. Looking down, the proof seemed written across that small, sunken face. He was so innocent, so helpless, and now, except for her and James, so totally alone.

During the predawn hours, the rain stopped, and everything became still. Even Dorothy was asleep, leaning against the hearth with Jethro still cradled in her arms.

At daybreak, their rooster Bartholomew crowed loudly from the water shelf on the back porch. Dorothy sat up with a start and glanced about the room. Brother Blanton sprang to his feet and grabbed his clothes from the drying rack near the fireplace. Devouring a piece of ham, he ran outside and unhitched the horse from the buggy. He threw the saddle over her, and shoving biscuits into the side-pockets, galloped out of the yard. His destination was the Blockhouse at Madison. Dorothy followed him to the cattle gap and watched him disappear down the lane.

A sunrise, pink and golden, began lighting the most beautiful sky she had ever seen. The world seemed unaware of the anguish in the cabin. She lingered, staring for a long time toward the distant bend in the lane. It was impossible for Matt, Isobel, and their two children, to be dead. Surely Jethro, half-conscious and traumatized, was not really curled up, twitching in her bed. If these things were so, the land would be weeping. The sky would be dark. But it wasn't. Nature acted as if nothing had happened. The contradiction was baffling.

She closed her eyes, hoping that when she opened them again the nightmare of the Hadleys' death would vanish like a forgotten dream.

Chapter Two

Dorothy sat motionless on a log, peering toward the bend where Brother Blanton had disappeared. All the important events of her life seemed to have come through that beautiful, tree-covered path. It had witnessed her greatest joys and sorrows. Mama, Papa, her brother Tom, and she had come down it that sparkling April morning she and James were married. Others had ridden it, bringing news of happiness and disaster. U.S. soldiers, Florida militia men, and Dr. Thad had all come through that tunnel of trees hundreds of times to their cabin.

The memory of her wedding was just as real now as the day it happened. She and James stood under the oak where the porch steps now stood. In her mind she could still hear Brother Blanton asking, "Will you, Dorothy Hapsburg, take this man, James Murray Danbury to be your lawfully wedded husband? Will you obey him, love, honor, and serve him until death divides you?"

"I will." She remembered how she gripped her cluster of daisies when those magic words came from her lips.

The pastor's wife, red-haired and sunburned Effie Blanton, caught Dorothy's eye and smiled approvingly. Effie had made the wedding dress; and it was perfect, white with a pink ribbon decorating the hemline and the neck. A large bow of the same pink was pinned on the left side of the bonnet. There wasn't another dress in Madison County as pretty as this one.

Effie's gaze lovingly studied the girl. Dorothy was well suited for life on the Florida frontier; she was energetic and strong but with a delicate beauty that would please any man. She knew how to laugh and have fun. Like her mother Malida Hapsburg, Dorothy was blessed with a lily-smooth complexion and thick, black eyelashes. And like her father Henry, she could be as determined as a mule. That was a quality she would need.

Effie's eyes moved to the groom who was nervously pressing his heels into the sand. Such a good looking man! His Scotch ancestry showed clearest in his blue eyes and heavy eyebrows; but best of all, his military career with General Jackson had taught him discipline. Dorothy was marrying a man who was strong as an ax handle with not an ounce of fat on him. Effie admired his well-trimmed mustache and wide smile. "What beautiful children they will have," she thought. James sensed Effie's stare, and squaring his shoulders nervously, moved closer to Dorothy. Slipping his hand around hers, he gave it a squeeze. Like an unfed yearling he hungered for her.

"James," the preacher spoke. "God took the woman from the man's side, beneath his arm and nearest his heart; and that," he emphasized, "is where she is supposed to remain, at his side! She is not above him, nor below him. Rather she stands with him."

He turned toward the witnesses, "If any of you knows any reason why these two ought not to be married, let's hear it now, or forever be quiet about it."

He waited as if expecting a reply. Not a breath was heard. His wife flashed a disapproving glare at him for daring to ask such a question. Everybody in Madison knew this couple's purity.

Closing his Bible abruptly, Pastor Blanton announced with a more official air, "By the authority vested in me by the United States Government, the Territory of Florida, and the God of Heaven, I pronounce that on this third day of April 1833, these two, James Murray Danbury and Dorothy Hapsburg, are man and wife! What God has joined together, let no man put asunder!"

Dorothy's father hurried toward James. "Son!" he spoke loudly, "there ain't no way to untie that knot! Sure as there's a God in Glory, you got her!" He gave James a vigorous hand shake. "And any man smart enough to marry a `Hapsburg' is bound to be a powerful smart man!"

James agreed with his new father-in-law, smiled, and pulled Dorothy aside. "It's my turn!" he said, leading her to the opposite side of the tree and hugging her tightly. "That part about you being taken from 'under my arm, nearest my heart' is exactly how I feel. For the first time in my life I feel whole, Dorothy, complete, like I've just found something that was always missing." He kissed her, "I never knew I could love anybody like I love you. I didn't know it was possible to feel this way, but I do!" He kissed her again, "You're the most wonderful thing that ever happened to me!"

"Son!" Dorothy's father interrupted again. "Come to my wagon and let me show you what I'm taking down to the Oklawaha!"

The two men left Dorothy with a group of ladies. As they walked away, Dorothy's brother Tom approached her, holding back his tears.

"Can we talk a minute," he asked, pointing in the direction of a fallen tree, "private, I mean?" There was a note of desperation in his voice.

"Of course, we can," Dorothy answered, taking his hand. "Let's step to the lane." Tom was fifteen and tall, his voice losing its boyish sound and his features transposing into those of a man. He had inherited his mother's well-proportioned face and his father's slight build. She studied his expression carefully, "You're really worried about going to the Ocala territory, aren't you, Tom?"

He waited a moment, "It's such a long way to the Oklawaha, Dorothy, more than a hundred miles!" Tom looked directly at her, "Dorothy, there's not another man on this place fool enough to do what he's making us do."

"I wouldn't say that he's a fool, Tom." She wished he had not used that word. It was a truth she wanted to ignore.

"No, you wouldn't call him a fool, Dorothy, but I will! There's not a bit of sense in it! We could homestead land right here close to you and James." He pointed toward the bend in the lane, "There's a good place a quarter-mile east of here, the soil is rich; it's got a good spot to build a pond." He dropped his hands. "Anywhere but down there! There ain't half a dozen white families on that whole danged river, Dorothy. It's the most dangerous place in Florida! And he calls it the 'Garden of Eden'."

Dorothy raised his face toward hers. "Would it do any good for me to talk to him again?"

"Not unless you want to ruin your wedding day," Tom answered. "The only reason Papa chose your wedding was so he would have a bigger audience to brag to. We have as much chance of changing his mind as taming a panther."

When they returned to the oak, a group of ladies had gathered around Mrs. Hapsburg. Dorothy's mother was a large, warm-hearted woman who never lacked for an audience. "Honey, I am as excited as Henry about moving down there on that river," she said to one of the younger women. "I hear tell it is just like the 'Garden of Eden!'" she said raising both hands as she spoke the word "Garden".

Tom gave his sister a defeated stare. It seemed hopeless to say anything.

Angry voices suddenly directed her attention toward the cabin site. Harlow Bentley and three other men were arguing loudly with her father. "You're a fool, Henry!" Harlow burst out. "A straight out fool!"

Henry snatched the cigar from his mouth. "What you mean is that I ain't a coward like the rest of you lily livers! I know there's Indians down there, and I also know that the best regiment in the whole United States Army is stationed right there at Fort King!"

Harlow gave him a censuring stare and began walking away. Henry tried to stop him. "Wait just a minute, Harlow!" he yelled. "Let's get this straight! I'm taking my wife and son down there because I want them to have the best. I ain't riskin' their lives! In the whole territory of Florida there ain't no better place to be."

Harlow ignored him and kept walking.

Angered, Henry persisted. "Ask Dr. Thad's son-in-law, Terrance Browning. He's a Lieutenant down there at the Fort! There ain't a better climate anywhere. There's wild oranges big as water dippers and Spanish cattle running loose as jay birds. All you got to do is claim 'em!"

Harlow stopped, spun around, and yelled back. "The Miccosukis are thicker than the seeds in those wild oranges you're so eager to pick. And they ain't letting nobody run off with their cattle."

"You think they're taking those cows to the Arkansas Reservation?!"

"Hell, no! Because they ain't going either," Harlow's face was red. "There'll be Indians in Florida a hundred years from now!"

"If you know so dang much about what the Seminoles are going to do, why don't you tell Governor DuVal or President Jackson!" Henry retorted. "It'd sure save the government a lot of money if they'd just ask you first!"

Harlow's eyes narrowed, he started to speak, but kept on walking.

Henry went on, "The Indians ain't fools. They know our Army has them overpowered." He looked around for approval from the other faces but found none. Undaunted he continued, "Anyway there ain't a Indian this side of the Caloosahatchee River that I'm feared of!"

If Dorothy's mother felt embarrassment at her husband's loud mouth, she never showed it. Her expression remained fixed, smiling, as if she had complete confidence in everything Henry said.

"No matter where we go," she whispered to the other ladies, "the good Lord has to take care of us. He can do that down there on the Oklawaha the same as He can here at the Blockhouse in Madison."

An uncomfortable silence fell. The group broke apart, and Dorothy's mother followed Dr. Thad to the food wagon. Dorothy approached them, stopping a short distance away. The man's voice was high-pitched and irritating; he reminded Dorothy of a nervous little bird. Even Mama's laughter could not overpower the doctor's shrill, annoying sound.

Mama was talking as excitedly as Dr. Thad. As Dorothy stepped near, Mama reached out, enfolding the girl in a bosomy hug. Dorothy took her mother's hand and led her to the edge of the clearing. She pleaded, "Mama, will it do any good to ask again? Do you have to do everything Papa says?!"

"No, Honey!" her mother interrupted quickly. "It won't do a bit of good to ask again! Your Pa's heart is fixed on going, has been for a long time."

Dorothy blinked back her tears.

"Sugar!" Malida consoled, "We're gonna' be just fine! The good Lord's gonna' take care of us! And Fort King and Fort Brooke are both close enough we can choose which one we wanna run to!"

Dorothy knew better. The forts were a hundred miles apart. But Mrs. Hapsburg did not wait for a different opinion. Instead she threw one arm tightly around her daughter and squeezed. With the other, she pressed Dorothy's face against her own. "Nobody's ever had a sweeter daughter than your Pa and me, and I couldn't leave if it weren't for that good man over there." She looked at James as she spoke. "He's gonna' take much better care of you than I *ever* have! Just watch. You'll see."

She pushed Dorothy back to arm's length, "Twenty-five years from now you won't be willing to leave him any more than I'm willing to leave your Pa. You'll go wherever James goes, regardless!" Again, she pulled the girl close, squeezed her tightly and kissed her cheek.

Dorothy pushed back. "Mama," she scolded, "you always win your arguments by hugging and kissing. That's not fair!"

"Sugar!" Mama laughed, "Anytime you can win a argument by lovin', that makes it fair." Patting Dorothy on both cheeks, she ran her fingers across the girl's temples and down her hair, "And don't you never forget it!"

"It may work with me, Mama, but it won't do any good with the Seminoles. You and Papa are taking poor Tom almost into the Reservation!"

Mama wiped back the tears and became very solemn. It was an expression Dorothy had rarely seen on her mother's face. "As you grow older, Sugar," she spoke softly, "you'll find that there are a lot of things in life that don't make sense. The day I married your Pa, my mama took to bed and said I ruined my life. To her it didn't make no sense. She said your pa was a `traipsing' man, and she was right. But I soon learned to traipse with him, and that's what I've been doin' ever since."

The woman hesitated as if pained by a memory, "But I learned something that my mama never knew, Sugar. I learned how to love a man! There ain't nothing more important, Nothing! Mama only wanted a `provider', not a mate. And that's all she ever got.

I decided I'd rather have a mate even if he didn't provide me with nothin' else but his love. And to this day, you've never heard me complain about your Pa."

She raised Dorothy's chin and held it firmly while she continued, "If he were to tell me we were going down to the saw grass swamp at Lake Okeechobee and die of Yellow Fever, I'd clap my hands, jus' like it's what I always wanted to do!" The woman's eyes were intense, "There ain't no stopping me, Sugar, no way, so don't even try." She paused a moment and then continued, "I love you and Tom, Honey, but I love your Pa in a different way." Reluctantly Dorothy nodded in agreement. "Someday you'll understand."

Mrs. Hapsburg pulled a handkerchief from the bosom of her dress. "Don't let folks see you crying on your wedding day, Sugar. It ain't proper."

By noon the walls of the house were halfway up. After lunch the men rested under the tree. Henry pulled their wagon closer to the house and began reciting his travel plans for the hundredth time. "By tomorrow night we'll be at Charles Ferry Crossing on the Suwanee River," he explained. "We'll camp there for several days until more wagons arrive that'll make up our train. And then we'll head south. Soldiers from Fort Atkinson will escort us as far as the Micanopy Trail, and then we'll be on our own. It's all that simple." Or so he made it sound.

Harlow walked around the wagon, studying its bulging sides disapprovingly and shaking his head. Weeping women clustered about Malida, hugging her tightly and smothering her in farewell kisses. It was the kind of send off Henry wanted.

Tom had already disappeared. He told James and Dorothy goodby privately and started walking toward the Bellamy Trail. He didn't want anyone to see him cry. Malida climbed into the wagon and pushed cushions around her back and hips. She sat as erect as an attendant in the Queen's Court. The team of two horses—an old pinto and a tan mare with a brown patch on her face—begrudgingly began to move. The wagon jolted forward as Henry slapped them with the reins. Dorothy seized her mother's hand and ran alongside.

"Remember everything I told you, Sugar," the woman whispered. "Love that James with everything you've got! That's what you promised God you'd do. Now do it!"

Dorothy gripped the woman's fingers with a frantic hold as she quickened her pace beside the wagon. When their hands parted, it was a pain unlike anything she had ever known. In one swift moment all her childhood security was ripped away; in that second she was forced into womanhood.

"Mama!" she cried. It all seemed like a dream flashing strangely from joy to sorrow, happiness to terror. If Mama, Papa, and Tom were going back to Richmond, it would be different. But they were heading into the Ocala wilderness. Standing statuesque in the middle of the lane with everyone else at her back, Dorothy looked longingly at the wagon lumbering away into the canopy of trees.

She was still standing in the lane, staring at the spot where the wagon disappeared, when an arm reached firmly around her. It was James. The grip was reassuring. Somehow it confirmed what mama had said, "There ain't nothing more important—nothing—than lovin' your man!"

Finally the two turned and walked back to the cabin where walls were rising. Teams of men worked to the square dance rhythm of Dr. Thad's banjo. Logs were notched to the lively cadence, and squads of four men took turns lifting them into place. The soldiers had stripped to the waist and were rolling timber to the notchers. Some of the women and a few of the older men were singing and clapping to the music. Others were busy at the food wagon where a large pot of stew simmered on the fire. From the grove of palm trees where the barn site had been cleared, the happy sounds of frolicking children pierced the air. Even Dorothy felt a surge of joy return.

She and James walked together to the edge of the garden where Pastor Blanton and Jeremiah were digging a well. James pulled off his shirt to help while Dorothy continued walking westward. A fence would later separate this site from the pasture. In the distance she could see the dark wall of cypress in the Stilippica Swamp wrapping around the south and west sides of their farm. The Gulf of Mexico was forty miles away. On the north the land was covered with pines and huge live oaks. She paused, looking toward the northwest, the direction of the territorial outpost of Madison. The town ten miles away consisted of a few houses, a small stockade, and the Blockhouse. While the protection of the militia was something they hoped never to need, it was still their first consideration in everything they did.

Between Dorothy and the swamp were mounds of burning pine logs sending columns of white smoke into the clear Florida sky. The field looked stripped, naked, like it had been wounded and left to die. It was hard to imagine cow pastures, rows of corn, beans, cotton, and open meadows replacing the scene of mutilation that lay before her.

A high-pitched cry overhead attracted her attention. Looking up she saw a large Red-shouldered Hawk darting frantically over the field. Her nest lay in ruins in the burning piles. The invaders below brought a message of disaster to the quiet Florida wilderness. The hawk was not the only one watching. Farther to the south, angry Miccosuki eyes saw the columns of smoke rising from their land. Unlike the hawk, they would not be mere observers to this intrusion.

Dorothy stood facing the west, wrapped in deep thought. As her eyes wandered across their homestead, she understood the Seminole's love for Florida. There was a drawing to the land she could not explain. It was as if a spiritual umbilical cord connected her to the soil, the trees, everything around her. This was where she belonged. Somehow the earth was trying to tell her that it also loved her, needed her, wanted her there. Perhaps it was this same feeling that drove Papa deeper into Florida's interior. For a moment she almost understood him.

Everyone in Florida had heard tales of the Oklawaha River's haunting beauty. Its banks overhung with palms, crystal clear water, giant fish that could be seen at a depth of twenty feet. But the Seminoles love for the ground and the river went far beyond a need for food or campsites. They believed the river to be sacred. For hundreds of generations the ashes of their ancestors had mixed with the soil, giving them a spiritual bonding that White Men could neither duplicate nor understand. It seemed strange to Dorothy that the Chiefs had actually signed Major Phagan's Treaty at Payne's Landing. But they had. And they agreed to begin migration within three years.

Chief Tuckose E'Mathala was already disposing of his cattle in preparation to leave. He, with other Seminole nobles, had traveled with Major Phagan to see their new home in the Arkansas Territory. Dorothy knew those facts well. Fort Brooke on Tampa Bay was designated as their departure point. From there the Indians would be transported by ship to the Mississippi River, then northward to the new reservation. Papa's claims were not without foundation, but she feared there were cracks in that foundation. If only there were some way that Indians and Whites could jointly share the land. How blessed that would be! Florida was huge. Surely there was room for all.

By mid-afternoon the cabin's walls were raised to their full height and the roof was covered. Though the singing died away in the afternoon, the men continued working with the same unbroken rhythm. James was busy with every aspect of the cabin's construction but still managed to include short visits with Dorothy. "It's going to be just like we planned," he told her, "big enough for the two of us and all our children. We're putting the kitchen window where you can see the barn."

The house faced the east looking toward the lane. When completed, it would have two large rooms downstairs and two loft rooms overhead. For the present, they were leaving the downstairs open as one large room. Dorothy stepped across the front porch and into the building. The fragrance of pine resin was an odor she enjoyed, and this house would have it for a long time. She moved to the south end of the building where the fireplace was under construction. All her cooking would be done here on the hearth; their dinning table and her kitchen shelves would be in the right-hand corner of the room. The stairway to the loft, made of two notched logs with board steps, rose between the back door and the southwest corner of the cabin. Holding to the handrail, she made her way up to the low-hung room. The flooring was in place and the roof finished on this end of the building. In the corner where they would sleep, someone had spread a quilt over a deep bed of corn shucks. This would be their mattress. The room had a cozy feeling; its only light came through the shotgun hole in the gable. It felt private. She inhaled deeply; the room smelled like the rich, green forest of Florida.

By late afternoon the roof was complete, its wide split board shingles ran the full width of the building. To Dorothy that transformed its appearance into that of a real home. Though the windows had no shutters and the cracks between the logs were yet to be chinked, it was their home. Their very own home!

When the men finally put away their tools, the women brought wedding gifts from the wagons. Hams, meal, quilts, dried fruit, vegetables, and furniture. A table and two benches were placed near the back door with fresh baked cakes and pies on them. Harlow Bentley was the last to bring a gift as he approached James and Dorothy on the front steps. "This is from Tom," he explained, placing a heavy item in their hands. "He asked me to give it to you."

Dorothy took the gift and hurriedly removed the brown paper twisted around it. "An iron fire poker!" she exclaimed as she held it up for everyone to see. "How sweet of him! I will always cherish it."

"He also sent a message," Harlow explained as he unfolded a small piece of paper and handed it to them. James read it aloud, recognizing the words from Scripture. It read, "The Lord watch between me and thee while we are absent one from the other." Dorothy took it, blinking back her tears as she silently read it again, and then slipped it carefully into the bosom of her dress.

Harlow walked to the edge of the porch, clapped his hands loudly and yelled, "We're goin' to give this couple the best gift of all! We're goin' home!" Everyone laughed and rushed forward for goodbye hugs. Effie hugged her in a long, motherly embrace and kissed her on the cheek. Gilbert and Odessa Mallory, just a few years older than James and Dorothy, were the last to leave.

"'Til my baby comes, I'm too heavy for light work and too light for heavy work," Odessa laughed. "And that don't leave nothing else!" James observed Odessa's lumbering movements as Gilbert waited at the bottom step. She was square from shoulders to hips, had no waist, and her legs were thin as corn stalks. A tightly twisted bun of hair on the back of her head completed the picture. James stepped ahead of her, taking her hand as she came down the steps. "I've been telling the Lord," she laughed, holding tightly to both men, "a woman with a house full of babies needs more than one man to help."

As the people climbed into their wagons, James stepped to the middle of the yard and thanked them. "You're all wonderful! Dorothy and I plan to live in this house the rest of our lives—however long God wills—and we will always remember today and everything you did for us. Thank you! God bless you!"

Pastor Blanton called from his saddle, "It's your blessing to live in that house, James; it was our blessing to build." With that he spurred his horse and galloped out of the yard. Mrs. Blanton was riding back to Madison in Marshall Townsend's buggy.

James and Dorothy stood in the yard looking at their cabin, "Our own private kingdom," he whispered.

The exhilaration of the day kept them from being tired; it seemed too wonderful to be real. They had each other and a home that smelled like the Florida forest. A warm glow of happiness descended on them as gently as the darkness falling on the countryside. In the distance a Whip-poor-will called from the swamp. James picked up Dorothy in his arms and started up the stairs. Carefully he made his way to the top, carried her to the pallet in the corner of the loft, and laid her down.

Moonlight shone through the cracks, creating streaks of light on the floor. From the branches of the oak, a thousand Katydids chorused together. It was a beautiful scene, and there, wrapped in the dark night of the wilderness, God took two lives, welded them to each other and to Himself.

Chapter Three

S treaks of early morning light shone through cracks in the cabin. Downstairs a moist breeze blew into the room. James stirred, and the corn shucks made a rustling sound as he turned toward Dorothy. "Wake up, Mrs. Danbury, to the best day of your life," he whispered in her ear.

Dorothy sat straight up, a piece of corn shuck hanging from her hair. It took a moment to put all the exciting parts together. This was her home. She was married! She lay back down, enjoying the fresh scent of morning. She was really married. James was her husband. Glorious!

James slid his arm under her and squeezed, "Have I ever told you when I first fell in love with you?" he asked. "It was before you stepped out of the wagon in Madison."

"Before I arrived in Madison?"

"In my heart I saw you, this farm, our family, that day with General Jackson in Pensacola when we raised our flag over Florida," he explained. "In my heart I saw you. Then when you stepped from your family's wagon at the Madison Square, something in me shouted, `Yes, Yes! She's the one!' You were the most beautiful girl I had ever seen." He pulled her closer to him, "You're all I've ever wanted, and more. Thank God, I found you!"

Dorothy was the first to climb downstairs. She felt like a child on Christmas morning. Strings of sausage, hams, onions, dried peppers, pots and pans, hung from the walls and rafters. Stalks of sugar cane stood in the corner. The sight of James' shoes at the door sent a shiver through her. A moment later James came down, held her in his arms, and kissed her. "I'll be right back," he explained, taking the fire tongs and heading to the log pile burning at the edge of the field. With one live coal, he started a fire in the hearth.

Dorothy dropped a thick slice of ham into a skillet, and within minutes the cabin was filled with the rich aroma of sizzling meat. James stood over the hearth, and Dorothy leaned against him, watching a whiff of smoke drifting toward the door. She felt the same kind of light-heartedness inside herself as the steam.

At breakfast he reminded her, "Governor DuVal is speaking at the Square in Madison today. I want to show off my new bride. What do you think?"

"Oh, I'd love to go," she answered. "I want to see what the ladies from Tallahassee are wearing."

Two hours later James pulled their wagon under the live oaks at the square. Stopping the horse, he looked around at the crowd. "What a mob of people!" he exclaimed.

Wagons, horses, buggies, and people jammed the area beneath the oaks. A thin vapor of dust filled the air. The speaker's platform was decorated with the United States flag and Florida's new state flag. Streamers of red, white, and blue fabric hung from the trees.

Madison Square was nothing more than a cleared area under the grove of huge oaks next to the blockhouse with a watering trough, hitching rail, and several dozen board benches. For today's official visit, a stage had been built on the north end. James tied the reins and helped Dorothy down from the wagon. Holding hands, they walked toward the podium where a crowd was gathering.

"Just look at the people," Dorothy exclaimed. "I had no idea there were this many people in the whole state." Her eyes moved across the crowd. She spotted several men in top hats with wives in satin dresses. "I've never seen such frilly bonnets and parasols in my life, James! I wonder how they pay for fancy clothes like that," Dorothy whispered.

"Most of these folks are from Tallahassee, maybe a few from Washington. See the one at the end, shaking hands. That's Governor DuVal."

Dorothy's eyes lingered on the man. He was short with a pumpkin-round face, and he seemed almost boyish when he laughed. But he laughed often with a joy that forced her to like him.

"Maybe he'll decide this is a good place and stay home a while. He's been gone so much that he doesn't really know what's happening in Florida."

James spotted Major John Phagan, Federal Agent to the Seminoles. "He's down at Fort King much of the time. You ought to tell him your folks are on their way to the river."

Dorothy nodded, but her eyes were on a slender, attractively dressed woman standing on the left of the speaker's platform. She appeared to be a few years older than Dorothy's age. The woman was not from Madison, but neither did she seem to be familiar with the other ladies in the crowd. Her dress was tailored, in better taste, Dorothy thought, than most of the wives of the government officials.

Dorothy made her way through the people, extending her hand to the woman. "I'm Dorothy . . . Dorothy Danbury."

"My name is Carolyn McKay." She took Dorothy's hand quickly. Her features were finely proportioned and elegant. She was more attractive close up than at a distance. Dorothy had never seen more beautiful eyes, a delicate shade of violet. Carolyn wore no hat and her auburn hair, turned under at the shoulders, had a copper sheen. Dorothy was impressed; this was a truly beautiful and refined lady.

"That's my husband John by the watering trough, the one with the crumpled suit. We've been traveling."

"Are you with the government officials?"

"Heavens, no!" Carolyn laughed. "John and I arrived in Madison yesterday to homestead land. We're from Virginia."

"Virginia!"

"Yes, I'm from Williamsburg. John is from Arlington."

"Welcome to Madison!" Dorothy answered warmly, still holding Carolyn's hand. "We're happy to have you here. Why did you choose Madison?"

Carolyn hesitated, ". . . we wanted to leave Virginia. John didn't want to go West. Florida seemed like a good choice."

"My husband James and I think this is a wonderful place. I came with my family from Richmond. He's from Massachusetts."

Dorothy half blushed as she held up her hand with the new wedding band, "We were married just yesterday and have a new farm on the Bellamy Trail about ten miles from here. Both of us loved Madison from the first day." Dorothy paused, "In fact, James and I met right here in this Square. My family and I had just arrived from Richmond.

"The county is well named. Mr. Madison was a wonderful man. My father knew him well . . . ."

"Really! Your father knew the President?"

"That's really nothing," Carolyn interrupted apologetically. "Most everyone up that way gets to know the President," she added with a laugh, "or so they claim."

She changed the subject quickly as if regretting what she had said. As John approached, she took his hand. He was dark-haired and well groomed with a pleasant smile. He was not as tall as James but more powerfully built.

"This is Dorothy Danbury" Carolyn said, "and this is my husband, John McKay."

Dorothy extended her hand. John had deep brown eyes and a black mustache. He was strikingly good looking and except for the name "McKay," Dorothy would have taken him to be Spanish. There was a dignity in these two that Dorothy had not seen in Madison, not even in the government officials.

James walked up in time to hear the name "McKay", and reached out his hand. "I'm James Danbury, and I see you have already met my wife."

"Yes," Carolyn answered with obvious pleasure. She turned to John, "They were married only yesterday! And they already have a house and land."

"Our cabin is a long way from being finished," James interrupted, "but it is ours! Our `private island'."

"We talked with Mr. Carlisle in the Land Office," John said. "There seems to be no shortage of good land here in Florida."

"We'd be pleased to have you look down our way," James replied. "We're about ten miles from here on the Bellamy Trail.

We like our part of the county mighty well. The soil is richer than some other areas, less sandy." Carolyn and John showed immediate interest. "And the land is well drained."

James looked toward the platform where the dignitaries were being seated. "After the speakers are finished, we can tell you why we chose that part of the county."

A moment later there was loud clapping and a voice calling for attention. Everyone was invited to the refreshment table to meet the special guests. As the two couples moved in that direction, Dorothy asked, "Why don't you come home with us. We have plenty of room for your wagon, plenty of food . . . and we'd enjoy having you. You could see the land down our way." There was a sound of eagerness in her voice, "James and I would love to have you."

"We would be an imposition on you!" Carolyn replied. "You're too generous to make such an offer. After all, you're still on your honeymoon."

"You'd be no imposition," James answered. "We'd be glad to have you. You'll be our first company. Besides," he looked at John, "I could use an extra hand on the place; there's lots to be done."

"Under those terms," John answered, "we accept! If I can help you for a few days, we'll come."

The men talked while Carolyn and Dorothy made their way to the receiving line. As the women neared the row of dignitaries, Carolyn took a look at Governor DuVal and spoke softly to Dorothy, "Remember that President Madison wasn't famous for good looks either."

A few minutes later the men joined their wives. Governor DuVal was charming. He had a brilliance that immediately made both couples appreciate him.

"How nice to be among such lovely people," he complimented, "and to be in such a beautiful place as Madison."

The women thanked him.

"You will write Washington favorably in my behalf, won't you?" he teased. He kissed their hands. "I like my appointment as Governor of Florida and want to stay."

Major Phagan was introduced next. There was something about him Dorothy did not trust. He was pleasant and smiled widely, but his eyes spoke a different message. The feeling was so strong that she did not mention her family. At the end of the line she pulled James aside, "There's more than just John Phagan looking out of those eyes."

The four had taken seats directly in front of the speaker's platform when a three-piece band burst into the National Anthem. As everyone stood with hats removed, James closed his eyes. He was back in Pensacola Plaza listening to a military band playing the same song. The sky was blue, sea gulls darted overhead, and the wind was whipping his uniform. Spain's flag made its final descent, and the American Flag unfurled for the whole world to see. Every detail of the memory was still there. From the USS Hornet in the bay, he heard the booming sound of a twenty-one cannon salute. James witnessed the state joining the Union, and now that piece of Florida that he had longed for was his own. No longer a dream, it was reality.

A familiar voice from the speaker's platform brought James back to Madison Square. Elder Blanton led the invocation. After proper introductions of special guests, Governor DuVal stepped to the lectern.

"Two of the major problems in Florida," he began, "are getting the Indians to leave . . . and the Governor to stay." The crowd laughed. "You may be underestimating the seriousness of that first statement. Until recently the Bureau of Indian Affairs had genuinely believed that we were well on our way to resolving our differences with the tribes in Florida. I need not tell you, that is no longer the case. The problem is vastly compounded. Nor can I promise you that new solutions, solutions acceptable to the Indians, will be found without difficulty."

An angry voice interrupted, "We don't care if the terms are acceptable to the Red Skins! We've got the Army! We can drive them buzzards out!"

A murmuring went through the crowd. The Governor moved the lectern slightly, but his voice showed no emotion as he replied. "I see you are not wearing a uniform. If you wish to be one of those slain in the process of `driving them buzzards out', come to Major Phagan immediately and volunteer." Not a breath of sound followed as Governor DuVal continued, "Responsible Floridians realize whites and Indians share a mutual obligation to each other. According to the terms of our treaty with Spain when we acquired the peninsula, we agreed to grant all inhabitants, reds and whites alike, `All privileges, rights, and immunities of the citizens of the United States.'"

The voice from the rear yelled again, "President Jackson won't agree to that!"

"Mr. Jackson was not President when the treaty was signed, and it is not his prerogative to agree or disagree!" DuVal's voice showed anger. "His Oath of Office mandates his responsibility to carry it out! I will be traveling to Washington, D.C. later this week to remind the President of his duty to both white and red Floridians!"

Several men in the rear rose angrily to their feet. DuVal hesitated. "Previously, as Governor," he resumed, "I forbad whites from migrating into Seminole territory. I believed then—as I do now—that if the two races were successfully kept apart there would be no conflict."

Dorothy closed her eyes; her father's foolishness had suddenly become more evident.

The Governor continued, "That effort failed." He addressed the hecklers in the rear, "But may I remind you that it was not the Seminoles who caused the failure. As a tribe they want to remain apart. It has been whites who supplied the Seminoles with illegal guns and ammunition. Irresponsible whites have deliberately encouraged the Indians to resist a peaceable migration West."

The Governor's voice was loud, demanding. "And most of us in this audience are aware of their scheme. When this territory passes into self-governing statehood and is free from the constraints incumbent upon it as a federally administered district, these men are plotting the capture and sale of the red men as slaves! I warn you that the practice of slavery, black or red, may yet bring this nation to the brink of disaster!"

Booing from several sections of the audience interrupted the Governor again. The heckler strode halfway up the aisle, "We're not only Floridians!" he yelled. "We're Jacksonian Floridians! We believe in Florida, Andrew Jackson, and God—in that order! And we've got no place for sympathizers with John Quincy Adams."

Everyone in the audience froze in deathly silence. Dorothy looked towards Carolyn and John as the two paled, almost as if the name, John Quincy Adams, involved them personally.

The Governor fired back, red-faced with rage, "Mr. Adams has nothing to do with my current administration or my policies!"

"Oh, Yeah? When he cheated Jackson out of the Presidency, you were Governor!" The man took several steps forward, shaking his fist at DuVal. "What did you do to help?"

Four blue-uniformed soldiers quickly moved into position between the Governor and the heckler. DuVal signaled them to step aside. Taking a sip of water, he made a deliberate effort to calm himself before replying. His voice was restrained and his words carefully enunciated. "There is no expediency in quarreling over problems related to President John Quincy Adams. We would do better to direct our energy to solving the problems most imminently concerning us, the issue with the Seminoles."

He paused, exhaled slowly, and then continued. "I became Governor of the Florida Territory in 1822, and four years later I went to Washington with Chief Tuckose E'mathala who very capably presented the Seminole cause to . . . President John Quincy Adams." He hesitated before speaking Adam's name, "I have no doubt that if Chief E'mathala's requests had been honored, we would be in a much more favorable position today. Unfortunately Chief E'mathala's wisdom was rejected, and in consequence, we are now nearer crisis than ever before. The Florida Seminoles do not want to be forced into joining the Georgia Creeks or the Arkansas Pawnees any more than we want to be joined to Spanish Mexico or the British Bahamas. They simply want to be given their part of Florida and be left alone."

He stopped and looked slowly across the audience. "And I must advise you that I am equally committed to seeking solutions that are agreeable to the Florida Seminoles."

The hecklers remained silent, awed that he would dare to speak so boldly. When Mr. DuVal concluded his message, the musicians began to play; and the audience rose applauding. The opposition dispersed; their strategy for the moment was to remain quiet.

Late that afternoon James and Dorothy returned home with John and Carolyn following them. The white canvas top of the McKay wagon was soiled with red Georgia clay and the gray stain of months on the trail. In the back were seven brass-hinged, round-top trunks along with numerous smaller bags. One of the smaller bags, Carolyn explained, contained lily bulbs, "I couldn't leave Virginia without them."

After they turned off the Bellamy Trail and reached the bend in the Danbury lane, James stopped the wagons. "Right over there is good land," he said, pointing toward the south. "That's the spot we want you to see. It's the richest land in this county. The swamp wraps around the southeast boundary, and our land joins that section in the center of the creek. Tomorrow we'll go look at it. If you like it, as soon as the Land Office approves, men from Blue Springs Church will help you with the cabin raisin'."

As the wagons approached James and Dorothy's cabin, Carolyn stood up, and John stopped the horse again.

"What a beautiful setting for their home!" she exclaimed. Carolyn was thrilled at the sight of the grove of trees, tall cabbage palms twisting over the lane, and the new Danbury cabin nestled under the oak as securely as a baby chick under a hen. "There must be a hundred palms. And they're so tall. Look how some of them curve out over the road. I understand why they love this part of the county, John!"

She took his hand, "I am so glad we came. This is what we've been looking for."

The two wagons pulled into the yard. "We plan to live here the rest of our lives," Dorothy explained. "First we'll show you around, and then you can come inside and see what the folks gave us for our wedding."

John and Carolyn parked their wagon in the opening southwest of the Danbury cabin. In the two weeks that followed, Carolyn and John explored the adjacent property and filed a homestead claim. They slept in their wagon at night and did some cooking on the tailgate.

James and John worked together long hours completing the Danbury's cabin, working on the new barn, the privy, and smoke-house. Brother Blanton and Jeremiah finished the well. Others from Blue Springs Church showed up regularly to help with whatever needed to be done. Dorothy and Carolyn mixed clay and chinked cracks between the logs, pulled up gallberry bushes, cut down scrub oaks, and cleaned out undergrowth in the palm grove surrounding the house.

The third Sunday in May was Elder Blanton's preaching appointment at Blue Springs Church. Other Sundays his circuit took him to Monticello, Ft. Wacissa, and Charles Ferry. Gilbert and Odessa Mallory were present with their new baby, Gilbert, Jr.; and John and Carolyn were there.

The McKays were delighted with Elder Blanton's sermon, the warmth of the congregation, and the sincerity of the worship. While the service was very different from the Episcopal churches Carolyn had known in Virginia, she recognized a strength in the worship that seemed adapted for life in the Florida wilderness.

During the singing, Carolyn slipped out to the edge of the woods for a moment alone. The log house and its tiny cemetery in the grove of pines and palms had an unusual appeal. There was a power here she could not identify. Her eyes turned to the north side of the building where a clear blue spring bubbled up from a sink-hole and flowed into the Oithlacoochee River a hundred yards away. The spot was idyllic. One fact became very clear to Carolyn—she would never return to Virginia. This was where she and John would stay. Here she found a sense of privacy—perhaps more of protection—she needed.

Carolyn's meditation was interrupted. Odessa approached, holding her baby in one arm, and reaching out with the other. The two women hugged as Odessa complimented Carolyn's dress.

Running her hand admiringly across the shoulder, Odessa admitted, "I come from a long line of fat ones. My papa weren't no taller than my mama was round! As you can tell," slapping her hips, "I taken the best from both of 'em," she laughed. Odessa's honest, disarming manner made Carolyn hug her again. Carolyn saw a lovely, sensitive girl locked in a cumbersome body.

Returning to the church, Carolyn slipped into her seat next to Dorothy as Elder Blanton rose to speak. He exhorted the congregation to pray for peaceful negotiations with the Indians and for Major Phagan, whom he did not trust. That was the first time Dorothy had ever heard Elder Blanton make such a comment.

The preaching hour was followed by dinner. Fried pies, molasses cakes, collard greens, dried meat, and a pot of catfish stew were shared from wagon tailgates. The men took their plates to the side of the meeting house. The women stayed close to the wagons shooing flies from the food and watching the children. Following the meal everyone returned to the building for an hour of singing.

When Dr. Thad offered to lead the song service, Mrs. Blanton rolled her eyes in a "please-help-us-Lord" expression. Jerry Baldwin, the regular Singing Clerk, quickly came to the rescue. Dr. Thad was a widower in his fifties whose wife had died with yellow fever nine years earlier. He was tall and thin with a high, squeaky voice. Elder Blanton suspected that Dr. Thad was at church primarily to look for unattached females, but widowed women his age were usually on the next stagecoach out of Florida.

As the congregation broke up in the early afternoon, Elder Blanton announced a cabin-raisin' at the McKay's homestead the following Saturday. Many volunteered, and everyone left the grounds looking forward to being together again soon.

Saturday morning the same enthusiasm and excitement that had been present at James and Dorothy's cabin raising was present at the McKay homestead. John and Carolyn were deeply touched by the warmth and love of their newly found church friends. By nightfall the trunks, bags, and lily bulbs were all in their new locations. Carolyn walked around the place, glowing with joy as she planned her yard.

"How wonderful it is, John," she said, glancing around to be certain that no one could hear her, "to have a place of our own again. It has been so long!"

"We must be a thousand miles from Hiram. If he ever looks for us, surely he'll go West." John hugged her as she continued. "Thank God, we are free of him at last!"

She had not intended to eavesdrop; but from where Dorothy stood, it was impossible not to overhear the exchange between Carolyn and John. Dorothy could not explain it, but somehow she knew in her heart that profound evil was connected to the name, "Hiram."

In the weeks that followed Carolyn searched the woods for wild flowers to landscape the yard. Lantana shrubs were placed at the chimney's base, and fragrant-smelling rosemary bushes, as round as if they had been pruned, substituted for boxwoods. These were placed at the four corners of the cabin and at each of the porch posts. Maypop vines, that she called "passion flowers", were planted along the split-rail fence. Swamp ferns in moss-lined baskets hung from porch rafters. Coco plums from the ridge on the north side of the field lined the garden fence. On each side of the front gate, saw palmettos stood proud as Royal Palms. Carolyn's eye missed no opportunity to beautify.

"Carolyn, you will have the only privy in Florida with Morning Glories on it," Dorothy laughed. Then she added in a more serious tone, "You have a gift from God to make everything lovely . . . and you touch people with that same graciousness."

Carolyn tried to discourage the compliment, but Dorothy continued. "It is easy to recognize your background of dignity and elegance, Carolyn. You could never have developed those qualities in the wilderness." Dorothy forced Carolyn to look at her, "I'm thankful you're here, but this is not the life your family prepared you for. You're a lady, Carolyn, a true Virginia blueblood. You're not a field hand."

Carolyn tried to stop her, but Dorothy persisted. "What really brought you to Florida, Carolyn? Why are you here?"

Carolyn twisted uncomfortably. For a moment it seemed she wanted to explain, but then she stiffened, ". . . this is where we chose to come . . . John thought it best . . . Florida seemed like the right choice."

Dorothy said no more, and the question remained unanswered.

A few weeks later, Carolyn invited Dorothy and Odessa for tea. The ladies were seated at the kitchen table, and Carolyn served tea with gilt-edged China cups and lace-fringed napkins. Dorothy and Odessa looked on in amazement.

"How in the world did you get these cups all the way from Virginia?" Odessa wanted to know. "When my tin plates weren't more than a month old, they looked like General Taylor had used them for target practice!" She held the saucer up to the light, "I'll bet there ain't nothin' in Tallahassee any fancier than this!"

After tea the women took a stroll through the yard. They stepped on a walkway formed of wooden blocks pressed into the ground. Odessa was impressed by the two large circular beds of milkweed planted between the fence and the house. "And to think that I must've pulled up a wagon load of them pests in my yard."

Around the south end of the cabin, a large rectangular enclosure of a formal garden greeted them. Paths covered with pine straw entered from each corner and converged in the center where a strangely pruned bush, tall as their heads, dominated the garden. "If that don't beat all!" Odessa exclaimed. "I know there ain't a garden in Tallahassee that pretty! Where ever did you get such an idea?!"

". . . Williamsburg," Carolyn answered reluctantly. "This is just a small copy of one I used to visit as a child. I couldn't have a fountain as the centerpiece, so I used that coco plum."

Dorothy moved nearer, touching the shiny leaves and examining the unusual manner Carolyn had pruned the stalk. It was a straight stem with three rounded balls of greenery; a small one on the top, a slightly larger one in the middle, and the largest at the bottom.

"It will take it a while," Carolyn explained, "but in time it will grow into shape."

Dorothy bent down and pointed to a circle of tiny flowering plants around the bottom of the centerpiece. "What are these?"

Carolyn laughed. "Those are bitter weeds—the same poisonous little plant that grows in the pastures and ruins the cows milk—but they can still be a bright spot in my garden." She pointed to several empty places in the garden. "I've already spotted some wild verbena on the ridge that I want to plant there. My lilies will be in an elevated bed behind them."

Dorothy marveled at Carolyn's handiwork. "It's just beautiful," she said. "I feel like Virginia has come to Madison."

That night after James and Dorothy were in bed, she talked about her visit with Carolyn. "James, she is like a flower that constantly gives a new fragrance. I've never known a more beautiful or more talented person." Dorothy moved nearer to him, "Carolyn is not like the rest of us. She's the type of Philadelphia or Washington woman you read about. Yet there is no one in Madison who seems to love—or need—the wilderness more than she does."

"I know what you mean. She and John are like a pair of swans in a flock of geese . . . they stand out from the rest of us." He put his arm over her, "The day we met them at the Blockhouse, I had the feeling they were two of the most genuine people I've ever known. And John is probably the best-educated man I've ever met. I know how to build a barn, but he knows how to build a mansion."

He rolled back, facing the ceiling. There was a long, studious pause. "There is much, much more to them than they have told us."

Chapter Four

Frightening news was about to send shock waves through the entire state. Accompanied by Private Marshall Townsend, Lieutenant Terrance Browning arrived at the little white frame Capitol Building in Tallahassee. The door to the Governor's office was ajar, and Private Townsend watched as Lieutenant Browning walked inside to deliver the news to Acting Governor Westcott.

"Fools! Fools that we are!" Westcott shouted, slamming his fist on the desktop. He grabbed the dispatch and read it again. "Lieutenant, can we be sure of this?!"

"Sir, you have General Arbuckle's statement . . . in his own handwriting."

"Why does William DuVal have to be out of the territory now? I'm only Acting Governor!" Westcott dropped into his chair. "Call that private in the hall for me."

Townsend entered, and Mr. Westcott shoved paper and quill toward him. "Write this quickly, *The Honorable Mr. Elbert Herring, Commissioner of Indian Affairs, Washington, D.C. Dear Commissioner: It is with regret I advise you that evidence of fraud and improper conduct has been disclosed on the part of Major John Phagan against the Seminoles.*"

The dictation continued, *"I need not express the jeopardy which this places upon the efforts of our government to peaceably remove the Seminoles to the West. Additionally it has brought imminent danger to our troops in the interior of the peninsular."*

Westcott paused, rose from his chair and stood looking out the window. *"Nor is it possible,"* he began again, *"to forecast the imme-*

diate threat to the white citizens of this territory. Your attention to this matter is of the most grave concern. The documents enclosed specify charges brought against Major Phagan by General Arbuckle. I await your instructions."

Westcott hurriedly signed the letter.

"Take this to the Express Post immediately. Tell them, by order of the Governor, they are to send a rider to overtake the coach that left an hour ago. It stops tonight at Monticello."

"Yes, Sir!"

"Advise Sergeant Billingsley to wait for additional instructions to be sent to all Forts between here and Fort King."

"Yes, Sir!"

The private rushed out the door, and the Governor closed it behind him. He turned back to the Lieutenant. "Sit down."

Westcott placed General Arbuckle's letter in the center of his desk, hunching over it. "How much of this do you personally know?"

Lieutenant Browning rose to his feet. "Only what I've seen in the ledgers, Sir. When Major Phagan accompanied the Chiefs to the Arkansas Territory, he entered cost payments against their names for services they never received. He took money that belonged to them."

"That dirty lying thief! And the Chiefs are aware of this?"

"Sir, not only the Chiefs but every Indian in Florida knows that Major Phagan cheated them. They are now convinced he lied about the treaty they signed at Payne's Landing . . . ."

"God help us!" Westcott dropped back into his chair. "God help us! I never liked that man Phagan or his interpreters."

"You mean the Negroes . . . Abraham and Pacheco?"

"That's right! I have no charge against either of them. But they're greasy devils. It's a rotten arrangement when the United States Government has to depend on the word of run-away Negro slaves to negotiate treaties with the enemy," Westcott yelled angrily.

"But, Sir, the Indians all trust Abraham and Pacheco."

"And I know of no better reason not to trust them!" Governor Westcott dipped his quill in the ink and began writing. A few minutes later he handed a note to the Lieutenant. "These are my instructions to the troops until we receive more explicit directions from Commissioner Herring in Washington. You will pass this word along to all the Forts between here and Fort King."

Lieutenant Browning took the piece of paper and read it silently.

To all troops in the Territory of Florida:

Greetings from Acting Governor Westcott. Serious complications now jeopardize the Army's plans to deport the Seminoles peaceably. You are placed on immediate alert for possible hostilities. Reinforcements will arrive as quickly as possible. Inventory your munitions supplies. Notify all white settlers to seek refuge in protected areas.

Very truly yours,
James D. Westcott

The Lieutenant looked up from the letter. "Sir, the garrisons at all the forts will be asking additional questions. What shall I tell them, Sir?"

"I don't know what to tell them! For the present they will have to be content with this. Nothing more, nothing less."

"Have you any word for Major Phagan, Sir?"

"Only that he is to remain at Fort King until Commissioner Herring contacts him personally." He paused. "You may also advise him that I will personally attend his court martial."

The Governor changed the subject abruptly. "Do you have family in Florida, Lieutenant?"

"Yes, Sir," he smiled. "My wife lives with her father in Madison."

"Warn the folks in Madison that circumstances have changed with the Seminoles. Give no more details than that. Who is your wife's father? What is his name?"

"Dr. Thaddeus Monroe, Sir. Most everyone knows him as `Dr. Thad'."

"I've heard of him. Good man. I remember something about his wife dying."

"She had yellow fever, Sir. There were complications that were never explained. We really don't know what killed her."

"I apologize, Lieutenant. Forgive my needless asking."

"Yes sir. Is there anything else?"

"I think not. That will be all . . . thank you, Lieutenant."

Terrance hurried from the building. At the rail, he mounted his horse and headed toward Fort Wacissa. Marshall Townsend was already on his way back to Madison with the news.

That evening the rider dispatched by order of Governor Westcott overtook the mail coach twenty-five miles east of Tallahassee. At daybreak the next morning, the message to the Commissioner of Indian Affairs traveled north from Monticello by way of Picolata on the St. Johns River. From St. Augustine it traveled by ship to Washington. The letter carried by Lieutenant Browning soon reached Fort Wacissa, Fort Noel, Fort Atkinson near the Suwanee River, Fort Wacahoota, Fort Micanopy, and other posts throughout the state.

Like prairie fire Governor Westcott's message spread to every cabin and farm. Panic settled over Central Florida like a shroud. Soldiers and citizens alike feared all-out war with the Indians.

Brother Blanton understood the seriousness of the situation, and he tried to comfort his flock. He assured them that though things looked bad for Central Florida, the northern part of the state—Madison, Monticello, and Tallahassee—would be safe.

Monday morning Brother Blanton rode out to James and Dorothy's place.

"Dorothy," he attempted to console her, "your folks have plenty of time to get out of Miccosuki territory."

It was not lack of time for her family to get to safety that concerned Dorothy. She knew all too well it would take much more than a plea from the Governor to discourage her father's quest for his "Garden of Eden."

Chapter Five

Henry, Malida, and Tom made it from Madison to Charles Ferry Crossing before nightfall, the day after Dorothy's wedding. First to join the Hapsburg wagon train was a couple from Tennessee, Calhoun and Gilda McElroy. Others arrived over the next few days.

Despite Henry's optimism, things were not "all that simple." Before the wagon train left Charles Ferry Crossing, the McElroy's lost a horse. The animal had to be put down after it was bitten by a water moccasin. Gilda took this as a bad omen. She had opposed her husband's decision from the beginning. Now more than ever she was convinced they were headed for disaster. She threatened to burn their wagon in a desperate attempt to coerce her husband into going north. She begged and cried, but Calhoun would not be persuaded. When soldiers from Fort Atkinson arrived to escort the wagon train, the group headed out with Gilda screaming and tossing Calhoun's clothes from the back of the wagon.

The Kanapaha Prairie was flooded when they reached it. Wheels sank into the mire, and there was damage to some of the wagons. Henry supervised the cutting of a new trail. The group went on, but more wheel spokes were broken by stumps; and their supply of replacements was seriously depleted. Repair work was slow, and mosquitoes swarmed as thick as fog.

When they got to the Micanopy Trail, their military escort left them. At that point Henry appointed himself foreman; and no one challenged him.

Later that same day soldiers dispatched from Fort Walker reached the area. After the wagon train set up camp for the night,

Henry went out on his own to explore an old Spanish trail. He was half a mile away from the campsite when he intercepted the troops.

"Are you traveling alone?" a soldier asked.

"No, I'm with a wagon train, eight schooners south of here," Henry replied confidently.

"Who is foreman?"

"That'd be me! Hapsburg's the name."

"I'm Sergeant Harold Middleton, and I have orders from the Governor. We are here to advise you that Governor Westcott has issued an emergency dispatch regarding white citizens traveling into the interior . . ."

"Westcott?!" Henry interrupted. "The last Governor I knowed anything about was DuVal!"

"Mr. DuVal has gone to Washington. Mr. James Westcott is now Acting Governor."

"Acting Governor! Well, what does the territory's Acting 'Great White Father' have to say?!"

"His recommendation is that all whites return to safer areas immediately."

"Return!?"

"That's right, Sir." The Sergeant removed a document from his pocket, "Shall I read his statement to you?"

"That won't be necessary! I'll take you boys' word for it."

Henry glared disapprovingly. The Sergeant folded the document and returned it to his pocket, "We'll be glad to escort you and your wagon train back to Fort Walker, Sir."

"That won't be necessary! We just had one escort leave us. They didn't seem to be scared like you boys."

"They had not received the Governor's orders, Sir. There are new developments with the Indians. Shall we advise the others in your train, Sir?"

"I said I was foreman! I'll take care of it!"

The soldiers spurred their horses and galloped northward. Henry watched them disappear. "Danged fools," he spat his words after them. "What else can you expect from the Seminoles when we ain't got nothin' but a bunch of wet-nosed young'uns and a 'Acting' Governor to fight them?!"

Henry never told the others of the warning. Early the next morning the wagon train headed southeast toward Lake Lochloosa.

Three weeks after leaving Charles Ferry Crossing on the Suwanee, the wagons finally reached Big Prairie twenty miles west of the Oklawaha. From here some would go to the St. John's River and others would head further south to Lake George. Most were only a few days from their destinations. Tomorrow they would go separate ways.

Mrs. McElroy still refused to get out of the wagon. Calhoun pleaded with her, and Malida tried to coax her. "Sugar," she said, "it's just like the 'Garden of Eden'!"

Grim-faced and nervous, Gilda clung to her seat. To her the dark line of trees along the horizon was a huge jungle mouth waiting to swallow them. "Oh, yes! The Garden!" she snapped, "with a snake hanging from every limb!" Her lips tightened. "Why did I marry a ramblin' man! My sisters all live within sight of where we were born! But where do I live? In a snake infested swamp!" She glared hatefully at her husband, "If you'd told me when we got married I was going to live like a savage, I would've scalped you then and been done with it!"

"Sugar! You'll come to love it here," Malida consoled. "Trust God! Just give yourself time."

"Time! I'd like to give my husband time! About twenty years in the Richmond Stockade!"

"But look at that sky, Honey! You ain't never seen one so blue! Why, I *like* this place."

"It won't be so pretty when it's black with Indian smoke," Gilda fired back. Then for a moment she fell silent. "You must not have left family."

"Oh, but we did! We left our only daughter in Madison, with a new husband."

"Now that's what I'm in favor of, a *new* husband! Right now, I'd settle for someone else's old one. Any husband, as long as he was headed north!"

Malida kept smiling. "Gilda, you're just upset and worried. You need to be thankful for the good things! Just think how warm it's going to be here in the winter."

"How warm it's gonna be?! I'm thinking how *hot* it's gonna be when the Indians burn the damned house down!" The other ladies looked away. Even in the wilderness there was no excuse for a woman to use profanity.

But Gilda wasn't through with her tirade. "None of us will have a neighbor in fifty miles! We'll all go up in smoke and never be missed."

The woman suddenly broke into loud crying. Malida climbed into the wagon and held her tightly.

"Sugar," she consoled, "more than your husband, your sisters, or anyone else, you need the Lord! I know Henry couldn't take care of me even if we were still in Richmond." Malida paused. She spoke affectionately, "But I'm not in Richmond. I'm here in this wilderness. And come what may, I'm going to trust the Lord! Henry is not the one my trust is in! I pray nothing bad happens to us, but I love my husband and I want to go where he goes."

Pushing her away, Gilda leaped through the flaps and disappeared into the wagon. Privately she envied Malida's faith. But for the moment, punishing her husband brought greater satisfaction than the prospect of finding peace for herself. She jerked the curtains shut and resumed her impassioned wailing.

Calhoun threw up his hands in despair, "She done just like that when we was living in her mama's house! Just like that! Only difference was I had to listen to her, her three sisters, and her mama! That was the reason we come to Florida." He walked away groaning, "Good Lord! What did I marry? What did I marry?"

That evening in the comfort of a strong east wind, the group shared their final meal around a campfire. Tall grass bowed in the breeze like an ocean of green. They sang, they laughed, and they talked about the troubles they were leaving behind. Before them lay the Promised Land. It was filled with fruits and flowers, clear rivers and abundant fish, wild game and lush gardens. They had arrived! Where others had failed, they had succeeded! Flooded prairies and broken wagon-wheel spokes had not stopped them.

At daybreak they broke camp. From the edge of the big prairie, lonely cypress hammocks and clumps of saw palmettos spread out toward the horizon. Each schooner slowly rumbled its way into the obscurity of high grass and scrub trees. Gilda was still screeching, convinced they were all riding into certain destruction.

Malida watched the McElroy wagon head off alone. "Lord," she prayed, "help her! And please, Lord, help that dear man!"

For several minutes no one in the Hapsburg wagon spoke, each was plunged into the deep reality of the utter loneliness and isolation of this place. A sense of total helplessness began to settle upon them. Though Henry would never have admitted it, even he felt the dark, heavy presence. Malida broke the silence with a song.

Oh, for a faith that will not shrink
Though pressed by every foe,
That will not tremble on the brink
of any earthly foe!
A faith that shines more bright and clear
When tempests rage without,
That when in darkness knows no fear,
In sorrow feels no doubt!

On the last line Henry joined her. Tom felt a surge of assurance. There was something in his mama's faith that filled him with a sense of security.

A month after leaving Madison the Hapsburgs reached the Oklawaha. To Henry it was like Joshua's arrival at the Jordan. He celebrated, talked excitedly, and repeated the same worn-out phrases that Tom and Malida had heard a thousand times. He climbed between the massive trunks of cypress trees on the river's banks and acted as if the entire stream were his personal possession.

Malida and Tom were genuinely impressed with the Oklawaha. They had to be. Henry killed the biggest turkey gobbler they had ever seen. They watched herds of deer drinking from the river and saw giant fish breaking the water. Panthers screamed at night, screech owls let out their blood-chilling sounds, and alligators bellowed from the swamp. There was a strange mixture of tranquility and terror; a mystical, almost hypnotic beauty seemed to float over the place. The Oklawaha exceeded even the most flamboyant descriptions.

There were no signs of Seminoles except for the few who harmlessly slipped by in dugout canoes. Soldiers from Fort King occasionally passed and sometimes came ashore for a short visit. Tom finally started to believe that his father had made a good decision.

"If only he's right about the Indians," Tom thought, "we really are in paradise."

They chose a spot on the bend with enough elevation to protect them from flooding and with an unobstructed view of the river in both directions. Cypress trees at their landing were forty feet tall and wide as their wagon. The branches reached the stream's opposite bank. This place had everything. Everything! Their only fear was losing their horses to panthers or alligators. Henry wished that Harlow could see him now. The soil was rich; in time they would have a prosperous farm. He envisioned an orange grove behind their house, a garden that grew oversized vegetables, and livestock—cows, pigs, chickens, guineas. If they should ever need an escape route, the Oklawaha gave them access to the St. John's River, Picolata, St. Augustine, and the Atlantic.

For the first two months while the house was under construction, they slept in the wagon. Fires burned for weeks in the south part of the field. On the north side they cut trees and let them lie. Malida removed palmettoes, gallberry bushes, sumac, ferns, and underbrush. She swept the yard to a white, sandy finish. She planted corn and collard greens, okra and tomatoes in scattered patches between fallen logs. Squash and pumpkin vines climbed over the debris.

There was little need for anything else. Henry shot whatever they wanted for meat. The river teemed with fish, turtles, alligators, and manatee; and Malida had a special recipe for each.

By October Henry and Tom had enclosed their two-room log house. It was built of long slender cypress logs light enough for the two of them to handle. Half of the roof was complete, and Tom chinked the cracks with clay and Spanish moss. There was no chimney or hearth; Malida cooked Seminole-style on an open fire in the yard.

Every day, sometimes every hour, she thought of Dorothy. Sitting on a fallen cypress and watching the flow of the Oklawaha, her imagination always turned to Madison. It was easy to picture Dorothy and James, their cabin, their farm. She could see their house with new rail fences, cleared pastures, and neat garden rows.

Malida's visualization of the Danbury homestead was not entirely accurate. Yes, good progress had been made on the fences, and the pastures were cleared. Dorothy's garden, however, was another story.

Certainly it was a prolific garden. Okra grew tall, bloomed, and bore heavily. Next to the okra, rows of tomatoes, corn, squash, and turnips thrived in the rich soil. As James described it, "There's not another garden like it in the whole territory of Florida."

From the beginning, Dorothy wanted the garden to be her very own project. She was determined to do it without help from anyone. To her great consternation, no matter how diligently she worked with hoe and garden tools, old roots held firm and resisted her every effort to pull them out.

No garden was going to get the best of her. She would find a way to do it on her own no matter what. Meanwhile she firmly admonished James, "Give me your word you will NOT go down to the okra patch!"

"That seems like a strange request."

"I don't care if it's strange! I don't want you down there, James!"

James recognized the bullheadedness of Henry Hapsburg in his wife's tone. Reluctantly he agreed to stay away.

James intended to keep his word, but curiosity finally got the best of him. Brother Blanton stopped by for a visit. While Dorothy was busy preparing dinner, the two slipped down to the garden.

At the sight of it, both men broke into side-splitting laughter. The rows were crooked, twisted paths around and between roots that Dorothy had never been able to remove. Her okra and other vegetables were blooming in zigzagging lines.

Their laughter was interrupted by Dorothy's voice behind them. "Don't you laugh!" she yelled. "I worked my fool hands to the bone on this okra patch! And all you can do is laugh!" With that she turned and headed back toward the house.

"Darling!" James ran after her and grabbed her arm. "I'm not laughing at the crooked rows . . . "

Before he could say another word, Dorothy tripped on the hem of her dress; and together they fell sprawling in the dirt. James rolled over, gripped his belly, and burst into howling. Dorothy sobbed as anger gave way to embarrassment.

She sprang to her feet and snatched her hem free. James stood up and looked her in the eye. Somehow he kept a straight face long enough to say, "Darling, okra grown in crooked rows will taste every bit as good as okra grown in straight rows . . . if you're the one cooking it. You could cook a pine cone good enough to feed Governor DuVal and all them important men in Tallahassee . . . "

That was as far as he got before a muffled chuckle slipped out.

"Then why are you laughing at me?!" Dorothy stormed.

"He's not laughing at you," Brother Blanton intervened. "That's just the joy of the Lord. Dorothy, look around us at the pine trees. God planted millions of them in Florida, and none of them are in straight rows."

James pulled Dorothy close to him. He kissed her lightly on the lips.

From then on, James and Brother Blanton were careful never to mention or go near the garden. But every time James thought of those crooked, zigzag rows, a smile crept across his face; and he felt that "joy of the Lord" all over again.

Each morning Dorothy walked down to her garden and brought back a basket of vegetables. One morning on her way to collect the daily produce, she stopped suddenly. A wave of nausea rolled over her, and she sat down on her bucket until it passed. The next morning it happened again. And then again.

A week later when James came in for lunch, Dorothy set a plateful of grits and sausage before him, "I cooked these just for you, Papa."

James looked up in surprise. "Papa?"

There was no answer, only a smile.

"Really?!" He leaped to his feet and grabbed her in his arms. "Really, Dorothy, really?!"

The next morning Dorothy walked to Carolyn's house. She joined Odessa at the table where Carolyn served them tea. She could hardly wait to share her news.

"I know you treasure this beautiful China," Odessa said holding up a cup.

"This set belonged to my grandmother," Carolyn responded. "She gave it to me when I was a little girl, and I have always. . . "

Dorothy interrupted before Carolyn could finish her sentence, "Speaking of little girls, or little boys, James and I are expecting!"

Carolyn leaped to her feet clapping her hands, "Wonderful! That's wonderful!"

"When? When?" Odessa asked. "And what do ya want? Girl or boy?"

"James has already told me that this baby is going to be named 'George' . . . even if it is a girl," Dorothy laughed. Her friends laughed with her as she explained, "His father was George, and James says his first has to be called that too."

"We'd better be praying for a boy!" Carolyn insisted.

"My Gilbert was supposed to be a girl," Odessa giggled. "But it's like my mama always said, 'When they're squalling in the middle of the night, you can't tell one from the other.'"

In the months that followed, Dorothy's excitement grew along with her waistline. Every week Dr. Thad made a house call to check on her and to visit with the McKays. One morning the doctor arrived waving an envelope in his hand.

Dorothy hurried towards him shouting, "Is it from Mama? Is it from Mama!? Please tell me it is!"

"It is indeed! It's from your mama, and it sure is thick. I ran into that traveling salesman, Doc Kupperman, on the Bellamy Trail, and he gave it to me. He got it from a soldier at Fort Wakahoota who got it from somebody in Picolata."

Dorothy wasn't interested in the details. Mama and Papa had been gone what seemed like a lifetime, and this was their first letter. Tearing into the soiled envelope, she eagerly devoured every word.

"Dear Dorothy, I sure hope you got all my other letters and know how well we all are, Sugar. We miss you and James lots but we're real happy. Just like papa said, we are in the Garden of Eden! I'm so glad we came. Our vegetables are growing faster than the jungle grows weeds. You've never seen such squash and pumpkins. There ain't no shortage of food down here. Deer come in our yard and there are so many turkeys we have to shoo them away. Tom has grown at least a inch. He's happy now and has a wonderful young soldier-friend, Kensley Dalton, who stops every month to visit with us. Kensley carries the mail from St. Augustine to Fort King. Tom sure looks forward to his visits. You'd never guess what Tom's new pet is! A bear cub! Tom named him Ahab. He is the cutest little rascal you ever seen! Poor little thing, he thinks Tom is his mama and follows him around everywhere he goes. Only God knows what we'll do when Ahab gets full growed! He'll probably be the worst thing we have to worry about in the Ocala Territory. We ain't heard from nobody since we left you and James, not even the folks who came down with us, but guess they is happy as we are. We love it here! Someday, Sugar, you and James can come visit us in paradise! Love, Mama."

Chapter Six

The Hapsburgs were not leaving the Oklawaha. Soldiers from Fort King delivered official warnings. Malida prayed. Tom begged, wept, and even threatened to leave without his parents.

"This ain't Europe! We ain't got a King to tell us where we can and can't go! We got a Republic, and citizens has got rights!" Henry stormed. "We ain't running like no scared rabbits!"

Weeks stretched into months without Indian conflict. Now, well over a year since leaving Madison, Henry was convinced that he was right again. He daily reminded Tom and Malida of his good judgment.

The federal Office of Indian Affairs had announced plans to close the Seminole agency. Chief Asi Yoholo, the most formidable opponent of the deportation plan, was now willing to cooperate. The tall and elegant Chief Coacoochee frequently appeared at social events in St. Augustine where he was introduced as "Florida's Prince of the Forest."

Henry was encouraged by these developments. His confidence was bolstered even further when the Legislative Council of Florida published an appeal for more white settlers to come to Florida and homestead land surrendered by the Seminoles.

Summers in the Oklawaha could be murderously humid and the sun as hot as a bronze searing plate. But every afternoon huge thunderclouds formed in the west. For an hour they dumped heavy rains that drenched the earth and cooled the breeze. Crops flourished in rich soil blessed by daily watering.

One August afternoon in 1834, Tom came in from the field, sweaty and dirty. Stripping off his grubby clothes, he dove from a cypress stump into the river and swam to midstream. In the clear water, Tom could see long streams of grass swaying on the river bottom fifteen feet below. Fish of all sizes darted in and out of the weeds. Manatees, eels, and turtles went about their business unconcerned with Tom's presence. Giant sea bass from the Atlantic moved slowly below him. He dived as deeply as he could and then shot to the surface like a cork. As much as he had resisted leaving Madison, every time Tom jumped into the river, he had to admit it felt a lot like paradise.

Tom was splashing like an otter when a boat rounded the bend. It was Kensley. His friend was barefooted and dressed in fatigue uniform with his pant legs rolled up to the calf. Kensley poled the boat toward the landing, and Tom swam to meet him.

"Get out of that river, Tom!" Kensley yelled. "I just counted a dozen gators big as this boat! "

Tom laughed, "They got better tastin' stuff than me to eat."

While Kensley secured the boat, Tom climbed out of the water and slipped into his clothes.

Malida came rushing out the door. "Come in, Kensley! Come in! Do you have any mail for us?"

"Yes, Ma'am, I do! A letter from your daughter in Madison."

Malida squealed, snatching the envelope from his hand. She could hardly believe the words she was reading! Dorothy and James had a little boy! George had been born earlier this year, and now there was another one on the way! Praise God, she and Henry were grandparents! Crops were excellent, and they had two new cows. Everyone at Blue Springs Church was well, and Elder Blanton was preaching once a month at the Hadley place on the Fenholloway River.

The letter closed with the same Scripture Tom included in his wedding gift, "The Lord watch between thee and me while we are absent one from the other."

Conversation over supper centered on Indians. Henry believed that the Indian problem was virtually resolved. Kensley disagreed.

"I hate to bring you bad news, Mr. Hapsburg, but Major Phagan cheated the Seminole Chiefs. Because of Phagan, negotiations with the tribes have broken down." Tom listened intently as Kensley talked. "But the Seminoles still want peace. They are willing to cooperate if the whites will give them a portion of the Florida land and leave them alone. In all honesty, Mr. Hapsburg, it's not the Indians who are creating the problem, it's us—the whites."

"But them Indians signed a treaty at Payne's Landing! They agreed to go west," Henry insisted. "They can't get out of that."

"They already have, Mr. Hapsburg. The Chiefs say the treaty is no longer binding because Phagan violated it. Unless our government comes up with answers real soon, there won't be any Indians leaving Florida voluntarily. And President Jackson has vowed they ain't staying."

Tom closed his eyes. Their stay in paradise had been short-lived. For a while he had been free of that knot in the pit of his stomach; suddenly it was back, and the forest towering over them was once again dark and horrific.

Months passed without incident. Then winter arrived with the hardest freeze in Florida history. At St. Augustine the temperature dropped to five degrees. Cattle and wildlife died; orange groves were destroyed. Farms on the Seminole reservation were decimated. Desperation drove Indians to a frenzied search for food.

Spring and summer brought better weather and more visits from Kensley. Malida and Henry always looked forward to seeing Kensley, but neither of them enjoyed those times of fellowship as much as Tom.

Late in the summer of 1835, Kensley delivered troublesome news. General Thompson had captured Asi Yoholo and put him in leg irons.

Tom and Henry fell silent. Malida finally spoke, "If God be for us, who can be against us?"

Kensley interrupted her, "That's what bothers me, Mrs. Hapsburg. I ain't so sure that God is for us in the way some white folks like to think He is. There's a lot going on in the army that sure ain't winnin' us any favor with God."

Henry frowned at him, but Kensley continued, "Soldiers set fire to a Seminole field at Peliklakaha, and Indian children were burned alive. I've heard white men brag about beating Seminole men and raping their women. Just a short while ago seven whites beat an Indian to death at Alachua."

"Why was the red skin off the reservation?" Henry demanded.

"He needed food for his family, Mr. Hapsburg. The freeze last February killed a lot of the Seminole cattle, and there's just not enough game left on the reservation for them to hunt." Kensley dropped his head and lowered his voice. "I know this much for sure . . . some of the things we're doin' ain't right. I've seen soldiers set fire to villages and farms just for the fun of it. The Indians clear land for crops, and whites force them off it. The Indians ain't doing nothing you and me wouldn't do if the situation was the other way around."

"God knows I don't want to be around when Miccosuki Hell breaks loose." Kensley shook his head. "Mr. Hapsburg, those savages know how to fight, and the word 'mercy' ain't in their language. They're buying up guns and ammunition as fast as they can from white traders."

"White traders!? White traders are selling guns to Indians!?" Malida was horrified. "Surely there ain't many white people who would do such a thing!"

"It only takes a few, Mrs. Hapsburg," Kensley replied soberly. "I've heard about one white trader who's sold hundreds of rifles to Indians. These men are powerful and dangerous. Worst of all, they've got friends in government."

Henry, Malida, and Tom sat silently as Kensley continued. "If Indians get defeated, there'll be lots of money to be made in selling them as slaves. Whites can take over all that Seminole cattle at the same time . . . maybe 20,000 head . . . lots of money . . . ."

Kensley finished off the last slice of sweet potato pie before he resumed. "There are a lot of good men in the Army and in government who want to do right by the Seminoles. Governor DuVal was one of them, but DuVal's not Governor anymore. I don't trust this new man. General Wiley Thompson is one of the finest military men I've ever known, but like it or not, he has to follow orders from the President. Men in Washington offices at the top don't always understand what it's like down here at the bottom."

Henry wanted to dismiss Kensley's words, but Henry was losing an inward struggle. The reality he had tried for years to ignore was now relentlessly confronting him. It hammered at his head and his heart.

He made an excuse about needing to finish some plowing before dark. But Henry did not go to his plow; instead he ran to a palmetto thicket. For the first time since arriving in the Ocala territory, he dropped to his knees. For several minutes he rocked back and forth, wrestling within himself.

Finally he cried out loud, "Lord, You know I ain't much of a man. I've struggled with this ugly disposition all my life, just like my papa. I try to be different, Lord, but it jus' don't happen. Honest, God! You know I try! I don't like the way I am. Oh, Lord! Oh, Lord! You know I didn't bring my family here to put 'em through all this worry. You know in my hardheaded way I was trying to do right. I just want 'em to have the best. Please, God, take care of my family . . . and, please, make me a better man . . .more like preacher Blanton . . . "

Henry would have prayed longer, but he was interrupted by the sound of Kensley's approaching footsteps.

"Well, boy," he spoke softly, "I'm gonna be thinkin' on those things you told us."

"Yes sir, Mr. Hapsburg," Kensley replied. "I'm glad to hear that."

At daybreak the next morning Kensley was back on the river. Tom's heart was heavy as he stood on the bank and watched the boat disappear. Kensley was not just Tom's friend. Although Kensley would never know it, Tom loved him as the brother he had always wanted.

Kensley traveled two days on the river. The banks teemed with wildlife. Deer were so numerous that he didn't bother to look up when he heard them splashing away. Anhinga birds dived from their perches into the river, swam for long distances under water, and then stuck their heads up snakelike. He even spotted two mother bears with cubs. "Too bad there's so little game inside the reservation," he thought aloud.

At nightfall he strung up a hammock between trees and slept until sunlight fell upon his face. All too soon lazy days on the river and peaceful nights under the stars came to an end. Kensley put ashore at the big Silver Spring and walked the foot trail to Fort King.

The stockade walls and Sutler's store were welcome sights, the first evidences of civilization since leaving the Hapsburgs. Kensley made a brief stop at the store and then continued the short distance to the Fort.

Fort King certainly did not merit Henry's bragging description. It was nothing more than a high-walled corral enclosing quarters for soldiers, a blacksmith shop, kitchen and dinning hall, stables for horses, and an ammunition storage shed. The walls were erect pine logs less than twenty feet high with a rampart running the perimeter of the inside. A separate building housed General Thompson's quarters and the office of the Federal Agent to the Seminoles.

The fort's walls were only a short distance from the forest, and even brave men were terrified by sounds of wild creatures prowling outside the perimeter at night. No one ever got used to it. Bull alligators bellowed from the marshes, and panthers let out tormented screams that sent a chill down the spine of the most veteran soldier.

In the dark of night, screech owl cries were by far the most unnerving. Indians imitated bird sounds perfectly and used them as signals. Even in sleep there was no escape; nightmares plagued all the men.

At the stockade gate, Kensley greeted the few men inside. Fort King was understaffed. Only one company of soldiers remained. All the others had been sent to protect General Clinch's plantation twenty miles away. Kensley looked appreciatively at the soldiers inside the compound. He watched as one exercised a horse, three worked together to repair the rear axle on a wagon, another shoed a mule, and the remainder sat on logs waiting for the evening meal. These were good men. Men who wanted to do right. Men who loved their wives and children.

Kensley knew each of these men. He knew that to the last man each longed to be home with family. He thought of the Seminole men, trying to provide for their wives and children, trying to protect the families they loved. He half prayed and half wondered, why do good men have to kill each other? Why do loving husbands and fathers have to take the lives of other husbands and fathers? If only all men—red, black, and white—could live together peaceably.

Kensley turned back momentarily and stared at the forest pressing close to the stockade walls. Kensley thought of the vastness of Florida and of the utter impossibility of driving the red men out. If the Indians chose to stay, they would stay. There was no way the United States Army could make them leave. The only choice the government had was whether or not there would be bloodshed.

There was no comfort in the fact that Fort King was seriously understaffed. Thankfully, Major Francis Dade would soon be bringing up a hundred reinforcements from Tampa Bay. Some of the men at Fort King would then be given long overdue furloughs.

Kensley walked to the Adjutant's office.

"You're a good soldier, Kensley. Right on time!" The officer motioned for the youth to sit down. "You have a new assignment; you will not be going back to St. Augustine. As soon as the rider comes from Old Town, you will leave for Ft. Brooke on Tampa Bay."

Kensley closed his eyes. He had hoped never to hear those words. In the whole of Florida, possibly in all of North America, there was no more dreaded assignment. The trail went through the heart of the Seminole Reservation. There were no white families along the way, and there was no river travel. The Wahoo Swamp north of Tampa was almost impenetrable. It would mean horseback or foot travel all the way.

He had heard horror tales from other carriers. It was easy for a soldier to get lost on the Fort King Trail. The jungle could obscure a newly cleared area over night. But Kensley understood that mail between the two Forts had to go through.

In the four days leading up to his departure, Kensley groomed his horse and wrote letters to his family. He wrote of the Hapsburgs, of his friend Tom, and of his new assignment. Kensley did not write about his overwhelming fear of the task assigned to him.

Kensley's first morning on the Trail he was drenched by thundering cloudbursts. Heavy rains were followed by glaring skies and stifling heat. Swarms of horseflies and biting gnats attacked as soon as the rain stopped. Kensley rode with a dog fennel in each hand, sweeping one across the neck of his horse and swatting his own back with the other. Only in rare open stretches of the swamp could the horse gallop fast enough to stay free of the pests.

His second night on the Trail, Kensley stopped at a campsite between Lake Panasoffkee and Tsala Apopka. Other mail carriers had camped here, and stones from old campfires were still in place.

He boiled coffee and ate jerky with dry bread. Then he cleared a spot on the ground and spread out his bedroll. Kensley brushed his horse, removed burrs from her tail, and checked the knot in her rein. A soldier in the Wahoo Sawmp abandoned by a run-away horse would be hopeless.

But it wasn't fear of losing his horse that troubled him. There was a terrifying stillness. No cricket sounds, no bird cries, not so much as a leaf moving. Never had he felt such an oppressive silence. An overwhelming sense of loneliness pressed in on him.

Then the realization came. Clearly it was not loneliness that gripped him. No, on the contrary, it was a feeling that he was being watched. He had no control of the situation.

Stamping out the fire, he lay down on his bedroll. He stuffed a ball of Spanish moss under his head and put his pistol beside it. He tried to find a comfortable position, but there was no comfort to be found. He sat up. He could see the moon dimly shining on marsh flats in the distance. A haze lay over the scene that took all beauty from it.

Kensley got up. He walked a short distance to an opening in the trees. Again he had the disturbing perception eyes were upon him. Staring into the darkness, a terrifying chill slid up his back. There was no mistaking it now. He knew he was being watched. Wishing for the gun he had tucked under his bedroll, he started back to the campsite.

At the trunk of a large oak Kensley slowly turned and looked behind him. Inches away he saw the war-painted face of a Seminole.

With one swift and precise blow of a tomahawk, Kensley's life was over.

A week later his body was found by soldiers traveling south to Fort Brooke. A short time after that the corpse of Chief Tuckose E'Mathala was discovered. Gold coins the Chief had accepted from whites in exchange for his birthright to Florida were scattered in the woods around him.

Two bodies—one the body of a white man and the other the body of a red man who had betrayed his heritage—were left on the Fort King Trail as a message. The unmistakable interpretation was: *Red men will not leave Florida. The ground will drink the blood of those—red or white—who try to force him out. White man, go away!*

Chapter Seven

The Hapsburgs learned of Kensley's murder several weeks later. A family on a flatboat came ashore and told them of the mail carrier who had been killed in the Wahoo Swamp. Malida desperately wanted to join the family in their flight northward, but Henry resisted. Even when Lieutenant Terrance Browning, leading a regiment to Picolata, stopped at their landing, Henry stood his ground.

"Kensley Dalton went right into the heart of the Seminole Reservation," Henry argued. "But we ain't goin' there! I got better sense! We're staying right here where it's safe!"

Sorrow filled Lieutenant Browning's eyes. "God help you, Mr. Hapsburg. I genuinely hope you are right and I am wrong . . . I genuinely hope you are right."

Henry shrugged as the Lieutenant and his men shoved off from the landing.

Four days later Tom came out of the house without speaking. He stood at his father's back on the edge of the river watching another boat as it disappeared at the bend. This last family had not even taken time to stop. Tom understood their urgency. The river was no longer beautiful. Worst of all he sensed an ominous message hovering in the wind, the trees, the sky. Nothing was untouched by the spirit of darkness that had descended upon the land.

Mr. Hapsburg turned and put his arm around Tom. "We've been here over two years, son," he reminded him, "and we ain't seen an Indian yet."

Tom stared. He felt that his father's words were unworthy of a reply.

Finally Tom turned to his father and spoke, "It's the Indians you don't see that you have to worry about."

For a moment the boy remained almost in a frozen position. "Papa," he began again, "you don't understand. Kensley was not just a friend, he was the only friend I've had in the two years we've been here . . . and now I don't have him." The boy's words ended in a suppressed sob, "And Papa, we don't even know what's gonna happen next."

"And that's the reason we don't need to run, least not yet." He squeezed Tom's shoulder as he spoke, "You and your mama both know I've been right so far. If I'd listened to everything I heard, we would've turned back when the soldiers stopped us on the Micanopy Trail."

Tom looked at him in surprise. That was the first he knew of the warning on the Trail.

Henry went on, "People are killed more often by stampeding than they are from standing still. Besides there's gonna be more soldiers at Fort King than ever before. You heard Dr. Thad's son-in-law. Major Dade's bringing up another hundred men from Fort Brooke."

"What's another hundred soldiers? There's more than *five thousand Seminoles.* And, Pa, you know what Kensley said about the men at Fort King being afraid."

"I heard a lot of stuff those dumb soldiers said. And I know some of them joined the Army 'cause they're too lazy to do anything else! Why, some of them would jump if they heard their stomach growl!"

Tom's anger flashed. "General Thompson's not like that!"

"I never said he was, son! And he ain't no fool either!" Henry glared at Tom, "You know where General Thompson is right now?! He's down there at Fort King! You know good and well if he was afraid he'd find himself a good reason to get to Washington!"

"It ain't no good, Pa!" Tom argued, "it just ain't no good!"

Tom glared at his father. His voice finally showed strength, "We need to get mama and get out of here now."

"Well, we ain't! Dammit, boy!" Henry's temper flared. "You wear a man's patience thinner than an old maid's hopes! You sound just like your grandma Farrell! That old woman worried herself to an early grave thinking that I had ruin't her daughter's life."

Tom was defeated and knew it. "Sorry, Pa."

"Apologizing ain't what I'm after! I'm wantin' you to be a man. A *Hapsburg* man! And if some paint-smeared savage puts his foot on this place, I'll blow his blasted head off! I swear to God I will!"

Tom never answered, and Henry stalked away.

Several weeks passed without incident. News was neither good nor bad, and Malida tried desperately to restore calm to the household. She sang, she prayed, she talked of God's grace. In spite of her own fears, she remained cheerful and encouraging to Tom and Henry. She wanted to be loyal to both of them. The problem, as she often told the Lord, was their needs were so different.

On a Tuesday evening she cooked a big supper. She wanted this to be a special meal for both her men. She fried a young turkey Tom had trapped. Henry preferred 'possum, and she cooked some with sweet potatoes. The sun had already disappeared when Henry lighted the lamp and set it on the table.

They were just sitting down to eat when a voice called from the river. All three sprang to their feet and rushed to the door.

"Halloo!" a man's voice yelled. "Can we come ashore?"

It was a family of four on a raft. The man was standing bare-chested and barefooted with pant legs rolled up to the calves. The woman and two children were seated. The smallest, a girl, appeared to be about five years old. Her brother looked to be seven or eight.

"Be glad to have you!" Henry shouted back, rushing toward the landing. "Pull in here and tie onto that stump!"

As they reached the shallow water, the man stepped into the stream. He pulled the raft to the edge and introduced himself.

"Doulos is the name," he said extending his hand. "I'm Michael. This is Gabriella. The children are Eleos and Charis. We need putting up for the night."

"Wonderful!" Malida exclaimed, rushing toward them and wiping her hands on her apron. "We are so glad to have you! And what beautiful children! Got lots of supper waitin'. Come right in and sit down!"

Tom helped Gabriella and the girl ashore, "Company is a luxury we don't get too often," he said lifting the child from the raft and stepping to the bank. "It'll be fun having you visit with us."

Eleos splashed through the water and climbed up on a cypress stump. From there he leaped to the bank.

Gabriella looked around marveling at the beauty of the place; she was seeing it the way Tom used to see it. "GOD is good! All the time!"

"Yes, He is! And we are so glad to have the four of you with us!" Malida laughed and hugged the woman. "Gabriella is such a pretty name, good enough for an angel . . . but I've never heard 'Doulos' before."

"You don't know how grateful we are," Gabriella responded. "We haven't seen another white face in weeks."

Malida studied the girl. Her face was attractive and freckled from sunburn. Charis was square jawed with pretty teeth and brown wavy hair. Though she was obviously exhausted, her eyes were alive with brightness. Malida couldn't help but notice that all four of them had the same sparkling eyes.

Michael, who appeared to be in his early thirties, had thick dark hair with a masculine, pleasant face. He was a rugged man but even Henry could not help but notice there was an unusual gentleness about him.

"We've got plenty to eat and a private room for everybody," Malida teased, "providing, of course, you don't mind sharing your privacy with everybody else. And we talk about the Lord a lot," she warned. "You'll have to put up with our evening worship."

"With all the scare about the Indians," Gabriella answered, "it's a joy to meet somebody who can talk about happy things."

"Well, Sugar," Malida replied, "I know them Indians is out there in the woods. And they're meaner than a whelped bear. But whether we're here, there, or somewhere else, the good Lord has got to take care of us."

"I am glad to hear you speak that way," Michael answered. "God is your refuge and strength and a very present help in time of trouble." Malida's eyes flashed approval as he quoted the Psalm.

"How far you folks traveling?" Henry asked. "What have you been doing in these parts?"

""We've been helping families get prepared to leave," Michael answered. "We won't go too far, and we'll be back when the time is right."

"Well, I imagine that won't be long," Henry answered confidently. "The Army is going to take care of them Seminoles!"

Michael looked at him studiously, "What about you? Are you folks leaving?"

"If things get serious enough," Henry answered reluctantly, ". . . but not right now."

It was dark when the two families sat down to eat. Henry, uncomfortable with the thought of praying in front of strangers, called on Michael to bless the food. When they bowed their heads, there was a short pause. Then the stranger began to pray.

It was unlike any prayer they had ever heard. The words were melodious, filled with grace and mercy. Great peace came over Henry, Malida, and Tom. All three raised their heads and stared intently at their guest.

Michael prayed, "The Angel of the Lord encamps 'round about those who fear Him and delivers them." The words were alive and powerful as he continued, "In time of trouble He shall hide you in His pavilion; In the secret place of His tabernacle He shall hide you; He shall set you high upon a rock. And now shall your heads be lifted up above your enemies round about you. Therefore you will offer sacrifices of joy in His tabernacle, you will sing, yes, you will sing praises to the Lord."

Somehow it seemed fitting and reassuring when Michael closed the prayer, "You shall have an abundant entrance into the everlasting Kingdom of your Lord and Savior Jesus Christ."

More than ever in her whole life, Malida felt the need to be absolutely quiet. In the stillness, she sensed a Presence so marvelous and powerful that she dared not defile the moment by speaking. Even the Whip-poor-will in the cypress at the river's edge fell silent.

But the Whip-poor-will had not quieted itself because of the prayer. The bird was aware five canoes had paddled quietly downstream. Without the sound of an oar, they nosed in among the cypress at the Hapsburg's landing. It was the same spot where Kensley Dalton had always come ashore.

Fourteen Seminole warriors, faces painted with dark smears of red, green, and black, stepped onto the farm. Brightly colored quills hung from their hair. Five held guns; the others were armed with knives and hatchets. The leader, a slender young warrior who stood a few inches taller than the others, stepped out first and studied the cabin. A yellow glow shone through its windows. The odor of food spilled into the night air. Inside an unsuspecting family ate their last supper.

With eyes narrowed and bodies tensed, the braves watched their leader's hand for the signal. At the flick of his fingers, they crouched low and rushed toward the cabin.

In the next second, there was an eruption of war whoops and screaming, gun blasts and slamming of tomahawks, shrieking and crashing furniture. Then sudden silence. Even the wild creatures in the forest fell quiet. The collision was over as quickly as it had begun. Two worlds had collided. One a world of ancient love for land, warpaint, and violence; the other a strange mixture of innocence, stubbornness, and greed. Both were wrong. Both were defending the only life they knew. Each drew the other into violence and death.

A victor's dance followed in the yard as the warriors pranced and leaped their way back to their boats.

But overhead another celebration was taking place. Malida, Tom, and even Henry, were snatched out of their bodies with the speed of light. The excitement of amazing and glorious music exploded around them, vibrating them with an unspeakable thrill. The dimensions of time and earth disappeared.

Henry's farm no longer mattered. Tom's haunting sense of inadequacy and frustration was left behind in the fire. Malida's shout was heard in both realms, "I am lifted up above my enemy! I am lifted up above my enemy! I am lifted up above my enemy! "

In the batting of an eye they were gone. They were now free to see "Heaven open and the Son of Man standing at the right hand of God". All that Malida had believed, had prayed for herself and her family, was now reality. "Yes! Yes! Yes!" She heard herself shouting, "All that was lost is recovered, All that was broken is whole!"

Days later two government boats loaded with men in uniforms, rifles and shovels in their hands, docked at the Hapsburg landing. Led by Dr. Thad's son-in-law, the soldiers came ashore and stared silently at the scene of desolation. A scorched area marked the site of Henry's dream house. Beyond the ruin the men saw the garden just as Malida, Tom, and Henry had left it. A row of tall sunflowers stood unharmed. Stalks of corn were still waiting to be harvested, squash and pumpkin vines scrambled over the logs, and tomato vines were weighted down with their fruit. Lieutenant Browning gazed for a long time and then said to the others, "The serpent came back to Henry's `Garden of Eden'."

The men dug one large grave for the charred remains of three bodies. The spot they chose was midway between the cabin and the river. Without speaking they hammered three slats into the ground to mark the site.

They removed their hats, placed their hands over their hearts, and silently bowed their heads. Lieutenant Browning spoke a muffled prayer, "He remembers that we are but dust, and our days are as grass. But the mercy of the Lord endures forever. Amen."

There were no other bodies to bury. No raft was at the landing. The horror of the carnage remained only in the minds of a handful of soldiers.

Chapter Eight

Two weeks later Elder Blanton rode his horse slowly up the Danbury lane. He searched his mind for words to say, explanations to make. There were no words adequate for the task ahead of him. Dorothy was clinging to the hope that her mother, father, and brother had escaped to St. Augustine. His mission was to shatter her hope.

As he approached the house, Dorothy ran to meet him. George, now a toddler, was tied in his swing. Baby Edward was lying on a quilt on the porch. From the day Kensley delivered it until the day she died, Malida cherished Dorothy's letter that brought the blessed news of a grandson named George and another baby on the way. The letter that would have told Malida all about her second grandchild never reached her.

"Is James around?" Brother Blanton asked, walking with Dorothy back towards the cabin.

"He's in the barn. I'll go get him."

"No, wait. Let's just the two of us talk." The pastor exhaled slowly. "Dorothy, you've heard me preach many times that there is no way for believers to lose. We are 'more than conquerors through Him Who loves us.'"

"Yes?" She looked at him quizzically.

"'We are persuaded that neither death nor life, nor angels, nor principalities, nor powers, nor things present, nor things to come, nor height, nor depth, nor any other creature shall be able to separate us from the love of God which is in Christ Jesus our Lord . . . '"

Dorothy grabbed his arm. "What are you saying, Brother Blanton?

"Dorothy," he began again. "I want you to get a firm grasp on that promise of God before I tell you what I must tell you."

Her eyes flashed with panic, "No! Brother Blanton! No! No!"

"I'm afraid so, Dorothy." He gripped her tightly as she leaned against him sobbing. "Dr. Thad's son-in-law sent word this morning. It happened about two weeks ago."

James rushed around the corner of the house in time to catch her as she dropped to the edge of the porch. "I begged them not to go! Tom and I both begged them not to do it! I tried to talk to Papa!" Dorothy slumped into James' lap, her body racking with hard sobs.

James carried her into the house and stretched her out on the bed.

Elder Blanton followed them. "I'll go get Carolyn. If anybody can help at a time like this, it's Carolyn."

The McKay's came immediately, as did other families from Blue Springs Church.

"Only God can heal a soul injury as profound as Dorothy's. And He usually takes a long time doing it," Pastor Blanton counseled. "What we can do is stay close and love her with all our hearts."

Church members filled the house with food and words of condolence. But underlying their sympathy for Dorothy was gut-wrenching fear. There was no escape from the oppressive knowledge that any one of them could be next to fall victim to the Miccosuki ax.

Overnight panic raced like a windblown wildfire through the state. Homes were attacked, and thriving pioneer farms were abandoned as their owners escaped with only the clothes on their backs. Vacated dwellings were ravaged and burned by Indians; crops were set ablaze. On the Suwanee, the Oklawaha, and the St. Johns, white families poled flatboats toward what they hoped would be safety. Even farms as far north as the Oithlacoochee River near Madison were abandoned.

Some were killed trying to escape. Those who traveled by wagons fought drenching rains, mud holes, and swollen creeks. Some made it; others did not. Axles broke. Boats overturned. Families were drowned, some pulled under the water by alligators.

Many fell prey to fatigue and illness. Others became lost in the wilderness and perished.

When his next preaching appointment at Blue Springs Church arrived, Brother Blanton was surprised to see Dorothy and James seated in their usual pew. The stubbornness the young woman inherited from her father could be an asset in difficult times. Despite her pervading grief, Dorothy was determined to return to her regular routine as quickly as possible. She forced herself to listen to Brother Blanton's preaching and even participated in small talk over dinner.

After the meal Dorothy climbed into the wagon for the trip home. Elder Blanton climbed up and sat next to her.

Dorothy was silent as she worked up enough self-control to speak without tears. "Why, Brother Blanton? Why did God permit it?"

"God did not permit this, Dorothy!" he shot back at her. "We did!"

Dorothy could no longer hold back the tears. "What do you mean? What did I do? What did I do, Brother Blanton?"

The pastor put his arm around her shoulders. The last thing in the world he wanted to do was add to this young woman's already unbearable burden.

"Oh, Dorothy," he began in a gentler tone. "I don't mean you personally; I am speaking of the Body of Christ collectively. Jesus gave us a direct command to take the gospel to every nation and every tribe. But instead of going to the Seminoles with the good news that Jesus died for them, we have gone to them armed with guns and empty words we call 'treaties.'"

Brother Blanton paused for a moment. "We have closed our eyes to the great suffering we have caused them. We have not even shown compassion for their widows and orphans . . . ."

He hung his head. The suffering on both sides was so great and so needless. He patted Dorothy on the shoulder, afraid that to say more would only add to her pain. But strangely Dorothy found comfort in his words. More than that, they ignited just a tiny spark of hope. It was a reborn hope that one day all Floridians—red, black, and white—would live in peace, together enjoying the blessing of the Lord.

Two days later the Governor held an emergency meeting at the Madison Square. The day was cold, and a north wind knifed through the group congregated near the Blockhouse. Stepping onto the back of a U.S. Army Wagon, the Governor called for a dozen volunteers to join a munitions train headed to Fort Wetumpka. Lieutenant Browning would accompany the train part of the way. There were not enough soldiers to provide protection; civilians were needed for the task.

According to the Governor, the volunteers would be gone no more than two weeks. "We do not anticipate any trouble with the Seminoles. We believe they have been driven far to the south, but we simply cannot take any changes with this shipment. This train is carrying ammunition that must be protected at all costs. The safety of our troops depends on it." The Governor paused and looked around the crowd. "Those of you who are single, or who have no children, are urgently needed."

There was a brief moment of silence, and then John McKay stepped forward. Carolyn was stunned; it happened so fast. There was no time to discuss it. They had no children, and John felt a responsibility to help. He was followed by more than a dozen others. As the wagons began to roll, Elder Blanton's son Jeremiah darted from the crowd and hopped aboard.

His mother ran after him; and he yelled back to her, "I gotta go, Mama! Tom Hapsburg was my best friend! I can't just let him die and do nothin'!"

The Governor's optimistic words brought little comfort to those who watched their loved ones riding away. The wagons disappeared in the dust of the Bellamy Trail leaving a despairing community behind. John and Jeremiah rode together in a wagon directly behind the one labeled, "Ammunition."

Carolyn climbed silently into James and Dorothy's wagon. She was numb with fear; there was no way she could have anticipated or prepared herself for this. Against James and Dorothy's protests, she demanded that they drop her off at her own home.

"I will be as safe in my house as I would be in yours," Carolyn insisted.

Colonel John Warren explained the travel plan for the ammunition train. The wagons would divide at Kanapaha Prairie. One section would travel from there to Wetumpka. Colonel Warren's convoy would head to Fort McCoy with the ammunition wagon.

Several days later under a clear December sky, the wagons arrived at the Kanapaha Prairie. The breeze moved the sea of grass like giant ocean waves. Men leaped from the wagons and eagerly stretched their legs. They exercised their bodies and briefly enjoyed the freedom to move around.

It was here the wagons separated. Colonel Warren went from wagon to wagon, repeating his instructions to the drivers. He spoke encouraging words to the men and bid each Godspeed on the journey.

As the Colonel approached, John McKay appeared from the flaps of his wagon, "We're ready to roll, Sir." John looked toward the southeast, "Beautiful day, isn't it?"

"Best I've ever seen!" the Colonel replied.

At the lead wagon the Colonel caught hold of the rail and raised his arm in a forward movement. Yodeling a long, musical, "Southward Hooo, the wagons!" he sprang into his seat.

As the wagons jolted forward, Jeremiah and John sat next to each other gazing toward the rim of trees on the southeast boundary of the prairie. A thin line of clouds looked like brush strokes across the sky.

"Sure hate to see the train split up here. Feels awfully lonesome without the others," John confessed. He turned and watched the white canvas tops moving away from them. Lieutenant Browning was riding in one of those wagons.

John and Jeremiah were not the only ones watching the train separate. From the south ridge under the protection of live oaks, eighty others on horseback, quills in their hair and paint on their faces, waited silently. They carefully studied the movement of the two convoys.

A young Miccosuki leader remained hidden under the trees until the first section of the train was beyond earshot. During his imprisonment Asi Yoholo had suffered the ultimate degradation; he had been chained like an animal. The angry Chief who had recently been released from prison was far more dangerous than the man General Thompson had captured. Today Asi Yoholo would avenge his honor. With a war whoop and a raised rifle, he led his warriors into battle.

Jeremiah was first to spot them. He grasped John's shoulder and shouted, "My God! John! Look!"

In that second Colonel Warren fired his rifle. "To the left!" he shouted. "Circle to the left!"

The wagons pulled into a tight ring, and men grabbed rifles. They hid themselves among crates and began firing as Seminoles wrapped their own ring tightly around the wagon train.

"Don't let them get the ammunition!" the Colonel shouted. "Whatever happens, don't let them get the ammunition! Blow it up if you have to! Just don't let them get it! "

For twenty minutes the firing continued. Horses brayed in panic. The two leading John and Jeremiah's wagon were writhing on the ground mortally wounded. Soldiers tried to yell to each other but their words were drowned out by the noise of war whoops and galloping Indian animals.

The smell of gunpowder filled John's lungs. Men around him had been shot, and some were dying. He heard calls for help but could not move from his cramped position. Even with the extra volunteers from Madison, the military escort was vastly outnumbered.

Blood covered John's face, but he had no time to think about it. He was oblivious to any pain. Jeremiah was somewhere close by; he had heard him yelling. Then John was seized by the sudden realization that the boy had grown quiet.

A moment later someone screamed, "Fire! Fire in the Ammunition Wagon!" John jerked up to see flames shooting through the canvas top.

Immediately the Seminoles retreated. John sprang from his hideout and leaped into the blazing ammunition wagon. He jerked the reins of the frantic horses and forced them into the open field away from the other men.

The shooting stopped as soon as the Indians were a safe distance from the wagons. There was a brief moment of quiet. Then suddenly a blast flattened the prairie grass and echoed a mile away. A plume of black, gunpowder smoke billowed into the winter sky.

From the protection of trees the red men watched the dark mushroom rise into the blue. Their numbers had been lessened in the battle, and some were severely wounded. Asi Yoholo gave the signal for his warriors to withdraw.

Frightening tales of the attack at Kanapaha reached Madison by horseback. Rumor after rumor preceded the return of crippled wagons and their cargo of injured. At the square wives and children, mothers and fathers, all waited out the long days of desperation. There was no official word. Even soldiers from Fort Noel had no news to share. Families waited, afraid to hope.

Carolyn stayed glued to Dorothy. Dorothy could feel the frantic tension in the body pressed close to her. When the beleaguered train finally rolled into the square, Carolyn broke free and ran to the wagons. Elder Blanton was close behind.

Carolyn's eye swept the men. "John!" she called desperately rushing from wagon to wagon, "John!" Colonel Warren stopped her. "Where is he?" she shouted. "Where is he?"

The Colonel dropped his gaze. "I'm so sorry, Mrs. McKay," he said regretfully. "Some of the men aren't coming back. They made the ultimate sacrifice."

"No! No!" Carolyn screamed. "He has to be here! He has to be here!"

The Colonel caught her under the shoulders as she slumped to the ground. Others were screaming and fainting. Mrs. Judson was laid across a buggy seat. The pound cake she had prepared for her son Harold was trampled in the dirt under the hooves of horses.

James carried Carolyn toward their wagon. He and Dorothy were both sobbing. As they reached the wagon, he turned back. "Where's Brother Blanton?" he asked glancing around.

In the last wagon he saw the pastor climbing through the tailgate and under the canvas. James left Carolyn in their wagon with

Dorothy and ran to the wagon where Elder Blanton disappeared. Inside he heard the man groaning. Jeremiah wasn't there. As James threw back the flaps, he saw Elder Blanton fallen face forward, clutching Jeremiah's duffle bag.

The preacher was sobbing, "Oh, my son! My son! Would God I had died for you Jeremiah, my son! My son!"

The next meeting day at Blue Springs Church the worship service was held in the cemetery. The sky was clear, the weather mild, and people sat on the ground or leaned against the palms as they listened. A gusty wind rattled the pages of Elder Blanton's Bible as he preached. At the end of the service as the congregation watched, a deacon erected five wooden grave markers.

They read:
John William McKay
1805 - 1835,
Jeremiah Samuel Blanton
1817 - 1835,
Henry Hapsburg
1793-1835,
Malida Hapsburg
1795-1835,
Thomas Hapsburg
1818-1835.

There were no bodies to bury. After the congregation dispersed, Carolyn knelt on the ground and laid a bouquet of flowers at John's marker. From where Dorothy stood a few feet away, she heard Carolyn say, "You are the only man in my life, John. There will never be another. I thought my life wasn't worth living after what Hiram did in Washington. But you brought love and joy into my life. You believed me when no one else would. I'll always love you, John."

Once again Dorothy sensed profound wickedness in that name, but this time she understood the Holy Spirit was forewarning her. Forewarning her of what, she did not know. She would have to wait for the answer.

The week before Christmas, Lieutenant Browning arrived back at Fort King; he had been there five days when the news of the explosion at Kanapaha Prairie and the deaths of John McKay, Jeremiah Blanton, and other volunteers from Madison reached the fort. He was grieved for his friends back home, restless and unhappy about being away during their time of crisis, but more distressed for his wife, Sarah. The only encouraging news was that Major Francis Dade and the replacements from Fort Brooke might arrive at any moment. And General Thompson had promised the best Christmas Dinner ever.

"There will be turkey and stuffing, wine and ambrosia, roast venison and every vegetable that grows in Florida," the General assured them. "And if we're a day or two late waiting for the other men to arrive, it will make the dinner taste that much better."

Christmas came and went. It was now December 28th, and Major Dade had not arrived. The men were fighting depression and boredom. Terrance Browning tried to fight off the monotony of the stockade walls by pitching horseshoes with Private Townsend who was also from Madison.

Most of the men were not willing to venture outside of the fort's protection, but a few ventured as far as Sutler's Store. General Thompson had no new information to offer. Privately he was fighting his own fears. The weather was cold, but it was sunny and dry. There was no apparent reason for Major Dade to be delayed.

That afternoon General Thompson and Lieutenant Constantine Smith walked from the stockade to the store, a little more than a mile away. The General spoke optimistically to the soldiers who opened the gate, "Tomorrow at the latest!" he half promised. "I'm certain they will be here by then!"

The two men strolled slowly through the woods to the store owned by the Hetzler family. Along the way they discussed changes that would come to the fort after Major Dade's arrival. Men who should have been received furloughs long ago would finally be free to leave. Constantine would be going home to see his wife and baby.

The General and the Lieutenant remained at the store for nearly an hour talking with Mr. and Mrs. Hetzler and the Rogers couple who operated it. General Thompson bought a supply of tobacco and a metal file as a gift for Major Dade.

He laughed as he explained to Lieutenant Smith,"The last time I was with Francis Dade his knife was the dullest I've ever known a soldier to carry. Maybe this file will help him keep it sharp." He smiled as he dropped it into his inside coat pocket.

Mrs. Hetzler stood on the porch and watched the two men as they left the store and headed back to the fort. She turned to Mrs. Rogers, "I never worried about General Thompson until that Hapsburg family got killed on the Oklawaha. Since then you'd think he'd be more careful than to walk in these woods like that." She shook her head, "If we weren't so close to the fort, my husband and I would have left for Savannah a long time ago."

As the two disappeared from view of the store, the General spoke, "Have you had any word from your family?"

"Yes, Sir," Lieutenant Smith answered. "My wife says our baby girl is getting prettier every day."

The General smiled, "There's nothing that makes a man feel more like a man than holding his own baby." He reached into his pocket and removed a gold coin. "Here," he said handing it to the Lieutenant. "When you get home buy something as my gift to your daughter."

The Lieutenant started to speak but a frown from the General silenced him. They froze in place as General Thompson listened. A bird whistle came through the woods on their right. The General knew it was not a bird. It was a dreaded Seminole signal. In that moment he knew Lieutenant Smith would never get home to his wife and daughter. Nor would he see his own family again.

Without breathing he whispered, "Your gun. Give me your gun!"

The Lieutenant's hand never touched the holster. Suddenly the forest exploded in a burst of rifle fire and war whoops. Fourteen bullets tore into Thompson's body. Nearly that many hit Smith.

As the men collapsed to the ground, sixty painted warriors leaped from the dense jungle and flooded into the path. One of them slammed his foot on the blood-splattered blue uniform. "Tell me now, General Thompson, who rules Florida? Now do you believe us when we say we will not leave?"

With a slash of his knife and a quick snatch, Asi Yoholo jerked General Thompson's scalp into the air. Immediately the others began dancing and rejoicing around the two bodies.

Strangely no one at Sutler's Store heard the gunfire nor did anyone at Fort King.

Mrs. Hetzler had just finished putting the evening meal on the table. She called the others to gather around. There were nine altogether including three soldiers from the fort.

As they sat down to eat, Asi Yoholo and his warriors raced toward the store. They stopped in the protection of the trees and waited momentarily. At Asi Yoholo's signal, they dashed across the yard, thrust their muzzles through the windows, and fired.

In one thunderous roar all nine were killed. The Indians looted the store, doused it with kerosene, and set it afire.

At Fort King, Private Townsend walked the narrow ramparts inside the stockade walls. Forty men in the yard below were waiting for their evening meal. Because of General Thompson's delayed return, dinner was already half an hour late. It was a clear, windless day and the late afternoon sky was as blue as any he had ever seen. The fading sunlight cast a golden glow across the landscape.

Townsend watched a whiff of smoke rising into the air. Chimney smoke coming from the store made him think of home and his mother's hearth. Most of all it made him think of Melody, his wonderful bride-to-be waiting for him at Madison.

Private Townsend continued his patrol, glancing periodically from the men below to the forest that stretched in every direction around them. When he rounded the corner and turned in the direction of the Sutler's Store, he froze in terror. The comforting chimney smoke had been replaced by black, ugly smoke belching into the sky.

"Captain! Captain!" he shouted nearly falling from the catwalk as he ran toward the men. "Fire! The store's on fire!"

Within seconds the soldiers scrambled to the top of the log stockade and stood transfixed. The billowing, black smoke explained why General Thompson and Lieutenant Smith had not returned. They were not coming back.

The soldiers instantly understood there only hope was Major Dade's imminent arrival. But fifty miles away near the Wahoo Swamp, the trail was littered with more than one hundred bodies of what had been Major Francis L. Dade's proud troops. Only a handful were still alive, desperately fighting for their lives. Of that number, only one would escape back to Fort Brooke. For the men inside Fort King, the stockade had just become their prison; more than that it had become their common grave.

Asi Yoholo's attack on Fort King began immediately. The men inside could not fire on the enemy except by exposing themselves from the top of the wall. Indians had the advantage of trees at various heights.

The Seminoles rained flaming arrows over the walls into the fort. The burning missiles landed among the horses, setting fire to bales of hay. The terrified animals broke down the walls of their corral and stampeded inside the fort. A soldier was as likely to be trampled by a horse as to be killed by a Seminole.

In desperation brave men fired from ramparts, but they were quickly knocked to the ground by Seminole bullets. More fire arrows landed inside the fort. This time there was a direct hit to the storage building, and soldiers worked frantically to remove the ammunition from the small shed.

When darkness fell, the Indians quit the battle. The blazing remains of the storage building lighted the inside of the fort. Working in the firelight, survivors dug a long grave to bury their dead. As each body was laid out, a corporal—the highest ranking soldier remaining—called out the name of the deceased. Each soldier's sword was shoved into the ground at his head.

"Private Marshall Townsend . . . Sergeant Nelson Sanford . . . Corporal Ernest Swilley." The young corporal fought to hold back his sobs. "Private Harlow McKinney . . . Private Harold O'Shields . . . "

After the last soldier was laid to rest, two more names were respectfully called, "General Wiley Thompson and Lieutenant Constantine Smith." The men stood at sorrowful attention as they gave a final military salute to their fallen comrades. The mournful notes of a bugler echoed across the dark Ocala forest.

Those still alive in the fort survived only for the night. At daybreak Asi Yoholo resumed the battle. Within a few hours he stood victoriously inside Fort King. The Seminoles celebrated. They carried off loot and a renewed supply of ammunition on Army horses.

With the fort behind them in flames, the Indians rushed out to conquer the rest of Florida. No part of the state would escape the terrifying reality that man for man and gun for gun, soldiers in blue uniforms had no advantage over red men in war paint.

Panic swept through the state. The Lasley family near Tallahassee was massacred. Sixty miles northeast of Madison near the Okeefenokee Swamp in Georgia, two more families were slaughtered. South of there on the Santa Fe River the remains of the Gwinn family were discovered. Mrs. Gwinn's lifeless arms still clutched her dead baby. It was evident that some of the Gwinns had survived the Indian assault only to be attacked and eaten by wild hogs. Just north of the state line, Indians fleeing Georgia to join their tribe in Florida, stormed the Columbia Church that lay in their path. No place in Florida was safe.

Chapter Nine

In the dark, the 'Wild Wind' traveled south on the St. John's River. The boat passed Welaka and stopped at a desolate location on Lake George. The bell gave five muffled signals. There was a pause, then three bells. Another pause, and one more bell. Minutes later a firelight directed the vessel to a landing. A band of Seminoles and a Negro interpreter met the boat. Behind them a large village lay hidden under the canopy of trees.

Through his black interpreter, Coacooche asked, "You have guns?"

"Fifty rifles, lead, and four barrels of gun powder," one of the five white men aboard responded. The man appeared to be in his forties. His hair was dingy, his beard dark and matted. He stank of sweat and river water. "Do you have gold to pay?"

The translation continued. "We have gold."

"You are going to need more guns and more powder," the white man said. "The Great White Father in Washington is sending ten-thousand men to destroy all of you. Your brothers who were captured are already dead."

The Chief bent low in despair as the translation continued, "All Seminoles who were put on ships at Tampa Bay were thrown overboard and drowned at sea. When the big Army comes they will kill your wives and little ones. You must fight!"

The 'Wild Wind' left the village by light of the moon. The gold coins stuffed into the white men's pockets had been looted from massacred white settlers. The gold wedding bands had been stripped from bodies of the slain.

The son of Coacoochee stood on the edge of the lake and watched the boat disappear. Unlike the white traders, Coosa Ico's body was clean. His skin was a clear bronze, and his long hair shone like the back of a crow. He was glad for the ammunition, but he knew these white men were not his friends. They were friends only to gold. White men who betrayed their own kind would betray red men even more quickly.

Coosa Ico had lived in seventeen different villages. Twelve of those villages had been burned by white men. Too many times he and his family had barely escaped with their lives. He had seen their chickees blazing, their old women trampled by soldiers on horseback, their fields set afire, and his cousins spilling their life blood from battle wounds.

Worst of all, his beautiful wife Noolitaka was defiled. She had been captured by three white men and raped. The baby she carried in her womb was the seed of a white man. Noolitaka no longer slept with her husband. She slept alone in another chickee. Soon she would give birth, and then the tribe would determine what was to be done with the baby.

Anger and grief flashed through the young warriors mind. He needed revenge! Yet he longed for the peace his ancestors had known before the white man came. He would someday become Chief in his father's place, but Chief of what? The tribe no longer had farms, villages, or tribal life. His children would inherit an even harsher life.

Coosa Ico turned and looked lovingly at the cluster of chickees hidden under the trees. More than thirty thatched-roof buildings ringed together in two tight circles under the covering of oaks and palms. Moonlight filtered through the treetops and bathed their palm frond roofs in a soft yellow haze. A thin curl of smoke was still rising from the coals of the evening meal in the center of the clearing.

A group of old men sat on stones near the fire examining the new weapons. Younger men stood behind them. Except for the laughter of girls, the village was quiet. Beyond the fire, garfish hung from the eves of the cookhouse. Raw hides of fox and raccoons were drying near the fish. In one corner, a mound of turtle shells was piled against a cypress pole.

A few minutes later the raspy voice of Pali Kapta, the village matriarch, ordered everyone to bed. The men rose obediently, hid their new rifles, and went to their chickees. Noolitaka rolled out Coosa Ico's straw pallet on the sleeping shelf and waited for him. After he lay down alone, she disappeared into the dark.

Coosa Ico's eyes would not close. Thoughts of white men robbed his sleep. He did not trust any of them. Their treaties always meant the red man would be forced to surrender more land. His brothers in the Yamacraw, Choctaw, Cherokee, and Creek tribes to the north had already lost their farms and been driven out like homeless cattle. Now the white man lusted for Florida. Someday, he thought, the white man will push us into the sea.

He meditated on the prophetic words of his grandfather, "You cannot fight the white man. His guns are stronger than your arrows. You must hide from him. Be patient. Someday the white man will come no more. Then peace will return." But white men kept coming. It troubled Coosa Ico that he no longer had faith in his grandfather's prophecy.

Then it happened. Lying there in the dark, a spirit of revelation came over Coosa Ico. He sat up straight. His grandfather now had new instructions for him; he knew it. He rose from the shelf and slid his feet into moccasins. He reached for his knife and tucked it under his belt. Although he had no use for the white trader who had given him the steel knife, he treasured the weapon. He had attached a small black feather and a tuft of fur to bring favor from the spirits and give the knife special power. Quietly he slipped out of the village.

Coosa Ico headed for a small flat-topped mound on the western side of the village. For many generations his ancestors had gathered on this hill for bonfires and dancing. Medicine men still came here to speak with spirits of the ancestors.

Under the bright moon, Coosa Ico walked to the top of the hill and stood facing west. Wind whipped through his hair and moved the tops of the knee-high bushes around him. For a long moment he waited; he listened intently for something beyond the noise of the wind.

He called the name of his grandfather. There was no reply. He called again, "My Grandfather! You must talk with me!"

Someone, or something, was with him on the mound. "Grandfather, I need your help," he spoke.

Coosa Ico's body lurched to the right. A form was materializing. The figure resembled his grandfather, but he found no comfort in its presence.

Coosa Ico bowed his head reverently. "You lived in peace with the white man, but now he takes all the land and forces red men to live in pens like cows and pigs. Soon he will put us on ships and take us to the land of the sunset beyond the Great Water."

The young man fell silent. A strange coldness in the wind gripped him. His body began to shake, and thick blackness enveloped the top of the mound.

Then he saw the others. Everywhere the air was filled with aged, wrinkled faces of red men and women. A vision of the Indian continent before the intrusion of white men opened before him. He saw a life of peace and freedom. Villages and campfires, lush farms and forests, lakes and wild rivers stretched out as far as his eye could see.

"Look around you," the voices of the wrinkled faces spoke in haunting unison. "Your fathers walked this land a thousand generations before the white man came from the Eastern Sea. Now you are like birds chased by a wolf. You fly to another field, and he chases you there. No matter where you go the wolf will come. This land is where you must fight and die. Do not believe the lying white tongue. You must never leave Florida!"

The apparition that resembled his grandfather began to change form. It swirled around Coosa Ico like a cyclone. There were flashes of fire and a suffocating darkness. The force grabbed him and threw him to the ground. Like a whirlwind it poured into him.

Coosa Ico choked and kicked the bushes. He writhed in the dirt. His body became rigid and paralyzed. The spirit now possessed him.

The beauty and gentleness of Coosa Ico were gone. As he rose to his feet, a man of war stood up inside of him. He felt a strange, violent power surge through his body. The heavy darkness was gone. The wind stopped, and the hilltop became still. The ancient voices were silent.

Coosa Ico stood trembling in the moonlight. Raising one arm he moved it in a wide, sweeping gesture toward the heavens, "I shall not leave this land where your sacred ashes are buried!" Reaching into his belt, he pulled out his knife and raised it toward the sky. "White man! You shall not live but die! You shall see the wrath of Coosa Ico, son of the Great Chief Coacoochee! The first blood of this knife shall be the seed of the white man planted in my wife!"

A week later at the stone fortress of Castillo de San Marcos in St. Augustine, Colonel William S. Harney rode his horse through the arched gate and into the courtyard. An elderly Indian woman, her hands tied to the saddle, and a black man dressed Indian style rode behind him. The black man and the Colonel quickly dismounted while two soldiers helped the woman to the ground. The Colonel hurried all of them into the office of General Walker Keith Armistead.

The General rose indignantly. "Who are these?"

"This woman has identified the village where whites are selling ammunition to the Indians . . ." Colonel Harney started to explain, but the General cut him off in mid-sentence.

"And you believe her?!" Armistead shouted. "I have informed you numerous times that the Department of the Navy has concluded that no such trading exists!"

"For God's sake, man!" Harney yelled back. "Tell me where the Seminoles are getting the bullets they shoot at me! It's your men they're killing. The Indians are getting ammunition somewhere!"

"Colonel!" the General blasted, "Your disrespect for my uniform can have you disciplined. Do you value the rank you hold?" He did not wait for a reply. "Tell me! Do you want to keep it?"

The Colonel swallowed hard. He stood up straight, arms locked at his sides. In a disciplined tone, he spoke, "I submit, Sir! Please accept my apologies."

General Armistead waved the back of his hand. "Dismissed. Get them out of here."

The Colonel did not move. Nor did he allow the others to leave. He waited until the General looked up again.

"It is my duty, Sir," Harney's voice was controlled and his words clearly enunciated, "to remind you that refusal on your part to adequately consider evidence brought to your attention can be considered treason."

Armistead looked at him in shocked disbelief. For a stunned moment, he stared at the Colonel. ". . . and what is that evidence?"

The Colonel turned to the interpreter. "Tell her to speak."

An exchange between the old Indian woman and the young black man followed. The black man translated. "Three weeks ago at Tsala, the village of Chief Mad Tiger on Lake George, Indians bought four barrels of gun powder, many boxes of lead, fifty rifles . . . "

The General interrupted, "From whom?! What is the name of the boat?"

"It named `Wild Wind'."

The General had seen the name of the vessel on his manifest. He spoke to Harney, "Find that village and destroy it! Locate the boat, sink it, and arrest the men. Keep me informed on your progress."

Colonel Harney and a battalion of men left together. Their destination was Tsala on Lake George. Once again Coosa Ico's village would be burned by the white man.

The Seminole woman and the Negro interpreter were taken inside the Spanish dungeon of San Marco. They were locked in adjacent cells. Each iron-barred cell was equipped with only a corn-shuck mattress on the floor, a jug of water, and a urinal pot.

Minutes later General Armistead walked into the dungeon. He spoke first to the interpreter. "Who is she?"

"She is mother of Coacoochee," the interpreter replied.

"My God!" Armistead shouted. "You mean `Chief' Coacoochee, the one they call 'Mad Tiger'?!"

"He the one."

"Does Colonel Harney know this?"

"He know."

"Find out what else she can tell us about Chief Mad Tiger," the General ordered.

A moment later the translation came back, "She know Coosa Ico, son of Coacoochee, he has war party with him. He goes to Tallahassee to kill all whites."

"How many warriors are with him?"

The woman held her hands wide and then clamped one fist together. "She think maybe fifteen."

Armistead walked back to his office and studied maps on the wall. With his finger he drew an imaginary line between Lake George and the Capital. The route passed over the Suwanee River near its juncture with the Santa Fe, the Estenahatchee, the Fenholloway, the Stillipica, and the Aucilla. Much of the area was wilderness, totally unknown and virtually inaccessible to the Army. The Indians would have a definite advantage. They slipped through impenetrable forest unseen and unheard. Without warning they appeared out of nowhere. They pounced their prey and then disappeared as suddenly as they had appeared. The General groaned aloud, "God have mercy on anyone in their path!"

When Colonel Harney and his men reached Tsala, they found it completely abandoned. Food, blankets, and a smoldering campfire were the only evidences of recent habitation. After a thorough search of the village, the Colonel shouted, "Burn it! Get the fire started on the back side of the village and work toward the boats. Don't leave anything for the Indians!"

The men lighted their torches from the village campfire and ignited the thatched huts. The blaze traveled rapidly from building to building. The fire roared like a drum roll under the heavy covering of trees. Overhead giant branches twisted in the currents of blistering heat.

The women and children of Tsala were safe in a jungle hideout sixteen miles from the burned-out Fort King. Mad Tiger and his men, armed with new guns and black powder, had set out in War parties headed in five different directions. The new Coosa Ico and his braves were headed to the white man's Capital, Tallahassee. With the fury of a storm and empowered by a demon of violence, Coosa Ico pushed northwest. Madison lay in his path.

Chapter Ten

A year after the Kanapaha Prairie disaster, the Army was routinely plundering Seminole villages and farms. Each time homes of red men were set ablaze and families forced deeper into the wilderness, it was considered yet another victory for the white man. Confidence mounted that Army troops had successfully driven the Indians south of Micanopy. Madison, Blue Springs Church, and San Pedro communities once again felt safe and secure. Families who had slept in wagons at the Blockhouse packed up and went home.

Matt and Isobel Hadley returned to the Fenholloway, and Carolyn was determined to get back to her own house. Since John's death, she had been staying with Dorothy and James.

Dorothy and James argued that it would be safer for Carolyn to stay with them a while longer.

"I know this isn't very consoling, but you have no way of knowing that I would be any safer at your house than at mine," Carolyn retorted.

"But James is here to protect us!" Dorothy insisted. "Over there you have no one!"

Carolyn interrupted, "I guess it seems that way . . ." she hesitated, "but Mrs. Gwinn's husband couldn't do anything to protect his family. And you, Dorothy, more than anyone else have taught me to trust the Lord in all things."

The next day James loaded Carolyn's trunk into the back of his wagon. He tethered her cow and horse to the tailgate. Dorothy and Carolyn rode on the seat with James, and the boys squeezed in behind them along with two crates filled with chickens.

When they arrived at her empty house, Carolyn stood motionless in the yard. So much had happened since that day she and John arrived here together. Memories screamed at her from every corner of the farm.

James went inside first. He opened the shutters and cleaned the fireplace. While he and the boys took the animals to the barn, Carolyn and Dorothy stepped inside. The house smelled stale. The photograph of Carolyn and John stared at them from the mantle next to a bouquet of dead flowers. Carolyn's life had changed drastically since that day she hurriedly left to meet the wagon train in Madison.

A clump of dog fennels had sprouted around the barn door, and James stopped to pull them up before opening the gate and leading the animals inside. He looked around at the stalls. Everything was just as John had left it. The two of them had spent many happy hours working here, and now the haunting emptiness mocked what had been a beautiful friendship.

Three weeks later Carolyn's house and grounds were back in order. There were no weeds in the yard, the garden had been hoed, and the shrubbery pruned. Carolyn still ate dinner with Dorothy and James every night; but for the most part, she was on her own.

If Carolyn had been tempted to lapse into depression and listlessness, she would not have had the time. Her cow was requiring a lot of attention. Dr. Thad made frequent visits but was never able to give a clear diagnosis.

Dr. Thad, like Carolyn, was still grieving over the loss of a spouse. Additionally Dr. Thad had lost his son-in-law Terrance Browning in the Fort King massacre. Now Dr. Thad's only child, the widow of Lieutenant Browning, had left for Pennsylvania. Like so many other women who became widows in Florida, she wanted to get as far away as possible. Dr. Thad knew his daughter would have a better life with her wealthy aunt up north. And he knew he would never see her again.

Dr. Thad tried several different remedies for Carolyn's cow with little success. He finally resorted to his special "All Purpose Tonic." This seemed to be the right match for the mysterious ailment. Nevertheless Dr. Thad still made frequent calls to check on the cow. Carolyn respected Dr. Thad's medical expertise, and she appreciated his friendship. Dr. Thad dreamed that someday, friendship would grow into something more.

Late one Saturday night, Carolyn was awakened by the noise of her cow groaning and slamming itself inside its stall. With lantern, quilt, and Dr. Thad's "All Purpose Tonic", she headed to the barn. The cow was on its side, writhing in the straw. Carolyn knelt beside the animal and poured the liquid down its throat.

"There, there," she said, stoking the cow gently. "Just relax. In half-an-hour, I'll give you another dose."

Carolyn spread the quilt on the straw and blew out the lamp. Then she lay down and waited. Twenty minutes passed. The cow was quiet, and the horse was sleeping.

Carolyn drifted off to sleep. In her dream she was back in Virginia. John was helping her pack for their move to Florida.

Suddenly she was awakened by a loud noise from her cabin. She heard it again. She jumped to her feet and opened the door just enough to see out. In the moonlight she saw half-a-dozen ponies tied to her front gate.

"Indians!" she gasped. "My God! They're in my house!"

The next instant she saw two Seminoles dash from her front door toward the barn. Pushing the door shut and dropping the bolt into place, she ran toward the horse. She grabbed his mane and jerked him toward the rear door. Shoving the door open with her foot, she leaped across the horse bareback and headed toward the pond. In a minute's time the Indians were in pursuit.

"God help me! God help me!" Carolyn cried as she clung desperately to the neck of the horse.

As they neared the pond, Carolyn began losing her grip. She was slipping from her horse's back.

"God! Help me!" she prayed. "Oh God! Please help me!"

As they reached the edge of the pond, the horse lost his footing in the mucky ground. He stumbled, and Carolyn slid off into the water. The frightened animal galloped away.

Pushing herself quickly into the mire and cattails, Carolyn sank as deeply as she could. Seconds later not more than ten feet from her, the Indians charged past.

"God!" she prayed, "Oh! God! Please keep them away from James and Dorothy's place! Please! Lord! Keep them away!"

Carolyn was shaking, her teeth were chattering, and her heart was pounding wildly. The water was freezing but she dared not move. The Indians might return. How long she stayed there, she didn't know.

Finally she rose from the pond. Her nightgown was drenched in black muck, and her body was jerking with cold. But she was alive!

"Thank You, Lord!" she praised. "Thank You! They missed me! Thank You, Lord!" Then her mind turned to James, Dorothy, and the children. "God, help them! Please, Lord! Keep the Seminoles away!"

Carolyn stumbled back toward the barn. Her stomach was cramping under a hard chill, and her body was shaking. She pulled down an armful of saddle blankets and peeled off the muddy gown. She wrapped herself in the covers and headed toward the woods on the north side of the farm. At a dead oak trunk she collapsed to the ground and fell into semi-consciousness.

At daybreak the next morning Carolyn started toward the Danbury house. She made it almost to the lane before collapsing again, and that is where James and Dorothy found her.

Dorothy was wearing her best dress for church, and the boys were Sunday clean. As they turned into Carolyn's lane, Dorothy sprang to her feet.

"James, what is that in the road?" she gasped. "It's Carolyn! It's Carolyn!"

James rushed the horse to the spot. Dorothy leaped out of the wagon and ran to Carolyn.

"She's alive!" Dorothy wept over her. "Thank You, Lord. She's alive!"

James carefully laid Carolyn in the back of the wagon, and Dorothy sat on the floor with Carolyn's head in her lap as they hurried back home.

When Carolyn roused, she tried to tell them what had happened. "Indians . . . eight or ten . . . ," She muttered weakly, "Thank God I had no fire in the house . . . they would have burned it down."

"Don't try to tell us now," Dorothy stopped her. "The important thing is that you are alive and will soon be well again."

The Danburys stopped at their house only long enough to load some food in the wagon, grab some clothing, and get James' two rifles. Then they headed for Madison. James rode with a rifle across his lap and Dorothy with the other across her lap. On the Bellamy Trail they met Harlow Bentley and his family on their way to Blue Springs.

"Tell everybody what happened!" James yelled. "Get everybody back to the Blockhouse."

When they arrived in Madison, they headed directly to Elder Blanton's house. Carolyn moved into the main house while James, Dorothy, and the boys slept in the barn. Word came that two more families, the Gilmersons and the Whatleys who lived between Carolyn's place and Charles Ferry Crossing on the Suwanee, had been massacred. By noon Madison Square was filled with families, wagons, oxen, horses, and mules, all camping near the Blockhouse.

In the late afternoon, Elder Blanton called a group together in the southeast corner of the square. He stood on a mounting block and announced, "Like it or not, we are going to worship!"

A large congregation gathered and joined Brother Blanton in a hymn. The singing was interrupted by soldiers on horseback galloping in their direction.

"We have good news!" their Captain yelled. "A band of Indians attacked the Army post at the Aucilla River this morning, and every last one of 'em was killed!"

A cheer went up from the crowd.

"Tell us what happened!" Elder Blanton shouted.

"They attacked the stockade right after daybreak," the officer explained. "It could've been bad, real bad, but about half our men bivouacked in the woods outside the fort last night. Them Indians didn't see 'em until it was too late. Whole thing was over in ten minutes!"

"How many were there?" James inquired.

"An even dozen, all of 'em young. Here, let me show you something." The soldier reached inside his coat pocket and removed a knife. "This is my souvenir," he announced proudly as he handed it to James. "Took it off the body of the leader."

It was an American-made steel blade, filed down Indian-style. A tuft of fur and a black feather hung from the handle.

"God only knows what this knife has done," James said softly.

Elder Blanton stared at it. A grimace moved across his face, "Except for the grace of God, we would have lost Carolyn to this knife."

"Well, it won't happen to no one else," The soldier replied, carefully returning the weapon to a sheath.

After the soldiers rode away, James stood by the watering trough in deep thought. Malida . . . Henry . . . Tom . . . people whose names he had heard but had never met . . . went through his mind. "Only God knows the blood on that knife," he mumbled to himself, "Only God knows."

The next morning as James was preparing to make a trip to the farm to care for the livestock, Dorothy made a sudden decision.

"James," she informed him, "I'm ready to go home. The Army killed that band of Seminoles, and there's no reason for us to stay here in town."

"Let's pray, and hear what the Lord says," James said as he took Dorothy's hands in his.

They bowed their heads together. A moment later James broke the silence, "Load up the boys. We're heading home."

Mrs. Blanton insisted that Carolyn stay with her a while longer. "I'd like her to stay at least long enough to give some of our church people a chance to go out and clean up her house before she sees it again."

"I'll be praying for your safety," Carolyn assured Dorothy as they parted. "The fact that I am still alive is proof of His care."

Dorothy nodded in agreement and kissed Carolyn on the cheek.

Back at home James built a fire on their hearth, drew fresh water from the well, and milked the cow. Then he rode to Carolyn's place.

As James reached the barn, he heard a whinny. Carolyn's horse was trotting towards him. "Thank you, Lord," James said, "her horse has come home!"

As he stepped inside the barn, the cow struggled to her feet. The poor animal desperately needed milking. James stroked her neck, checked her eyes, and looked into her mouth. "And you'll be good as new after I've milked you!"

The next day a group from Blue Springs Church arrived to help with Carolyn's house. Dr. Thad appointed himself supervisor. By mid-afternoon little evidence remained of the Indian attack.

A few days later James and Dorothy brought Carolyn home. As they walked through the front door of Carolyn's house, all three were struck by a conspicuous and puzzling absence on the mantle.

"Why in the world would Indians take a picture of you and John?" Dorothy wondered.

"I can't imagine," Carolyn replied. Standing on her tiptoes, she reached for something pressed against the wall on a shelf. "But they missed my Bible!"

Carolyn grabbed the Bible off the shelf and opened it. She pulled out a photo of John and handed it to Dorothy.

"I always preferred this picture, but John loved that photo of the two of us together," Carolyn's voice choked up. "And after he died . . ." Carolyn fought to hold back tears. "After he died I couldn't bear to change things. But now I'll just have to find a frame for this picture."

Dorothy looked intently at the picture of John. He was wearing an official-looking suit. There hadn't been a suit like that in Madison since the Governor's last visit. Dorothy recognized the White House in the background of the photo. Washington, D. C., she thought. Carolyn was the best friend Dorothy had ever had. Yet so much about this wonderful woman whom Dorothy loved with all her heart was a mystery.

Chapter Eleven

In less than four years, the Danbury household had grown to a family of five. George had been born a month before James and Dorothy's first anniversary. Edward arrived a year and a half later. Then less than six months after the deaths of Dorothy's mother, father, and brother, Dorothy gave birth to little Franklin.

By the time Franklin came along, James had developed a routine. As soon as Dorothy went into labor, he ran for Carolyn. Carolyn stayed with Dorothy while James rode into town to fetch Dr. Thaddeus. Once Dr. Thad was there, James did his best to make himself scarce.

While Dorothy struggled in labor, James paced the front porch. Over and over again, he walked to the barn and back. He checked on the animals. He checked the crops. Now with the birth of a third child, James paced off a perimeter where a room would someday be added to their home.

James' thoughts were interrupted by Dorothy's screams. Children are one of God's best gifts, James thought. Why does so much pain and agony come with a gift? Before he had time to contemplate any further, he was interrupted again.

Carolyn yelled from the front door, "James! Come inside! It's another boy!"

James broke into a cold sweat at the sight of the tiny, helpless little person. James was convinced this one would not survive.

"He's healthy as a wild deer," Dr. Thad assured him. "He'll probably turn out to be the cutest pea in the pod."

James stared at the little squirming bundle. "He's as red as a scalded pig!"

Though he was smaller than the others at birth, this new one had well-developed lungs and a healthy appetite. He screamed louder than the others; and as James would soon find out, he always seemed to be "as hungry as a full-growed hog".

James shook his head, "He's so little. He looks awful to me."

Dorothy managed a smile. "James," she chided, "don't talk that way about our pretty baby boy, our little Franklin."

"'Franklin!" Dr. Thad frowned, "Are you sure that's what you want to call him? I don't know why anybody would name a child 'Franklin!'"

"Your only job," James jumped to Dorothy's defense, "is to deliver, not to label."

"Well! If he were my child . . . "

"If he were your child," James crossed his arms in feigned seriousness, "I'd have already run you out of the county!"

Dorothy raised her hands and covered her face. "Oh! James!" she scolded. "Shame on you!"

As Dr. Thad predicted, Franklin did 'turn out to be the cutest pea in the pod.' James came to refer to him as his 'prize piglet'.

The baby grew, and it became more and more apparent that Franklin had inherited Malida's sanguine disposition. He laughed and enjoyed things others never noticed. By the time he was three years old he could giggle during a dinner blessing or church service so innocently that correction seemed a sacrilege. When others frowned at James for his failure to discipline, James recalled a time in an okra patch when Brother Blanton had come to his rescue. James greeted disapproving looks with, "Franklin is just rejoicing in the Lord."

Wherever Franklin went, he brought the atmosphere of a party. He was so much like Malida that Dorothy found she could often anticipate what he would do or say. The daily reminders of her mother brought Dorothy both pain and joy.

Of the three boys George was the most athletic. He climbed trees at every opportunity, enjoyed helping his father, and was always eager to show off his strength. He proved to be more stubborn than his brothers. Once his mind was made up, there was no room for discussion. Edward, on the other hand, was quiet and reserved. He was a deep thinker. On those rare occasions when Edward had something to say, it was usually worth hearing. Most of the time Edward was content to delegate his share of conversation to Franklin.

The birth of Joseph was the quickest and easiest delivery for Dorothy, and it was by far the least traumatic for James. As Dorothy reached her sixth month, James decided it was time to have a family talk.

"Your mother is going to have a baby," James announced.

"Wow!" George exclaimed, "We're gettin' a baby brother."

Franklin clapped his chubby hands, "Baby brother! Baby brother!"

"I didn't say it was a boy," James interjected. "This one could be a girl."

"A girl!" George was horrified. "We can't have no girl in our house!"

"May I remind you," James said with a smile, "that your mother is a 'girl.'"

"No, she ain't!" George insisted. "She's our Mama!"

James shook his head. Edward took it all in stoically, and Franklin 'rejoiced in the Lord.' Undaunted by the exchange between James and George, Franklin clapped his hands and did a little dance around the room. "My baby brother! My baby brother! I love him already! I love him already!"

On a house call near the end of the pregnancy, Dr. Thad gave strict instructions for Dorothy to refrain from riding in the wagon until after she had given birth. The next Sunday, however, was Brother Blanton's preaching appointment at Blue Springs Church.

"I'll know when it's not safe for me to ride in a wagon!" Dorothy protested. "I want to hear the sermon, and I want to be there for dinner afterwards!"

James knew there was no point in arguing.

Thankfully Carolyn was able to reason with Dorothy. "I'll stay home with you, Dorothy. There's no need to take any chances," Carolyn consoled her. "We can have our own Bible Study on the book of Esther. I've been reading Esther, and I have so much to share with you."

Dorothy and Carolyn spent all day Saturday preparing food for James and the boys to take to the church dinner. Although Dorothy would never have admitted it, by the end of the day, she was looking forward to a restful Sunday at home.

The next morning James headed for church with the three boys and the food. Dorothy and Carolyn sat down for a leisurely cup of tea and Bible Study. As it turned out, there would be no rest for Dorothy on this particular Sunday.

When James and the boys walked through the front door later that afternoon, they were greeted by the sight of Dorothy propped up in bed, holding the new baby.

"Come meet little Joseph," Dorothy said.

Franklin ran ahead of the others. He climbed into the bed, hugged his mother, and kissed the baby on his head.

"I love you, Joseph," Franklin said as he patted the newborn gently.

George and Edward looked on from a safe distance.

"Well, Dr. Carolyn," James teased. "Looks like Dr. Thad may have some competition."

Carolyn threw her arms into the air. "Oh! No! This is not my calling! I made it through this one without Dr. Thad only by the grace of God! I wouldn't do it again for anyone!" Then she added, "except Dorothy, that is."

That evening James sat down at the table with the family Bible. On the same page that recorded their wedding and the births of George, Edward, and Franklin, he wrote a new name, "Joseph Thomas Danbury."

The birth of a fourth son prompted James to finally begin the addition on the house. Over the next several months, he worked in the early evening hours after all the regular farm work and chores were completed. George, of course, wanted to help. James at first assigned him only small tasks he thought suitable for a six-year-old. It quickly became evident that the boy had a natural sense for construction work, and George proved to be a genuine asset in completing the project.

Had it been up to George, he would have spent a lot more time helping his father. But it was around this same time Dorothy determined George should begin his schooling. George was required to complete his lesson for the day before going outside to work with James. George's curriculum included "The Lectures of Thomas Jefferson", the Bible, a copy of the Constitution, a McGuffy Reader, and ragged sheets entitled "Principles of Arithmetic." Edward voluntarily sat down next to George during the lessons, and Franklin entertained Joseph.

George never showed much interest in schooling, but this was not the case with Edward. The next year Dorothy decided it was time for Edward to become a participant rather than just an observer. Edward amazed her by reading through the entire McGuffy reader on his first attempt. This thoughtful child had been quietly absorbing everything she taught George. In a short time the two boys were working together on the same lessons.

Franklin still kept Joseph occupied while schooling was going on. For the time being, it was an ideal arrangement. But Dorothy planned to begin Franklin's education soon and was concerned about getting him to sit still long enough for reading, writing, and arithmetic lessons. She knew that would be a real challenge. Dorothy did not know that one night very soon, she and her family would be confronted with a far greater challenge.

Chapter Twelve

A new crisis was about to erupt in the Danbury household. A heavy cloud cover moved in from the Gulf. By midday James, Dorothy, and the boys were confined indoors by heavy rain. The storm intensified in the afternoon and continued into the evening hours.

The boys were tucked in for the night when James thought he heard footsteps on the front porch. It must be the wind, he told himself. Then there was no mistaking it; he heard someone call his name.

James picked up his rifle and cautiously opened the door. "Elder Blanton! What are you doing out in this weather?"

The pastor rushed past him carrying a leather-wrapped bundle. He dropped onto the hearth and threw back the covering

"Jethro!" James and Dorothy exclaimed. "That's Jethro! Brother Blanton! What happened?"

"I've just walked through Hell! There's been a massacre at the Hadley place. Little Jimmy, Sandra Dee, every one of 'em, butchered in their own yard. Jethro's mama and papa are gone, carried off by the Seminoles—would've gotten Jethro too if he hadn't hid in the chicken coop."

For days on end, Jethro hovered near death. Although he had escaped physical injury, the trauma had robbed him of the will and desire to live. He hung in semi-consciousness, unable or unwilling to eat or drink. Dorothy forced small amounts of broth and liquor into his mouth.

The Danbury home was suddenly filled with strangers and never-ending talk of Indian massacres. Wagons loaded with soldiers and supplies passed daily on the Bellamy Trail. Many nights the new addition to the house was filled with soldiers. Troops bivouacked under the oak tree, and others slept in the barn. For several days the Florida Militia camped in the pasture while awaiting reinforcements from Jefferson County.

The military presence comforted Dorothy; she saw it as a shield of protection. The boys, on the other hand, felt anything but protected. Their lives had been disrupted and changed in ways they did not understand. Their daily routine of chores, schooling, and family worship had been replaced by frantic activity and unfamiliar faces. Nothing was the same. Even Jethro was different. He was no longer the energetic child who ran and played with them after church dinners on Sunday afternoons. Now he was silent, distant. Worse yet, Jethro had stolen their mother's time and attention when they most needed her.

The boys were afraid. They did not like what was happening around them, and they partly blamed Jethro. After all, everything was fine until he showed up. George and Edward sulked; they were easily moved to tears. Joseph wanted to be held constantly. Only Franklin seemed to be taking it all in stride.

Two months after Jethro's arrival, news reached Madison of another massacre, this one on the Estenahatchee River. White families had been slaughtered and their homes burned. As word spread, more refugees came northward on the Bellamy Trail. Fleeing settlers stopped to rest their weary bodies and water their horses. Many had abandoned their homes with little more than the clothes on their backs. Some planned to set up camp at the Blockhouse in Madison and hope the Army would soon get things under control. Others were determined to press on until they reached northern states where all of this would be only a bad memory.

In the midst of the tumult, Jethro made no effort to talk. He stared aimlessly when he was awake; and he slept in short, troubled spurts. Jethro's brief periods of sleep were punctuated by nightmares ending with frantic thrashing about. James and Dorothy moved Jethro's pallet next to their bed so they could wake him when the thrashing began. His dreams left him wild-eyed and terrified but still not speaking. Dorothy held him and rocked him back and forth, whispering reassurances in his ear.

"Do you think he will ever talk again?" James asked her.

"By the Grace of God, he will," she replied. "I just know he will."

"You sound pretty confident."

"If love can heal, then someday this child will be as normal as the others. It has to be that way! And I know it will be!"

At times Dorothy thought she saw evidence in Jethro's bewildered expression that he was remembering. Perhaps a memory of his parents had flashed across his mind. Maybe it was a thought of the Hadleys or their home on the Fenholloway River.

Despite his demanding schedule, Pastor Blanton visited Jethro as often as possible. Refugees needed food, shelter, clothing, and spiritual direction. The Florida Militia was depending on him to relay messages from Fort Atkinson to Lieutenant Garansak at the Blockhouse. His own church members, still overcome with grief and fear, desperately depended on him for comfort and counsel. But he knew that Jethro needed him, too.

On a Friday morning Brother Blanton rode up the Danbury lane and dismounted at the big oak. Jethro was sitting on the porch with James and George. The boy focused his gaze on the pastor.

Deep in Jethro's mind a dark veil blocked his memory, protecting him from reliving the night of horror. At the same time, a battle was underway to recover his identity and to piece together the strange partial memories that floated just beyond his reach.

Elder Blanton waited. The child stared intently at the old man.

"Jethro," the pastor spoke. "It's me. Brother Blanton. Do you remember me?"

A befuddled look crept across Jethro's face.

"I baptized your mama and your papa in the Fenholloway River, Jethro," Pastor Blanton continued gently. "Do you remember me rocking you on the Hadley's front porch?"

Jethro scooted backwards until he was leaning hard against the house. He clamped his teeth as if in pain. He pulled his knees up close to his chest and wrapped his arms tightly around his legs. A fleeting recognition seemed to flash through the child's mind. He closed his eyes and rocked back and forth, banging his head against the wall.

Then he stopped abruptly. "Brother Blandon! Brother Blandon! Where you bin, Brother Blandon? Where you bin?"

Jethro jumped up and ran toward him. The pastor picked up the boy. He squeezed the child gently and kissed him. "I am so glad to see you, Jethro."

"He's talking!" James shouted. "Dorothy! Come here! He's talking!"

Dorothy rushed from the house and threw her arms around Jethro. The child held tightly to the pastor and turned his face away from Dorothy.

Jethro looked pleadingly into the old man's face. "Take me home, Brother Blandon! Take me back to my mama and papa. I wants to go home!"

The old man fought back tears. "Tell me, Jethro, where are your mama and papa?"

"They's at the Hadley's, Brother Blandon. You know where we lives! Don't you 'member?"

"Of course, I remember!" Brother Blanton replied, his emotions about to explode. "I will never forget that, Jethro, never!"

Jethro's stare became glazed again, as if something painful were pressing on his brain. "Take me home, Brother Blandon. I ain't never been gone from home before. My mama and papa is gonna worry. We gots to go now!"

Elder Blanton walked to the steps with the boy in his arms and sat down. Dorothy hung her head, and James closed his eyes.

"Someday, Jethro," Elder Blanton began softly. "All of us will see your mama and papa again. We'll see Mr. and Mrs. Hadley, Little Jimmy, Sandra Dee. Everybody!" His words broke off abruptly as Dorothy fled into the house sobbing.

"I promise you, Jethro, you will see them again!" Brother Blanton forced a smile. "And it will be wonderful! We'll have the best time we've ever had."

"When, Brother Blandon? When? Brother Blandon, I wants to go now!" Jethro insisted.

The pastor hugged the child, "Right now you need to stay here with Miss Dorothy and Mr. Jim."

"But I don't want to! I wants to go home!"

Brother Blanton swallowed hard. "You can't go back to the Hadleys, Jethro. They aren't there anymore. They're in Heaven with Jesus."

"No! Brother Blandon, they ain't!" The boy raised his voice defiantly and pushed the man's arms away. "Mistah and Mis' Hadley and my mama and papa is at the house! I know they is. They ain't gone off and left me! They wouldn't do that!"

The pastor held him tightly. How he wished! How he wished they were all at the house, and he could take Jethro home right now.

In the weeks that followed, Jethro showed some improvement. His conversation sometimes seemed confused, and he stumbled over words; but he was talking more and more frequently.

One morning he sat down at the table where Dorothy was shelling peas. "Mis' Darthy," he asked, "Where is my papa and my mama? An' why ain't I living with the Hadleys?"

"You really don't know, Jethro?" she asked, pulling him beside her. He shook his head. "You don't remember Indians coming to the Hadley farm?"

He looked up in surprise. "No, M'am! I don't remember nothin' like that!" His words were defiant. "They ain't been no Indians at the Hadley place, Mis' Darthy! If they had I'd seen 'em!"

Dorothy hugged him again, holding back her tears. "I don't know where your mama and papa are, Jethro. I really don't. But until they come back, we want you to stay here with us. We love you, Jethro," she assured him. "We want you to stay with us until your mama and papa return."

For the moment he sat glaring, eyes unblinking. "When they gets back, you be sure to tell me, Mis' Darthy."

"Yes, Jethro," she promised. "I'll tell you."

There was such innocence behind those distressed eyes. Perhaps he would never know. Maybe God was protecting him by keeping the memory locked away. So many things she simply did not know.

But one thing she knew for certain—if Jethro failed to recover, it would not be for lack of love.

On George's ninth birthday nearly a year after Jethro's arrival, Dorothy sent the boys to catch chickens for supper. "Bring me back three frying-sized pullets."

Jethro pursued one under the fence and into the cow lot before he caught it. Holding the bird by its legs, he proudly announced, "This one thought he got away, Mis' Darthy . . . ."

Jethro froze in mid-sentence, his body paralyzed. A terrified expression gripped his face.

"What is it, Jethro?" Dorothy asked.

Without answering, the boy moved away from her in rigid, tense steps. His hand loosened, and the frightened chicken ran away squawking. For a long moment Jethro stood motionless, staring blankly across the field. A vague memory was tormenting him. It was close enough to stalk him, yet it alluded him.

At supper that night he had little to say. When the family sang, "Happy Birthday to George", Jethro was silent.

After everyone was tucked in for the night, James blew out the lamp. He and Dorothy drifted off to sleep, and the cabin was quiet.

On his bed near the fireplace, Jethro was twitching. He was struggling with chickens. Mis' Darthy was standing on the porch. But, no, it wasn't Mis' Darthy. It was Mis' Hadley! "You and Sandra Dee catch that chicken," she said. "Whoever gets it can have first choice for supper!"

But he couldn't catch the chicken. It flew into the garden where his mama and papa were working. Something was wrong. Bad wrong! Sandra Dee was running! The chickens were chasing Sandra. Chickens were everywhere! Mean chickens with guns and knives.

Mrs. Hadley was screaming. Mama was screaming. They were both running from the chickens. "Run, Jethro! Run!" he heard his mama yell. More noise. Everybody was screaming now. Chickens were flying everywhere. In the yard. On the porch.

Jethro ran. He kicked the covers off his bed. He ran as fast as he could. He had to hide. He dove into the palmettoes. An Indian ran past his hideout. There was blood all over the Indian's chest and face.

Then there was no more noise. Jethro was scared. He slid on his belly into the chicken coop and hid in the darkness.

The Danbury household was awakened by a bloodcurdling scream. James and Dorothy leaped to their feet.

"Jethro! Wake up! You're having a bad dream!" James grabbed the boy in his arms. "It's me! It's Papa Jim! You're alright, Jethro. It's just a bad dream!"

Dorothy lighted a candle. The child was shaking violently. George, Edward, and Franklin, wide eyed with fright, climbed down from the loft.

"I thought somebody got killed!" George exclaimed.

Dorothy and James looked at each other. "I think they did," she said.

James held the boy, rocking him back and forth. James could feel Jethro's small body tremble with each breath he inhaled. A sobbing moan accompanied each breath he exhaled. James sang to him softly until the child, exhausted and emotionally spent, could no longer resist sleep.

Jethro's memory had fully returned. There was no more mystery about the Hadleys, his parents, or why he was living with the Danburys. Now he had the truth, and only by the Grace of God would he ever be able to live with it.

Over time Jethro seemed to accept his new life and his new family. But the boys, other than Franklin, were not ready to accept Jethro. George and Edward were often insensitive, teasing or ignoring Jethro. Joseph was threatened. He clung to his mother whenever Jethro was around, afraid that this outsider was stealing his mother's affection.

Franklin was the only one who genuinely enjoyed Jethro. More kids meant more fun.

Dorothy and James admonished George and Edward to treat Jethro with kindness and respect. But friction, especially between George and Jethro, increased; and it reached the ignition point on a Sunday after church.

"You ain't the owner of me! Mistah' Jim is my owner!" Dorothy heard Jethro yelling in the barn.

As she ran toward the door, she heard it again.

"Mistah' Jim is my owner! He's the only one what can tell me what to do!" Jethro's voice was loud and angry. "And he's the boss of you!"

Dorothy heard George's voice, "If you're saying you're the same as me, darkey, I'll bust you in the mouth!"

"I'ze saying if you busts me in the mouth yo' papa's gonna' bust you in the butt! Go ahead! See what he do! I double-dog dare you!"

George lunged, catching Jethro around the waist and crashing him against the barn wall. Jethro grabbed George's hair and jerked him backward. Together they tumbled into the straw, scrapping and yelling.

Dorothy stormed through the barn door and pulled the boys apart. She grabbed each one firmly by an ear and dragged them out of the barn.

"My ear! My ear!" George yelled. "You're going to pull it off!"

"Don't you dare touch each other again!" she ordered.

"It's all his fault, Mis' Darthy," Jethro whined. "I wasn't doin' nothin'!"

"Don't give me that!" she snapped back. "It takes two to have a fight! You're both to blame!" She shoved them down on the porch step. "And don't you dare move until I tell you to!"

Dorothy was grieved by the hostility between the boys, but something troubled her even more. Her heart ached when she thought of Jethro's words, "Mistah' Jim is my owner!" She and James loved this child. They had taken him into their home and their hearts. They had tried to make him part of the family. Yet Jethro still saw himself as property, as their slave. Where had they gone wrong? Would Jethro ever understand they loved him like he was their own?

Either the fight wore them out or the boys feared incurring Dorothy's anger again. Whatever the reason, things were quiet over the next few days.

One afternoon Dorothy picked up Joseph and headed out the back door.

"Jethro," she called, "get the wooden tub and come to the garden with me. We need peas for supper."

Dorothy led the way to the garden, Joseph on one hip and a hamper in the other hand.

"I can help with the baby, Mis' Darthy," Jethro volunteered. "And pick peas, too."

"You're a good helper, Jethro, a good helper!"

"Yassum, I wants to be."

Dorothy worked a row of peas. Jethro settled in three rows away, picking peas and playing with Joseph at the same time. By the time Dorothy's hamper was half full, she was already fatigued from the overbearing heat.

"Come empty your tub into mine," she called to Jethro. "Let's see how much more we'll need."

The boy stepped across the rows and emptied his peas into her hamper.

"You are really a good worker!" she complimented him. "You've picked as much as I have, and you were taking care of Joseph at the same time."

Dorothy bent over to scoop up peas that had fallen to the ground. "This should be enough, Jethro. Let's get Joseph and go back to the house."

But Joseph was gone. Then she saw him, running through the garden towards the swamp.

"Joseph!" she yelled. "Come back here!"

As she watched, Joseph stopped short and pointed a pea flower stem at something on the ground. He bent down, poking the stem at whatever he had discovered. Dorothy's maternal instinct compelled her to run like she had never run in her entire life.

She was almost to Joseph when she caught a glimpse of the diamonds on the back of a rattler glistening in the bright sunlight. The snake was coiled, prepared to defend itself against what it perceived as an attacker.

Her eyes locked on the snake, she did not even see what knocked her sideways to the ground. Out of nowhere Jethro lunged between Joseph and the reptile. Jethro slammed his tub upside down, capturing the rattlesnake underneath.

Jethro threw his body over the tub as the panicked animal underneath struck at the wooden slats.

"Hold him, Jethro!" Dorothy shouted. "Hold him!"

Dorothy snatched up Joseph and screamed for James. "The gun! It's a rattler! Bring the gun!"

James charged across the field with the boys close behind him. "Get back, Jethro!" he yelled. He pointed the muzzle of his Blunderbuss at the tub.

The blast shook the field. Lead shot sent dirt and splattered wood in every direction. As the smoke cleared, the mangled form of a dying rattler thrashed in the dirt.

The next moment Jethro was in James' arms. "You saved his life, Jethro! You saved Joseph's life!"

Once they were all thoroughly convinced no life remained in the creature, George stretched it out and measured it with a corn stalk. "He's as long as Papa is tall! Over six feet!"

George cut off the rattles and counted. "Fourteen! Wow! Fourteen rattles and a button!" As they walked back to the house the boys took turns holding it.

"We don't ever want to lose this," Edward commented. "You won't never see a bigger one."

Jethro rolled his eyes upward, "Oh, Lawd! I sho' hope I don't never! "

The boys would never see Jethro the same way again. On the way back to the house, Franklin, Edward, and George jostled against each other for the privilege of walking next to Jethro. He had become their hero.

As they bowed their heads for the blessing over dinner that evening, James prayed, "Lord, we thank you for the great deliverance of this day. We thank you for protecting Joseph from the snake!" He paused, "And Lord, we're especially grateful to You for sending Jethro to us and for making him part of our family."

At the end of the prayer all the boys joined in an enthusiastic "Amen!"

After dinner Jethro approached James privately. "Mistah' Jim, I gots to ask you somethin'. That thing in the prayer about making me part of yo' family . . ."

"Yes, Jethro," James slipped his arm around Jethro's shoulders. "We believe God sent you to us, and we love you like you are one of our own."

"But I'ze a darkey, Mistah' James. Ain't no white folks I ever seed got darkies in their family. White peoples owns black peoples."

"Jethro," James turned and looked the boy directly in the eye. "We believe slavery is wrong. Brother Blanton hates slavery. We do not believe that one human being has the right to own another, because God made us all equal."

"Mr. and Mrs. Hadley never told me nothin' like that!" Jethro protested. "My mama said they was the bestest owners she ever had. And they was always nice to me, too!"

"Jethro, the Hadleys were my friends," James struggled to find words to explain to a child the ugly dilemma that was dividing the church and destined to tear apart a whole nation. "They were good Christian people . . . but sometimes good people get caught up in bad ideas."

Jethro looked puzzled as James continued, "We would like you to consider us family. You can call us 'Mama' and 'Papa' just like the other boys."

"Mistah' Jim, I thanks you for that," Jethro said through tears, "but I gots my own mama and papa."

James could no long hold back his own tears.

"Mistah' Jim, I could still love you and Mis' Darthy like a mama and a papa," somehow the roles had been reversed, and Jethro was comforting James. ". . . until my own mama and papa gets back."

"That'd be fine, Jethro," James hugged him. "Just fine."

Chapter Thirteen

The war with the Seminoles was in its dying hours. On May 1, 1841, a great American Indian Chief came face to face with a young American military officer. A flag of truce guaranteed the safety of Chief Coacoochee as he arrived in Ft. Pierce, Florida to meet Lieutenant William Tecumseh Sherman. The Lieutenant, in a display of contempt for the Chief and for the agreement, glared down at Coacoochee, never dismounting his stallion.

On June 4, 1841, little more than a month later, the Chief and the Lieutenant met again. This time the flag of truce proved to be a worthless fraud. Coacoochee was clamped in heavy chains and led away as a U.S. prisoner of war. At Tampa Bay the mighty Chief was forced up a gangplank and onto a ship that carried him and his warriors to the Arkansas territory. Unable to step but a few inches at a time, he bowed his head to the rail and wept.

Through deception and trickery, Florida's "Prince of the Forest" was captured but never conquered. "They may shoot us, drive our women and children night and day; they may chain our hands and our feet, but the red man's heart will always be free."

With salt spray in his face and longing in his heart, Coacoochee watched his beloved Florida vanish from sight. At that same moment, passersby in New York City gawked at the head of Asi Yoholo impaled on a stick for public display.

An uncounted number of Indians died on the soil of their beloved Florida. Four thousand Miccosukis were deported to reservations in the west. They were paid two cents an acre for their land. Those who suffered most were the Seminole children. Fatigued and unfed, many died of exposure or starvation. At times Indian mothers killed their own infants to spare them the tragedy of the life they were doomed to endure. Only a small, determined remnant escaped both deportation and death. They fled to the Everglades where the white men could not find them.

In battle, the Chiefs lost; in integrity and honor, the Seminoles proved themselves superior to those who clamped leg irons around their ankles.

In 1842 with the war still unwon, the U.S. Army quit the field. After seven years of fighting at a cost of nearly $40,000,000 and the loss of untold white civilian and Seminole lives, the troops withdrew. Nearly 1,500 soldiers remained behind in wilderness graves.

James and Dorothy stood at the end of their lane as long caravans of wagons passed by on the Bellamy Trail. They watched soldiers in bandages, some sitting in caissons with crutches beside them and the least fortunate jostling along on stretchers in white-covered hospital wagons. Those who had escaped battle wounds marched wearily behind the caravans.

No treaty was ever signed. Had one been offered, the Seminoles would have rejected it. The white man's treaties had lost all meaning of truth and value for the red man.

Ignoring the treachery committed against the Seminoles, white settlers praised Lieutenant Sherman for bringing an end to the hostilities. Sherman's treatment of the Indians should have been a prophetic warning to all Floridians. Years later white Floridians would encounter this Army officer once again. He would return as General, striking hearts with more terror than Coacoochee and Asi Yoholo combined.

By August 1843 life for the Blue Springs Church congregation was in many ways as it had been before the war. Brother Blanton had resumed his regular preaching circuit. Farmers were tending crops and raising livestock. Dr. Thad was delivering babies and treating common ailments with his unique concoctions.

On a Sunday morning James and Dorothy stepped down from their wagon and unloaded the boys. They followed the crowd toward the spring on the north side of the church building. Today,

Dorothy thanked the Lord, we will sing and worship without guards stationed at church doors and windows.

Though Brother Blanton's preaching had grown more powerful and anointed over the years, a spirit of heaviness overshadowed the church services. The conspicuous absence of fathers, husbands, and sons was a perpetual reminder of the great loss the community had suffered. It seemed there was no escape from sorrow, not even in the House of the Lord.

This morning Elder Blanton was scheduled to baptize Norman Bentley, son of charter members of Blue Springs Church, Harlow and Hazel Bentley. Slowly the congregation gathered on the white sandy shore of the spring, waiting for Elder Blanton and Norman to arrive. The water was clear as glass; it was a dark iridescent blue in the deepest part of the pool. A cliff dropped sharply to the surface of the spring at one end. At the other end, the stream burrowed through a canopy of tall palms and flowed into the Oithlacoochee River.

Dorothy never tired of being here. A hallowed feeling was permanently attached to this place. She, James, Tom, and her mother had all been baptized here. Shortly before John McKay volunteered for the ill-fated Army mission, he and Carolyn had stepped into the spring together. Memories hovered over this site like a beautiful fragrance.

Elder Blanton approached James, "Will you help me with my baptismal clothes?"

"I'll be glad to, Pastor."

"Take my dry clothes over to the oak thicket so I can change there later."

James hurried back to the preacher's wagon. He grabbed the clothing basket and delivered it to the spot where the pastor always dressed after baptisms.

Elder Blanton and Norman waded into the water as the congregation sang,

"On Jordan's stormy banks I stand
And cast a wishful eye,
To Canaan's fair and happy land

Where my possessions lie;
I am bound for the Promised Land,
I am bound for the Promised Land,
Oh, who will come and go with me?
I am bound for the Promised Land!"

For a fleeting moment the congregation felt as though they were Israelites entering the Promised Land. Elder Blanton and Norman stood together in the water. The young man crossed his hands on his chest and tilted his face upward.

"Holy Spirit," Elder Blanton prayed, "You came upon Jesus at His baptism. Come upon this young man today. Bury him with Christ in this liquid grave. Raise him to walk in newness of life, and fill him with Your Power!" He paused momentarily and then added prayerfully, "I baptize you my brother in the Name of the Father, the Son, and the Holy Spirit!"

The pastor plunged the youth out of sight. A wave burst out from the spot, and Norman came up shouting. His arms shot upright as he let out another yell and fell back into the water. Elder Blanton caught the boy's shoulder and supported him as his body floated effortlessly in the water. Shouts of praise went up from the crowd.

When the pastor and Norman stepped from the stream, three deacons rushed forward with towels. Two men escorted Norman to a private place in the woods. The other walked Brother Blanton to the spot where his basket awaited him.

"That water is always cold!" Brother Blanton said to the man behind him. "As soon as I get out of these wet clothes, take them to my wagon."

A moment later a pair of wet overalls, a blue work shirt, and a towel came hurling over the bushes. The deacon grasped them and hurried to the wagon. Meanwhile Norman finished changing into dry clothes and headed for the Meeting House.

From his private spot in the woods, Elder Blanton could hear the congregation singing. He did not hurry to get dressed; he let himself get caught up in the beauty of the hymns and the serenity of the moment. He stood there alone with God, enjoying the worship music and basking in the warmth of the sun on his naked body.

His thoughts were filled with the joy of Norman's baptism in water and in the Spirit.

He would have stayed longer, but he knew his congregation was expecting him. Reluctantly he removed his shoes from the top of the basket and prepared to dress.

Then he opened the basket lid. "Fried chicken! Potato salad!" His eyes stared in unbelief. "That James! He brought the wrong basket!"

He searched frantically through the basket only to find cornbread, chicken, and collard greens. "Wait 'til I get my hands on that rascal!" he threatened. "He won't forget this day!"

He let out a yell, but the sound went unheard. He called again. The only response from the Meeting House was the singing of the congregation, *"How tedious and tasteless the hours when Jesus no longer I see."*

"Somebody come here!" he screamed.

But the singing continued, *"The midsummer sun shines but dim, the fields strive in vain to look gay."*

He waited for a pause in the song and hollered louder, "I need help!" No one answered. "Dadburnit! Somebody come back! James brought the wrong basket!"

There was no reply, and the singing went on. *"When I am happy in Him, December's as pleasant as May."*

"James! Harlow! Somebody come here now!"

Gritting his teeth, he searched through the basket furiously. Underneath the food he found a folded red and white tablecloth. He jerked it out and tied it around his waist.

"Wait 'til I get my hands on that James!" he threatened again. "Just wait!"

He unwrapped the napkin from the cornbread and used it to wipe the sand off his feet. Then he slipped into his shoes. As he bent over to tie them, the tablecloth fell off.

"Dadburnit!" he muttered angrily. With his shoes untied, he twisted the cloth more tightly around himself. "I'll just go to the wagon and get that dadburned basket myself!"

But things did not work out that way. Odessa Mallory was sitting by the window on the north side of the building. From the corner of her eye, she caught a glimpse of something sneaking through the bushes. It was crouching low, dressed in red and white. She looked intently; there it was again. And it was coming toward the Meeting House!

Dr. Thad was seated directly in front of her. She gouged him in the back, "Doc! Doc! Look! What is that?!"

The doctor looked up in time to see a bent figure slipping through the underbrush.

"*Indians! Indians!*" he screamed leaping to his feet. "God A'Mighty! Grab your guns!"

Singing exploded into screaming and shouting. Benches over-turned, women fell to the floor shrieking, and children scattered. The only two men who had brought guns into the building that morning grabbed them and raced to the windows. Stumbling against a stack of hymnbooks, the first fell backward, accidentally firing his gun through the roof. Hazel Bentley dropped in the corner screaming a prayer at the top of her voice as she fainted.

"Stop! Don't shoot!" Elder Blanton yelled. "Don't shoot! It's me! Don't shoot! "

Effie Blanton raised up eye level to the window. "Benjamin! For Heaven's sake," she shrieked in horror at what she saw. "Put on your clothes!!"

The preacher made no response. Instead he burst into the open and raced toward the wagons with all his might. The congregation rushed to the windows on the opposite side of the building and watched in utter astonishment as their spiritual leader darted past them, shoes untied and tablecloth flapping in the breeze.

When he reached his wagon, Elder Blanton did not even look for the dry clothing. He snatched up his wet overalls and dashed to the nearest woods. A moment later he reappeared. Snatching the reins free, he yelled for Effie and clambered into the wagon. With his humiliated wife seated beside him, he rode out of the yard.

James rushed from the building and ran alongside the wagon. "I'm so sorry, Brother Blanton. I wouldn't have done that to you for the world!"

Without so much as a nod in James' direction, Elder Blanton slapped the horse with the reins. As the Blanton wagon hurriedly disappeared behind the trees, James turned back to the Meeting House. The shocked congregation stared wide-eyed and aghast from the building.

Then it happened. The church fell into side-splitting, foot-stomping laughter. Proper, elderly ladies doubled over and giggled uncontrollably. Parishioners dropped to their knees at the pulpit, rocking back and forth. Others tumbled across upturned benches. Laughing children held their bellies and rolled on the floor. Gladness rolled over the congregation like a crashing wave of healing, thera-peutic oil. Sunlight streamed through the gaping hole in the roof, as if confirmation that the mantle of darkness had been broken. Never, absolutely never, had such sounds of hilarity come out of a church building.

For Blue Springs Church the Seminole War had officially ended. But a new battle was about to begin at the Danbury homestead.

A few days later, James came in from the fields carrying a ball of yellow and brown fur.

"What in the world?!" Dorothy exclaimed as she and the chil-dren gathered around.

"A bobcat," James answered, holding the tiny kitten up for all to see. "I found him down by the creek . . . can't imagine what hap-pened to his mother."

"Papa!" Franklin pleaded. "Can I keep him? Can I keep him? Please! Papa! Please!"

"Not on your life!" Dorothy declared emphatically. "One thing I can tell you for sure! We will *not* have a wild cat in *this* house!"

"But, Mama!" all the boys argued. "He's so cute!"

"And just how cute do you think he'll be when he kills every chicken on this place?"

"Please! Mama! Please!"

"No! No! No! Absolutely not!

James could see Dorothy's determination in the set of her jaw and the tension in her shoulders. There was no use arguing, but he had other options.

James walked up behind Dorothy and slipped his arms around her waist. Kissing her gently on the ear, he said, "There's a full moon tonight."

"Oh, no, you don't! James Danbury!" Dorothy protested and pulled away.

James bent down and whispered to Franklin, "Take him to the barn, and put him in that old crate for tonight."

"Yes, Papa!" Franklin whispered back enthusiastically. "I'll make him a bed from some straw, and give him some milk!"

That evening without any prompting, the boys put themselves to bed earlier than usual. They pretended to be asleep when James, a quilt thrown over his shoulder, led Dorothy out the back door.

With their parents safely out of earshot, Edward philosophized, "Mama must really like looking at the moon and stars with Papa. She's always real happy the next day."

Over breakfast the following morning, it was settled. The bobcat would stay, and Franklin would take responsibility for its care.

The boys built a pen in the corner of the barn. At night the bobcat slept in the pen. By day he was leashed to the oak tree. Chickens, geese, and ducks rapidly learned to stay clear of the area. Franklin named the cat, "Sen", for a Florida senator he had heard his father criticize. The boys thoroughly enjoyed Sen; and over time even Dorothy, though she would never have admitted it, grew fond of the creature.

Jethro was adjusting to family life, and Dorothy had an inner confidence that the future held good times for the whole family. The crops were doing well. The bushes she and Carolyn had planted around the house were thriving. Everything looked healthy and green. In fact, as she mentioned several times to James, some things were doing too well. A fern had sprouted in the shingles over the back porch and was growing heartily.

"Will you pull that thing out before it damages the roof?" she asked. "It's been there most of the summer."

"I'll get to it soon," he promised. "I really need to keep working in the field right now."

"That's what you told me last time."

"Dorothy, I will get that bush off the roof! Just have a little patience!"

A week passed and the plant was still there. James had time to play with Sen and to pitch horseshoes with the boys, but somehow he never found time to deal with the growing problem over the porch.

One afternoon after finishing up in the field for the day, James stopped in the pasture to enjoy a game of kickball with the boys. Then he headed towards the cabin. As he came around the corner of the barn, he jolted to a stop. There was Dorothy perched on the roof of the cabin a few feet from the edge. Using her fire poker—the treasured wedding present from her brother—she was aggressively digging at the fern.

Cautiously James slipped into the outhouse where he could watch through a crack in the door. Dorothy had devised her own safety line for roof work. A rope with one end tied around her waist extended over the top of the house. At the other end, the rope was securely attached to a post on the front porch. James could barely keep from laughing out loud at the sight of Dorothy struggling with the annoying weed. Each time a splinter caught in her dress or her hand, her level of aggravation increased. James could hear his name spoken angrily with colorful adjectives.

Several minutes later Dorothy sat triumphantly on top of the cabin, the fern in her hand. With great satisfaction she tossed it to the ground. Then she untied herself and twisted around backward.

James prayed aloud as he saw Dorothy ease herself toward the ladder that was leaning against the eaves. "Oh, Lord! Help her!" He held his breath until she had made her way down the ladder and was safely standing on the ground.

Dorothy quickly removed the ladder and disappeared around the end of the cabin. James used the opportunity to make his escape and sneak back to the field.

He gathered the boys and ambled back to the cabin. Not a word about the fern was spoken.

A week later James came in from the pasture and found Dorothy searching through the woodpile.

"Did you lose something?"

Dorothy was almost in tears as she responded, "The fire poker, the one Tom gave us. I can't find it anywhere."

"Later, we'll look for it later," James responded confidently. "But first I need you to help me with something. Wait here for a moment."

Dorothy sat down on the steps while James stepped inside. She was still in deep thought when suddenly a brown, snake-like object flew over the house and landed in her lap. She screamed and jumped before she realized it was the rope.

From the other end James hollered, "Catch hold, and I'll pull you up to get the fire poker!"

Dorothy's fear flashed to embarrassment and then to anger. James had been watching her that day! Racing around the house she collided with him at the corner.

"James!" she shouted, "you, you . . . "

The rest of her threat was never spoken. James grabbed her and kissed her. "Darling," he said, "it's going to be a beautiful, clear night tonight."

Chapter Fourteen

Dorothy became increasingly concerned about Jethro's schooling. He obediently sat at the table with George, Edward, and Franklin during instruction time; but Jethro simply would not participate. Dorothy attributed it to the trauma he had suffered, and for some time she restrained her urge to push him.

"Give him more time. He's suffered so much." Carolyn seemed to have a special discernment for Jethro's situation. "You just don't know what it's like to lose everything, to have to start a whole new life."

Day after day, Dorothy pondered the situation. There were no more nightmares, and Jethro seemed fully adapted to family life . . . with the exception of his education. She respected Carolyn's advice, but she could find no good reason to delay any longer.

One afternoon Dorothy reached the limit of her patience. There was no way a child in Dorothy's household was going to grow up illiterate. Shoving a tablet and pencil in front of him, Dorothy insisted, "Jethro, you are going to write the letters of the alphabet *today*!"

Jethro pulled back from the tablet, "Oh, Mis' Darthy," he pleaded. "I'ze too afraid for you and Mistah James!"

"What in the world are you talking about, Jethro?"

"Mis' Darthy, my mama tol' me 'bout some white folks what got hanged for teaching a darkey to read." Jethro broke into tears. "And they beat that darkey with a horse whip real bad!"

Dorothy put her arms around the child. "Oh, Jethro! Jethro! God is our Refuge and our Protector!" Her voice was filled with the faith and confidence—and even the tone—of her mother Malida.

Then Dorothy added, with an irony that would not be revealed for years to come, "Jethro, no one in our family is going to get hanged. And no one, absolutely no one, is ever going to beat you with a horse whip!"

Jethro was unconvinced. Dorothy grabbed his chin and turned his head so he was forced to look directly into her eyes. "You know the Bible is the Word of God, don't you Jethro?"

"Oh, yes, Ma'am! My mama always tol' me that, and Brother Blandon, too! My mama loved to hear Brother Blandon teach the Bible!"

"Jethro, we all love Brother Blanton's teaching. But don't you think God wants you to read His Word for yourself? Don't you think Your Heavenly Father wants to speak to you personally through His Word?"

"Well . . . I needs to think on that, Mis' Darthy . . . . "

Apparently Jethro did think on it, and gradually he began to take part in the daily lessons. But it was not until Joseph began his schooling that Jethro showed any real enthusiasm for learning.

A special bond connected Joseph and Jethro. The whole family had experienced a breakthrough when Jethro saved Joseph from the rattlesnake, but something far greater had happened for Jethro and Joseph that day. It was the birthing of a bond between souls. The unconditional love of Joseph began to nurture Jethro's broken spirit back to life. The love that grew transcended the six-year age gap and the difference in skin colors.

This must be like the friendship of David and Jonathan in the Bible, Dorothy thought. There were so many reasons Jonathan and David could have—perhaps should have—been enemies, yet, "The soul of Jonathan was knit with the soul of David, and Jonathan loved him as his own soul." Likewise with Jethro and Joseph, there was no earthly logic to explain the love between the two of them.

It was a great relief to Dorothy to finally have all five boys involved in schooling. George and Edward were far enough along to do most of the teaching of Franklin, Jethro, and Joseph. Dorothy was beginning to enjoy those evenings when she could sit in her chair knitting or mending while the boys worked on their lessons across the room. She often chuckled to herself as George and

Edward struggled to keep Franklin's attention on reading and math. Franklin was maturing, but his first priority was still having fun.

All the boys were growing, and Joseph was doing his best to keep up with the others. With Jethro as his mentor, Joseph was learning to tend crops and care for farm animals. By the time he was seven years old, Joseph figured he could do just about anything the older boys could do.

One afternoon Dorothy and James looked out the kitchen window to see Joseph running desperately toward the house, right through the garden. As they watched, he fell head first between the rows of vegetables, scrambled to his feet, and then took off running again.

"That child!" she exclaimed, raising her hands to her face. "What has he thought of now?!"

"Well, at the rate he's coming, it won't be long before we find out!" James laughed. "Whatever it is, it must be powerful important!"

"With Joseph there is nothing unimportant! Everything is an emergency."

Joseph sprinted up the aisle of turnips and jumped across the onions.

"My poor garden!" Dorothy smiled lovingly, "I've told him a thousand times not to race across that patch. And just look at him!"

James stepped from the porch and met Joseph at the back gate.

"Can I go, Pa? Let me go with them this time, Pa!" He was out of breath and could hardly speak. "Last time you promised, remember?"

"Slow down a minute, son!" James laughed. "I promised what?"

"Say 'yes' before they get here, Papa, so there won't be no arguin'. You've gotta let me go 'cause you promised!" There was a judicial tone in his voice. "They're goin' trapping Friday night with Gilbert Mallory in the Rocky Creek swamp, and I have to go with them!"

"I never promised anything like that!"

"Pa, you always let them do stuff like that," Joseph's words were matter-of-fact. "And you know it's time for me to go, too."

"I only let them—and you—do what I think is safe and worthwhile. Nothing more and nothing less. Understood?"

"Yes, Sir," Joseph muttered, hanging his head dejectedly.

"If they're willing to be responsible for you, then I might consider it."

Dorothy interrupted, "That's not fair, James! Don't make the older boys take the blame. You tell him! Joseph is too young, and he knows it!"

Joseph stood still for a moment. Then, angry and disappointed, he stalked away.

"I'm not saying he's too young," James explained. "I did more dangerous things than that when I was his age. I'm just saying that the other boys need to be included in the decision."

"But I don't want him to go, James! I think he's too young!"

"Then you should be the one to tell him," James snapped.

"Then I will!" she fired back. Tossing her dishtowel onto the porch, she marched toward the barn. Joseph was standing by a palm tree, methodically thumping ants off the trunk with his finger. He didn't look up as Dorothy approached.

"Can't go, can I?"

"Not this time."

"I knew it. I'm not old enough. I wasn't last year, and I won't be next year, or the next."

"Joseph, stop it!" she ordered. "You should be glad your parents love you enough to care about your safety." She was angry, but her anger was towards her husband for putting her in this situation; and her heart went out to her young son. When she attempted to hug Joseph, he pulled away. Frustrated and annoyed over the whole matter, Dorothy marched back to the house.

Friday arrived; and just as Joseph had predicted, the older boys got to go trapping. He stood on the rail of the cow stall, watching them load gear and saddle horses.

Jethro tried his best to console him, "I'm gonna stay home with you. You and me can go fishing in Mis' Caroline's pond. One of these days we're gonna catch that granddaddy bass." There was no answer. "Joe!" he went on, "There ain't no use pouting. When you can't do what you wanna do, you do something else!"

"I ain't wanting to go fishing!"

"Not even if you could catch that big bass?"

"You fish there all the time, and you ain't never caught him!"

"And I never will if I sit on the fence the rest of my life."

Joseph jumped down. He turned his back to Jethro and began walking away.

"Joseph, when you get's ugly, you gets real ugly," Jethro called after him.

"You'd get ugly, too, if all you ever heard was `wait a few more years, wait a few years'!"

Secretly, Joseph knew Jethro was right, and he was grateful that he was staying home so that the two of them could go fishing together. But he wasn't ready to surrender.

A little later the boys rode out of the yard. Jethro took his cane pole and started toward Carolyn's pond. Confident that eventually Joseph would calm down and join him, he called back to him, "You know where to find me, Joe!"

Joseph stood stubbornly at the oak. He watched until everyone was out of sight. He teased the bobcat for a few minutes before heading back to the barn.

On the ground where the boys had saddled their horses, Joseph spotted a spring trap with the initials, "F.D.", scratched on it. "Franklin sure is going to be disappointed," Joseph mumbled sarcastically. "Too bad for him."

Joseph stood for a moment with the trap in his hand. A tempting idea flooded his thoughts. He could set the trap in their own swamp. Joseph's hesitation was brief, far too brief. He looked toward the house to make certain his mother and father were not watching.

He stopped at the hen house long enough to snatch two eggs for bait. Then he climbed over the corral fence, and with the barn shielding him, ran toward the southwest. Once he was behind the ridge he turned northward again and skirted along the edge of the swamp. He had heard his brothers talk about a second fork of the swamp that lay northwest of their farm.

Entering what appeared to be the narrowest strip of swamp, he hiked toward the opposite side. The water here was only ankle deep, and beyond it lay another ridge. The main flow of the swamp would be just beyond the ridge. He would set the trap and then join Jethro at the pond. He could come back tomorrow to check the trap.

Half an hour later, Joseph stepped up onto a sandy ridge. A short distance away he spotted the tallest cypress trees he had ever seen. There was nothing growing on the ridge but scrubby bushes, and he easily crossed it. He startled a covey of quail. The birds took noisily to the air, and the sound of their beating wings frightened him.

His heart was still racing when he reached a wall of bushes at the water's edge. For a moment he stopped, hesitant to go farther. Maybe he should turn back right now and just go fishing with Jethro. After all, Jethro had stayed home just for him.

Resisting the momentary pang of conscience, Joseph cautiously pushed his way into what looked like a huge, high-vaulted room of the swamp. Simultaneously he sensed the danger and absorbed the beauty that surrounded him. Standing there alone, danger warned him to leave immediately; but beauty held him fast.

Again he thought of Jethro, sitting alone by the pond, expecting him at any moment. Joseph started to turn back; but as he did, his attention was drawn to his brother's metal trap, hanging from his belt. He could set up the trap and then run all the way back. If he hurried, he'd still have time to fish with Jethro before sunset.

He unhooked the trap from his belt. Then he knelt down and gazed into the still, tea-colored pool. The riverbed sloped down rapidly directly in front of him, and the water was clear enough to see minnows darting about the bottom. Joseph was engulfed in serenity and absolute silence. He stared in awe at the huge cypress trees before him. He had never seen a garden so beautiful, and he wanted to take in every bit of it.

Joseph's were not the only eyes fastened on the scene. A short distance away, shielded by low-hanging swamp apples, a giant alligator rose on short muscular legs and slid unseen into the water. With hardly a ripple, it submerged itself and moved swiftly in Joseph's direction.

Joseph's fear returned suddenly, and this time it was stronger. He somehow knew that incredible peril was about to lay hold of him. He glanced nervously over his shoulder. When he turned back towards the water, he froze. Just below the surface, ghost-like and only two feet from where he knelt, he saw the terrifying head and bulbous eyes of a monstrous reptile. In that split-second the pond exploded. The alligator burst from the water. Its massive jaws clamped down on the boy.

Before he had time to scream, Joseph was gone. The swamp quickly returned to its deceptive tranquility. The only evidence Joseph had ever been there was his brother's trap, resting at the edge of the water.

In the late afternoon, Jethro returned from Carolyn's pond with two small catfish and a brim.

"Have you seen Joseph?" James called as he entered the gate.

"No, Sir, Mistah' Jim," Jethro answered with a troubled look. "I waited and waited for him, Mistah Jim. I was so sho' he would settle down and come on over to the pond. But he ain't never."

Dorothy stepped across the porch and into the yard, "You don't think he tried to follow the others, do you?"

"He couldn't without a horse," James reminded her. "He'll be back shortly. Let's not worry needlessly."

"But James, he's been gone all afternoon. It'll be dark in half an hour!" She looked nervously at the sky. The sun was already low in the west.

"Take the fish, Dorothy. Jethro and I will go looking for him."

Dorothy watched from the well as the two rode their horses bareback toward the west. "Lord, Oh, Lord!" she whispered. "Please don't let anything happen to that precious boy. Lord, please, he's my baby."

As James and Jethro disappeared, she hurried toward the south side of the farm. "Joseph! Come home! Joseph, where are you? Come home!" she yelled as loudly as she could. In the distance, her voice mockingly echoed from the trees.

Long after the sun had set and the stars were out, James and Jethro combed the woods. They searched the oak grove on the north side of the farm, sloshed through swamp water, and scoured the lane from their house to the Bellamy Trail. The boy was nowhere to be found, and there was not even a hint of what direction he had taken.

No one slept that night, or even undressed. James paced the floor praying, and Dorothy sat numbed in her chair. Dorothy imagined every terrifying possibility. He had drowned, had broken his leg, had fallen into a ravine, had been bitten by a snake, or a thousand other horrors. Jethro went from the cabin to the barn, field to lane, calling for Joseph.

Before daybreak the next morning, Jethro rode into town to spread the word. By ten o'clock the yard was filled with friends and even strangers who heard the news and came to help. Elder Blanton, Harlow Bentley, Dr. Thad, and most of the congregation from Blue Springs Church gathered at the Danbury homestead. They set out in pairs, diligently searching the woods. No possibility was overlooked.

Late that afternoon George, Edward, and Franklin returned from their hunting trip and were greeted with the tragic news. "We'll find him, Mama!" they promised. "Don't you worry! He's going to be O.K. We won't quit until we find him!"

People were everywhere, combing the countryside, milling about the yard, all desperately wanting to help. Every hint of a clue, including Franklin's missing trap, was pursued to exhaustion. The frantic searching over the next few weeks brought not the slightest trace of Joseph, and every shred of evidence disintegrated.

Elder Blanton offered what consolation he could; Dr. Thad prescribed medication. Friends came and sat silently on the porch. Each family member endured his own personal heartache. Dorothy went to bed; James sat beside her. The brothers blamed themselves for not taking Joseph with them. James and Dorothy blamed themselves for not letting him go.

For a while, Jethro's nightmares returned. He wept, prayed, and groaned for the little brother he dearly loved. Why had he gone to the pond without Joseph? How could he have been so foolish to think that Joseph would follow? Why had he left him alone? Why did life go on? This was too much to bear.

Carolyn stayed at James and Dorothy's house for the first few weeks. She wanted to comfort Dorothy and take care of the household chores; but her own sorrow was so intense, she could barely function. She grieved as though she were grieving for her own son. Some days she sat in Dorothy's chair and rocked for hours on end without speaking a word. Carolyn had held and rocked each of Dorothy's babies in this chair. With heaviness of heart, she recalled the secret about the chair she and Joseph had shared. Though he would never have wanted his brothers to know, at almost eight years of age, Joseph still sometimes let "Auntie Carolyn" hold him and rock him. Carolyn's arms ached to hold that precious child once more.

She could not get the picture of what she affectionately called Joseph's "pouty face" out of her thoughts. When Joseph was unhappy, his lower lip protruded, and his forehead wrinkled. Whenever Joseph made that face, it reminded Carolyn of the very first time she had held him in her arms, on the Sunday morning when he had arrived unexpectedly with no opportunity to run for Dr. Thad. How could it even be possible that she might never again see that little "pouty face?"

Sometimes Dorothy thought she heard Joseph laughing in the next room. At night Dorothy and James both dreamed that Joseph was home again, sleeping securely in his bed. In the morning when sunlight streamed through the windows, it jolted them back to bitter reality and crushing despondency.

Elder Blanton comforted the family with the same comfort that sustained him in the death of his own son Jeremiah. Over and over he recited David's words at the death of his infant son, "He cannot come to me, but I shall go to him."

"We will see Joseph again! God says it, and I believe!" Brother Blanton exhorted. "This sorrow will pass!"

The days that followed were filled with torturous agony. There was no respite from the pain, and no way to stop the passing of time. Each tick of the clock was a merciless blow to any fragment of hope that remained.

A month after Joseph's disappearance, the community gathered at Blue Springs Church for a memorial service. "A precious light is gone from the Danbury farm . . . a light that can never be replaced, but neither can it ever truly be extinguished. This little light will shine its blessing as long as any Danbury lives," Elder Blanton spoke from a heart familiar with its own sorrow and with a faith purified by fire. "It is only after the sun has set, that it paints the sky with its most beautiful colors. Joseph has gone beyond the horizon, but the happiness he leaves behind will always be with us."

The congregation wept loudly.

"As surely as the sun goes down, it will rise again! Jesus Himself promised it, and it is so! You will meet Joseph in Glory!" the old man declared. "Instead of each passing day pushing you farther and farther from him, each day brings you closer to him! Closer to that glorious reunion!"

Brother Blanton came down from the pulpit and stepped next to James. The preacher laid his hand on the shoulder of the bereaved father, "I believe with all my heart that Joseph is with the Lord, and we shall see him again! I know it is so!"

James was slumped over with his face in his hands; Dorothy and the boys sat immobile beside him. Elder Blanton spoke with great compassion, "James, I know what it's like to lose a son . . . I lost Jeremiah . . . and I also know what it's like to trust the Lord! And I do! With all my heart! James, I can tell you, in time, your strength will be renewed. Your faith will be restored!"

He closed his sermon with one of his favorite quotations,

"Time will heal, God will bless,
Turn loose thy fretful anxiousness!
He who knows the present wrong,
Also knows tomorrow's song!"

On a Sunday evening five months after Joseph's disappearance, Dorothy put aside her Bible and went to bed early. She slipped immediately into a deep sleep. She did not rouse when James climbed into bed next to her and kissed her.

The cabin was quiet, and it was a little after two a.m. when Dorothy awoke suddenly and sat upright in bed.

"James!" she called loudly. "James! Wake up! Wake up!"

He opened his eyes and turned toward her.

"I saw him, James! I saw him!" Dorothy cried out excitedly.

James, still half-asleep, raised himself up on one elbow. "Who, Dorothy? What are you talking about?"

Dorothy was laughing and crying. "Joseph! I saw Joseph! James, I saw him! I saw him!"

James was wide awake now. "You saw Joseph?"

"Oh, yes! Oh, yes! James, it was so beautiful I can't even describe it! He was with Mama, Papa, and Tom. They were laughing. It was so beautiful! Even the air looked like gold!" Dorothy leaped out of bed, danced through the house shouting, clapping her hands, and singing, "Lord! You let me see him! You let me see where he is! Thank you Lord!"

James ran after her, "Tell me everything! Tell me everything!"

"It started like a dream except I was leaving my body and being pulled upward with incredible speed. I could see our house and farm from above, everything, James, everything!"

Dorothy paused to catch her breath. "All of a sudden I was surrounded by light so magnificent, so bright . . . . but it didn't hurt my eyes . . . and the music, James! It was the most wonderful sound. You can't even imagine! The grass was emerald green . . . that's when I saw Joseph! He was coming toward me, not running, just 'coming'. How, I don't know how, but there he was! And he was laughing like he was happier than he'd ever been. Mama, Papa, and Tom, they were just beyond him, they were coming towards me. Everything around them was sparkling with golden mist. Just as we got close to each other, something pulled me back. James, I didn't want to leave! I didn't want to leave!"

James was in tears. An anointing came over him as he soaked in every word she spoke. "Praise God! Thank You, thank You, Jesus!"

The anointing was so powerful that Dorothy could no longer stand. She sat down on the edge of the bed with James next to her. "Oh, James! Joseph was so safe, and so happy! He was immersed in a Love so intense and so pure that it permeated everything. It was as if there was no gravity; everything was held together by this intense Love! Joseph was breathing Love instead of air! My mother was clapping her hands and laughing. She was jubilant at the sight of Joseph! James, I wouldn't have brought him back here if I could have! No! It's too marvelous! ' He cannot come to me, but I shall go to him!' "

Dorothy fell into James' arms weeping for joy. "Then the next thing I knew, I was back here in my body! Oh, James! Joseph is right where we want him to be!"

"You really saw him!" James laughed through his tears, "You *really* saw our boy! Joseph is still alive! He's up there, and he's alive! We don't have to worry about looking for him anymore. We know where he is! Praise God!"

Dorothy's vision impacted every member of the family. As Elder Blanton had prophesied and sooner than anyone had anticipated, James found his strength renewed and his faith revived.

At hearing Dorothy describe her vision, Carolyn shouted, "'Thou has turned my mourning into dancing! Thou has put off my sack-cloth!' John is there, too! I know John is there with Joseph!" Carolyn insisted that Dorothy repeat every detail of the vision over and over again. Each retelling brought fresh anointing. Dorothy and Carolyn both somehow understood that this vision was meant to do more than give reassurance about Joseph; a mighty anointing was establishing them and building them in faith for some future time.

The boys were genuinely comforted in the knowledge that Joseph was laughing and rejoicing with the uncle and grandparents none of them had ever met. They longed for the day when all three generations would be celebrating together in Glory. In the meantime, their love for each other deepened. Losing one brother made them value and cherish those who remained.

In time, Dorothy's vision did more than comfort the boys; it challenged them. No longer satisfied with superficial platitudes, they were compelled to pursue truth to its origin.

The boys needed answers. How could slavery be justified in the light of God's Word? It was inconceivable that Jethro had once been considered "property." Why had Seminoles been denied rights guaranteed to them in the acquisition of Florida from Spain? And who or what gave the United States government the authority to deport native Floridians from their own homes? Why had the church been silent on these issues?

James cautioned the boys in their quest. "You can be right in a way that makes you more wrong than those you oppose. The most dangerous rebel is the one who is blind to his own rebellious spirit, the one who does not see that it is rebellion and resentment within himself that is challenging the wrong in others." With fatherly concern, he added, "If you pursue a righteous cause in a wrong spirit, you can end up making a bad situation even worse."

Chapter Fifteen

Joseph was missed, but his absence never again brought despondency. Sometimes loneliness crept in; but loneliness was quickly displaced by the joy of knowing that Joseph was alive and well, in the Presence of the Lord. They longed for the day when they would be reunited in Glory; but for now, each member of the Danbury family embraced life on earth with a new sense of purpose and enthusiasm.

George, Jethro, Edward, and Franklin directed their energies into finishing the addition on the house. James and George had completed the outer structure and the roof. The room had provided shelter from the elements for soldiers during the war; but it remained little more than an empty, enclosed area. Dorothy vetoed the boys' idea to turn it into a home for their bobcat. Now the boys set out to convert it into a dwelling of their very own.

Under George's capable direction and with Edward as architect, the boys constructed a loft bed in each corner of the room. Beneath each loft, they built shelving along the wall. With notched logs and board steps, four ladders were assembled. At Edward's design, the ladders were secured to the wall as vertical stairways leading up to the overhead beds.

"I never had so much room for myself." Jethro marveled. "It's like we got our own house."

"Yeah," Edward observed, "a house with no place to cook."

"And we don't want any place to cook," George warned. "Mama might make us learn to fix our own food!"

Finally it was time to turn their attention to furnishings. While the boys worked on tables and benches, Dorothy and Carolyn worked on bedding, tablecloths, and window dressings.

Odessa Mallory brought a pitcher and washbasin. "The pitcher's got a couple of cracks in it, but it don't leak," Odessa laughed. "I figured the boys won't notice anyhow."

Mrs. Blanton contributed three wall hangings. In colorful, meticulous needlepoint, they displayed the Lord's prayer, the ten commandments, and the twenty-third Psalm. "These were Jeremiah's. His grandmother made them, and he cherished them." Mrs. Blanton explained, her eyes moist. "Tom Hapsburg was Jeremiah's closest friend. I know Jeremiah would be pleased for Tom's nephews to have these."

Carolyn brought flowers from her garden, and Dorothy made a cake to celebrate the day the boys moved into their new room.

Their first night alone in the main house, James put his arms around Dorothy and whispered, "We haven't had this much privacy since we were newly weds."

"And don't you go getting any ideas, James Danbury," Dorothy coyly and unconvincingly protested.

"Oh, but I already have an idea, a wonderful idea." James grinned as he kissed Dorothy firmly on the lips and pulled her body close to his. "And tonight we won't have to take a quilt out to the okra patch."

The next morning, the boys gathered around the table in the main house for breakfast.

"I wasn't expecting you," Dorothy joked. "I thought you all had moved away."

"We could never move away, Mama!" Franklin replied, with a wink to George. "We'd miss your cooking too much!"

The new living arrangement suited everyone. Having their own quarters gave the boys a feeling of independence and maturity. And James and Dorothy were enjoying a second honeymoon.

One morning as James read the Bible and Dorothy worked on the quilts she was preparing as a Christmas surprise for the boys, a thought abruptly interrupted James' concentration.

"Dorothy, when was the last time you saw Carolyn?" he asked.

"Now that I think about it," Dorothy answered, "it's been several days . . . at least . . . I've been so busy with these quilts . . ."

"I think we need to check on her. It's strange for her to stay away like this."

Dorothy dropped her quilting into the basket. "I'm going over there right now. Don't let those potatoes in the fireplace burn," she called to James as she headed out the front door. "They should be ready in about an hour."

At the bend in the lane, Dorothy saw smoke rising from Carolyn's chimney. From a distance, the scene appeared normal and usual. But the closer she got to Carolyn's house, the more evident it became that things were anything but normal or usual.

The wash, always carefully hung along the fence, looked as though it had been thrown at the fence haphazardly. The front porch, no longer neat and attractive, was littered with garden tools, vegetables, and an empty basket. Dorothy froze in her tracks at the sight of a ragged pair of men's boots next to the front door.

Fear engulfed Dorothy as she scanned the yard. A large, unfamiliar wagon was parked on the south side of the barn, partially shielded by the cedar tree. Should she run home for James? Should she call for Carolyn? Dorothy did not have to make a decision.

Two unkempt young men—probably a few years older than her own boys—appeared at the window. Their hair was long and dirty. They stared silently at Dorothy from vacant eyes.

"Is Carolyn here?" Dorothy hesitantly called. "I came to see Carolyn."

The two continued to peer at her without responding. Dorothy was about to call for Carolyn when a dark-haired man stepped to the window. Older than the others, Dorothy surmised he was their father. He, too, was dirty and disheveled; and Dorothy perceived something ominous and sinister about this man.

Before Dorothy could speak, Carolyn rushed out the front door onto the porch. She lingered momentarily and then came down the steps toward Dorothy.

Without opening the gate or inviting Dorothy inside, Carolyn stammered, "Dorothy, my sister and her family are here."

"Your sister!" Dorothy gasped in shocked surprise. "I never knew you had a sister. You never told me."

"She's my only sister. Her name is Francina."

"When did they get here, Carolyn? You didn't tell me you were expecting company." Dorothy was confused and hurt to think that her closest friend had kept a secret of this magnitude from her.

"They're from Virginia . . . I wasn't expecting them . . . I . . . I haven't been in touch with them since I got to Florida . . . I suppose they found me through the land grant records in Washington, D.C." Carolyn's expression was lifeless and unchanging. "They'll be staying with me for a while. Francina is not well . . . ."

"Carolyn, if your sister is not well, you need my help. I'm coming in." Dorothy reached for the gate, but Carolyn grasped her hand.

"No, Dorothy! Please," Carolyn resisted, "I can manage on my own." She held tightly to Dorothy's hand. "If I need anything, I'll let you know. It's just that I have to take care of this myself."

Dorothy had encountered this stubbornness in Carolyn during the Seminole War days when she tried to convince Carolyn it was not safe for a woman to be living alone. She knew it would be futile to challenge Carolyn. "Will you come get me if there is anything I can do to help? Anything at all?" Dorothy pleaded.

"I will, Dorothy. I promise."

Without opening the gate, Carolyn hugged Dorothy over the fence.

Dorothy watched as Carolyn turned and walked back to the house. From the window, the two young men stared at Dorothy again. The oldest was dark-haired like his father; the younger had sandy-colored hair.

The emptiness in their eyes captured Dorothy's attention and sent a chill through her body. She recognized a cry for help, a need to be loved. At the same time, she perceived coldness, almost heartlessness.

"God help!" Dorothy prayed. "God help Carolyn and that family!"

It was as if a dark power had taken control of Carolyn and her home, and Dorothy's fears had not been relieved by weak explanations offered over the front gate. Everything Dorothy had heard and seen told her Carolyn was in serious danger.

Her heart was throbbing in her throat as Dorothy turned to leave. She had moved only a few steps from the gate when she overheard voices from the cabin. Dorothy could not hear well enough to follow the conversation, but one thing she heard clearly and distinctly; and it terrified her. She heard Carolyn call out the name, "Hiram."

That name—it was the name Carolyn whispered to John so many years ago at the cabin raising. It was the name Carolyn had spoken at John's grave marker. The first time Dorothy heard that name from Carolyn's lips, the Holy Spirit had immediately given her a warning. The warning was still powerful and intense. Hiram was a dangerous man; she and James would need special wisdom to deal with him.

Dorothy clutched her skirt and ran all the way home. Surely the Holy Spirit's forewarning was intended to prepare her. But she wasn't prepared. Worse yet, she didn't know how to prepare. And why was Carolyn so unwilling to be helped?

When Dorothy reached home, she ran across the yard, through the house, and into the back yard calling for James. He appeared at the door of the barn; and she ran to him, gasping for breath.

"There's an awful man at Carolyn's house! He's evil! We've got to do something! Carolyn wouldn't even let me come in the gate!"

James held her in his arms as she told to him everything that had happened. Silently he prayed for wisdom and direction.

"From what you're telling me, Carolyn feels she doesn't need our help," he tried to comfort Dorothy. "Carolyn's no fool, and we can't do anything against her will."

"James, I know something is terribly wrong! You have to do something!" she demanded.

He hesitated for a moment. "All right. I'll get a group of men to come here to our place, and we'll send Brother Blanton over to Carolyn's. If Brother Blanton needs our help, we'll be available."

Saturday morning a dozen men from Blue Springs Church gathered at the Danbury farm and prayed while Brother Blanton made a call on Carolyn. Half an hour after he left the Danbury place, Brother Blanton returned, Carolyn with him.

Carolyn looked thin and drawn. Dorothy rushed out and took her hand. When their eyes met, Dorothy knew immediately that Carolyn was still as resolute and unyielding as when she had last seen her.

"I'm grateful for your concern, but please try to understand that I must handle this situation myself," Carolyn asserted before all those who had gathered out of concern for her. "If I need your help, I will let you know. In the meantime, you must trust me to make the right decisions."

Carolyn turned to Dorothy. She hugged her as tightly and as warmly as in the past, and assured her of her love. "We're like sisters, Dorothy, and we always will be . . . please trust me . . . just trust me."

The men listened earnestly. It was evident that Carolyn would not be dissuaded. Brother Blanton, nevertheless, persisted, "Carolyn, if we find out that you are in danger, we will override you and take action. As your church family, we owe you that much. It is our duty as Christians."

"I'm grateful for that, Brother Blanton." Carolyn replied. "I know you mean it sincerely." Then in an almost convincing tone, she added, "I promise you, if there is danger, I will tell you."

Carolyn hugged Dorothy once more and then walked home alone.

Elder Blanton threw up his hands. "There's nothing else we can do . . . except pray."

Dorothy shook her head. This was all wrong. Carolyn was saying the right things, but there was no sincerity in her words. Deep inside, Dorothy knew Carolyn was afraid. Others might not recognize it, but Dorothy could feel it. Carolyn was struggling to give the appearance of confidence. Dorothy's instincts told her that Carolyn's pride was preventing her from asking for the help she needed. Somewhere in Carolyn's past, Dorothy thought, there was an injury—an injury so grievous it still controls every part of Carolyn's life. So much of Carolyn's past was shrouded in mystery. Her father had been a judge during President Madison's administration. Carolyn's words at John's gravesite resounded in Dorothy's mind. Hiram had done something in Washington, D.C., something so horrific that Carolyn had been running ever since. It was apparent that Carolyn was willing to do almost anything to protect her secret past.

Occasionally Carolyn was seen in Madison, and she visited Dorothy from time to time. Carolyn continued to attend church, but she was no longer the elegant lady Dorothy had met in Madison Square the day of Governor DuVal's visit. Carolyn's dignity—like a beautiful flower struck by an unseasonable frost—had faded. It was evident in her clothing, in the way she carried herself, and in her uneasy smile.

The Danbury boys were no longer welcome to fish in Carolyn's pond, and the infrequent visits between Carolyn and Dorothy took place only in the Danbury home.

No one ever saw Carolyn's sister, Francina; but Hiram began to make himself more public. Sometimes when Hiram showed up in Madison, he was clean, well dressed, and seemingly well-versed on any subject of conversation. Other times, he was withdrawn, sloven in appearance, and unshaven.

On rare occasions, Hiram Jr. and Leroy accompanied their father into town. Each time Dorothy saw them, she felt she was watching desperate, caged animals. In the two years following the arrival of Hiram and his family, Hiram Jr. and Leroy were seen in public no more than half a dozen times. They never attended church. They frequently prowled through the south side of the swamp bordering James and Dorothy's land, but they were careful to avoid the Danbury farm.

Hiram's presence on the adjoining property was like a plague of darkness over the once bright and beautiful lane and the friendship that joined the two homesteads. Hiram's dogs were a continual reminder of the danger that lurked so close by. They were large, fierce mongrels; and the sound of their vicious, ceaseless barking echoed through the woods day and night.

Carolyn assured Dorothy the dogs were no danger to anyone as they were kept in pens, but Dorothy was neither convinced nor consoled.

In the summer of 1851, for a while at least, Dorothy was too busy to worry about Carolyn. She was engrossed in preparations for two major events. One event involved the whole community, and in fact, the entire country. The Diamond Jubilee—the seventy-fifth anniversary—of the Declaration of Independence was approaching. The other event was personal to the Danbury household.

Jethro had been born into slavery, and there was no record of his date of birth. For that matter, no one even knew for sure where Jethro had been born. Any hope of finding out had been carried off along with his natural parents in the Seminole raid that left all four of the Hadley's dead.

When Jethro became part of the Danbury family, Dorothy determined that Jethro's birthday would be celebrated annually just like all the other boys.

"Jethro, you're the only one in the whole family who gets to choose his birthday!" Dorothy announced.

"But Mis' Darthy," Jethro protested, "that don't seem right. I can't just go makin' up my birthday."

"Jethro, when do we celebrate the birth of Jesus?" Dorothy countered.

"Oh, I knows that, Mis' Darthy," Jethro proudly responded. "Christmas! December 25!"

"That's right, Jethro," Dorothy lured him in. "And is that the day Jesus was born? December 25?"

"Why, sho! The Bible say so!"

"No, Jethro, the Bible doesn't say that. There's nothing in the Bible to tell us what day Jesus was born," Dorothy instructed the child. "December 25 is just the day the church chose to honor His birth."

Jethro tilted his head and wrinkled his forehead. This was new information, and he needed to ponder it.

"Jethro," Dorothy pushed on. "The church loves Jesus, so the church celebrates his birth every year, even though no one really knows his birthday. We love you, Jethro; and we want to celebrate your birth every year just like we celebrate the birth of every member of our family."

Jethro did not take the task lightly. Only after serious consideration did Jethro choose July 4th as his birthday.

"And why did you settle on July 4th, Jethro," James asked.

"July 4th is the day this country got free, and that's sump'in ever'body wants . . . to be free," Jethro answered.

Many years had passed since Jethro's first birthday celebration as part of the Danbury family. Now it was an annual family tradition. As destiny would have it, Jethro's seventeenth birthday would be the biggest celebration in the history of the nation.

When the Danbury wagon rolled into town on the afternoon of July 4, 1851, it looked as though the whole world had converged upon Madison. The entire town was decorated. Banners hung from the blockhouse, the courthouse, the buggy shop, the tavern, the general store, the livery stable, the half-finished town hall, and from trees around the square. Flags waved in the breeze from the front porch of Elder Blanton's house on Moseley Hall Road.

The speaker's platform in the center of the town square was draped with red, white, and blue banners and flanked by a large cannon. Everyone talked excitedly about the fireworks display that would climax the evening. It would be the biggest fireworks show that Florida had ever seen, and people had come from miles around to watch. Families planned to camp overnight in Madsion Square and along roadsides leading into town.

"How Madison has changed," James spoke half reverently. "Who would have thought so many people would come to Florida . . . ."

Dorothy did not answer; for the moment she was lost in her own remembrance. The ancient live oaks still hung with as much Spanish moss as they had the day her parents' wagon pulled into Madison Square nearly twenty years earlier. She loved the square. The first time she ever saw James, it was right here.

The boys were ecstatic. They wanted to examine the cannon and see who else was there, but they did not want to get too far from the enormous cake that sat near the tailgate of the wagon. The cake had three tiers covered in thick, white icing. It was lined with green fern and pink flowers from Dorothy's coral vine.

"There's Gilbert Mallory!" George yelled, "Maybe we can spend the night with them. They've got lots of room."

As the boys started to leave, James called them back. "Pay attention to what the Senator has to say! Florida is no longer a territory. We are now a state. You can't be good citizens unless you know what's going on."

"We'll have our supper and cut the cake as soon as Senator Wilford has finished speaking." Dorothy added. "I've got fried chicken. If you want any, you'd better be on time. We're not waiting for anybody!"

As James tied the horse, the boys raced toward the speaker's platform and the cannon. Gilbert Mallory was already exploring the wheels, the barrel, and the ramrod of the giant weapon and was eager to share his authoritative opinion. "When that thing explodes, it's gonna ring bells all the way to Tallahassee!"

Two hours later, after Senator Wilford's long-winded speech had finally come to an end, the boys drifted back to the wagon.

"That man has the soul of a wood rat!" Franklin mumbled angrily as he climbed over the rail. "I wouldn't trust him farther than I could throw a plough stock."

James laughed. "What makes you say that, son?"

"He bragged—right there in front of everybody—he bragged that his father used to beat slaves with a surrey whip! He called that 'authority'!! He says that's the kind of 'authority' Florida needs to show the rest of the nation!"

The other boys were eager to express their disapproval as well, but Dorothy quickly changed the subject. She had already endured all she could stomach of the senator's remarks. "Light the lantern, and let's eat. If we don't get started soon, the fireworks will start before we can finish dinner."

"The soldiers are going to shoot the cannon at sunset," Franklin announced. "I bet it'll scare the chickens all the way back at our barn. The Lieutenant told me it came from the fort at Fernandina. It can shoot a twenty pound cannon ball all the way across the bay!"

Why is it that even in times of peace, Dorothy wondered, there must be constant reminders of war? As she spread out the dinner on the tailgate, she remembered the words of Jesus, ". . . wars and rumors of wars . . . ." With a mother's heart, she looked at the four boys, so filled with joy and excitement. Lord, she prayed silently, let it be only "rumors of wars" in their lives.

The family gathered at the end of the wagon. "Give your attention, boys," James said, "Let's bow our heads for the blessing."

"Let's all hold hands," Dorothy quickly interjected. "We're thankful for God's blessing on our nation, on our farm, on each other . . . and for Jethro." She squeezed Jethro's hand and smiled widely, "You are a wonderful blessing in our lives. We thank the Lord, Jethro, that He chose us to be the ones to raise you."

Jethro lowered his eyes modestly, "I'm thankful, too, Mis' Darthy."

The sun was setting as the little circle pulled tightly together with bowed heads. "O Lord," James prayed, "for these Thy blessings, we give Thee thanks . . . "

The cannon exploded and rocked the square with a roar that echoed a mile away. Cutting his prayer short, James threw up his hands and yelled, "In the Name of Jesus, Amen! Hold the horse, George! Dorothy, grab the cake!"

The cannon erupted a second time, and the wagon shook. George held the reins tightly as the horse reared. Dogs howled, and people shouted.

Dorothy served dinner to a background of cheering and celebrating. She handed Jethro his plate first. The drumstick was Jethro's favorite piece of chicken, and the other boys looked on with concern as Jethro received two drumsticks and a large serving of sweet potato pie.

"There's plenty for everybody," Dorothy laughed. "I cooked enough cornbread and black-eyed peas to feed the county."

As they finished the meal, James pulled the cake to the edge of the tailgate; and Dorothy lit the candles.

"When I give the signal everybody sing, and sing loud!" Dorothy said. "Now!"

The singing was accompanied by a hissing sound coming from the courthouse. Everyone turned to see a skyrocket zipping up into the night. A flash of light filled the sky and a booming sound shook the square.

"Happy Birthday, dear Jethro! Happy birthday to you!" They finished the song as the cannon exploded and the night sky was set ablaze with a shower of fireworks. The nation was celebrating its seventy-fifth birthday, and Jethro was celebrating his seventeenth.

Late that night the Danbury wagon pulled under the Mallory's shed. Dorothy and James went into the house to sleep, and the boys slept in the wagon. The next morning at first light, they headed back to the farm to milk the cow and begin daily chores.

When they arrived home, James unhitched the horse. The boys ran directly into the barn to tend to the cow and feed the chickens.

Dorothy stepped inside the house alone. The scene she encountered made her wonder if there had been a fireworks show inside the cabin while they were gone. A thin layer of white powder covered everything. The dinning table, the chairs, and the floor were dusted with it.

Dorothy ran her finger across the mantle. She raised her finger to her mouth and cautiously tasted the powdery substance. "Flour!" she exclaimed. "What on earth happened here?"

She stepped towards the flour barrel at the end of the counter and was met by a flurry of white powder. From inside the barrel, she heard sounds of scratching and clawing.

"Sen!" she yelled. Grabbing her broom, she attacked the barrel with several sharp blows.

With a howl, the bobcat sprang from the flour barrel to the cupboard, knocking Dorothy's kneading bowl to the floor. Sen snarled, warning Dorothy to keep her distance.

"Franklin! Franklin!" Dorothy screamed. "Come get this beast!"

The animal snarled again and let out a full-grown bobcat wail as Dorothy swung her broom and chased him toward the door.

James and the boys rushed out of the barn in time to see Sen, white as a snowstorm, escaping from Dorothy's fury. Leaving a flour trail behind him, he scattered chickens and geese in every direction as he raced to the oak and shot straight upward. Safely out of Dorothy's reach, he spun around on a limb and let out another wail, as if to get in the last word, before settling down on his perch.

The noise from the house, however, did not let up. Plates, bowls, cups, and a rolling pin were heard slamming against walls and crashing to the floor.

"That cat has got to go!" Dorothy shouted. "Either that beast goes, or James goes! Look at my house! It's worse than a cotton gin!"

James and the boys sank back into the barn and peeked around the edge of a hay bale. "I think this is where we should stay for a while," James advised the boys. "The cat is safe in the tree, mama is in the house, and we are all safe here in the barn . . . at least I think we're safe . . . ."

There was no lunch that day; but in the late afternoon, Dorothy stepped to the back door and called James and boys. Her voice was pleasant, as if nothing had ever happened. "Wash up!" she called, clanging on the dinner bell. "The food is on the table."

"Either she's repented, or this is a trap," Edward whispered.

"I think it's a trap," George concluded. "She knows we're all starving. We ain't had nothing to eat all day!"

Apprehensively James and the boys slipped into the house. Dorothy was in her best dress, and a bouquet of flowers sat in the middle of the table.

"I cooked more of that sweet potato pie," Dorothy spoke with an unusual sweetness in her voice. "You seemed to enjoy it so much yesterday in Madison. I thought you might like to have it again today."

James and the boys exchanged glances. Fear and suspicion filled their eyes.

As they sat down at the table, James said, "You give the blessing, Franklin." There was no response, and James repeated his instruction, "Say the blessing, Franklin." Still no response.

James looked at Franklin and then around the table. All the boys were suppressing snickers, trying their hardest not to laugh out loud.

Then James looked down at his own plate, and he understood. His tin dish was bent and wrinkled. Scanning the other dishes, he saw that none of the plates or cups sat flatly on the table. Every plate and every cup was bent. Some looked as though they had suffered a beating with a fire poker. Even the tin cup holding the flowers tilted to one side from a large dent near the bottom.

For a brief moment, James maintained his composure. He didn't want to laugh. Not now, Lord, he thought, not now! But it happened. There was no way to hold it in. He leaned back from the table and roared.

Instantly, the boys let go and joined him. George bent forward with his face just inches above the table. The others slapped their knees, stomped their feet, and held their bellies.

Dorothy rose abruptly from her place at the end of the table, and for a fleeting moment almost burst into tears. But she didn't. She couldn't.

Suddenly she saw the table as they saw it. Instead of crying, she laughed with them. But she laughed louder. How silly it all looked . . . flowers, her best dress, a delicious meal . . . contrasted with irreparably bent and dented dishes and streaks of white flour in the floorboards. She looked at the beautiful flowers in the beat up cup and her mouth-watering sweet potato pie in a dish that would never again sit flat. And she laughed even harder.

"We'll never forget this day!" Franklin blurted out. "Every time we eat something in these banged up dishes, we're gonna remember this, Mama!"

In the pandemonium, James rose from his seat and took Dorothy in his arms. He nuzzled her hair and kissed her. "You are the most wonderful wife any man ever had," he said through tears and laughter. "No one ever had a more wonderful wife than you!"

Then feeling brave and safe again, he added, "Colonel Zachery Taylor could have ended the Seminole War a whole lot sooner . . . if he'd let you teach his soldiers how to fight!"

Chapter Sixteen

George rushed into the barn where the other boys were tossing hay up to the loft. "I just saw him! Hiram was in our lane!" George was out of breath. "I ain't never seen a monster, but if there is such a thing, that man is one! He makes my skin crawl!"

Edward expressed what they were all thinking, "Why ain't the men folks around here doin' something? Everybody knows Miss Carolyn's lying. That man has got her trapped inside her own house, and she's too scared to do anything about it."

Jethro and Franklin listened as George responded. "If the men in this county won't help her, then we will!"

"Us?" they gasped.

"Yes, us!" George replied in an authoritative tone.

"But what will Papa think?" Franklin asked.

"We ain't gonna tell him. We're old enough to handle this ourselves."

"Not tell Papa?"

This was the most dangerous-sounding talk the other boys had ever heard.

"We can't. He wouldn't understand. And if he finds out what we're gonna do, he won't let us."

Jethro dropped down from the hay loft, "What're you gonna' do?"

"Not me! Us!" George corrected. "It'll take all four of us!"

The other three knotted around George. They had never seen him so determined.

"I have a plan," he spoke in a hushed voice, "something I heard Harlow Bentley talking about at the fireworks last month."

"What is it?" Edward whispered.

"When he was our age, Harlow Bentley and his two brothers scared a whole troop of Gypsies clear out of Hampton, Virginia. And they did it with a Whang-doodle."

"I've heard of that," Edward laughed. "Mama said grandpa Hapsburg made one."

"I ain't heard of it," Jethro said, "and I ain't sure I want to."

George described the device. "It's made with a hollow log, a piece of leather, and a violin string. At night it sounds like Hell has split wide open, and you can hear it for a mile. Harlow said it'll stampede horses and cows faster than a cave full of bats!"

"But what about Miss Caroline?" Jethro asked.

"We'll figure it out . . . we'll think of something . . ." George hesitated. He could almost hear his father's voice, 'If you pursue a righteous cause in a wrong spirit, you can end up making a bad situation even worse.' He made himself focus on the task at hand. "The thing we got to worry about is getting Hiram and his family clear out of Florida."

Franklin thumped George on the shoulder, "Aren't you forgetting something? We ain't never even seen a violin!"

"Like I said," George went on, "we'll figure it out."

In the weeks that followed, there was no more discussion on the Whang-doodle; but there was plenty of talk about Hiram. Elder Blanton sat at James and Dorothy's dinning table one evening, deep in thought. He hung his head, showing little interest in the delicious meal Dorothy had set before him.

The boys listened intently when their pastor spoke of Carolyn. "I've been by her house several times," he worried aloud. "She always gives me her word everything's fine . . . just fine . . . but I know it ain't so!" He put down his fork, "Carolyn has aged ten years since those rogues moved themselves into her house."

George glared at the other boys. They all knew what he was thinking.

Another month passed. Over breakfast one morning, Dorothy said, "James, the new town hall in Madison will be dedicated

Saturday evening. The boys' chorus from Tallahassee will be singing, and I'd like for us all to attend the concert."

George's ears perked up. Concert, he thought, they have violins at concerts. "Hmmm, that might be interesting," George commented coolly. He was straining to hide his excitement. "I bet Gilbert Mallory will be there."

"I can't imagine Gilbert Mallory sitting through an evening like that," Dorothy interrupted, a little puzzled at the lack of resistance to her suggestion. "You know you have to wear neckties to a concert, don't you?"

"Neckties!" Edward and Franklin were horrified at the thought. This was going to be more challenging than George had anticipated.

"Yes, and you will sit through the entire concert without leaving or making noise." Dorothy asserted. "It's settled; we're going."

Saturday afternoon, the Danbury wagon pulled onto the Bellamy Trail. With the exception of Jethro, they were all dressed in their best clothes.

George wondered if Miss Carolyn would ever understand what great sacrifices were being made for her. Along with Edward and Franklin, he wore a bright green homemade necktie. Franklin tugged on his tie as though he were choking. Edward sat quietly, straightening his tie every time the wind moved it.

Only Jethro was relaxed and comfortable. Dressed in overalls, he dangled his legs from the wagon's tailgate. Negroes would not be allowed in the new town hall, so Jethro didn't have to deal with a necktie or with sitting still all evening. But those green homespun ties are kinda pretty, he thought. He wondered how one would look tucked under the bib of his overalls.

As the wagon rolled along the trail and splashed through the creek, Franklin continued to grimace and fidget.

"It's kind of like having lace on your drawers, ain't it?" George teased.

"Well, Precious," Franklin answered in an effeminate voice, "I wouldn't know. How does the lace on your drawers feel?"

George punched him in the shoulder. "One more crack like that, and I'll strangle you with that green tie!"

"Boys! That's enough!" James snapped. "Don't worry, Franklin," he added. "If you choke to death, you'll already be dressed for your funeral."

"Uh, huh, and I'll be the only corpse ever buried in Madison County with wide-open, blood shot eyes." Franklin looked at his mother, "Please, can't I loosen it just a little? Please!"

"No, you may not!" Dorothy answered. "If you're going to a concert, you're not going dressed like a field hand."

"I'd rather be in a field picking cotton any ole day than sitting in a stuffy building listening to a bunch of boys sounding like screeching girls," Franklin complained, with a hard look in George's direction.

At the junction of Bellamy Trail and Moseley Hall Road, they turned north and rode past the Mallory home. "Boys, don't be disappointed if you don't see Gilbert this evening," James commented. "I really doubt the Mallory's will be interested in going to a concert."

"Some guys have all the luck!" Franklin lamented.

"You're the fortunate ones," Dorothy corrected him. "Not everybody gets to hear singing like the Tallahassee Seminary Boys' Chorus."

Edward leaned over to Franklin and whispered, "What you think them seminary boys got on their drawers, pink or yellow lace?"

In Madison, a hand-painted cloth sign hung above the front door of the new town hall and flapped loosely in the breeze. The sign read, "Madison County Cultural Society." A soft yellow glow of oil lamps lighted the inside of the building.

"There's Gilbert!" George yelled, pointing to a wagon at a watering trough north of the building, "The Mallory's are here!"

"Does he have a tie on?" Franklin asked, "If he ain't . . . ."

"If he doesn't, he ought to," James replied. "And you're going to wear yours regardless."

The unpainted pine board interior of the hall was decorated with bouquets of flowers, magnolia branches, and kerosene lamps flickering across the front of the stage. Tree limbs decorated each side of the stage from floor to ceiling. The scents of women's perfumes blended with the smells of pine resin, magnolia blossoms, and kerosene smoke. The boys would never have admitted it, but they were impressed.

James and Dorothy led the way down the aisle. They chose a row near the middle of the hall, on the left. They stepped between the wooden benches, and the three boys followed.

Franklin looked disdainfully at the seats and whispered to Edward, "Your butt is gonna hurt like the devil for the next two hours."

Concert goers twisted in their fancy clothes and looked as uncomfortable and out of place as Franklin. As he scanned the crowd, he was relieved to see that he was not the only one suffering with a miserable tie.

Near the front, several men in black suits and dressy bow ties sat facing the audience. George suspected they all had lace on their drawers.

After about ten minutes, one of the black-suited men, Mr. Gillison, rose to address the audience. "We will all please stand," he announced ceremoniously, "to pledge our allegiance to the flag. Then please remain standing for the invocation by the Reverend Amos Albritton."

George sprang to his feet. He flexed his shoulder blades; they were already beginning to ache from leaning against the hard bench back.

Following the pledge, the Reverend began, "O Lord." In a dull and monotonous drone, he petitioned the Lord about politicians who were dividing the nation, on behalf of the unsaved in the Hawaiian Islands, and for an end to the outbreak of malaria fever in the middle of the state. When George thought there couldn't possibly be anything left to pray over, the Reverend inhaled deeply and prayed on. Finally, to a background of coughs, shuffling feet, and clearing of throats, Reverend Albritton delivered the long-awaited, "Amen!"

Mr. Gillison made another announcement. In addition to the pleasure of hearing the Tallahassee Seminary Boys' Chorus, the crowd tonight would be favored by five special performances.

Five additional performances, George groaned to himself. How long was this thing going to last? Oh, Miss Carolyn, if you only knew . . . .

The first special performance was given by a teenage girl who, according to Franklin, sounded like she was wearing his tie. Next a young man played a flute. Several times he faltered and missed his note.

It was the third special performance that captured the attention of all three boys and caused them to sit erect on their hard, bench seats.

"Mrs. Hagin from Marianna," Mr. Gillison told the audience, "will play a selection from Mozart on her violin."

James and Dorothy were pleased at the boys' show of interest in classical music. How handsome they look in their Sunday shirts and green ties, Dorothy thought, and how wonderful for them to experience the biggest cultural event ever in Madison.

Mrs. Hagin strutted onto the platform. She clutched her violin, a handkerchief, and a bulky music book. She was more mature than the other performers, squatty in build, and filled with self-assurance.

She proudly introduced her selections, "I shall play Mozart's 'Minuet in G', followed by, `All We Like Sheep Have Gone Astray' from Handel's Messiah." Then Mrs. Hagin began to play, alternating between vigorous sawing and quick, lilting motions with her bow.

Dorothy turned to James and whispered in his ear, "Look how the boys are enjoying the violin!"

After her selections, Mrs. Hagin tucked her violin under her left arm and bowed to the audience with the finesse of a professional musician. In response to enthusiastic applause, Mrs. Hagin played an encore.

Two vocal performances followed Mrs. Hagin. An older man, in a voice Franklin and Edward thought sounded exactly like Dr. Thad, presented a solo. Finally the special performances concluded with a song by a trio of young girls.

Mr. Gillison dismissed the crowd for a twenty-minute inter-mission. "You are invited to the reception room on my right. You will have the opportunity to enjoy cookies and fruit punch with our guest musicians and our feature performers, the Tallahassee Seminary Boys' Chorus."

As the audience rose in applause, the boys pushed their way through the crowd. They rushed down the front steps and hurried to the side room. Franklin was first in line at the refreshment table. He walked away dejectedly with one small ginger cookie in each hand.

"This ain't enough to draw ants," he grumbled. He made his way outside with the two tiny cookies and a half-filled cup of punch. George and Edward followed with their meager ration of refreshments.

From outside the building, George peered through a window. "There it is! There is it!" he whispered, pointing at the violin case unprotected on a chair near the stage. "That's where we're gonna get the string for our Whang-doodle!"

"She probably ain't gonna give us one," Edward surmised.

"Of course not, Idiot!" George whispered angrily. "Franklin's going to steal it."

"Me?" Franklin panicked. "Me? Steal it! Why me?"

"Because Ed and I are going to be busy watching both doors while you do it. I'll stand here at the front door, and Ed will guard the one that goes into the refreshment room."

"But I'll get caught!"

"No, you won't. If anybody comes, we'll cough real loud. All you have to do is pull out the pegs, and the strings will fall off in your hand."

"But that old lady will find out!" Franklin argued. "Papa will kill us!"

"Nope," George assured, "she'll be back in Marianna before she even knows they're gone." He grabbed Franklin by the arm and shoved him, "Now get down there!"

The hall was empty. It looked like everyone was busy visiting in the reception room. Franklin was still reluctant, "I ain't never stole anything before . . . ."

"And you ain't never had to live next to Hiram Crowley before either! Go! Go!"

George's argument convinced him. If anything would motivate Franklin to steal, it was the prospect of getting rid of Hiram and his brood. Edward walked to the side entrance, stepped into the refreshment hall, and leaned against the door. George disappeared into the dark of the front steps to stand guard and make certain Franklin carried out the operation.

Every board in the floor creaked like planking on a bridge as Franklin worked his way to the front of the hall. He felt every eye in Florida was peering through the windows, watching him steal a piece of wire from an unsuspecting lady. He stopped and turned back toward the front door. He was met by George's menacing frown. There was no way out; he had to go through with it.

Franklin eased himself to the front of the room and cautiously picked up the violin case. He took a quick look around the hall. Then he squatted on the floor behind the magnolia limbs and opened the case. The violin and bow were there, but he stared in unbelief at what wasn't there. Spinning around toward the front door with the case still in his lap, he locked eyes with George. Franklin slammed the case shut, dropped it back onto the chair, and rushed down the aisle.

George met him midway up the steps, "You stupid Idiot!" he yelled as Franklin rushed past him. "You could've gotten it!" George followed Franklin to the edge of the yard. "You blew it! You crazy fool! You had the perfect opportunity!"

"I swear to God! George!" Franklin stammered. "There ain't a string on that violin!"

"You expect me to believe that?" George half-shouted. "You ain't no good as a thief but you're the bravest liar in all of Florida! You think I'm dumb enough to believe that a fiddler can saw across plain wood and get music like Mrs. Hagin did? What kind of an idiot do you think I am?"

"I swear to God, George, that's the truth! She don't have no strings on that violin."

George shoved him against an oak tree, "I'll show you!" He grabbed Franklin by the tie and jerked him forward, "Stand at the door! If anybody comes, you cough, or I'll run that violin bow through both your ears!"

George left Franklin standing at the top step as he dashed into the building and hurried down the aisle. When George reached the platform, there was a sudden burst of gagging and coughing as Edward's door opened and Mrs. Hagin stepped into the hall. She was still clutching her handkerchief as Mr. Gillison led her to her seat. George stumbled to a halt. He reached down and picked up a hat—whose, he did not know—and carefully brushed it off before placing it again on the bench.

"Sure is a nice program, Mr. Gillison," he complimented. "And you, too, Mrs. Hagin. That was some mighty fine fiddlin'." Mrs. Hagin's smile dropped. "I mean to say, good violin playing, Ma'am. Mighty good."

Mrs. Hagin's smile returned. She thanked him as she stuffed her handkerchief into the bosom of her dress.

George spent a moment inspecting the decorations with feigned admiration. Then he stepped out the door and looked vainly for Franklin. His brother was nowhere to be found. It wasn't until the program was under way again and the boys' chorus was singing that Franklin entered the hall. He took a seat between his parents.

His mother looked at the disheveled tie. Franklin did not reply when she whispered, "Franklin! What have you done? Your tie looks as twisted as a rag mop." In a whisper, she consoled him, "At least you're not dead yet."

"I ain't home yet either," he replied with a weary exhale.

"Be still," his father warned, tapping the boy on the knee. "Maybe you'd better loosen that collar if it bothers you that much."

Franklin's knuckles dug into his throat as he gouged under the tie for the button. The tie was loosened, but his problems could not be solved so easily. He could still feel George's fierce glare from the opposite end of the bench.

The boys' chorus sang, but Franklin did not hear them. It was not until the last song had ended that Mr. Gillison's voice pulled his attention back to the front. "And now," the master of ceremonies addressed the audience, "our surprise finale will be 'The Star Spangled Banner'. The chorus will be accompanied by all of the special performers! Everyone please stand!"

As the audience rose applauding, George's eyes met Franklin's. The singers waited as Mrs. Hagin lifted her violin case from the floor, perched it on her knees, and opened it. A moment of confusion followed. Mr. Gillison rushed to Mrs. Hagin. The two of them exchanged whispered messages while the audience and the performers waited.

Mr. Gillison returned to center stage and explained hesitantly, "Unfortunately, it will be necessary to present this last number without Mrs. Hagin's beautiful playing." Mrs. Hagin frowned angrily, and Mr. Gillison stumbled for words as he glanced in her direction. "There is . . . there is . . . a problem with her violin . . . and Mrs. Hagin will be unable to perform."

As the Danbury family piled into the wagon and headed for home, Dorothy was still enthralled with the last song. "It was worth the trip into town just to hear that! Didn't you love that song?" She burst into singing, "O, say can you see, by the dawn's early light, what so proudly we hailed at the twilight's last gleaming . . . ."

"It was something, all right," George answered. "The whole thing turned out a lot different than I ever thought it would." He looked apologetically at Franklin.

"Move over, Jethro," Edward pushed his way between the others and into the pile of straw. "It's time to sleep. Make room." Jethro yawned and moved to one side.

"How was it?" Jethro asked.

"It was the most unusual event we ever went to," George answered.

As they left town, the wagon rattled over the new railroad bed. Under the full moon, the road stretched before them like a lighted white path. A few miles beyond, they reached the junction of the Bellamy Trail and headed southeast towards home.

Dorothy felt invigorated by the concert and the clear night sky with its scattering of white clouds. "Why don't we sing, James," she suggested. "Let's sing, 'Home, Sweet Home'."

While James and Dorothy sang, the boys lay face up in the back, studying the myriad of stars across the sky.

"I bet there's more than a thousand." Jethro estimated.

"Probably even more than that," Franklin guessed as he stared at a bright, diamond-like star just above the horizon. He was fascinated by its dazzling blue color. For a long while, Jethro and Franklin lay side by side, staring at the same wonderful western star.

Ordinarily George and Edward would have shown more interest in stargazing. Tonight their thoughts were absorbed in bewilderment over the strange events of the concert.

Dorothy gazed lovingly at James in the moonlight. She put her arms around his waist and pulled herself closer to him. We must be doing something right, Dorothy thought. Our boys have developed an appreciation for fine music and an admiration for God's handiwork in the heavenlies. What a wonderful night this had been.

James, so close to her, was strong and muscular. He's more handsome now than when I married him, she thought. She nestled her head against his shoulder. He leaned over and kissed her . . . longer than he probably should have with the boys in the back of the wagon. Then James looked at her and winked, sending a thrill through her body. What a truly wonderful night . . . and the best part, Dorothy smiled, is still ahead.

The burr of crickets from the roadside and the clopping of the mare's hooves were too pleasant to be disturbed by conversation.

But less than a mile from their lane, the tranquility was disrupted by the sound of a horse approaching. "He's sure traveling fast," James said as he pulled the wagon to a halt.

"Somebody may be sick," Dorothy spoke with concern. "We must offer to help, James."

The boys rose to their knees and watched as the rider galloped nearer. "He doesn't look like he's going to slow down," Edward worried aloud. "Who in the world . . . ."

"Hello!" James called. "Is there trouble? Can we help?" There was no reply as the rider darted past.

"Hiram Crowley! That was Hiram!" Dorothy was troubled and confused. "Why is he out prowling around this time of night? What is that man up to?"

"Heaven only knows," James tried to sound unconcerned. "He's a strange one. But don't you worry about it."

As the wagon moved forward again, James put his arm around Dorothy. "This is where my arm is always going to be," he assured her, "right here, all your life." He leaned over and whispered in her ear, "Now let's get back to where we were before Hiram interrupted us."

The boys sat at the rear, dangling their legs from the end of the wagon. Hiram's sudden appearance seemed to mock them; it was a cruel reminder of their failure at the concert.

"You saw me, George," Franklin whispered. "There ain't never been anything so strange in all my life. When I opened that case and saw all those little pegs lying loose around the violin and the strings gone, I felt like I had seen a ghost!"

Jethro bent close to Franklin. "You think you seen a ghost?" He reached into his overalls and pulled out a fistful of tangled violin strings, "I is your ghost!"

"You!" they all whispered in amazement. "You!"

Chapter Seventeen

Sunrise announced a new morning with a fiery-red explosion across the full length of the eastern sky. The earth awoke fresh, and every bird in Florida sang to its glory. In times past, Carolyn would have reveled in the breaking dawn and breathed in its beauty.

This morning, she never raised her eyes. With head down, a milk pail in each hand, and bitterness in her heart, she walked toward the barn. As she passed the well, a hen flapped to the ground and hurried toward her.

"Not now!" The bird continued clucking, and Carolyn swung at it with a pail. "I said, not now!"

Carolyn had loved the life she and John had built here on this farm in Florida. Now she hated the farm and everything about it. All joy in Carolyn's life had vanished the hour Hiram and Francina pulled up to her gate. How wrong she and John had been to think they could hide in Florida—or anywhere else—and escape the nightmare of this man.

Why couldn't Francina stand up to him? Why did Francina have to be his mindless slave? Carolyn stopped and turned towards her cabin. For a brief moment, she took pleasure in imagining the house and all its occupants in flames. She shook herself out of her daydream; her own thoughts frightened her. How could she despise Hiram so much she had actually allowed herself to wish for the death of her own sister?

"O, Lord, help me!" she prayed. "Forgive me! Forgive me for wishing evil upon my sister and her family! Please, Lord, give me strength!"

In the barn, the sweet fragrance of hay welcomed her. She stood in the quiet. At peace for the moment, she basked in her memories. John loved this barn. He spent many happy hours here, and every board spoke of him. A reverential presence filled this place. Shafts of sunlight fell through cracks in the walls, reminding her of light filtering through the stained glass windows of her church in Virginia.

Setting the buckets on the ground, Carolyn spoke affectionately to her cow, "You've eaten every bit of your hay. I can't expect you to give me milk, if I don't give you enough to eat!"

With her rake, she pulled a generous heap of hay to the floor and began tossing it into the trough. Her hands were filled with hay, and her arms were swung upward, when Carolyn was seized from behind. She was pulled backwards, against the bare chest of the man who had been hiding, out of her sight, behind the open barn door.

"Hiram!" Carolyn inhaled in fright. "Let me go!"

"There ain't no use fighting," he told her calmly. "Won't do you a bit of good." He spun her around so that she was facing him.

She struggled to get loose. "No! No! Let me go!"

He forced her face toward his. For an eternity of seconds, she could not make herself breathe. Then, gasping for air, she tried again to break free.

"You gotta' resist, 'cause you're a lady, but if I was to leave you right now, you'd hate me all the worse for it!"

Carolyn felt like she was going to vomit. Every place his body touched hers, she felt defiled, unclean. Nausea burned in her stomach. She wanted to push away from him, but somehow, her arms seemed to have lost their strength. She wanted to yell; but tightness clutched her throat, and confusion gripped her mind.

Her head began to spin. A terrible weakness, an overwhelming tiredness, came over her. It washed over her like a wave, from the top of her head to the bottom of her feet. She tried to speak, she wanted to fight, but weariness grasped even her mind. She could not think. She could not move.

She was scarcely aware that her knees were giving way beneath her and she was slumping downward. Hiram turned loose and let her fall to the ground. He stood over her, leering at her body, lying limp and motionless in the straw.

"See," he bragged, "I knew it all the time! And you thought you had me fooled."

Hiram fell on her like a wild animal tearing into its prey. Carolyn never moved.

When Hiram rose to leave, he laughed at her again. "In the morning, you'll probably be waiting right here in the barn for more."

At the door, he stopped. "If you get any ideas about not cooperating, just remember, that's your only sister in the house. And don't try any tricks like you pulled on me in Washington."

Carolyn never heard a word he said. He stared at her, as she lay numb and perfectly still. He waited for a response. Annoyed by her silence, he stepped through the door and closed it behind him.

Three days later, Dorothy stood at Carolyn's gate, reluctant to break the strange silence that hung in the air. She carried a large platter of baked sweet potatoes and ham.

"Carolyn!" she called. "Carolyn, I have something for you."

There was no reply. Dorothy started to speak again when Hiram strode onto the porch.

"She ain't here!" he yelled. Spying the food, he walked quickly to the gate and snatched the platter from Dorothy's hands. "But I'll be sure to tell her you brought these."

"Where is she?" Dorothy looked him straight in the eye. "When will she be back?"

"I don't know!" Hiram answered abruptly. "I don't ask her nothin', and she don't tell me nothin'. But as soon as she comes back, I'll tell her you came over."

The two stared at each other unspeaking; and in a startling moment, Dorothy lost all fear of the man. He was as villainous and threatening as ever; but from somewhere deep inside, she felt strength arise, strength greater than the evil in this man. No longer intimidated by his wicked glare, she had to resist the impulse to reach across the fence and grab him.

"How long has she been gone? You surely know when she left!" A righteous indignation welled up in Dorothy. She was shocked by her own boldness. "Carolyn is my best friend! I insist that you tell me where she is and how long she has been gone!"

Like a snake trying to hypnotize his prey, Hiram's eyes locked into Dorothy's. The vessels in his temples and neck bulged. "Carolyn can tell you herself when she comes back, woman! Now get the hell out of here!"

"I'm leaving, but you can be certain I will be back!" Dorothy yelled at him. "I'm not afraid of you, Hiram! And don't ever think that my family or I will back down one inch from you. We won't! You're not welcome in Madison! This is Carolyn's home, and we won't allow vagrants to come in and steal it from her! "

"I'm her brother-in-law!" he yelled. "And you ain't telling me I got no right here! You're the one leaving, Mis' Danbury! Not me!"

For a tense moment she glared at him across the fence, totally unafraid. Then she turned away. As she ran towards home, she could feel his hateful, vindictive stare following her. She could hear the vileness in his laughter, the heinous sound of delight in another's pain.

An authority had fallen around Dorothy like a shield. She heard herself quoting the promise of Jesus, "I give you power to tread on serpents and scorpions and over all the power of the enemy; nothing shall by any means hurt you." By the time she reached home, Dorothy was no longer concerned about Hiram. Her only thought was of Carolyn.

She raced through the gate and yelled for James. "Carolyn's gone! Hiram won't tell me where she is! We've got to find her!" Dorothy was sobbing, "We should never have listened to Carolyn! We should have run that beast out of Florida the first day he got here! Oh, James! What if he's killed her?!"

"O, God!" James cried out, "Lord! How did we let this happen?"

George was sitting by the oak, holding Sen's leash, as he listened to his mother. He rushed to his parents and started to speak, but then he stopped himself. Somehow he knew his father would not approve of his plan to scare Hiram away, despite this turn of events.

James spoke with anguish in his voice, "Why did this have to happen when Elder Blanton and most of the church men are away?"

"When do they come back?" Dorothy asked, wiping her eyes with her sleeve.

"Day after tomorrow, unless we can get word to them. They're up at Columbia Church for the association meeting." James shook his head. "Regardless, we've got to find Carolyn! Finding her is more important than getting rid of Hiram."

George almost spoke. But, again, he stopped himself. He knew what had to be done, and he knew he would have to leave his father out of it.

James turned toward George, "Saddle the horse for me, son. I'll go into town and see if I can find some other men to help. I'll spread the word about Carolyn. Maybe someone has seen her."

In the late afternoon, Dorothy and the boys were sitting down to an early supper when James returned with Harlow Bentley and Dr. Thad. The three men squeezed in at the table. Dr. Thad talked frantically in his shrill voice, "If he's harmed Carolyn, there won't be any need to run him out of Florida! After I get through with him, you can throw what's left in the swamp!"

"We can't do this alone," Harlow warned. "Just the three of us won't work. We need a posse of all the men around here. Hiram is dangerous, and he needs to know the whole county feels the same way about him. Thad and I will stay here tonight. First thing in the morning we'll start our search for Carolyn."

Dorothy agreed. "I know the Lord is with us, James," she said, "but we mustn't do anything hasty or foolish. Harlow is right. We need to wait for the other men."

George rose from the table and put his plate in the dishpan. "Papa," he interjected, "Edward, Franklin, Jethro, and me could camp out overnight. Dr. Thad and Mr. Bentley could have our room.

"That might be a good idea," James answered. "But make sure you stay on our land, and get back early to do your chores."

"We will, Papa," the boys assured their parents.

"And be careful," Dorothy added.

"Yes, Mama," they replied.

"I'll get the trap," Edward said, to disguise the true purpose of their camping trip.

Franklin packed a lard can with ham and biscuits, and Jethro filled a jug with water. George slipped into the barn and grabbed the piece of deer hide leather from the corner of the barn where he had covered it with straw. Jethro gathered up the violin strings from beneath his corn shuck mattress. And Edward made a show of carrying the steel trap. A short time later, the boys disappeared through the garden and headed southwest toward the swamp.

George stopped at the edge of the woods where he had concealed a two-foot section of a hollow, hickory log in a cypress tree. Then he took inventory.

"Edward, you got the saw?"

Edward nodded. He pulled the wooden handle into view from under his armpit.

"Pliers? Hammer? Strings?" George went through the list.

Edward and Franklin displayed their smuggled tools, and Jethro pulled the violin strings from his pocket.

George looked at the deer hide. He knew his father had tanned the leather for chair bottoms, and he worried what Papa might do when he discovered it missing. More than that, his conscience still troubled him over the theft of Mrs. Hagin's violin strings. Even this emergency, somehow, didn't make it feel right. But if Mrs. Hagin understood the importance of their mission, he rationalized, she would be glad for them to have the wires.

As they worked their way deeper into the swamp, they found themselves in a dense forest, engulfed by a mesmerizing silence. The place was so deathly silent, and they spontaneously dropped their voices to whispers. As they pushed their way between huge cypress trees laden with heavy moss, the setting sun cast eerie shadows around them.

The water was shallow, reaching just above their ankles; but with each step, their feet were sucked into the muck.

"We could never get away from an alligator in this stuff," Edward whispered nervously. "How are we even gonna know when we get to the right place, George?"

"There ain't another creek that runs into the swamp between the one on our farm and the one on Miss Carolyn's." George was glad he had solved that problem ahead of time. "When we come to a creek, that'll be the right place."

"I never knew it got this scary!" Franklin's voice was barely audible. He gazed at the gnarled swamp-apple trees with banks of fern clinging to their trunks. "It looks like a picture I saw in one of them books of horror . . . ."

Franklin never completed his sentence. Out of nowhere, a white cape-like form swooped over their heads with a whir of air that sent them sprawling into the water. They came up with mud covering their faces and dripping from their hair and clothing.

"It was an owl!" George yelled, his own heart racing from fright, "It was only an owl! Let's get going. We can't stop now!"

After another ten minutes of trudging through marsh, Edward exclaimed, "The saw! I don't have the saw!"

They stared at each other and then headed back to the place where they had fallen in the water.

"It's got to be here," Edward hoped out loud. "I remember having it until then."

Each boy bent down and ran his hands under the muddy water, gingerly feeling for the saw. Jethro was dragging his fingers carefully along the bottom when suddenly his hand struck something familiar. He gasped as he realized what he had discovered.

"The violin strings!" he mumbled under his breath. His eyes darted toward the others. Each was intent on finding the saw, and no one was looking his way. Quickly he pulled the wires from the water and shoved them into his pocket. This time, he made certain the flap was securely fastened.

"O, Lord! O, Lord!" he thought. "What if we hadn't come back?"

Seconds later Edward let out a cheer as he lifted the saw from the marsh, "I found it! I found it!"

"All we need now," Franklin quipped, "is for Jethro to lose the violin strings."

"Oh, no!" Jethro assured, patting his buttoned-down pocket. "Them strings is safe and sound right here!"

The boys plodded back over the same ground they had covered before Edward discovered the saw missing. A short distance beyond that, they reached the creek. They followed it upstream toward Carolyn's house.

Before dark they found a fallen tree wedged between two cypress knees.

"This looks like a good place for a Whang-doodle," George decided. In a few minutes, the instrument was set up and ready to go.

"Let's hear how it sounds," Edward suggested, "You can do it real easy so it won't be too loud."

George plucked the wire gently; and the hollow, hickory log let out a deep growl. They stared wide-eyed at each other. The sound was awesome. Again George touched the string. This time he used a little more force. A wailing groan rose from the Whang-doodle, and chill bumps rose on the boys' skin. From somewhere nearby, they heard frantic splashing as an animal leaped away.

"A deer," Franklin concluded. "If this thing don't scare the devil out of Hiram, nothing will."

"Don't do it again!" Edward cautioned. "Save it until tonight!"

On the bank of Carolyn's creek, a hundred feet from the Whang-doodle, the boys made a hideout in a palmetto thicket. They spread a bed of Spanish moss on the ground. Tonight, they would sleep close together.

They settled into their shelter, and Franklin pried the lid off the lard can. They passed around ham and biscuits, and Jethro offered the blessing.

"O Lord," he prayed, "don't leave us now. Protect us from Hiram. Find Mis' Caroline, and bless the food. Amen!"

By the time they finished their meal, night had fallen over the swamp. The moon was blocked from view by the canopy of cypress limbs overhead. But its light filtered through, casting soft yellow splotches and shadowy reflections of tree trunks on the water.

Strange birds let out their calls, and bull frogs grunted from the darkness surrounding them.

No one admitted it; but secretly, they all wished they were home. This had seemed like a much better idea, at home, in the daylight. George lay back, pretending to be unafraid. Inside his chest, his heart pounded with fear.

Fireflies flickered through the trees. Somewhere in the southwest, the silence was broken by the tormented cry of a screech owl.

"If I live to be four hundred years old," Edward said, "I'll never get used to that sound."

"Me neither!" Franklin agreed.

George could sense a mutiny in the making. "We're here, and we're staying 'til we get this thing done," George said with the authority of an older brother. "This is our one and only chance. Like it or not, we ain't leaving until we've scared the living daylights out of Hiram Crowley and his gang."

The others definitely did not like it, but they realized George was right. It was tonight or never.

"How long are we gonna wait?" Franklin asked.

""We'll wait until after midnight," George answered, "when they're all in a snoring sleep. Then we'll make 'em think Judgment Day has arrived."

"In the middle of the night?" Edward laughed, his anxiety evident.

The boys resigned themselves to the situation and tried to settle down for a few hours of sleep. They lay side by side with their eyes closed, but no one was sleeping. The silence was interrupted when a large tree limb broke loose from high above. On the way down, it pulled smaller branches with it and crashed to the ground. All four boys bolted upright.

"What was that?" Edward screamed, his heart pounding in his throat. "Did Hiram find us?"

George let out a heavy sigh, "Just a tree limb . . . I think . . . ."

"We gotta pray!" Jethro pleaded. He was about to begin when a screech owl let out another shrill call. This time it was closer. The boys lunged together and huddled on the moss.

"Good God A'Mighty!" Jethro's voice echoed through the swamp. "Save us, Jesus! Save us!"

"Stop it! Stop it!" George ordered. "There ain't nothing happening in this swamp tonight that doesn't happen every single night! You're letting screech owls and tree limbs make you act like a bunch of sissy fools!" George sounded angry; but in truth, he was as scared as the others.

"I'm gonna tell you something else! We ain't heard the worst of it yet," George warned. "There's bull alligators out here that make the ground shake when they bellow. There's panthers out there that sound worse than a crazy woman screaming! And if it happens, it happens! We ain't running! We ain't budging! Now, go to sleep!"

George fell back on the mattress, and the others followed his example. They tried to sleep, but their eyelids simply would not stay closed. There was no comfortable spot on their lumpy, moss mattress. Bugs whizzed around their heads, gnats flew up their noses, and ants crawled into their ears.

The four boys lay there, each in silent agony. Edward thought he felt a snake slither under his neck. *It's my imagination,* he convinced himself. *I will not scream.*

Then suddenly, George leaped to his feet and shrieked, "Snake!" He jerked the slender body of a rat snake from between his legs and hurled it into the air. The others sprang to their feet, yelling, jumping up and down, and stomping their feet.

"That's it!" Franklin gasped. "That's it! We can't do this! Hiram would have to be deaf not to know somebody's out here!"

"We can do it!" George was adamant. "We are gonna make it work! Hiram can't tell the difference between a screech owl and your sissy yelling! We ain't leaving!"

Once more, the boys lay down. This time there was no pretense of trying to sleep. When the owl screeched again, and when an alligator bellowed in the distance, they all remained still and silent. The moon was now visible through the canopy. Lying there on their backs for the next several hours, they watched it glide slowly overhead.

It was well past midnight when George finally rose from the campsite. "Here goes," he announced. "You all wait right here. No matter what happens, don't move!"

George cautiously stepped into the water and slowly made his way to the fallen tree. He was about to touch the string, when the memory of Mrs. Hagin, sitting in the concert hall staring into her violin case, flashed across his mind. Then he had another thought. Would this really work? Just because it worked on a bunch of Gypsies, how could he be sure it would work on Hiram? Maybe Hiram had made a Whang-doodle himself.

For a moment, George struggled with guilt and doubt. In the bushes a hundred feet away, three hearts beat wildly as George hesitated.

George made his decision. Suddenly the stillness of the Stillipicca Swamp was shattered by hellish growling. It sounded like some ancient, blood-hungry dinosaur emerging from the swampland, intent on killing everything in its path.

Frenzied cries of birds, howlings of fox and wolves, and screams of panthers filled the night. Birds took frantically to the air. Disoriented bats swooped wildly over their hideout. The boys peered through the palmetto fronds at George. Even though they knew what it was, more bumps popped up on their arms and legs than on the skin of a plucked chicken.

George bore down more fiercely on the string. From the McKay farm, horses whinnied, and cows bellowed. Even the ground around them seemed to be vibrating from the sound.

"Good God!" Franklin called to George, "Stop it! There won't be an animal left in Madison County!" From every direction, frightened animals brayed and howled in fear.

George looked back toward the others, his face wet with sweat. He leaned against a tree and caught his breath before stumbling back to the hideout.

George dropped in a heap on the ground. "The only thing we can do now is wait until daylight, to see what Hiram does."

"I ain't never heard anything that awful!" Edward exclaimed. "Never! And I hope I never hear it again!"

George took two more ham and biscuit sandwiches from the lard can and stuffed them into his mouth. "Now maybe we can sleep," he said, "I sure will be glad to see daylight."

So exhausted they did not notice the lumps, the boys dropped back onto their moss mattress. Crickets resumed their chirping, and fireflies blinked in the dark. The moon dropped behind the bank of clouds in the west, and the boys slept soundly.

Had the boys been awake, they would have seen the flickering light in the distance. Slowly it moved in the direction of their hideout. A torch in one hand and a multiple-firing, flintlock pistol in the other, Hiram stepped deliberately through the water. He paused. Like a bear sniffing for the scent of his prey, he seemed to wait for unseen guidance. Then, as if directed by a spirit guide, he made his way directly to the hickory log, wedged between the cypress knees.

Hiram laughed with the satisfaction of a predator about to devour its prey. He raised the torch over his head, and his eyes diligently searched the area. He knew his prey was close at hand.

Edward was the first to awaken. In the stillness he heard the muffled sloshing. He raised his head slightly and saw the glow of light through the cypress. Terror gripped him at the sight of the hulk of a man, only a short distance away.

With his left hand, Edward grabbed Franklin's shoulder, and at the same time, cupped his right hand over his brother's mouth. Instinctively, George and Jethro awoke at the same time. They stared wide-eyed at the menacing outline of a huge figure in the ghostly light.

"Don't move!" George whispered. "If he finds us, we don't have a chance."

They huddled together as Hiram holstered his ivory-handled pistol. Then he stepped back to the Whang-doodle, grabbed it in his arms, and smashed it against a tree. The hollow log splattered with a crash, sending broken pieces in all directions.

"You wanna play scare games?" he roared like a bull alligator. "You ain't scarin' me with no damned toy! I'll find you! You ain't getting away!"

Edward gasped aloud at the incredible strength of the man. Instantly, Hiram spun around as if he had heard the sound. The boys were frozen with fear. They huddled together like four baby birds, stalked by a cat.

George whimpered in terror, "Cover your eyes. Peak through your fingers, and don't move!"

Jethro did not need to cover his eyes; they were already clinched tightly shut, and his fingers were pressed over his nose and mouth. "Jesus!" he prayed, "Jesus, please help us." The others joined Jethro in wrenching, agonizing prayer.

A short distance from them, Hiram brandished his pistol in one hand and his torch in the other. "You're still here!" he yelled. "I know you are! And I'll find you!"

As Hiram rampaged through the waters, Jethro's memory flashed back to the night of the concert. Oh, if only he hadn't taken those strings! God hates stealing, and look where it had gotten them!

Then it hit him. Disobeying God had brought them here, and trusting God was their only way out, their only hope of deliverance. Deliverance, Jethro thought. He remembered Brother Blandon praying a prayer of deliverance . . . but he could not remember much of it . . .

Just then Hiram spun around and locked his eyes on their hideout. "Aha! Aha! I found you!" he howled triumphantly. Waving his torch and his pistol, he slammed his way through the palmetto fronds.

Jethro jumped to his feet and stood looking up at the massive form towering over him. He searched his mind for the words of that prayer. Frantically he shouted out all he could remember. "Jesus! The Blood of Jesus! The Blood of Jesus!"

As the Name—Jesus—crossed Jethro's lips, an owl swooped down and collided with Hiram's face. Hiram yelled and fell backward, flailing his arms. His head hit against the blunt end of a cypress knee as he landed face up in the ooze. The torch settled in the water and went out with a hissing sound. The pistol disappeared in the muck.

Momentarily transfixed, the boys stared at the form sprawled out in a dim patch of moonlight. Then they looked at each other. No one spoke, but they all knew what to do. They ran. Stumbling and falling, they ran through the swamp and all the way home.

When they reached their gate, they were panting for breath; but they did not stop until they were inside the barn. They closed the door and collapsed on the straw.

"Good God A'Mighty!" George gasped, finally getting his breath enough to speak, "Where did that bird come from? We'd be dead if that owl hadn't hit Hiram in the face!!"

"I ain't never seen nothing like that! Never!" Franklin exclaimed

"Did you see him lying there in the water? Was he dead?" Edward worried.

"I'm bleeding from both my legs," Jethro complained.

"I'm all scratched up, too," Franklin added.

"Keep your voices down, we don' t want Papa and Mama to know we're back . . . ." George whispered a little too late.

Light from a lamp appeared in the kitchen window of the cabin, and James called, "Is that you boys out there in the barn?"

"Yes, Sir. It's us," George replied. "We're back early . . . something was prowling around out there in the swamp . . . so we ran home . . . but we wanna sleep the rest of the night out here."

"Are you sure you want to stay out there? Are you alright?" James asked.

"We're fine," George lied.

The next morning, Brother Blanton, James, and nearly forty others rode out together from the Danbury farm.

"We only wanted to chase him away," Edward worried. "We never meant to kill Hiram."

"We didn't kill him!" George corrected his brother. "If he's dead, it was the bird that killed him!"

"All I know," Franklin added, "is we'd all be dead if it hadn't been for that bird."

"That wasn't just a bird," Jethro spoke up. "God sent that bird to rescue us. That was the Hand of God."

Carolyn's house was quiet as a tomb when the posse arrived. No one dismounted.

"Hiram! Come out!" James yelled. "Come out, and don't give us any trouble!"

There was no response.

"We're taking you to the Florida line, Hiram!" James yelled louder. "Come out into the yard now!"

There was still no response from inside the house, but a shuffling sound from the woods behind them caught the attention of the posse. They looked around to see Hiram pushing his way through the bushes. His face was swollen, and his eyes were as red as raw meat.

"Get all your junk and load it in the wagon!" Elder Blanton ordered. "We're sending you north! You're leaving Florida!"

"Suppose I choose not to go!" Hiram growled.

"You ain't got no choice! We decided for you! You're leaving now!"

Hiram eyed the posse. All the men were armed. He limped through the gate and went inside the house.

"Leroy!" they heard him yell. "Get the wagon up to the kitchen door!"

Leroy slipped from the rear of the house and pulled the wagon to the step. As the two boys began tossing their ragged belongings onto the floorboard, Harlow, Elder Blanton, and James rode their horses up to the wagon.

"We're watching to see that you don't get anything that belongs to Carolyn," James informed them. "Take your own stuff, and get ready to roll!"

Hiram stood at the door with a bloody rag tied around his head. "Get the dogs!" he ordered Hiram Jr.

"Don't even think about trying anything with those dogs." Harlow Bentley yelled. "We'll shoot them beasts quicker'n you can say 'sic'!"

Half an hour later Hiram curled up in the back of the wagon, and the boys hitched up the mule. Hiram propped his head with a rolled-up quilt and pulled the bloody cloth over his eyes. Then Elder Blanton, Harlow, and Dr. Thad saw Francina for the first time.

She stepped out the door last, dressed in a thin black dress with a bonnet pulled low over her face. Frail and colorless, she held a shawl tightly around her body. She did not speak or even look in the direction of the men.

As the wagon rolled out of the yard, James—rifle at his side and accompanied by three others—took the lead. The rest of the posse followed behind the wagon. Elder Blanton and Dr. Thad went through the house, closing the shutters and doors. A few minutes later, they caught up with the rearguard of the posse.

At the Bellamy Trail they turned northwest to Madison and the Georgia line. As they passed through town, people stopped to stare; and others cheered. Hiram never looked up.

North of town, a few more men joined the escort. The posse followed the Cherry Lake Road towards Quitman.

Midway between Madison and their destination, James' attention was drawn to a sagging old house behind a grove of low-hanging live oaks. With its front door swung open and an unshuttered window on either side, the house made him think of a skull. Perhaps it was the fearsomeness of this mission and the loss of Carolyn. There was no particular reason he should feel a special foreboding about that house. But even after the house was out of sight, James could not shake the feeling.

In the mid-afternoon, hot and wearied, they reached the rock pile marking the Georgia line. James raised his rifle over his head, bringing the posse to a halt.

"Hiram!" he yelled. "Keep going and don't ever come back to Florida! You'll regret it if we ever catch you here again! Do you hear?"

The men waited on the Florida side of the state line. Hiram finally rose up on one elbow and stared at them through swollen eyes. He spat at them and shook his fist. He looked as though he were about to speak. Instead, he clutched his head in pain and fell back.

As the horses galloped away, Hiram rose briefly once more. Though none of the posse heard him, he called after them, "I'll be back, James Danbury! You can count on it! I've got unfinished business!"

The next day was a special Sunday for Blue Springs Church. As James and Dorothy's wagon pulled into the yard, a large crowd had already gathered for the "Fifth Sunday Union Meeting." Horses, oxen, and mules were tied to palms. The churchyard was filled with wagons covered in white canvas, some open wagons, and even a few fine buggies. An arbor of pine limbs had been built on either side of the building to accommodate those who would not be permitted to sit inside the building. Between the north side of the building and the spring, long tables had been setup for the dinner.

"Such a mob," Dorothy said with concern, "I hope we have enough food!"

James laughed. He had never known them to be undersupplied, nor had he ever known the women not to worry.

As they stepped from the wagon, Dr. Thad waved to them. "We have news about Carolyn!"

Dorothy and James hurried toward him. "Tell us!"

"Doc Kupperman talked with a stage coach driver in Picolata. He remembered Carolyn riding that far with him."

"Was she alright?" Dorothy wanted to know.

"He didn't notice anything unusual. He said she was real quiet, kept to herself."

"Where did she go from Picolata? Did she go on to St. Augustine?"

"He didn't know. Maybe she went on to St. Augustine. She might have taken a boat north."

"That Carolyn!" Dorothy shook her head. "That beautiful, wonderful, bull-headed woman!"

The boys jumped down from the wagon and headed toward the crowd.

"Come in the Meeting House as soon as the singing starts," James called.

George, Franklin, and Edward acknowledged his instruction and kept running. Jethro lagged behind. He walked toward the black people, congregated outside the building.

Jethro found a spot under an arbor, near a window. He stood up on a split log bench by a corner post. From there he had an unobstructed view of the front end of the church. The pulpit reached nearly from wall to wall, and visiting preachers were lined up behind it. Other black people crowded around to see through the windows.

When the singing began, Jethro could feel something coming over him, flooding every ounce of his being. It was the same wonderful peace he had experienced in the swamp, when he called on the Name of Jesus. In that terrifying moment—when he fully understood his only hope was in God—a glorious assurance had manifested itself. Standing there outside the church, he knew he was in that Presence again, being bathed in it and cleansed by it.

Without instrumental music, voices blended in worshipful sounds. Rich, beautiful harmony echoed into the woods. Jethro joined in the first song, along with all the black people on the outside. He knew the words well; Mis' Darthy had sung the song a thousand times at home.

> *"There shall I bathe my weary soul in seas of Heavenly rest,*
> *And not a wave of trouble roll across my peaceful breast*
> *. . . ."*

The hymn came to an end, and the voices trailed off. A few seconds of absolute, holy silence followed. Then the singing clerk led into the next song, the twenty-seventh Psalm.

> *"The Lord is my light and my salvation;*
> *Whom shall I fear?*
> *The Lord is the strength of my life;*
> *Of whom shall I be afraid?*
> *When the wicked came against me*
> *To eat up my flesh,*
> *My enemies and my foes,*
> *They stumbled and fell . . . ."*

Jethro was hearing the words with his ears; but, somehow, he was hearing the message with his heart. "My enemies . . . stumbled and fell . . ." He saw Hiram, stumbling backwards and falling into the mire. He remembered so many years ago, Mis' Darthy had told him, God could speak to him personally through His Word.

This was like the light of dawn, piercing the darkness. For the first time, Jethro heard God's Word, somewhere deep inside, speaking to him, personally. O, Lord! O, Lord, he thought, hanging onto the post to steady himself, You were there. You were faithful even when I wasn't . . . when I caused the problem by my own disobedience to You!

Jethro held tightly to the post for the rest of the singing and worship, overwhelmed by the Grace of God. It wasn't until Brother Blanton stepped to the pulpit that Jethro left his private thoughts and came back to the meeting. Brother Blanton introduced a young, muscular man with a brown, square-cropped beard that hung down to his chest.

"This is Pastor Sheffield of Fellowship Church, the new church on the Fenholloway River," Brother Blanton announced.

At the mention of the Fenholloway River, a flurry of happy memories burst from Jethro's mind. He fondly remembered his parents. He thought of the Hadley's. Even though they had been his "owners", he had loved them; and he missed them. He remembered the homestead where they all lived together, on the river.

Pastor Sheffield's message touched his heart even more than his own memories. Brother Sheffield spoke about a run-away slave named Onesimus. The Apostle Paul sent the slave back to his master with instructions that Onesimus be received no longer as a slave, but as "a brother beloved."

The Scripture seemed to be talking about him; and for the first time, Jethro could understand it. God saw him as a "brother beloved"; he was not a piece of property. In God's eyes, he was not black and the other brothers white; he was simply a "brother beloved." This is what Mistah Jim and Mis' Darthy had been trying to tell him all along!

Jethro listened intently as Elder Sheffield continued. "Jesus said, "Ye shall know the truth, and the truth shall make you free.'"

The preacher stopped momentarily and looked around at the congregation. "Truth alone will not set you free. Make no mistake about that. You must know the truth! The truth works only for those who know it!"

Someone inside the building shouted, "Amen!"

"What is the truth a slave like Onesimus needs to know?" His eyes searched the congregation. "This is that truth: All slaves— whether they be slaves of fear, slaves of sin, slaves of hatred—all slaves need to know that true freedom begins in the heart. Black people aren't the only slaves. I have known white masters living in greater bondage than the black men and women they owned."

A hush fell over the building. "There are many kinds of slavery. I cannot say that one is worse than another. Slavery is slavery! Consider the Roman slave chained to the oar of a ship all his life. That slave lived and died without ever knowing physical freedom. But the moment he knew 'the truth' that Jesus 'came to set the captives free'," Brother Sheffield's eyes scanned the congregation. ". . . that moment, the slave chained to the oar stepped into a freedom far greater than any of his captors knew. It is only when a slave knows 'the Truth' that the Holy Spirit can safely begin to work God's freedom in every area of life."

Elder Sheffield paused before he continued. "Men and women who discover their physical freedom first, sometimes never move into the wonderful freedom of the Holy Spirit." Eyes in the audience were glued on him. "Once we have truly found freedom in Christ, there is no limit to what the Holy Spirit can teach us or where He can lead us! The 'good news' of the gospel is that once our hearts are free, there is no power on earth or in hell that can stop us! We are free! Black men can be free in a slave-culture! White men can be free in a king's tyranny! Roman slaves can be free on a galley ship!" His voice was strong and powerful as he shouted, "Jesus came that we might have life, and have it more abundantly! That abundance is not limited by human slavery—wrong as it is! God moves beyond the human realm! Regardless of our situation, Jesus said we shall know the truth, and the truth shall set us free!"

Elder Sheffield raised both arms in the air, "Once our hearts are free," he shouted, "we are free!"

Inside and outside the building, weeping spread through the congregation. Jethro was among the weeping. He grasped the post, closed his eyes, and pressed his forehead against the wood.

Then it happened. As the congregation sang, Jethro sobbed; and the words of the hymn captured his heart.

"Come ye sinners, poor and needy,
Weak and wounded, sick and sore,
Jesus ready stands to save you,
Full of pity, love and power.
Let not conscience make you linger,
Or of fitness fondly dream,
All the fitness He requireth
Is to feel your need of Him."

Jethro wasn't singing. He couldn't. Nor did he see the elderly black woman who stepped up beside him. She put her arms around his waist and pulled him loose from the post.

"You go on, boy," she whispered, "God tol' you to go, and now you gotta' go!" Jethro didn't budge. "You ain't answering the call of a white preacher! You is answering the call of Jesus! You is goin' to Jesus, givin' yourself to Him! You got to confess Him before men! He's got a work for you to do, boy. Ain't nobody else can do it but you! Now you go!"

With the discernment of one who has walked with the Lord for many years, she understood exactly what to do. She did not wait for Jethro to respond. She led him to the steps of the building, and then she pushed him forward.

The next thing Jethro knew, he was all the way down front. Elder Blanton grabbed him. He held him tightly. Brother Blanton recalled that rainy night years ago, and he shouted. With one arm around the boy and the other raised over his head, the preacher danced. He laughed and cried at the same time.

"There is neither Jew nor Greek, bond nor free," Elder Blanton wept aloud, "but we are all one in Christ Jesus!"

Others flocked to the front, dropping at the mourner's bench, sobbing out old grief, and breathing in new joy. George ran forward and fell on his knees. Edward and Franklin shoved their way to the front and fell into the arms of their dad.

In the midst of the joyous confusion, the congregation broke into singing.

"I will arise and go to Jesus,
He will embrace me in His arms,
In the arms of my dear Savior,
Oh! There are ten thousand charms!"

When Elder Blanton let loose of him, Jethro dropped to the floor as if in a faint. Dorothy rushed toward him, weeping and singing, and fell beside him. Harlow Bentley went down with a crash. Franklin and Edward slumped from their father's arms as they passed out.

The spontaneous burst of singing was replaced by a solemn still-ness. Every sound was hushed, and no one moved. A holy energy swept through the building and beyond. The congregation in the arbors fell silent. Three men who had gone to the spring fell on their knees, midway in the yard, and broke into tears. Even birds became quiet, and horses ceased their braying. For twenty minutes, Glory gripped the place and held everything perfectly still.

After a period of time, the Presence slowly lifted. Jethro and Franklin sat up and looked around. No one was standing. The log building itself seemed different. Even the air around them had changed. They could not explain it; they knew they had been in the Presence of God. And He was still hovering over them.

Another twenty minutes passed. In the southeast corner of the building, someone began to sing softly. Voices from every direction joined in.

"Come Holy Comforter! Thy sacred witness bear!
In this glad hour, Thou who Almighty art,
Now rule in every heart, And n'er from us depart,
Spirit of Power!"

Soon, people were on their feet again. They hugged each other, sang, and rejoiced.

Elder Blanton waved his hand, "Follow me to the spring. These who have died in Christ must be buried in baptism and raised in newness of life!"

Elder Blanton led a group of twenty new believers—Jethro and five other black people among them—into the spring,

Jethro tugged on his shirtsleeve. "Brother Blandon, would it be alright if Elder Sheffield comes into the water with us . . . if I becomes a member of Fellowship Church . . . instead of here at Blue Springs?"

Elder Blanton squeezed the boy against his chest. "Of course! Jethro! All the churches are represented here, and you can join whichever one you like!"

"I was jus' thinking . . . if my mama and papa were still here . . ." Jethro dropped his head. ". . . that's where they would be members . . . maybe I can take their place." Jethro raised his head and looked at the pastor, "Do you think that Mis' Darthy and Mistah Jim will understand?"

"Of course, Jethro! They will rejoice with you!" Elder Blanton turned toward the bank and called, "Sheff! Come in the water and help me. Jethro wants to be a member at Fellowship Church!"

With Elder Sheffield on the opposite side, Elder Blanton made the pronouncement of baptism. Together they dipped Jethro under the spring. Jethro was followed by George, Franklin, Edward, and then sixteen more.

On the way home that evening, the boys sprawled out in the back of the wagon. James held the reins, and Dorothy leaned against him.

"There has never been a more blessed day, James," Dorothy spoke. "Never!" For a moment, she was silent. "There is only one thing that steals its joy."

James nodded understandingly. He knew what she was about to say.

"If only our dear, precious Carolyn were here. If only we could know where she is right now . . . .

"Carolyn! Oh, Carolyn! Wherever you are!" Dorothy called aloud, "Come home to Madison!"

Chapter Eighteen

⁕

Carolyn had been gone over a year. Little was known of her whereabouts other than what had been reported by a stage-coach driver. Doc Kupperman, the traveling salesman, relayed the news that Carolyn—without giving the driver any indication of her intentions beyond that point—had ridden the stage to Picolatta.

Dorothy prayed daily for Carolyn's safe return. She wondered, does Carolyn know Hiram is gone? Does she realize how much she is wanted and needed here in Madison? Dorothy was pregnant for the fifth time, but her joy was overshadowed by constant worry about Carolyn.

"Dorothy! You're not a young woman!" Dr. Thad scolded her. "Your boys are almost grown! And James is too old to be raising another baby!"

"Apparently God decided otherwise," Dorothy replied.

"Oh, don't act like you and James didn't have anything to do with this!" Dr. Thad was immediately embarrassed by his own remark. He should never have spoken that way to a lady.

Dorothy just smiled, "I'll be fine," she assured him. She decided not to mention the persistent morning sickness. It was more intense and more frequent than with her previous pregnancies. Dr. Thad is worried enough already, she thought.

A few days later, a wagon pulled into the front yard. Doc Kupperman folded down the side panels of his wagon to reveal an abundant supply of pots, pans, medicines, sewing supplies, farm tools, cosmetics, and ladies hats.

"Do you have any word about Mrs. McKay?" Dorothy asked.

"Nothing! Nothing!" he answered. "I travel all the 'vay from Marianna to St. Augustine asking questions, but nobody knows even one thing about her." He gestured with both hands. "Poof! She is gone! Like magic!"

Dorothy scanned Doc Kupperman's medicines. "Do you have anything for morning sickness?"

"Morning sickness! Another little Danbury! 'Vunderful! 'Vunderful!" Doc Kupperman picked up a small bottle of dark-colored liquid. "If you are needing something to settle the morning stomach, this is best! Always it is good for that!"

Dorothy paid him and dropped the little bottle into her apron pocket. Franklin stood nearby, looking at Doc Kupperman's merchandise with disinterest.

The traveling salesman turned his attention to Franklin. "Young man! You are 'vanting the young ladies to be noticing you? This 'vill do it!" Doc Kupperman held up a bottle of lilac water.

"No, thanks, Doc. You don't sell what I'm lookin' to buy." Franklin thought of the six dollars he had earned trapping otters. The five-dollar gold piece and the dollar in silver change were tucked safely under his mattress.

"And 'vat is it you are 'vanting to buy, young man?"

"A horse," Franklin replied as he waved goodbye.

A few days later, Franklin met someone who was selling exactly what he wanted to buy, or so it seemed.

James needed farm supplies, and Franklin rode along with him into Madison. While James went into the General Store, Franklin headed down the street to the livery stable. A slender black boy about his own age met Franklin at the door of the barn.

"Is you gots a horse in here?" the boy asked.

"No, but I'm going to buy one . . . uh, someday, that is . . . I've got six dollars saved up." Franklin felt important hearing himself talk about purchasing a horse.

The other boy was impressed. "How'd you get all dat money?"

"Trappin' otters." Franklin didn't mention that it had taken him an entire winter to earn the money.

"Mistah' Fromley come all the way from New Orleans to sell horses. Maybe you could buy one from . . . ."

The boy was interrupted by a dumpy, middle-aged man. "I'm Mr. Fromley," he grasped Franklin's hand in a firm handshake. "I deal in rare horses, mostly purebred Arabians."

"Wow! I ain't never even seen a purebred Arabian horse!" Franklin was obviously impressed.

"I was taking a nice stallion to Virginia. Got a breeder up there who really wants him, but it looks like I'm gonna have to take him back to New Orleans." The horse trader shook his head and frowned. "These purebreds are high strung, and they don't take well to ocean travel. This one had such a bad case of seasickness, I had to take him off the steamer in St. Augustine."

Mr. Fromley continued, "Such a pity. That stallion could sire a whole herd of purebred Arabians, but a lot of people can't recognize purebred quality if the animal is a little lean. Why, rather than put that poor horse back on the ship, I'd almost be willing to sell him for the cost of shipboard hay."

"How much is the cost of shipboard hay?"

Mr. Fromley gave Franklin a sympathetic look. "Boy, I think you're in the right place at the right time. I just might decide to let you have a real deal." He looked directly into Franklin's eyes. "It would do my heart good to come back someday and find you the owner of the finest horse breeding farm in Florida! And you could do it all for . . . hmmm . . . probably for . . . say . . . six dollars . . . ."

"Sold!" Franklin beamed, "When can I get him?"

Mr. Fromley waited as Franklin dug into his pocket and pulled out a tightly wrapped handkerchief. He opened it to reveal the gold coin and the silver pieces.

"Elijah," the New Orleans stranger addressed the black boy. "Take this young businessman back to stall number seven, and show him Starfire."

"Starfire!" Franklin's heart leaped with excitement. "A purebred Arabian stallion named Starfire!"

Mr. Fromley called Franklin back to the door, "Now remember, boy, this horse has been seasick. Don't expect him to act like a trotter for a few days. He still has sea legs."

"Oh, I understand, Mr. Fromley," Franklin assured the horse trader, "I'll take good care of him." As Elijah and Franklin walked to the stall, Mr. Fromley dropped the money into his pocket and hurried away.

Franklin looked through the slats of stall number seven. It was evident that Starfire was still suffering from a serious case of seasickness. His ears flopped, his eyes were sunken; and his thin legs wobbled.

Franklin tried to hide his disappointment, "After a few days in our pasture, he'll be good as new."

"How long'd it take to earn dat much money?" Elijah asked.

Franklin did not answer. Somehow the question made his pocket—and his heart—feel empty.

An hour later James stared intently at the "purebred Arabian" as Elijah led the animal into the street. James shook his head. "Well, boy, this may be the best six-dollar lesson you ever learn."

"He might not look so good now, Papa," Franklin replied defensively, "but in a few weeks he'll be just like new." Even to Franklin, his words sounded hollow.

George, Jethro, and Edward were not as kind about Starfire as their father had been. When the wagon pulled into the gate with Starfire plodding wearily behind it, the three boys studied the animal in disbelief.

"There ain't enough hide on that skeleton to make a Whangdoodle!" George laughed. "Franklin, you just bought yourself a purebred, six-dollar bone rack!"

Without a word, Franklin led Starfire to the barn.

"How you gonna' tell when he's dead?" George called after him. "He can't look any worse than he looks right now!"

Franklin stepped inside the barn and closed the door behind him. He felt sorry for the frail creature, but he felt worse for himself. He gently stroked Starfire's neck, "It ain't your fault. You can't help being a dumb animal. And I got no excuse for being dummer 'an you."

That evening after dinner, James uncorked the little medicine bottle and sniffed the dark liquid. "Smells like it would make you have morning sickness!" He twisted his face, "The colic medicine I give the calves doesn't smell this bad."

Dorothy laughed, "Maybe I'll try some of your remedy!

After a few days, Dorothy thought she might be improving; but Starfire was not responding to Franklin's care. The 'seasickness' was getting progressively worse. Over the weeks that followed, Starfire became more feeble and lost even more weight.

It was Edward who came in from milking the cows early one morning with the news that Starfire had died during the night.

George couldn't resist a last jab at Franklin's foolishness, "How did you know he was dead?"

Undestanding how difficult it was for Franklin, James interrupted the taunting. "I'm sorry, son," he said to Franklin. Then he turned to the other boys, "As soon as you finish eating, get your shovels and help your brother. That horse'll stiffen up in the next few hours. And if you wait too long, you'll have flies and swelling . . . ."

"James! Please!" Dorothy scolded, cupping her hands over her mouth. "That kind of talk over breakfast isn't helping my stomach!"

Three hours later the boys were exhausted, sweaty, and dirty. They stood beside the carcass of the horse, on an unshaded hilltop in the pasture, next to a hole seven feet deep and nearly five feet across.

"Alright," George ordered, "let's drag him into the hole."

"Wait a minute! Wait a minute!" Jethro yelled. "Look at them legs!" As James had warned, rigor mortis had set in; and the legs were stiff as boards. "He ain't gonna fit in that hole now!"

They all groaned when they saw it.

"Ain't but one thing to do," George muttered disdainfully. "Gotta cut off his legs."

Jethro protested, "Not me! I ain't cutting legs off 'a nothin'!"

"You don't have to," George replied, "Franklin's gonna do it."

"Me? Why me?" Franklin clinched his fists and stuck out his chest as he spoke. "It's your idea! You do it!"

George snapped, "It's your horse! You're the only one fool enough to buy a 'purebred Arabian' bag of bones!"

"But what will Papa think?"

"He's not going to know." George turned to Edward, "Go get the saw and the ax."

A few minutes later, Edward returned with the tools. He could see the distress in Franklin's face and felt compassion for his younger brother. "I've got an idea," he said, "there are four of us, and the horse has four legs . . . ."

"O.K., Edward, it's your idea, you go first," George said. ". . . at least dead horses don't bleed . . . ."

In another two hours, the four boys stood beside a neatly packed mound of earth. Starfire had finally been laid to rest. A tobacco stake marked the head of his grave.

"This is the worst funeral I ever seen," Jethro shook his head as he stared at the mound. Edward spoke reverently, "Starfire, may he rest in peace."

"Not 'in peace'," George corrected him, "in pieces."

Sadly Franklin's best efforts had not saved Starfire; and Doc Kupperman's medication had provided only temporary relief for Dorothy's problem. Dorothy was still fighting nausea. She had an uneasiness about this baby. It was far too late in the pregnancy for morning sickness, and she decided it was time to consult Dr. Thad.

"It's different," she told the doctor. "I never went through anything like this with my other babies."

"And no wonder!" Dr. Thad said in a chiding tone. "You're twenty years older than you were the first time you got pregnant!"

Dr. Thad tried to conceal his concern. Something was wrong. He could not diagnose it, and he certainly did not have a remedy for it. Though neither of them said it, Dr. Thad and Dorothy were thinking the same thing . . . if only Carolyn were here.

"Dorothy," he advised his long-time patient and friend, "you're going to have to spend more time off your feet. You cannot work in the garden, and you really should let the boys take over most of the cooking and housework."

"The boys? Cook?" Dorothy chuckled. "Oh, my! We'll all starve!"

Several weeks later, James sent George for Dr. Thad. When the doctor arrived, he hurried into the house to find Dorothy wrenching in pain. He recognized immediately that these were not normal labor pains. There was no pattern to the contractions. Sometimes they were so close together, Dorothy could not even catch her breath in between.

"Pray hard that she will deliver this baby quickly and get out of this agony," he instructed James and the boys. "She can't go on like this very long!"

"But it's too soon," James protested. "Can't you do something to stop the contractions? The baby might not live if it comes this early!"

"That's in God's Hands," Dr. Thad replied. "Just pray hard!"

Suddenly it hit Franklin. This was not just about losing the baby—the little brother or sister he had never met—his mother's life was in danger. In a panic, he grabbed Jethro, "You've got to pray, Jethro! There's special power when you pray! I know it's true! I can't never forget what happened with Hiram in the swamp!"

Franklin knew when he mentioned the night in the swamp, sooner or later, he would have to explain the whole Whang-doodle episode to his father; but he didn't care. Right now, all he cared about was his mother. And, tonight at least, his father wasn't asking questions.

"Jethro," George spoke up. "Franklin's right. Even when you say the blessing over dinner, I feel something special."

"We all need to pray in agreement," Jethro said softly.

"Then let's do it!" Edward spoke up. "The four of us can go to our room, get on our knees, and you can lead us in prayer until Mama gets through this."

Before sunset, the westbound stage drew to a stop at the Danbury lane, and a passenger stepped out. The driver climbed to the roof, untied two small bags, and handed them to the rider. Then he swung back into his seat and headed toward Tallahassee. As the coach rode out of sight, the rider turned and walked slowly toward the house. In the twilight, no one saw her approaching. Nor was she seen when she stepped onto the porch and waited quietly, as though gathering courage before opening the door.

Dorothy was staring blankly at James and Dr. Thad when an angelic-like face appeared between them. The woman's features blurred in and out of focus, as though Dorothy were dreaming.

"Come home! Carolyn!" Dorothy called aloud, "Wherever you are, come home!"

"I'm home, darling," Carolyn softly replied. "I'm home." She pushed between the two men and knelt at the bedside. "You'll never know how much I've missed you, Dorothy. You'll never know," Carolyn wept.

Dr. Thad was overcome with emotion. He had done his best to appear calm for Dorothy's sake, but now there was no holding back. He hugged Carolyn and wept openly. Then he laughed, and then he cried some more.

James embraced Carolyn silently. She was thinner, the luster was gone from her face, and her hair was pulled back carelessly into a bun. "Hiram is gone," James told her. "Your house is waiting. We always knew you would be back someday, and we've taken care of everything."

Daybreak marked the end of a long ordeal. Carolyn woke with a start, still dressed in her traveling clothes. She looked down from the loft where she had slept. The cabin was quiet, and Dorothy was resting peacefully. James was asleep in his chair. Dr. Thad lay sprawled out on the floor with a pillow wadded under his head.

"Thank you, Lord!" Carolyn prayed quietly, "Thank you, Lord. I'm home where I belong."

She climbed down the stariway and eased over to Dorothy's bedside. She gently laid her hand on Dorothy's cheek. Dorothy was breathing normally and her coloring had returned. "Thank you, Lord. Thank you, Lord, for saving her."

Carolyn lifted the tiny bundle from the bed and held it mournfully to her breast. The soul hangs by such a narrow thread between life and death, she thought as she looked into the precious face of the lifeless little girl. Dorothy struggled so hard to give life to this child, yet the little one could not keep it for herself. Tenderly and reverently, Carolyn returned the bundle to the bed next to Dorothy. Then she took Dorothy's apron from the kitchen wall, and went to the well to draw water. She would begin her first day back at home, cooking breakfast for everyone.

Three weeks later, Dorothy was well enough to make the ride to church. She, James, Carolyn, and the boys headed out together in the wagon. When they rounded the bend into the churchyard, singing spilled from the little building like a sweet fragrance flowing from a garden.

Silently they made their way to the cemetery. Elder Blanton saw them arrive, slipped out while the congregation was still singing, and joined them at the family grave plot. James knelt down and placed his hand on the little mound of earth. Dollie's grave was marked with a wooden cross and a seashell decoration made by Franklin.

Brother Blanton put his arm around Dorothy, "The Lord doesn't expect us to give thanks for Dollie's death, but we can give Him thanks because we know where she is right now."

Carolyn grasped Dorothy's hand, "Yes! Yes! And Joseph was there to greet her when she arrived!" Carolyn's eyes blurred with tears, "And they're waiting for us, Dorothy. When it's our time, they will be there to greet us!"

Dorothy scanned the row of grave markers. It seemed her whole life story was recorded here. James sensed what she was thinking. "This is not our life story," he said pointing toward the graves. "These markers remind us of the wonderful memories we have of those who have gone on ahead of us, but this is not the end. Dorothy, hear me when I tell you, the Lord will once again make you 'a joyful mother of children.'"

James stood up and took Dorothy in his arms. He held her tightly as he prayed, "Lord, we thank You for life! We thank You for each other, we thank You for our home, for health, for our wonderful boys, and all the other good things You've given us. We wish we could have kept Dollie . . ." James paused to regain his composure, ". . . but we couldn't . . . so now . . . so now we give thanks that she is with You forever. We thank You for every good and perfect gift You've brought our way. Amen."

Dorothy dropped to her knees. She stroked the ground as gently as she would have touched Dollie's hair and placed a fresh bouquet of flowers against the cross. Then she bent forward and kissed the mound. As she stood up, Dorothy whispered, "She shall not return to me, but I shall go to her."

When Autumn came, the sumac and dogwood trees turned fiery red, and the poplars were a golden yellow. The entire lane between the Danbury farm and the Bellamy Trail was ablaze in shades of orange, green, purple, red, and yellow. James and the boys worked long hours in the field gathering crops and preparing the smoke house for the winter months. Dorothy and Carolyn were busy putting up vegetables.

It was late in the day when the Danbury wagon returned from a trip into town for supplies. James, Dorothy, and Carolyn sat in the front, and the boys were stretched out in the back.

At the bend in the lane, where a gap in the trees gave a view of the sky, Dorothy caught sight of a thin grey mist of smoke. "James, what is that?"

James turned to see a sudden burst of black soot, rising above the treetops. "That's Carolyn's place!" He slapped the horse with the reins and urged the animal in the direction of the McKay homestead.

"Lord, no!" Carolyn wept aloud. "Lord! Please! Not my house! Not my house!"

"It's the barn!" James shouted as they broke into the clearing. "The barn is on fire!"

"Thank God it's not the house!" Carolyn yelled, "Thank You, Lord!"

"Stay away from that barn!" James yelled to the boys as they piled out of the wagon. "It's ready to fall!"

Carolyn ran frantically to the well and grabbed a water bucket. "It's too late!" James shouted above the noise of the fire and pulled her back, "No amount of water will save the barn! It's too late!"

"But the mare is in there!" Carolyn yelled. "The mare is in there!"

"You can't go in, Carolyn," James shouted, "There's nothing you can do for that mare!"

The mare's four-month-old colt darted nervously about the yard, as though hypnotized by the fire. Dorothy yelled to the boys, "Catch the colt! Don't let him get near the barn!"

The boys sprang for the colt, but the young horse was quicker. He darted around them, knocking George to the ground. Then the colt raced back into the blazing inferno, just as the roof and walls collapsed with a roar.

"Why did he do that?" George screamed in horror. "Why?"

"God only knows! But we've got to get water on the roof!" James yelled, pointing to the house. "Pull the wagon up to the back porch, and let's get water on the shingles!"

Edward got to the well first and began drawing water. Franklin, Jethro, and George formed a bucket brigade. They passed the buckets of water down the line and up to their father. James splashed the water onto the section of the house nearest the barn, protecting it from flying sparks.

Dorothy held Carolyn in her arms, "Everything you've lost can be replaced. I'm just thankful you still have your home."

"Oh, I am, too!" Carolyn replied. ". . . I was just thinking how much I owe you and James and how little opportunity I've had to repay you. Since that first day when John and I met you at the Madison Square, you have been God's blessing in my life . . . ."

"And that's the way it's supposed to be," Dorothy hugged Carolyn. "We are here to love and be loved . . . it's like my mother always told me, 'There ain't nothing more important than loving!'"

The next morning James and George rode back into Madison to recruit volunteers. The following Saturday, eight men—all of them eager to help Carolyn—joined James and the boys at the McKay farm.

"I'd like my barn in a different spot," Carolyn informed them.

"There's no need to change the site," James told her. "It'll be easy to clear away the debris and build a new barn in the same place. We can build it just like the first one; you won't know the difference."

"I like the idea of a brand new barn, in a brand new place." Carolyn was firm, and James knew there was no use arguing.

Throughout the day, Dorothy and Carolyn kept the men fed. The two women had spent most of Friday cooking and baking. As always, Dorothy's sweet potato pie was a big hit. Thankfully, she had made plenty.

By nightfall, Carolyn had a beautiful, new barn, in a new location.

"I don't understand why she wouldn't let us rebuild it right where John built the first one," James wondered.

Dorothy smiled, "It's all part of the mystery of our wonderful Carolyn."

Chapter Nineteen

In 1859, the Danbury family celebrated James' sixtieth birthday. His hair was white and thinning; but when Dorothy looked at him, she still saw the best-looking man in the county.

For Dorothy and James, the past few years had been some of the best in their life together. Settlers in North Florida slept peacefully, without fear of Indian raids. Carolyn, after an unexplained two-year absence, had returned just as mysteriously as she had disappeared. The boys were now young men, and Dorothy was grateful to have Carolyn back in their lives.

On the third Sunday in September, James and George left at daybreak for the Association Meeting at Old Columbia Church, fifteen miles north of Madison. The meeting house was just inside the Georgia line. George wore his best clothes, complemented by a dash of Doc Kupperman's lilac water.

As they pulled into the yard and approached the log structure with its wide pine-bough arbor, James reminisced, "Soon after your mama and I married, a band of Creeks raided the church and killed several members." He pointed to a large oak, "Mr. Edward Henderson was one of them. He's buried under that tree. His son-in-law, Joel Morris, operates the tannery in Madison."

George nodded. He knew Mr. Morris well. But at the moment, he wasn't interested in the cemetery's past. He was looking at a girl standing near the well right now.

"Papa, do you know anything about her?" George interrupted his father's history lesson, "The girl with the long blond hair?"

"Nothing more than she's as pretty as any girl as I've ever seen," James smiled. George turned sideways on the seat so he could watch her as the wagon moved through the crowd. He hoped she would still be at the well when he could get back there for a drink.

George jumped from the wagon, and James called to him. "Remember, you are a delegate from Blue Springs Church; and you have to be in the house for all the business sessions."

George nodded as he rushed back to the well. By the time he got there, the girl was gone. He tried not to appear obvious as he searched the grounds. When the singing began, George went inside the building and sat down next to his father. When everyone else had their heads bowed for prayer, he opened his eyes and scanned the crowd. He couldn't find the golden-haired girl anywhere in the room.

After the service, George carried the basket of food his mother had prepared to the dinner tables. He was about to set it down, when a thin woman with a harsh tongue scolded him, "Give that to me! We'll spread the victuals!" She motioned for George to get out of the way. "You get over there with the men folks! Leave the food to the ladies."

The woman turned her back to George and called, "Elizabeth! Come help me with this food!"

George was about to walk away when he saw something that stopped him in his tracks. The girl he had seen at the well was standing mere inches from him. She was even more beautiful up close. Her hair was like corn silk gold, and her eyes were bright blue.

George thrust out his hand, "I'm . . . uh . . . George Danbury," he stammered, ". . . from Madison."

"You're one of the delegates!" the girl smiled, "I remember hearing your name. None of the other churches have such a young representative." She was obviously impressed.

"Papa and I were elected . . . ," he stumbled over his words, ". . . I really don't know why . . . ."

"I'm Elizabeth Darnell," she introduced herself. "I live with my aunt Bessie Hackett in Quitman." For a terrifying moment George could not speak.

Finally Elizabeth broke the awkward silence, "I've never been to Madison. I've heard it's a pretty place."

When she smiled, something inside George melted; and his knees felt weak. He hoped she couldn't tell how fast his heart was racing.

They were abruptly interrupted by chiding words from Aunt Bessie. "Elizabeth! You can save that visiting until the dinner hour! Help me with this food!" She pointed to an open spot on the serving table, "Set that boy's victuals right there! Most of this food will be wasted, but some women just have to show off their cooking."

Elizabeth looked away, embarrassed by her aunt's cutting remark. Before George could say anything else—even if he could have thought of something to say—Elder Blanton called for everyone's attention, "Let's bow our heads for the blessing."

After the prayer, Elizabeth served George a piece of sweet potato pie she had baked herself. "That's my favorite pie!" he exclaimed, "My favorite!" He took a deep breath. "Will you sit with me?" he asked, motioning toward the far side of the cemetery. "There's a good spot near our wagon."

The two sat on a cedar log, George straddling it with his plate in front of him and Elizabeth sitting sideways with the plate balanced on her knees. Her dress was the same intoxicating blue as her eyes.

"How long have you lived with your Aunt Bessie?" he asked.

"Since I was eight years old . . . my parents died of yellow fever at St. Marks . . . that's half my life . . . ." Elizabeth dropped her voice as she told him more about her family. "I'd rather live with my Aunt Clarabelle . . . but Aunt Bessie is sick a lot . . . and she needs me . . . ."

George wasn't sure what to say, so he talked about his own family. "I live with my parents and my brothers."

"That's nice," Elizabeth looked at him and smiled. "How many brothers do you have?"

"Two brothers . . . really three. A negro boy, Jethro, came to live with us after he lost his parents . . . he was only eight years old . . . just like you when you lost your parents . . . Jethro grew up with us. We love him like a brother, and he loves us back."

"Aunt Bessie wouldn't like that," Elizabeth shook her head. "I have to do all the house work myself because she won't allow any black folks on her property."

George changed the subject. "Your dress sure is pretty."

"Thank you," she answered, straightening her skirt. "My aunt Clarabelle gave it to me. She's always doing nice things for me."

When the two finished eating, they wandered through the cemetery. On the way back, Elizabeth stopped at a grave. The ground was slightly sunken. There was no marker, only a rim of aged seashells. "That's my great-uncle Harding's grave. He fought in the Revolution and got wounded in the hip. My papa showed me this grave when I was real small . . . don't know why I remember it so well."

"War makes us remember things," George explained. "My dad talks a lot about the Indian War."

"I'm glad we're not living in war times. And I hope we never do."

"That's one of the good things about living in Florida . . . or South Georgia," George added quickly, "We're away from everybody else. With the Gulf on three sides, we ain't got neighbors to worry about."

"Aunt Bessie says the Union is going to divide. She hates the North and says we ought split away from it. Even if we have to fight . . . ."

"Won't never happen!" George quickly assured her. They sat down together on a wooden bench near the grave. "And even if the country did get in a war, we'd hardly know it, all the way down here."

Elizabeth exhaled with relief. This young delegate spoke with confidence and authority. She was glad Aunt Bessie had insisted on attending the Association Meeting.

Elizabeth turned suddenly on the bench, "How long have we been gone?" She gave a troubled look in the direction of the meeting house, "Aunt Bessie will be worried about me!"

As she stood up to leave, her foot sank into the loose sand, and she fell toward George. He caught her around the waist.

"You alright? You didn't hurt your ankle did you?"

"No, I'm fine," she laughed, holding his arm as she steadied herself. "But I've got a shoe full of sand!"

George held her elbow as she emptied her shoe. Then the two hurried toward the meeting house, their hearts racing. Elizabeth's heart pounded in fear of Aunt Bessie; George's heart with the excitement of the wonderful moment when he had touched her.

At the door before they stepped inside, Elizabeth promised to visit with him again. George watched from the entrance until she sat down next to her aunt. Then he took a seat in the rear where he could have a clear view of her. Everything about Elizabeth made him feel good.

On the way home, George held the reins for miles without speaking. He was lost in deep thought, and his father understood perfectly. James had seen his son and the girl with the golden hair sitting together on the bench in the cemetery, and he liked what he saw.

As their wagon pulled onto the Cherry Lake Road, James gave his son some fatherly advice. "Son," he said, "it was God who gave you all those wonderful feelings for that beautiful girl. Keep your mind pure, and He will let you discover other exciting things about her and yourself." George was amazed. How had his father known what was going on in his mind? James responded to the unspoken question, "The day I first saw your mother get out of the Hapsburg wagon in the Madison Square, I felt all the same things you're feeling right now. God made you a man. He made Elizabeth a girl. And He never meant for either men or women to live without the joy and happiness of the other."

The next spring, James and Dorothy celebrated their twenty-seventh anniversary, and the following month, George's twenty-sixth birthday. George had been writing to Elizabeth since the association meeting in September. He had been exploring the property on the opposite side of the Bellamy Lane, directly across from his family's lane. Dorothy knew he had been asking questions at the land grant office, and she wondered how much longer she and James would have all four boys living at home.

By summer George was making several trips a month to the post office. One hot summer afternoon George rode into town to check for letters from Elizabeth. As he approached the front door, he heard loud, hostile voices coming from inside.

"If them federals want war, I say there ain't no need to disappoint them! A couple of weeks of fighting is way better'n losing our rights! Florida don't need nothin' Washington has to offer!"

George cringed as he heard another voice speak in agreement, "We can sure make our own decisions down here better'n they can make 'em for us up there!"

George walked past the men without speaking. He stepped to the window, "Good morning, Mr. Bentley," he greeted the Post Master. "Any mail for me?"

"Yes, indeed!" Harlow answered, holding up a white envelope, "and another one for your folks." He eyed George carefully, "Lot of letters going back and forth between you and that girl. Looks to me like things are getting mighty serious."

George avoided his gaze. He took the envelopes and darted out the door. He ran to a large tree at the corner of the square and opened the envelope addressed to him.

May 27, 1860
Dearest George,

I am almost too excited to live! I told Aunt Clarabelle that you have asked me to marry you and that I wrote back, YES! YES! YES! Aunt Clarabelle has written to your mother and father inviting them to visit her next month in Quitman. And even if your parents cannot make the trip, she still wants you to come. It seems too good to be true!

Aunt Bessie hasn't been well at all. She has weak spells, can't eat or sleep, and has to rest most of the time. Poor thing! I can't imagine what ails her, the problem is so strange. She won't let Doctor Marlow visit her. He is the only doctor in town but she doesn't trust him. I hope and pray that she will be improved by the time you arrive.

If your parents agree to come visit, you and your parents will be staying at Aunt Clarabelle's house. I think Aunt Clarabelle is almost as excited as I am! Her house is large and you will be very comfortable there.

I pray, when you arrive, Aunt Bessie will be strong enough to talk about setting a date for the wedding. There are problems I try not to think about. Darling, remember how much I love you.

Lovingly,
Elizabeth

That evening after dinner, George sat at the table with his parents. He talked excitedly about the invitation from Aunt Clarabelle.

"Son, are we going up there to plan a wedding?" James asked.

George grinned, "Yes, Papa . . . I've been trying to find the right words to tell you . . . ."

"Oh, Praise the Lord!" Dorothy jumped up and hugged George. "So that's why you've been so interested in the homestead across the way! It will be wonderful to have grandchildren so close! And they can spend the night with 'Grandma' any time they like!"

"I suppose we knew without you saying anything," James smiled and hugged his son. "In fact, I think I knew last September when I saw you and Elizabeth, sitting on that bench in the church cemetery. And I guess it goes without us saying it, your mother and I approve. You and Elizabeth have our blessing."

The weeks leading up to the trip were filled with activity and excitement. George applied for homesteading rights on the land on the other side of the Bellamy Trail. His brothers helped him explore it and look for the best spot for a cabin. Carolyn was as thrilled as Dorothy at the thought of grandchildren just across the way.

Carolyn agreed to stay in James and Dorothy's house while they were gone. She would cook for Jethro, Edward, and Franklin during Dorothy's absence, and make sure they wore clean clothes . . . at least once in awhile.

The night before the trip, George slept in spurts. Over and over again, he awoke thinking of the words in Elizabeth's letter, *"I am almost too excited to live!"* George felt the same way. He did not let himself dwell on the words in the last paragraph, *"There are problems I try not to think about."*

George had the wagon loaded and ready to go shortly after daybreak. "Have you ever seen a sky so blue?" he asked his father. "And look how green the trees are!"

North of Madison, the wagon passed the dismal-looking house on the west side of the road, the house that had captured James' attention the day the posse drove Hiram out of the state.

"Everything about that place feels evil," George observed as they passed. He turned to his father, "Why is that, Papa? What makes an ordinary house look different from other houses?"

"The evil that you sense isn't the house," James answered. "You're discerning the 'spirit' of the people who live there. Probably, the place has a dark past . . . and it will have a dark future."

George continued to stare at it. Even on this wonderful day in his life, George shivered at the ghastliness of the place. "That grimness," James explained, "will attract people who have the same darkness in their own lives. They'll find a familiar presence there."

Several miles later, the wagon passed the rock pile identifying the Florida-Georgia state line. Shortly thereafter, they entered a large swamp. Here the road narrowed to a mucky trail and wound through a cavern of cypress trees. Giant ferns clung to the trunks of the cypress, and moss hung from the limbs overhead. The air was cool and blessed with the fragrance of jasmine. Dorothy inhaled deeply. A welcome shade fell across the wagon, and the mare seemed to appreciate the moist ground beneath her hooves.

On the north side of the swamp, they emerged again into the sunlight. They followed the road leading to Columbia Church.

At noontime, they stopped at the church well and drank from it. While the mare rested, George wandered through the cemetery. Privately, he was reliving the day he met Elizabeth. He sat down on the same bench and envisioned Elizabeth sitting next to him, the two of them eating dinner together. He remembered the dress she was wearing, a gift from Aunt Clarabelle. He would never forget how beautiful she was, with the sun's rays falling on her golden hair. He remembered, too, how he had assured her that the nation would never go to war. He had been so confident then . . . but no more. Somehow, everything had changed. Now war seemed almost inevitable.

When they arrived in Quitman, George pulled out the map Elizabeth had sent to him. They had no trouble finding the landmarks she had identified, and they quickly made their way to Aunt Bessie's house.

George was disheartened at the sight of the home. It gave him the same feeling as the house on the Cherry Lake Road. Two stories and dreary brown house, it was built from sawmill boards, with steep, sharp-pointed gables on the roof. George could not imagine his beautiful, bright Elizabeth living in such a dark, dismal place.

He was even more dispirited when he was turned away at the front door. A barefoot, elderly white woman, wearing a soiled, torn dress greeted him.

"Miss Hackett's doing poorly," she informed George, "and she ain't able to see no company. Miss `Lizabeth can't come to the door neither. She says for you to go on down to her Aunt Clarabelle's house, and she'll come as soon as she can get away."

"Elizabeth can't come to the door even for a minute?" George asked painfully. He couldn't believe his ears.

"No, sir," the woman responded. "She can't leave Mis' Bessie at all, not even for a minute."

"Then may I come in for a moment?" George pleaded.

"No sir. Miss Bessie won't have no folks coming in when the house ain't ready. And Miss `Lizabeth ain't had time to do it. She's been kept mighty busy with her auntie. She said for me to tell you that she will meet you down there at her Aunt Clarabelle's." The woman gestured toward the west before she closed the door. "You can see the house from here."

George backed away. He couldn't believe this was happening. Never would he have expected such a greeting! Every distrusting suspicion he had about Aunt Bessie had just been confirmed. He had not liked her from the first day they met over the dinner table at Columbia Church, and now he knew why. Without any explanation to his parents, he directed the horse out of the yard and onto the street. He headed straight to Aunt Clarabelle's house.

As they neared the house, George and his parents stared in amazement. It was an elegant colonial mansion with tall white columns and a fan-shaped yard that radiated out from the front steps.

A border of boxwoods lined the circle on each side of the house, and a row of large Crepe Myrtle trees stood behind the hedge. "I had no idea," Dorothy said, "that Aunt Clarabelle lived in such a lovely home."

"Sure looks better than Aunt Bessie's house!" George replied. "That place gives me the creeps."

"Careful, son!" his father corrected. "Don't say anything you'll regret later."

This time when George ran the bell, he was welcomed warmly. An elderly black butler invited him inside.

As the two greeted each other, a woman's voice called from upstairs. "Is that George?" Without waiting for a reply, she hurried down the staircase, "Do come in! I am thrilled you are here."

George was impressed with the lady. Though she was probably older than his parents, she still had the same beautiful blonde hair and bright blue eyes as Elizabeth. "I am Elizabeth's Aunt Clarabelle!" she introduced herself and took George's hand. "I'm so thrilled you are here!" She glanced beyond him, "I do hope your parents are with you!"

"Yes, Ma'am," he replied. He was trying his best to make a good impression, "They're in the wagon."

Aunt Clarabelle rushed out the door and across the porch toward James and Dorothy. "Oh, come in! Please, come in!" she spoke with affection and sincerity. "I am so honored to have you visit!"

She took both of Dorothy's hands and gripped them lovingly. "It is such a long ride from Madison, and you must be weary. Do come in!" She turned to the butler, "Josiah, please get the bags and take them to their rooms upstairs."

Aunt Clarabelle looked at James and Dorothy, "I think my niece Elizabeth has wonderful taste in choosing a beau!"

Josiah held the door as they entered the house, and Clarabelle led them into a large, circular parlor with heavy maroon drapes and velvet chairs. "Did you stop at my sister Bessie's house?"

"Yes. Ma'am. We did," George replied.

"I had hoped," Aunt Clarabelle went on, "that you would come here first . . . ."

"Yes, Ma'am . . ." George paused midway in his sentence, ". . . what's wrong with Miss Hackett? When will I see Elizabeth?"

"You will see her right away, George," Aunt Clarabelle assured him. "She will be here quickly. As for my sister Bessie, I wish I could give you an answer . . . but I can't. Ever since we were children, Bessie has had . . . health problems . . . ."

Dorothy interrupted, "Is it serious?"

"Darling," Clarabelle drew a long breath, "according to Bessie, it's always serious. But the good news is that Elizabeth is fine!"

Josiah entered the room, carrying a silver tray with tea and cookies. George eagerly accepted the refreshments. He set down his cup when he heard footsteps moving hurriedly across the porch. The door opened, and Elizabeth stepped inside. She stood in the entrance in a white dress, with the elegant cut glass of the doorway and heavy velvet drapes surrounding her. She looked as regal as a royal bride, and George could scarcely believe his eyes. Was it possible she could be even more beautiful than he remembered?

He rose, bumping the coffee table with his knee, and hurried toward her.

"George!" She extended her hand, "I'm so sorry that I couldn't see you at Aunt Bessie's house . . . ."

"It's alright, Elizabeth," he gripped her hand and desperately wanted to take her in his arms, "so long as you're doing well."

"I'm fine!" Elizabeth smiled as they stepped into the parlor together. Elizabeth embraced Dorothy warmly, extended her hand to James, and hugged her Aunt Clarabelle.

They visited a few minutes while Elizabeth had a cup of tea. Then Aunt Clarabelle made a suggestion, "Elizabeth, why don't you take George out to the grape arbor while I have a visit with George's parents?" She smiled to James and Dorothy, "I know this young man didn't come all the way to Quitman to sit in my parlor! He and Elizabeth have a lot to talk about!"

The grape arbor was built like a dome-shaped gazebo. Stepping under it was like stepping beneath a large green umbrella. George picked several large, ripe scuppernongs and put them in Elizabeth's hand.

"We stopped at Columbia Church on the way here," he told her, "and I went back to every spot where you and I were that day. It was almost like I could remember each word you said." He looked longingly at her, "I love you, Elizabeth, and I want to spend the rest of my life with you. I can't live without you . . . and I don't want to wait."

He glanced nervously toward the house and then grabbed her firmly around the waist. He pulled her close and kissed her on the lips. She quickly pulled away.

"Not here!" she protested. "Someone might see us!" He wasn't listening. Instead, he kissed her again. And again. Elizabeth dropped the grapes from her hand and melted into his embrace.

"Elizabeth! Let's get married right away! Everything will work out! God will help us! I know He will!" He kissed her again. "Why should we wait? Let's do it right away!"

"Let me talk with Aunt Clarabelle . . . she always has good ideas . . . ." Elizabeth hesitated. "And I'll have to tell Aunt Bessie . . . that's the part I dread."

"Why?"

"Aunt Bessie has never been well, but in the past few months she's been much worse."

"What's wrong with her?"

"Fainting, dizzy spells, can't eat well, doesn't sleep. Just about everything you've ever heard of."

"Is she really sick?"

"Oh, yes, George!"

"But she doesn't want you to get married, does she?"

His question took Elizabeth by surprise. "She's never said anything like that. Never! She always tells me that she's concerned only for me."

"But she got worse about the same time as we started writing each other . . . ."

"That only happened by coincidence!" Elizabeth answered defensively. "Aunt Bessie wants the best for me. She will want us to be married just as soon as she's well enough to care for herself."

"But that may never be, Elizabeth! What if she never gets well enough to take care of herself?"

"Then we'll marry anyway!" Elizabeth promised.

The next day, after a great deal of persuasion from Elizabeth, Aunt Bessie allowed George and his parents to visit in her home. She entered the parlor on the arms of her niece and the woman who had met George at the door. Aunt Bessie breathed heavily as she was lowered into a chair and made it clear that she only had strength for a short visit.

Clarabelle spoke first, "We have wonderful news, Bessie. You're going to get a new nephew! Elizabeth and George want our blessing on their marriage."

There was a pause. Bessie made no response and showed no emotion. Her face remained absolutely expressionless.

Elizabeth broke the silence. "I want your approval, Aunt Bessie. You have been so good to me since Papa and Mama died—you are like my mother—and I want you to be pleased with the man I marry."

"I'm sure you do." Bessie finally replied in a pained voice, "I'm sure you do. I just hope I live until the wedding."

"But you will!" Elizabeth assured her, "I won't leave until you're better . . . ."

Clarabelle interrupted. "Bessie, we have all discussed this, and we'd like it to be a September first wedding. That is long enough for you to get your strength back." She motioned toward the woman who had seated herself next to Bessie, "Maggie and I will take good care of you after the wedding. You will get along just fine!"

Bessie stared hard at Elizabeth but did not speak. Again, Clarabelle broke the silence. "Why not come to my house for dinner tonight, Bessie? It would be good for you to get out. You can spend the night with me and have more time to visit with George's family. We can all be together for a wonderful evening."

Bessie stared angrily at Clarabelle. Then she directed her attention back to Elizabeth. Patting herself on the chest, she wheezed, "My heart is acting weak again . . . I had better get back to my room and lie down. Elizabeth, dear, help me get back to bed. Then you can leave me here and go back to Clarabelle's."

With the assistance of Elizabeth and Maggie, Bessie left the room. The others watched silently as the three disappeared into the hallway. In her room, Bessie dropped onto her bed and motioned for Maggie to leave. "Elizabeth, dear," Bessie gasped for breath between words, "You've heard . . . all the talk about war . . . if I were you . . . I wouldn't start a family until . . . it's over."

"No, Aunt Bessie, I won't wait that long! And if I knew for sure there was going to be war with the North, and that George might be called away, I would marry him today!"

"Elizabeth!" she scolded, rising from the pillow, "that's not sensible talk! No man is worth that kind of risk!"

"George isn't just any man, Aunt Bessie! He is a wonderful man, the man I want to spend my life with!"

Miss Hackett's eyes narrowed. "But are you sure he is worthy of you, Elizabeth?"

"Oh, yes, Aunt Bessie, you know the Danbury's are good people. We met them at the association meeting! George and his father are both delegates for Blue Springs Church!"

"I've been deceived many times by 'good people', Elizabeth, people I thought I could trust." She sat straight up in the bed. There was no evidence of any weakness or illness. "And you will do well to think about these Danbury's before marrying into that family!" The old woman's eyes glared at Elizabeth as she continued. "I've never known any decent Southerners who would consider a darkey part of their family!"

"You mean Jethro?!"

"I mean that darkey boy who lives with them! I don't know his name, and I hope I never learn it!"

"Aunt Bessie, how you feel about Jethro has no bearing on my love for George!"

Bessie took hold of the girl's arm and gripped it firmly. "There is no man worth loving, Elizabeth, if you are marrying down! You can bring disgrace on your name by marrying into the wrong family!" The old woman fell back onto the pillow—as if overcome with exhaustion—and lowered her voice, "I promised your mother and father before they died that I would take good care of you. Don't throw away all my years of effort, please, Elizabeth." Bessie closed her eyes and gasped for breath. ". . . I won't be here long, Elizabeth," she whispered, ". . . just promise me you won't marry until I'm well enough . . . ."

"I already promised that . . ." For a fleeting moment, Elizabeth wondered if George was right, if Aunt Bessie was only pretending to be ill, to keep her from marrying. She pushed the thought out of her mind. "Aunt Bessie, September first is still a long time away. You will be well by then."

Elizabeth never told George about the conversation in Aunt Bessie's bedroom. When the Danbury wagon left Quitman the next day, she assured George, on the first day of September, she would become Mrs. George Danbury. They would be married in the entrance hall of Aunt Clarabelle's house, and their reception would be in the garden near the grape arbor.

On the way home, Elizabeth's words kept ringing in his ears, ". . . Mrs. George Danbury . . . ." He repeated it over and over under his breath, "Mrs. George Danbury . . . Elizabeth Darnell Danbury." The words were music! Nothing could be more wonderful than for the most beautiful girl in all of Florida and Georgia to become "Mrs. George Danbury!"

At the new bridge over the Okapilco, they stopped and watered the horse. George stood on the planking and looked down into the tea-colored water churning around the pilings below. If time could only move as fast as the stream, he thought, how soon Elizabeth would be his! Elizabeth! Elizabeth! He could not keep from singing that beautiful name.

Late in the afternoon, the Danbury horse wearily pulled the wagon through the gate and into the yard. George dropped from the driver's seat and looked lovingly at the place. It was the only home he had ever known. Smoke was rising from the chimney, laughter was coming from the barn, the corn was green, and a halo of joy seemed to wrap around the place. It was everything he wanted his own home to be. With Elizabeth, he knew it could be that way. Mama and Papa had given him the best possible example—a home where God was honored, where love directed every action, and a place where people lived openly and unafraid.

Chapter Twenty

J ames stood by the well, looking toward the north. The sky was a clear blue with not a cloud in sight, but what he sensed was dark and malevolent. A calamitous storm was rising over the land. In his heart, he heard the thunder of war. Everywhere, people talked of it. Politicians screamed it. In the sermon the previous meeting day at Blue Springs Church, Elder Blanton had preached about it.

Florida had seemed so remote, so detached from the rest of the nation. What happened in the rest of the country had little to do with the southern peninsula. Now, somehow, all that had changed.

Several weeks passed without word from Elizabeth. George now had homesteading rights for the property on the opposite side of the Bellamy Trail, directly across from his family's lane. Norton Creek passed through the property; and he chose a cabin site on a rise of ground, just south of the stream. Like his parents' place, his homestead had a grove of huge oaks and palms.

On July Fourth, the family celebrated Jethro's birthday with a party in Carolyn's barn. Carolyn decorated the barn with pine limbs and magnolia blossoms. She served cinnamon tea with ginger cookies and a huge upside-down cake. Elder Blanton and Effie joined the family for the celebration.

After dark they sat on the ground by Carolyn's pond and watched the boys shoot fireworks. The largest, a skyrocket, was fired as they sang, "Happy Birthday." Afterward, Brother Blanton prayed for Jethro and for the nation.

When the prayer ended, he pulled Jethro to his side, "Son, you have a wonderful life before you, but you can find it only by asking the Holy Spirit to guide you." He hesitated a moment, "And He will, Jethro! No matter what happens, always remember that! And always remember that He has given you the heart of an intercessor. Be faithful to your calling!"

Jethro didn't need the pastor to remind him of his calling; he couldn't get away from it if he wanted to. Lately he had been waking up at night, overwhelmed by an urgency to pray. Jethro was glad to have his own, private loft bed in the corner of the large room he shared with his three brothers. Many nights he muffled his sobs with the quilt Carolyn had made for him, as he lay there, agonizing in prayer. He knew something big was about to happen. He felt increasingly compelled to pray for his family, his church, the state, and even the whole nation.

He had overheard men talking in the General Store; they were mocking a new political party, called, the "Republican Party". It was an abolitionist party, and the Republicans had a candidate running for President. The men at the store said there was no way a "Republican abolitionist" would ever be President of the United States of America.

At the Danbury home, with Miss Carolyn, with Elder and Mrs. Blanton, Jethro was "a beloved brother." They all understood true freedom in Christ, where "there is neither bond nor free." But anywhere else he went, everyone—black and white—looked at him as a slave. White people expected him to turn his eyes downward and answer respectfully, speaking only when spoken to. At church, he was forced to stand outside the building and listen through the windows. Jethro suspected that even some of the black slaves in Madison resented his relationship with the Danbury family. What would it be like, Jethro wondered, to walk through the middle of town and have everyone know that he was a free man? If the "Republican" candidate wins the next election, Jethro thought, was it really possible slavery might end? Could his dream become a reality? And at what price . . . at what terrible price?

As they walked home late that evening, George talked about the homestead and his plans for the cabin.

"As soon as our crops are finished," James spoke, "we can build the house for you and Elizabeth. Your brothers and I will help you clear the land."

Then James brought up an unpleasant subject. "Have you and Elizabeth discussed what you will do if Florida secedes from the Union and you have to serve in the army?"

"James!" Dorothy scolded immediately, "You would have been the last person to let politics stand in the way of getting married! Do you remember what you told my father? You said, 'the only thing a young man needs to get married is a girl!'"

George laughed, "I agree with that!"

"And I still believe it," James answered. "But politics isn't the same these days. In those days we were a territory; now we're a state. If these boys are called upon to serve in the Army, they'll have to go. God help them if they don't! Elizabeth needs to know that."

Dorothy fell silent for a moment. "But, James, you don't really think it will come to that, do you?"

"I wish I could say, no . . . but we never believed the Seminoles would fight like they did . . . your papa sure didn't think it would happen . . . I just don't know, Dorothy . . . ."

"Are you willing for the boys to fight?" Dorothy pressed him for an answer.

"It's not whether I'm willing or not. If we have to defend our farm from Union soldiers—like we did from Miccosukis—then, yes, I'll fight. And the boys will have to fight. We won't have a choice."

"But are you willing to defend the cause of slavery?" Dorothy persisted.

"Absolutely not! I don't believe in making men or states the slaves of others. No, I will not defend the cause of human slavery; but yes, I will defend Florida and our farm."

"That's confusing!"

"It's very confusing; and there is no easy way out of this mess. The Tenth Amendment to the Constitution guarantees the right of each state to make its own decisions . . . here is the predicament . . . ," James paused and shook his head, ". . . southern states have

hidden behind the Tenth Amendment to protect the wicked practice of slavery . . . ."

"We would never fight to support slavery!" Edward asserted.

"But we'd have to fight to protect our home and family!" Franklin
added.

"Southern states have used . . . abused . . . the Tenth Amendment
. . ." James went on,

". . . . to justify the terrible practice of human bondage . . . I just
don't see how this can ever be resolved peaceably . . . ."

"'With God, all things are possible,'" Dorothy reminded him.

James turned to George, "Son, I'm not suggesting that you and
Elizabeth shouldn't marry. I very much want you to marry. But you
need to remember what happened to John McKay and so many
others during the Seminole War." He looked at Dorothy with foreboding in his eyes, "Darling, we have to be realistic."

When they reached home, they all went inside and sat down
at the kitchen table. "There's a real danger the South may organize
itself into a separate nation," James continued. "If that happens,
Florida's militia will become part of a `Southern' army. They will be
fighting not just for Florida, but for slavery."

George interrupted. "Papa, I haven't heard anything like that.
The only talk I'm hearing is about protecting Florida. If I don't protect Elizabeth from foreign invaders, I'm not much of a husband!
People in Florida just want sovereignty—independence—from the
other states!"

"Yeah!" Franklin added. "State sovereignty! That was part of the
deal when Florida became a state. Like you said, Papa, the Tenth
Amendment! They can't be changing that now!"

"Son," James replied in a serious tone, "It was 'part of the deal'
for Indians to have, `*All privileges, rights, and immunities of the
citizens of the United States.*' Sometimes things change in ways we
never thought they could . . . ."

"Then maybe we should secede," George said, "and become a
separate nation."

"If states can't resolve their differences and learn to live together
harmoniously, how do you suppose two separate nations could?"
James replied.

"But, Papa, what would you do if a Yankee army came to Florida, burning our farms?" Edward asked.

"I'd protect you boys and your mama with everything I've got! And I would fight for state sovereignty! But try to understand what has happened here. Something good and righteous, the Tenth Amendment, has been used to support something evil and ungodly, human slavery. God cannot ignore this grievous sin indefinitely . . . ."

"James," Dorothy looked at him with concern in her eyes, "isn't there some way this can be resolved in peace . . . not in war?"

"Dorothy," James replied, "I believe there is a way. If pastors, north and south, would preach against slavery like Brother Blanton and Brother Sheffield preach . . . if church members throughout the nation would repent and stand united against slavery . . . if Christian slave owners would set an example and start paying their slaves a fair wage and teaching the slave children to read . . . I believe it could happen . . . it could be done over a period of years . . . gradually . . . we could rid this nation of the scourge of slavery . . . especially if that new anti-slavery, Republican party wins the White House . . . ."

"I don't think that Lincoln fellow has much of a chance!" Dorothy said. "From what I hear, he's lost nearly every time he's tried to run for any office!"

James put his arm around her and smiled as he reminded Dorothy of her own words, "'With God, all things are possible.'"

Dorothy changed the subject. "George," she said, "When Elizabeth comes, Carolyn wants to ask her about quilts for your house. She plans to make something nice for Elizabeth," George nodded his approval as Dorothy continued, "I didn't know until the other day that Carolyn's samplers are in the Governor's Mansion in Virginia! That Carolyn! She's so talented and so secretive! "

Mention of Virginia brought George's thoughts back to the earlier topic. "Papa," he asked, "if it happens, will Virginia go with the South or with the North?"

"Robert E. Lee is one of the finest military officers this country has ever known; and he is a Virginian," James replied. "If it comes to war, a lot will be determined by which way Virginia goes . . . if

Virginia and Robert E. Lee go with the North, it will be a short war
...."

In the weeks that followed, it became apparent to Dorothy that
she could not hide from the discussion. War was the topic of discussion at home, at church, and on Saturdays when they went into
town to shop. There was no escaping it.

There was always lively discussion outside the post office. Many
expressed concern over the tyranny of an oppressive federal government. If called upon, they were willing to fight for state sovereignty. Some believed black people were "cursed by God" and
destined to live their lives in slavery. Others simply wanted to free
themselves of debts to northern creditors and gave no thought to
the lives that would be lost in order to save their bank accounts.

On the other side, most kept their opinions silent and prayed
desperately there would be no war. They knew this argument
could not be won by human logic or persuasiveness. They understood that conscience would compel them to set aside all other
concerns, to sacrifice everything, and fight against the great evil of
human slavery. Surely they loved Florida and treasured the Tenth
Amendment as much as—if not more than—anyone else. But if
they were forced to make a choice, they knew what they would
have to do.

As Dorothy approached the post office, she saw a crowd gathered around Mrs. Gibson, a strongly-opinionated woman who lived
on the Monticello Road.

"We have to fight now!" Mrs. Gibson declared loudly. "If we'd
go ahead and do it now, it would all be over in time for spring
planting."

Dorothy spun around. "Do you have any idea, Mrs. Gibson, what
war is like?"

"Well," she answered haughtily, "certainly I've never served in
the army!"

"Nor have I!" Dorothy retorted. "But I can tell you some things
about war! We are standing under the same oak trees where the
wounded of the Seminole War were nursed! Their wagons came up
that road!" Dorothy pointed to the main street through Madison.
"Many of them died right here! And when the war was over, the

names of all the dead were posted on that blockhouse! Mrs. Gibson, I saw far too many widows and mothers crying for their dead husbands and sons right here in this square!"

"My dear," Mrs. Gibson answered condescendingly, "I had no idea you were so unwilling to defend Florida from the Yankees! Are you a Union sympathizer?"

"I'm a sympathizer for the wounded! For the dead and dying! But I have no sympathy for the fools who send them to their graves!"

"I hardly think you are entitled to call the rest of us fools, Mrs. Danbury!"

James stepped onto the porch and took Dorothy by the arm. "There's no need to start a war right here in Madison," James whispered, "if you get Mrs. Gibson riled up enough, there will be no way to preserve the Union! Why don't you let the men do the fighting?"

James led Dorothy back to the wagon, and a moment later, George joined them. George slumped into the front seat. Too distressed to read it aloud for his parents, he handed James the letter he had just received from Elizabeth.

It read:

August 10, 1860
My Dearest George,

Last Tuesday morning, soon after I received your last letter, I found Aunt Bessie unconscious on the floor and for the last four days she has seemed at the point of death. The malady is so strange. Dr. Marlow has finally seen her, but he doesn't know how to treat it. I am distressed to death. Aunt Clarabelle is at St. Marks and will stay another three weeks on the coast. I would feel so much better if she were here. I had to promise Aunt Bessie that I would postpone the wedding just a little longer. Under these circumstances, I know you'll understand. Remember how much I love you.

Yours always,
Elizabeth

"What do you think, son?" James asked.

"I think that old woman is a witch!"

"George!" his mother cautioned him.

"It's the truth, Mama! The only medicine that'll do that old woman any good is a kick in the butt!"

"George!" Dorothy reproved him. "That's not the way you were raised! You've never heard your father or me talk like that!"

"No! And you and Papa never had a hateful old lady like Miss Hackett trying to keep you apart! That old woman is fooling Elizabeth. I know she is!" George was losing control of his emotions, and his chin began to quiver.

"Even if she is hateful, you mustn't become that way, too. Surely Elizabeth would know if Aunt Bessie were pretending!"

James intervened. "Dorothy, I think George's reaction to Miss Hackett is no different than your reaction to Mrs. Gibson; and I happen to think you're both right. Miss Hackett and Mrs. Gibson are the kind of women who are dangerous to everyone."

George jumped out of the wagon and started out of the square ahead of them. "Pick me up later . . . I need to be alone . . . ."

"Don't say anything, Dorothy," James cautioned her, "Let him go. That's a harsh blow to a young man. When you're in love, it's the worst possible disappointment." They sat together, watching their son plod slowly out of Madison Square, head dropped forward and hands in his pockets.

The first of September came like a magic autumn day across North Florida. Golden Rods were blooming in every field, and the morning was clear and bright. But there was no beauty in it for George. Two more letters from Elizabeth had arrived, each assuring him of her love, but there was still no wedding date. Aunt Bessie thought they should think about spring. If not April, then surely she would be better by the end of May. Aunt Clarabelle urged Elizabeth and George to go ahead with the wedding right away, but Aunt Bessie was determined to make them wait.

George wrote back and suggested a Christmas wedding. In the middle of November, George received Elizabeth's response. Aunt Bessie saw no way she could be well enough for a Christmas wedding. It would have to be spring, at the earliest.

Around that same time, news that Lincoln had won the election reached Madison. Tempers were short, and opinions were strong. Fear was pervasive.

Mrs. Gibson again used the post office steps as her speaker's platform. "We need to fight now! If we wait until after he's inaugurated on March 4, it'll only make things worse! We know what he's gonna do!"

As Dorothy approached the steps, Mrs. Gibson seemed to direct her ranting in Dorothy's direction, "No Southerner voted for him! Not a one! If seventeen Northern states want him to be their President, let 'em have him! Why, that Republican only got thirty-nine percent of the popular vote! He's got no right to tell us what to do!"

This time, Dorothy held her peace. It would not have mattered to Mrs. Gibson that thirteen out of fifteen Southern states did not even list Abraham Lincoln's name on their election ballots. Nor would it have mattered to her that in those two Southern states where Lincoln's name appeared on the ballot, given the opportunity in the privacy of the voting booth, enough Southerners voted for the Republican, abolitionist candidate that he carried three counties. All too soon it would become apparent that many Southerners quietly detested the practice of slavery. Churches would be split apart, neighbors would never again speak to each other, and families would be forever divided. The whole nation would suffer for the sins of the one person out of every seventy who owned slaves.

At Christmastime, Dorothy and Jethro greeted James on the front porch as he returned from a trip to town.

"Darling," she asked, "why didn't the boys come back with you?"

He avoided eye contact.

"James, what is it?" she questioned him again. "What happened? Don't keep anything from me!"

He still tried not to look at her. "It's the boys . . . ."

"What about them?" she grabbed his arm, overcome by sudden dread.

"They volunteered for the Florida Militia . . . all three of them."

"James! No!" she screamed, fear tightening her face. "Why? Why?"

Jethro stood in the doorway. Last month when he had first heard the news about Lincoln winning the election, he knew troubled times lay ahead. Yet, he had hoped furiously and prayed desperately that, somehow, his family might be spared. Now he knew that would not be the case.

James and Dorothy entered the house, and Jethro followed. The three of them dropped onto the bench at the kitchen table.

"I didn't want them to do it," James grieved aloud. "There was too much excitement and emotion. They needed more time, much more time, to make a decision this big!"

"But, why? James, why did they do it?" Dorothy sobbed. "How did it happen?"

"It was like a revival meeting at the Court House. There were speeches. There was lots of music, shouting, and carrying on."

"Who else volunteered?"

"Nearly every young man in Madison County, and some old ones, too. A lot from Jefferson and Hamilton Counties. They're calling themselves the `Minute Men'. They've already signed a petition asking Governor Perry to officially charter them into the Florida Militia and give them arms."

"Who spoke?"

"Lots of people. No surprise, Mrs. Gibson's husband was the loudest. He's for seizing the federal arsenals in Florida and killing the Yankees with their own bullets. Everybody knows he's a hothead, just like his wife, but today they listened to him like he was some kind of authority on warfare and politics."

Dorothy leaned forward, holding her head in her hands. "What did George say?" she asked.

"He said it's his duty to defend his wife-to-be and his parents," James paused. "There's a lot of good folks, Dorothy, who feel that way. I fear they may be underestimating how bad this war could be and how long it may last."

"But why couldn't the boys have waited?" Dorothy asked.

"Darling, our boys joined for noble reasons. What else could they do when they were asked, `Are you willing to protect your mama and papa from invasion'?" James shook his head, "Maybe we need them to defend our home. God only knows! I don't!"

When James rose from the table, Jethro left to find a private place to pray. Only God can help us now, Jethro thought. He took solace in the words of the Psalmist, a man who loved God deeply yet fully understood the pain of war, "God is . . . a very present help in trouble."

The boys returned late in the day, eager to defend their decision. They were convinced there was no other reasonable course of action.

George spoke first, "We didn't join because we want to fight, or even expect to fight. Mama, we have to let the North know we're ready and willing to defend ourselves. It's the only way we can prevent a war."

Franklin added his perspective on the situation, "We aren't going to fight to defend slavery, because we aren't going to fight at all! Governor Perry said Washington hasn't been listening to us. Now maybe they will. At least they'll know better than to invade us!"

During the winter months the boys met regularly for training with the Florida Militia at the Mosley Hall Post. On occasion, they traveled to Monticello for training exercises; and once they went all the way to Tallahassee. The news from Washington and state capitals around the nation was not encouraging, and it intensified their resolve. They were prepared to protect and defend their home from invasion.

Edward explained to his father, "I don't want to kill anybody, and there's not but one thing that would make me do it—if they attacked our family."

Despite the deteriorating national situation, the second week of January was a time of jubilation for George. He was ecstatic. A letter from Elizabeth set the wedding date; it would be April 23, 1861. Aunt Bessie had given her assurance that nothing would interfere, and the wedding would not be postponed again. George spent his spare time clearing the new land and getting timber ready to build the house. He sang, he whistled, and he wrote more frequently to Elizabeth.

April came gloriously. Dogwoods and redbuds bloomed in the woods, and the scent of wildflowers filled the air. Dorothy tried to focus on the wedding and not let herself think about war. But on April thirteenth, an unexplained feeling of distress clung to her like a shadow. She tried to keep herself busy with housework. She prepared lunch early. She swept all the floors. She worked on her pile of mending. Anything to draw her thoughts away from war. But she could not escape it.

She walked to the henhouse to gather eggs. As she returned to the cabin, an unfamiliar rider galloped toward her. Dorothy recognized the dark coat and wide-brimmed, three-cornered hat of a Florida Militia officer.

"You Miz' Danbury?" he asked her, without dismounting.

"Yes."

"Is this where George, Edward, and Franklin Danbury live?"

She forced herself to answer, "It is."

"I'm Lieutenant Neal McGuire of the Florida Militia, Ma'am," he explained. "Under orders of Governor Perry, your sons are to report for duty at Fort Hamilton by four o'clock this afternoon."

"Four o'clock! This afternoon?" Dorothy drew back from him in unbelief. "But, why?"

"God A'Mighty, woman! This country's been at war since yesterday! Ain't you heard?"

"War?" she repeated the dreaded word unbelievingly, "War!"

"That's right. Started yesterday at Fort Sumter, South Carolina. Governor Perry has instructed Florida to prepare for a federal invasion. All members of the Florida Militia are ordered into active duty." The soldier studied Dorothy's expression and added a warning. "Failure for your sons to appear can result in court martial and punishment. You will tell them that?"

"Yes," she answered weakly, "yes, I will tell them."

The soldier tried to encourage her. "I know this is hard on you, Ma'am. But try to be proud that you got sons who were willing to join up. There's a whole lot of Florida, and there ain't many of us to defend it. Thank you, Ma'am."

At noon, James and the boys returned from the field. They found the table spread with as much food as Thanksgiving Day. Chicken with dumplings, fried ham, raisin pie, baked sweet potatoes, vegetables, and all their favorite dishes.

As they looked around the room, they saw two suitcases and an old medical bag Dr. Thad had given them, all lying open on the floor. The boys' clothes and their Bibles were packed.

"What's this all about?" James asked.

"They're going to need them," Dorothy replied.

"Why?" Franklin hurried toward her, "Why, Mama? What's wrong?"

"We're at war . . . . have been since yesterday."

"And how long have you known this?" James asked.

"A couple of hours."

"Why didn't you tell us sooner?" George asked.

"I wanted you boys to spend every minute you could with your papa," she answered, "And I needed a few more hours of knowing where you were."

The boys looked at their bags. "When do we have to leave?"

"As soon as you eat. That's why I packed for you. All three of you have to report to Fort Hamilton by four o'clock."

They all stood staring at Dorothy. She looked as bereaved as a mother duck robbed of her ducklings. The boys blinked back tears.

"Will you write Elizabeth for me, Mama?" As hard as George tried, he could not keep from crying. "Tell her I'll be back soon. Tell her the war won't last long. We'll get married just like we planned."

Dorothy hugged him and assured him she would save every one of Elizabeth's letters. Then she motioned for all of them to sit down at the table.

"I want you to leave here having had a good meal," she told them. "Even if you don't feel like eating, Papa and I want you to go away remembering that the Lord has prepared 'a table before you in the presence of your enemies'. Regardless of what happens to you boys, wherever you go, whatever you do, whatever you see, we want you to remember that 'goodness and mercy' has followed you 'all the days of your life.' And someday, you will 'dwell in the house of the Lord forever'."

"The promise of the Scripture is the most important thing we can give you," James added. "If Mama and I had provided you with a house, food, and physical needs; but we had not shared God's truth with you, we would have failed you as parents. We have raised you 'in the nurture and admonition of the Lord', and now as you go out to face the worst crisis of your life, you carry the Truth with you."

After lunch, James, Dorothy, and Jethro stood at the gate and watched as George, Edward, and Franklin vanished into the shadows of their lane. Along with the three boys, their joy and purpose in life rode out of the yard that April afternoon.

Chapter Twenty-One

After their arrival at Fort Wacissa that April afternoon in 1861, the boys were hurriedly transferred to defensive posts around the state. Franklin was sent to Pensacola Bay, directly across the harbor from the federally-occupied Fort Pickins. George was assigned to Fort Hamilton on the Atlantic coast, and Edward was stationed with a garrison on the St. John's River.

Florida's thousand-mile coast could not be defended by the Florida Militia. The Union Army maintained control of Key West, Fort Pickins, and other strategic defense posts scattered around the state where they received a constant influx of ammunition. Residents watched helplessly as the noose of the Union Army drew more tightly around them. Fighting had not yet broken out in Florida, but the incoming tide of armaments to federal posts dashed any remaining hope that conflict might be avoided.

Many of the coastal towns were deserted in fear of the Union convoys prowling the shore. The population crowded into the central part of Florida, a mocking reminder of the days when Seminoles had been forced from their homes and confined to reservations in the state's interior. Unfamiliar faces of refugees in ragged clothing began to fill the Madison Square. Nameless people drifted about the center of town, talking of their abandoned homes on the coast and the inevitability of attack by federal troops.

Dorothy avoided Madison, except for trips into town to check the post office for mail from the boys. She read and re-read each letter. Edward wrote as sparingly as he talked, with few words but with depth and tenderness. George's notes were matter-of-fact and to the point; Elizabeth commanded all of his writing time.

Franklin's letters were long and detailed, and often included a poem. His writing was so descriptive, Dorothy felt like she had seen Santa Rosa Island. Franklin told of his evening visits to the water, to pray and reminisce.

Nighttime on Pensacola Bay, with its million stars overhead, made the terror of warfare seem remote. One night he gazed longingly at a bright diamond of a star, hanging low in the west. He remembered lying next to his brother Jethro, in the back of the wagon, looking at the same star on their way home form the concert. He smiled as he recalled the violin strings and the Whang-doodle.

Where the currents of Santa Rosa Sound and Pensacola Bay came together, Franklin stared at Fort Pickins on the opposite side of the channel. Light from torches reflected on the water and made the dark outline of the fort seem out of place in the serene setting.

Only a narrow strip of water separated him from the Union battery at the fort. From a peninsula of mud and marsh grass, Franklin could scan the two-mile stretch of beach where a thousand Confederate campfires sparkled like fireflies on the water. It looked as if the whole southern army were congregated on that one, curving stretch of beach. How many Union soldiers were entrenched at Fort Pickins, he did not know; but from the activity at the fort and the number of lights flickering from the camp, it appeared the entire war could be fought and finished at Pensacola Bay.

"Must not be anybody left in New York," Franklin thought aloud, as he studied the encampment of Colonel Wilson's Sixth New York "Zouaves" occupying the sandbar island. From the fortress at the western tip of Santa Rosa Island, the narrow strip of land extended some forty miles to the east, paralleling the mainland. In another direction, he saw the grey hulk of the Confederate dry docks rising out of the bay like an island.

Franklin removed his boots. He tied the laces together, swung them over his shoulder, and stepped into the water. It was good to feel mud squeezing between his toes. A light rain began to fall, but he did not return to his tent.

His eyes scanned the horizon. He knew Union soldiers were pacing the fort's north wall, looking back in his direction. From the Confederate dry docks, another Southerner gazed across the water as he finished his last hour of guard duty. He looked at the thousand lights of the Confederate encampment. "I'm glad they're here," the soldier said to himself as he strode over the rough planking of the dock. "God, help us, if the federals ever set fire to this tinder box!"

At the far end of the pier, he stopped and turned around. Campfires on Santa Rosa Island had become dim as the mist from the sea spread over the harbor. Checking his pocket watch to be certain he was not leaving his post early, the soldier quickened his step and hurried away. The rain began falling more heavily, but even so, he stopped to look back. His duty shift had ended, but he had an uneasy feeling about leaving Florida's most valuable naval building unguarded.

Across the bay at Fort Pickins, Union soldiers were moving about in the darkness. "Lieutenant Shipley!" a voice called. "Colonel Wilson has given the order! The tides are right. You are to set out immediately."

"Alright!" the Lieutenant answered. Then he called to a group of men waiting nearby, "Let's go! It's time to bring this war to Florida!"

Eleven men dressed in dark clothing hurriedly joined the Lieutenant and lifted a rowboat into the channel. "Listen again to the instructions," Shipley ordered. "Brotsky, O'Halloran, and Fields will stand guard while the rest of you pour on the fuel. If you're not back in the boat when the time comes for Leipold to throw the torch, you'll go up with it! Do you understand? We're not waiting for anyone. We're here to win a war and go home!"

The men acknowledged his instructions and climbed into the skiff. At midpoint of the bay, the boat rose and fell in the current of the outgoing tide.

"Row hard!" the Lieutenant ordered. "That tide will take us a hundred miles into the Gulf! Pull against it!"

The men fought the driving action of the channel, stabbing their oars at full strength. As they neared their target, the force of the current subsided; and the men drew their oars back into the boat.

They pulled the skiff up to the unguarded dry dock. O'Halloran dropped a hook over the step of a ladder that reached from the waterline to the planking. He climbed to the top and crouched low. Nervously, he scanned the pier to make certain there was no sentry before extending his hand to the others.

"Start at the far ends with the fuel, and work your way back to the boat," the Lieutenant ordered. "Be careful with those drums, and make no noise."

Brotsky and Fields lifted the cargo of oil from the boat and handed it carefully to waiting arms. Silently the men disappeared into the darkness. This is easy, Shipley thought. Too easy. He looked back at the bay. There was no way to know how quickly the wind might change, making their return to Santa Rosa Island difficult, if not impossible. The speed of the outgoing tide would increase by the time they returned; and, equal to the danger of being captured or shot, was the danger of being carried out to sea. Everything had to work perfectly.

Before Shipley had time to think about what else might go wrong, two men rushed out of the darkness toward him. "All finished on our end, Sir," they reported.

"You got oil on the warehouse walls?"

"Yes, Sir!"

"Get in the boat," he ordered. "Where in hell are the others?"

"They had a little farther to go, Sir," one of the men reminded him. "We had the short end of the dock."

"Here they come now," the Lieutenant whispered at the sound of muffled steps running toward them. As they came into sight, he began counting under his breath, "Eight . . . nine . . . ten . . . and there's the last one!"

The men scrambled back into the boat. The Lieutenant loosened the hook and shoved them free of the dock.

"Leipold!" he ordered, "Get ready!"

The young Pole grabbed the handle of an oily rag mop. He held it over the side of the boat as Lieutenant Shipley touched it with fire. A burst of yellow flame lighted the faces of the men and reflected on the water. Leipold stood up. Supported by the other men, and with all his strength, he swung the torch over his head and hurled it toward the dock. It landed with a direct hit, the fire splattering onto the oil and instantly racing in all directions along the planking and up the sides of the warehouse. In a flash, the night was lighted by rising tongues of flame.

"Row, fools. Row!" Shipley shouted as their boat, now illuminated in the light of the fire, became fully visible to the Confederate batteries. "Get us out of here!"

A mile away Franklin was still standing ankle deep in the water with his back toward the dock. His face and hair were wet with rain; he felt cleansed from the dirt and grime of pup tents. Most of the campfires had died away. He bent down to wash the grit from his hands. As he rose, the whole end of the bay burst into an explosion of fire. For a second Franklin was mesmerized—unmoving and unbelieving.

"God, no!" he yelled. "They've done it! The Yankees have set the dock on fire!"

Franklin sloshed through the water toward the tents, waving his arms and yelling, as men in their underwear scrambled into the night. The soldiers stared helplessly at the fire as it destroyed their treasured dock and lighted the dark Florida sky. Anger swept through the crowd as they rampaged through the shallows, shouting defiance and shaking fists at the distant enemy. Some began to cry. They well knew, in spite of their curses and threats of revenge, the fire announced a terrifying reality. The war in Florida had begun.

A few weeks later on the night of September 13, 1861, an unusually cold wind blew across the bay and whipped mounds of foam onto the beaches around Pensacola. Darryl Wiggins, a young man from Monticello whom Franklin had befriended, was assigned to stand guard on the deck of the Confederate ship Judah, anchored in the bay. For a man who had never lived on the coast, the sounds of the sea were unnerving; and Darryl dreaded his post on the vessel. That night, with the wind whipping against him and his fists hidden deeply in his pockets, he paced back and forth on the deck of the Judah. Unobserved by Darryl, three federal launches, loaded with armed troops, had been lowered from the warship Colorado and were approaching the Judah. The noise of tackling hitting the masts overhead and nighttime sounds of the ship groaning in the wind muffled the sloshing of the invaders as they eased alongside the ship.

Darryl pulled his scarf closer to his face as he walked the deck. Then, above the blast of the wind, he heard the distinct sound of feet running in his direction. Darryl spun around in time to see a band of men in blue uniforms bearing down on him. Before he could utter a warning, a knife flashed in the dark and disappeared into the heavy folds of his coat. Darryl lay dying on Judah's deck.

Almost instantly the Judah was swarmed with Union attackers who fought hand-to-hand with the poorly-outfitted Confederates. The Southerners tried desperately to defend their ship. A distance away at the Confederate camp, the long roll of drums jarred the sleeping men to their feet. They watched helplessly as the Judah died.

Franklin was frantic at the sight of fire and smoke belching from the ship. He knew Darryl was on board. The Florida Naval Yard batteries remained quiet, powerless to do anything. The struggle finally ended, and what remained of the defeated crew leaped half-naked into the water.

General Braxton Bragg, Commander of the Pensacola Army, plotted his counter attack for the night of October eighth. He planned to attack the troops camped on Santa Rosa Island and move toward the fort. Brigadier General Richard H. Anderson was assigned to divide the army of one thousand soldiers into three separate battalions. Franklin was detailed to the first battalion. They would cross the island and push westward on the Gulf side toward Fort Pickins. The second and third battalions would take the center and bay side of the island, respectively.

For the first time, the weapon Franklin gripped in his hand was there for the specific purpose of killing someone. This was no longer practice; this was real. He thought about the sentry he had seen earlier on the ramparts of the fort. Many of the Union men behind those walls were his age. They had parents and loved ones. It had never been his desire to take the life of another. He thought about Darryl Wiggins. Darryl never wanted to hurt anyone; he just wanted to get this over and go home.

The night of the invasion, troops were moved secretly onto barges. Franklin was assigned to the ship, Neaffle. His twenty-seven-year-old Lieutenant, Wallace Castleberry, had been born in Tampa and trained at West Point. Castleberry, like Franklin, carried a Bible and spoke of his church and his love for God.

The ship pulled a convoy of barges, crowded with men. Some were grandfathers, others were teenage boys; and all of them were afraid. Franklin leaned against the starboard rail, watching the outline of the island in the distance. Below him he heard the rhythm of the water, slapping against the hull of the ship. "Oh, God!" he cried under his breath. How he wished that sound could have been the clopping of his mare's hooves.

Men were pressed about him, huddling against the wind and protecting their eyes from the salt spray. Few were talking.

"Ever been on a ship before?" an old man crowded against his left shoulder asked.

"No," Franklin didn't look up. The man was probably a grandfather.

"Scared?"

Franklin looked at him. He needed to talk to someone. "Yes," he finally replied, "but there are so many different feelings inside me that I can't seem to separate them."

"Like what, boy?"

"Like I've never killed anybody before . . . ."

"You ain't alone. There's probably lots of boys on that island who ain't never killed anybody, until tonight. But all you gotta' do is pull the trigger," He nodded toward Santa Rosa, "'cause that's what they're going to do to you. If you don't kill 'em first, they'll sure kill you."

"I worry about both possibilities . . . killing and being killed."

The old man looked hard at Franklin. "That's the way war is, boy, that's the way it is. It don't matter who they are, or how old they are. Remember one thing, boy," he pointed to the island in the distance, "them Yankees is invaders! They got no business in Florida!" He raised his rifle, "And you and me is gonna tell 'em so!"

Franklin looked down at the bow of the ship, peeling back folds of water. It was dark and fearful looking; but at the same time, it strangely reminded him of the plough turning up soil on their farm. He didn't turn toward the old man, but he felt his gaze locked onto him.

"Boy, we may carry a load of bad memories away from that island," the man said. "that is, if we come away. And that's one reason I'm glad I'm old. I ain't gotta' live with the recollections of this war as long as you will." He touched Franklin on the shoulder and made the boy look at him, "But one thing I don't ever want to have to remember is that I let my family down. It ain't just you that them Union men will kill. It's your papa and your mama."

The ship bumped up and down as they entered the channel coming out of Santa Rosa Sound. "Another mile or so, and we'll turn due south toward the island," The man explained. "Them federal campfires is already way to our right."

At midnight the barges struck the marshy beach on the bay side of the island. The men swarmed ashore into its palmetto thickets and fanned out to straddle the full width of its sandy dunes. On the Gulf side where Franklin's regiment was assigned, the waves broke against the beach and spread a layer of water a foot deep up to the edge of the pines and scrub growth. The light was pale, and the sea foam left by the retreating waves was strangely beautiful in the soft glow. Troops on the bay side battled against the marshy ground that sucked them to their ankles and slowed their movement to a crawl. Men trudging through the island's center encountered cactus plants,with three-inch long spines, stabbing into their legs, and sharp-tipped palmetto fronds, striking them at eye level. Some men fell back clutching their ankles, victims of rattle snakes that infested the thickets.

The troops advanced slowly toward the rim of federal lights. The sound of their movement was drowned in the noise of the surf, crashing onto the beach, and the wind whistling through the trees. For nearly three hours, they struggled toward the sleeping federal encampment. Franklin's battalion finally curved inland from the Gulf in time to close the gap with the center regiment. It was just before 4 a.m. when a weary federal picket, stationed on the extreme eastern end of the compound, heard a strange noise.

The sentinel looked up, and through the trees, he saw the low-crouching forms of hundreds of men. He shouted and began firing. Instantly tent flaps burst open, and unarmed Union soldiers piled into the night. Under a barrage of Confederate rifle fire, men leaped into the dark and collided with each other in their effort to escape. Many fell to the ground mortally wounded. From three sides, the attackers fired into retreating flanks of Union soldiers.

Lieutenant Castleberry yelled to his troops, "This way! This way! Circle around the dune and head them off!"

With rifle fire flashing from behind trees and palmettos, a disoriented soldier in the middle flank began firing wildly. Castleberry screamed orders, "Knock him down! Knock him down!"

It was too late. The man spun toward the Lieutenant and fired point-blank. Lieutenant Castleberry lurched sideways. He gripped his face and fell against Franklin. The two dropped to the ground as more shots dashed over their heads and dug into the trees around them. Franklin screamed, pressing his hand tightly over Castleberry's forehead, in a vain attempt to stop the blood spurting from his Lieutenant's mortal wound. Almost instantaneously another spray of gunfire tore through the palmettos. Franklin lay motionless across the body of his Lieutenant. Blood covered them both and formed a crimson border about their bodies.

The three Confederate battalions fought their way toward the fort. The dead and dying were left behind in the scrubby growth of the island. There were no medics to treat the injured; there was no means for transporting bodies of deceased. Enemies in life, Union and Confederate soldiers rested together in death, their bodies sprawled one upon the other.

Chapter Twenty-Two

Reports of Confederate losses across the South reached Madison well in advance of the dreaded government letters. Daily, the townspeople gathered in the Madison Square, awaiting and fearing news from the battlefield. When the mail carrier arrived, his horse was surrounded by eager hands and desperate pleas.

"I don't know whose mail I got," the rider informed Odessa Mallory as she ran up to his horse and clutched at him. "You'll have to wait until it's posted inside."

Rushing into the post office, she pressed against the window grate. "Is there any word from my Gilbert?" she begged, as Harlow Bentley carefully sorted the mail into three piles on the counter below him. Her eyes flashed from his face to his hands and then back to his face again.

"Is there? Look careful."

"Sorry, Mrs. Mallory," he sympathized, "there's nothing for you." She turned her back to the partition and wept.

"Odum," The Post Master called, "Blanton, Townsend, Danbury, O'Reilly." Trembling hands snatched the yellow envelopes from his grasp and tore into them.

Dorothy was waiting in the wagon as James passed slowly down the steps toward her. He climbed into the wagon and dropped onto the seat. Not until that moment did she see the corner of a yellow government envelope, protruding from his hand.

"James!" she gasped and reached toward it. His fingers squeezed more tightly about it.

"I haven't read it yet."

He picked up the reins with the rolled paper still clutched in his palm and slapped the mare on her flank. Pulling her to the left, he made a wide circle toward a private spot at the square, under George's favorite tree. Just then violent shrieks rose from the porch of the post office.

"Odessa!" Dorothy jerked around in the seat, "That's Odessa!" James pulled the mare back to the steps where a crowd had gathered around the convulsing form of the grieving mother. "Oh, God!" Dorothy exclaimed, raising her hands to her mouth, "It must have happened. It must have happened!"

"My Gilbert!" Odessa screamed. She collapsed to the floor and threw her head back against the wall, "My Gilbert! He's dead! He's dead! They killed him! They killed my baby!"

Dorothy jumped from the wagon and rushed through the crowd to join Brother Blanton as he bent over Odessa.

"Better get Dr. Thad," the pastor called out. "Some of you men help get her over to the buggy shop." He rose with a crumpled piece of paper in his hand. The brief message from an unknown soldier in Virginia told of Gilbert's death in a field hospital near Richmond. Gilbert's last request had been for his minister to be the one to inform his mother.

The crowd dispersed, some followed Odessa to the buggy shop, while others milled about the post office porch weeping. Several buggies and a bareback rider left slowly down the Cherry Lake Road with no news, neither good nor bad. They plodded away despondently, grieved for Odessa, and fearful that in tomorrow's mail, they, too, might receive a government envelope.

Elder Blanton lagged behind the crowd and stopped to rest for a moment at the rear end of a wagon.

"Brother Blanton," James called as they neared.

"Yes. James?" He turned partway toward them, his eyes squinting.

"Would you, Pastor?" He held the crumpled envelope toward him.

"Oh, no. You, too!" His voice broke when he saw the despicable yellow of the envelope.

James nodded as Dorothy stood beside him, her arm locked tightly into his.

Elder Blanton did not allow his mind to consider which of the three boys it might be as he pulled the letter apart. From trembling lips, he softly whispered the word, "Pensacola."

"Franklin!" Dorothy grabbed Elder Blanton's arm, "No! No! He's only a boy! Only a boy!" As the old man fought for composure, James snatched the note from his hands.

As Commanding Officer it is my sad duty to inform you that your son, Franklin Danbury, was engaged in battle against the enemy forces on Santa Rosa Island on the eighth day of October, 1861, and was killed.

"My boy! My boy!" James sobbed, "That's my boy, my youngest boy!" He stood swaying, stunned by the message, with the paper jerking in his hand. It wasn't so! A message of Franklin's death was not here. Not on a scrap of paper! Life did not end so abruptly! So needlessly! Death and life, hope and despair, did not hang on a fragment of official-looking paper. It couldn't be so!

"No . . . James . . ." Dorothy exhaled and crumpled to the ground. Dropping to his knees beside her, he lifted her and stumbled toward their wagon.

"Oh, God!" he wept, his face buried in her hair, "Franklin's our baby boy! Our baby boy! He wouldn't hurt nobody! Nobody!"

Soon after the battle at Santa Rosa Island, the South was shaken by news Fort Donelson on the Cumberland River had fallen to the Union. The loss of this strategic ground was a staggering blow to the Confederacy. Nashville, Tennessee, was left defenseless. Protecting the railroad between Memphis and Richmond became the South's most immediate concern. General Robert E. Lee and the Confederate War Department ordered the entire coastline of Florida stripped of all military and defense equipment.

The governor screamed. The legislature held emergency sessions to stop it. Frightened citizens protested the betrayal, but there was no reconsideration. Florida became the pawn of sacrifice.

At General Lee's order, the cannons, military supplies, and ammunition were all removed from fortresses for shipment northward. Military personnel protecting the peninsula were transferred immediately to General Johnson's beleaguered Army in Tennessee. Jacksonville, St. Augustine, and all coastal defenses were left powerless. Florida was abandoned to the enemy.

In Pensacola, women and children ran screaming to the docks and rail yards as they watched six thousand, five hundred soldiers marching out of the city. Townspeople lined the streets in disbelief as soldiers filed onto ships and boxcars for transfer to Tennessee. Only a token guard was left. Southern Alabama and Georgia had relied on the Florida buffer zone for their defense, and now that was gone.

Colonel John Beard, left in command of Pensacola, met with the remaining city fathers. "It is only a matter of time," he advised, "until we are occupied by Union Troops. I am ordering the destruction of every saw mill, boat yard, lumber yard, or anything else that will be of value to the enemy."

Within hours, the sky over Pensacola was black from fires of self-destruction. Across the bay at Fort Pickins, Union soldiers gathered on the ramparts to watch Florida burn. At two o'clock in the morning, anyone fortunate enough to be asleep was jarred from bed by the booms of exploding oil drums. Rockets fired from the Confederate Marine Hospital hit the huge tanks and sent shrapnel and blazing fuel into the night sky. Mushrooms of flame, greater than what the federal forces had ignited on the Naval dock, rose above the city. The light could be seen for miles.

Charred buildings on Fort McRee, in the Navy yard, and throughout the city of Pensacola greeted the daybreak. In the middle of the morning, acting Mayor Brosenham boarded a launch for the federal warship, Harriet Lane, anchored in the bay. He formally surrendered the smoking ruins to the Union. Commander David Porter accepted the abdication. The next day, federal troops entered the Pensacola Plaza and returned the American flag to the city's staff. A few elderly citizens, who remembered the 1821 flag raising in that same plaza, silently witnessed America's determination to keep Florida under the Stars and Stripes.

At Fort Clinch on the Atlantic coast north of Jacksonville, George assisted in the frantic removal of cannons and large artillery for transportation to Tennessee. As part of a meager crew left behind, he helped complete the stripping of the state's defenses. Union ships were bearing down upon the fort, and attack was imminent. By command of the war department, Florida had been left defenseless.

At a whistle blast from the train, the last soldiers rushed frantically from the fort and clambered aboard. People from Fernandina crowded into the cars, screaming and shoving; some were clutching bags, carrying children, or helping the elderly. As the train crossed the bridge, a federal gunboat sped in their direction. Passengers screamed and crowded down below the windows.

"Somebody pray!" a terrified woman screeched, "Somebody pray!" George fell across her, shouting his prayer above the noise. A second later, his words were drowned out by a whistling sound and an explosion that shook the trestle. It was followed by another piercing sound. This one came closer. People screamed louder, prayed harder, and cowered on the floor when the third shell struck the end car. The blast was deafening. Glass scattered everywhere. Shrieking passengers were covered with blood as the engine limped onto the mainland. When it came to a halt, they fought to get off and ran screaming to the woods.

Along with a few other soldiers, George escaped to Jacksonville. Together they walked to Baldwin, the major railroad terminus west of the city. The depot was in mass confusion. Military reports were filled with so many discrepancies, it was impossible for officers to redirect troops. At the rail yard, George and two hundred other men, were put on a train for Tallahassee. From there, they were to be dispatched to Tennessee. At Lake City, the train was stopped and everyone ordered off. The Confederate post at Lake City was in panic and confusion. A telegram from General Trapier advised that the city of Jacksonville had been abandoned and burned.

As George stood waiting outside the Adjutant's Office, Colonel William Bradley rushed onto the porch and yelled. "I cannot tell you where to go! I have no orders!" He shook General Trapier's telegram at them, "If you have a home in Florida, go defend it!"

"Yes, Sir!" George saluted, and left running. Madison was only fifty miles away. Elizabeth, a few more than that.

Dawn found Jacksonville in smoking ruins. It had been ripped apart, gutted, and burned by Confederate hands. The citizens were in terror. They feared men in grey as much as those in blue. An official delegation formally surrendered the sprawling bed of ashes that had been the city of Jacksonville.

South of Jacksonville, attack on the old city of St. Augustine was imminent; and its fall certain. The city fathers wanted to spare St. Augustine the fate of other coastal towns and prepared for a peaceful surrender. But when federal authorities, led by Commander Rodgers, came ashore, sentiment among townspeople was still bitterly divided. As the mayor and city council escorted the Union authorities from the ship to the town hall, they were confronted by a band of zealous Confederate women. Waving placards and Confederate flags, the women blocked the street. The spokesperson for the group—a tall, thin woman with a high-pitched, piercing voice—rushed up to the Union Commander.

"These men are cowards!" the woman waved her arms accusingly at the council members. "They are not worth your capturing! They are too weak to fight! But remember one thing!" she yelled, beating her breast, "There are still stout hearts in women's bosoms!"

Commander Rodgers ignored her and pushed his way through the blockade of women. As the delegation from the ship sat down in the chamber with the mayor and the council, the women invaded the room.

"Where is your chivalry?" the speaker for the women demanded of the council. "Why your sudden willingness to leave us women defenseless before these Yankees?" Her rage turned toward Commander Rodgers, "And you! What would your mother think of your bringing wicked men to our shores to cause molesting! And rape!" The other ladies gasped at her boldness to use that word in front of a group of men.

Commander Rodgers slammed his fist on the desk and sprang to his feet, "My dear Madam," he yelled, "I can assure you that there will be no raping! If my soldiers can fight off your men on the battle field, then they can certainly fight off your women in the brothels!"

There was shocked silence. The Commander yelled louder, "Besides! You'll find most of my men willing to volunteer!" In a flurry of flags and handkerchiefs, the ladies left the room.

Later, when Commander Rodgers and his troops prepared to raise the American banner over the fort, they discovered the women had chopped down the flagpole.

With the surrender of Pensacola, Jacksonville, and St. Augustine, Floridians lost all hope. They had been betrayed by the Confederacy. The state's young males were far from home, separated from farm and family, unable to protect the ones they loved. Florida's isolation from the rest of the country had not protected her. Rather, it had made her the most difficult to defend and caused her to become the first to be abandoned to the enemy.

Seminoles who had avoided deportation by escaping to the Everglades, now stood on beaches and watched the stream of warships. This time, thankfully, they were not the white man's target. Army Lieutenant William Tecumesh Sherman, who captured Chief Coacoochee and shipped him away from his ancestral home in leg irons, was back. Now General of the Union Army and commanding operations from a distant post, Sherman's conquering hand once again reached into Florida.

With the fall of St. Augustine, Edward's garrison on the St. John's River at Picolata fled. Their Commanding Officer disappeared without a word of explanation or instruction to his men.

Separately, George and Edward traveled homeward. Unknown to anyone, Franklin was also making his way home.

Left behind and presumed dead on Santa Rosa Island, Franklin had awakened hours later, his uniform soaked in Lieutenant Castleberry's blood. Dazed and confused, Franklin tried to stand up. Dizziness forced him to his knees. He waited before attempting to stand again. This time, he rose slowly, grabbing onto a pine tree to steady himself.

He walked the full length of the island. Finally, he stood on Santa Rosa's eastern tip, looking across the channel to the mainland. A much greater and more dangerous crossing lay before him. His mind was confused, his thoughts clouded, and his body weary; but in his heart, one thing had become perfectly and painfully clear. It was not possible to fight for Florida's sovereignty without also fighting for slavery. Removing his shirt, he took hold of the Confederate insignias on the sleeves and ripped them from the fabric. Reverently, almost prayerfully, he tossed the patches into the channel and watched the current carry them out to sea. As much as possible, he washed his Lieutenant's blood from his shirt. He waited until low tide, and then swam to the other side where he climbed out into the Choctawhatchee Swamp. Exhausted, but determined to reach home, he began the two-hundred-mile walk to Madison.

George was first to run up the lane and across the yard. "I'm home! I'm home!" he hollered at the top of his lungs. He grabbed his mother at the well, picked her up in his arms, and buried his face in her neck. Dorothy slapped her arms around him, glued herself tightly to his grimy body, and hugged him with all her strength. James locked arms around him and broke into weeping. Jethro embraced George with all his might and shouted out praise and thanksgiving to the Lord.

Through tears, they told him of Franklin's fate.

Two nights later, they were sitting at the supper table, doors and windows locked, and heads bowed. A light tapping interrupted the prayer and drew James to the front door.

"It's me!" Edward announced as James opened the door.

Edward wept for hours at the news of Franklin. For a week, the brothers struggled with their anguish, fluctuating from denial to grief and then to denial again.

Dorothy and Carolyn were preparing dinner when they heard a loud knock at the front door. "James! James! Come quickly," Carolyn called.

"Franklin!" James screamed as he opened the door. "My God! Son, it's you! It's you!" Dorothy passed out. Carolyn dropped a pan of biscuits. Jethro, George, and Edward heard the commotion and ran inside.

The scene that followed was rapturous chaos. Ecstacy erupted, temporarily obliterating all pain of war. Shouting, rejoicing, praise, and prayer simultaneously shook the cabin.

Their joy was tempered by news Franklin brought with him.

"Hiram's back," Franklin told them. "He passed me not far from here on the Bellamy Trail."

"Oh, God!" Carolyn exclaimed. "Oh, God! No!"

"Yes, I'm afraid so," Franklin went on. "And it's bad. He saw my uniform . . . with the Confederate patches torn off . . . ."

"Did he say anything to you?" Fear overwhelmed Dorothy's heart as she asked the question.

"He called me a traitor," Franklin answered softly. "He said traitors will be hanged."

"You boys have to get out of here," James said mournfully, "before Hiram can get back with a posse."

Chapter Twenty-three

An hour after he arrived, Franklin—clean for the first time in weeks and wearing fresh clothing—was ready to leave. George and Edward stood with him on the front porch, as the three brothers prepared to depart. Dorothy and Carolyn packed all the available food in the house—ham, biscuits, and potatoes—and the boys hurriedly stuffed it into their saddlebags. Jethro saddled the horses and led them to the front porch. Through tears, Dorothy, James, Jethro, and Carolyn hugged the boys. James prayed over each one individually.

As they mounted their horses, James spoke a blessing, "Your mother and I commend you to God and to the Word of His Grace which is able to build you up. May He give His angels charge over you to keep you in all your ways. We bless you in the Name of the Father, the Son, and the Holy Spirit. Amen."

When they reached the Bellamy Trail, George signaled the others to stop.

"What's the trouble?" Franklin asked.

George hesitated for a moment, ". . . This is as far as I'm going with you."

"George! What's wrong? We all agreed to do this!" Franklin protested.

"And I'm gonna do it, but there's something I've got to do first . . . it's Elizabeth . . . ."

"Oh, no," Edward groaned. "You can't go to Quitman, George."

"Even if you make it to Quitman, you'll never be able to get to Union lines before they catch you. Never!" Franklin shook his head. "You won't be going to Elizabeth, you'll be going to your grave!"

"That's the chance I have to take. There's nothing more important to me than marrying Elizabeth." He looked at both of them, "I'm not running out on you. You're my brothers . . . but Elizabeth is going to be my wife."

"But you won't make it, George," Edward pleaded.

"If I don't, I don't! But I'd rather have one night with Elizabeth than all my future without her."

For a long moment, no one spoke. Their horses stood motionless in the moonlight. Franklin reached out and took George's hand, and Edward moved his horse to the opposite side. They gripped their brother's hands lovingly.

"Kiss her for us, George," Franklin said, "And tell her that when this war is over, we'll all be together again."

George nodded. Edward closed his eyes and prayed. So much was at stake, so much already lost.

"Goodbye, Edward," George spoke, still clutching his brother's hand, "Goodbye, Franklin. We're all gonna help win this war."

George spurred his horse and galloped westward into the night.

Franklin looked at Edward, "It's you and me, Ed. Let's go!" They slapped their horses and turned southeast toward Charles Ferry Crossing on the Suwanee River. Their destination was St. Augustine.

George avoided Madison by cutting across hay fields on the east side of town. He joined the Cherry Lake Road north of the dismal shack. It was past midnight when he reached the half dozen buildings of the Hamburg community; here he turned northwest toward the Georgia line. As the road wound through the marsh of cypress trees south of the state boundary, he slowed the horse to a walk. Less than an hour later he emerged from the swamp and headed toward Columbia Church. The road was open, and the horse made good time. When the log building appeared before him in the moonlight, he looked lovingly at the spot where he had first seen Elizabeth.

A feeling of apprehension, almost fear, hung over the building. Ignoring his inner warning, he rode directly to the well. He dismounted and lowered the bucket.

He poured water into the trough for his horse. As he was about to take a drink himself, a voice yelled, "Don't move! Danbury!"

George spun around and stared into the dark. The forms of a dozen men rose from behind gravestones and came toward him, their muskets aimed directly at him.

"No! No!" George groaned. "Please, God! No!"

"Stay away from that horse, or we'll blow your Yankee-loving guts all over this cemetery!" George spun around to find himself face to face with Hiram's son Leroy.

"Don't let our prize get away!" Leroy laughed as he stabbed the barrel of his gun in George's stomach.

The others grabbed his arms and held them behind his back. Four of them were upon him, pinning him to the ground. One of them jerked a rope tightly about George's neck while two others tied his hands and feet.

George gasped, stretching his neck for air, "You've got no right to do this!"

"We got all the right we need, Danbury! You're a Yankee turncoat!" He spat in George's face.

At ten o'clock the next morning, a mob gathered in front of the livery stable in Quitman. Word spread through town that a posse had captured a Yankee spy at Columbia Church. A crowd rapidly assembled for the hanging.

A block away, Elizabeth looked from the upstairs rear porch of Aunt Bessie's house. "Mrs. Simms!" she called to the neighbor next door, "What's happening? What's all the commotion?"

"Ira told me a Yankee spy was caught down at Columbia Church last night," Mrs. Simms yelled back. "Probably came here to blow up the railroad, or worse. They're gonna hang him." A look of terror crossed Elizabeth's face, and Mrs. Simms tried to console her. "Don't worry, child. It's alright. These men from Florida are Confederate soldiers. They know what they're doing!"

"He was hiding at Columbia Church?"

"That's right! That's where they found him. Good thing, too! He might have killed somebody else!"

Elizabeth stepped away from the porch and backed into the house. The thought in her mind was too awful to consider.

A few minutes later, Aunt Bessie came through the front door. She rushed up the steps and began closing all the shutters.

"Aunt Bessie!" Elizabeth called to her, "Mrs. Simms says there's going to be a lynching at the livery stable!"

"Not a `lynching', Elizabeth," Aunt Bessie corrected her angrily, "a `hanging'. There's a difference!"

Elizabeth frowned, "What are you saying, Aunt Bessie?"

"A `hanging' is the legitimate disposal of a man who is a threat to society, Elizabeth." Aunt Bessie answered pompously.

"You talk as if you know about it."

"By nightfall, everybody in the county will know about it."

Elizabeth hurried back to the window and opened the shutter. She heard people shouting and dogs barking. Aunt Bessie was immediately behind her, pushing the shutter closed again.

Elizabeth pulled it open. "Hush! Aunt Bessie! I need to hear! I think I recognize a voice . . . ."

Aunt Bessie pushed her aside, slammed the shutter hard against the frame, and attempted to fasten it. There was no weakness in Bessie's thin fingers as she grappled the latch from Elizabeth's hand.

Elizabeth ran past her aunt, through the porch door, and onto the balcony. She turned back in horror. "That's George! Aunt Bessie!" Elizabeth shrieked. "That's George, and he's calling for me!"

In a frenzy, Elizabeth ran back into the house and toward the stairs. Bessie blocked her way. "That man is white trash, Elizabeth! He's a traitor! He's no good for you!" Bessie shouted, "He'll ruin our good name!"

Elizabeth screamed for George and shoved the old woman against the wall. She leaped down the stairs, taking several steps at a time. Suddenly she stopped. The shouting had ceased, and the town had fallen quiet. Elizabeth paled as the blood drained from her face, and her heart felt it might never beat again.

Bessie, again showing no lack of strength, rushed down the stairs to Elizabeth, "It's all for the best, dear," she said in a gentle, comforting tone. "In time, you'll understand. He was just white trash. He was no good for you."

Elizabeth grabbed the old woman by the shoulders, "No good for me! He loved me! Something you never did!" She shook her aunt, "No good for me! You heartless witch! You kept me from marrying him while he was alive! You kept me from going to him when he was dying!"

"Elizabeth! You're hurting me!" Aunt Bessie lapsed back into her weak, sickly tone.

The girl's fingers dug deeper, and she shook harder. "You let him die without me! You let him die when I was this close to him!" Elizabeth thrust the old woman against the staircase and ran from the building screaming George's name.

At daybreak the same morning on the other side of the Gerogia-Florida line, Carolyn told James and Dorothy she needed to go home. Without explanation, she took her satchel and left. Carolyn did not go home. She went instead to the Bellamy Trail, caught a ride to Madison, and then another ride out of town.

She headed north to the home of Hiram and her sister Francina on Cherry Lake Road. Carolyn arrived at noon and found Francina alone. The house was as gloomy inside as out. It was nearly vacant of furniture. The foul odor of the squalid cages where Hiram kept his underfed dogs permeated the air. Francina was more pale and fragile than Carolyn had ever seen her. Tenderly and pityingly, Carolyn held her sister in her arms.

At that same moment on the Danbury farm, Dorothy was in the garden, Jethro in the back field, and James at the kitchen table, filing saw blades. The sound of horses galloping up the lane disrupted the tranquility. James grabbed his gun from the mantle and stepped to the door. Eighteen men on horseback filled the yard, all armed with rifles. Five wore Confederate uniforms. Hiram, with the insignia of a low-ranking officer on his collar, rode the lead horse.

"Danbury!" Hiram yelled. "Throw down your gun, and come out with your hands up!"

James did not move. From the doorway, he leveled his gun on Hiram.

"We ain't leaving until we do what we came to do!" Hiram yelled again.

"You're trespassing on private property!" James threatened, holding firmly to his rifle, "You'd better get going now!"

"We're going, alright!" Hiram yelled as he dismounted. "We're going over every inch of this place until we find them Yankee-loving, traitor sons of yours."

James followed Hiram's movements, keeping the sights of his firearm fixed on him, "I'm warning you, Hiram. Get off my property!"

In that instant, Dorothy came around the corner of the house. Too late, she recognized Hiram and turned to run.

"Grab her!" Hiram yelled.

Two men ran after Dorothy. They caught her, scattering her basket of okra. As James turned toward her, several men leaped upon him. They knocked his rifle out of his arms and pinned him to the floor

"James! James!" Dorothy screamed, fighting and kicking against the men.

As James struggled to get to Dorothy, a rifle butt slammed against his head.

Hiram kicked him in the face, "Tell us where they're at or we'll beat you to death!"

"They're gone!" James yelled. "And you'll never catch up with them!"

"Tie 'em both up!" Hiram ordered. "You heard what he said! That's a confession to 'aiding and abetting the enemy!' They helped traitors escape!"

With the two wrapped tightly in ropes, Hiram slapped James across the face.

"Darling, remember that I love you!" James called to Dorothy. "No matter what happens, remember that I love you!"

"And I love you!"

Hiram backhanded James across the jaw. "We didn't come to hear you make love," he scowled angrily. "I'm giving you one more chance! Where are they at?"

"They're in God's Hands!" James shouted, "And you can't pluck them out!"

"Oh, yeah? Let's see how your God takes care of you!" Hiram laughed. "Bring the wagon here to the tree! We're gonna get this dirty work done and get out'a here!"

Hiram climbed into the wagon. The men forced James to his feet and dragged him to the wagon. One soldier grabbed his feet, and two others took his arms. They swung him into the wagon. While they held him erect, Hiram made a noose and slipped it around James' neck.

"If you've got anything to say, Danbury," Hiram yelled, "you'd better talk in a hurry!"

Hiram was knocked off balance as Jethro lunged into the wagon. Jethro threw Hiram to the ground, kicked one of the men in the groin, and grabbed for the rope.

"Save him, Jethro!" Dorothy screamed, "Save him!"

Hiram Jr. leaped onto the wagon. He smashed his rifle butt into Jethro's head, and Jethro tumbled out of the wagon.

A man in a Confederate uniform slapped the horse, and the wagon jerked forward. The rope snapped tight. The struggle was over. Dorothy and Jethro were unconscious. James was dead.

"I didn't bargain for this," a man in civilian clothing said softly. "He told us he was only gonna scare 'em." Several men mounted their horses and rode closemouthed out of the yard.

One of the soldiers turned to Hiram, "What about the nigger?"

"Tie him good. I know someone who'll pay a good price for him."

"He's too dangerous to sell and get turned loose in a field," the man warned Hiram. "He'll come back looking for us."

"We'll make sure he spends the rest of his life padlocked to a chain. There won't be no getting away." Hiram turned to the others, "Let's finish up and get out'a here. I don't like fooling around."

Jethro was tied with his body arched over one of James' horses. Dorothy was carried to the backside of the well. The body of her husband was dropped next to her.

James and Dorothy's cabin—the one built on their wedding day and expanded as the boys matured, the one where their children had been born and reared, the one where they had lived and loved for nearly thirty years—was ransacked and treated like public trash. Hiram's men emptied drawers, scattered clothes about the floor, and took whatever they wanted. Dorothy's few dresses were examined, dropped, and trampled. Hiram grabbed the large gold-framed family portrait from the mantle. He smashed it across the top of a chair and hurled it against the wall. A few gold coins in a small tin under the bed were stuffed into his pocket. Treasured letters—from Dorothy's mother, from Elizabeth, and from the boys—were dumped from the metal box and strewn about the cabin. A brass fireplace screen, given to Dorothy by James as an anniversary gift, was tied to a saddlebag. Her best pots and pans, and a small quilting frame, hung from another saddle. Boot prints through a layer of white flour on the kitchen floor recorded the steps of the pillagers. Broken dishes, metal pans, Tom's iron fire poker, knives, and forks were tossed about the large room.

When there was nothing further to loot inside the house, the men turned their attention to the barn. They rounded up the milk cow, the mule, and the rest of the horses. They tied the animals to the rear of the Danbury wagon. The sow was shot, and her piglets tied in hemp sacks. Chickens escaped to the fields and barn rafters while Guinea hens flew to the top branches of the oak.

"We got everything we want," a man addressed Hiram. "Ready for the fire?"

"Yeah," he grunted, "burn everything but the well house."

One of the men entered the cabin with a can of kerosene and poured a trail through the two rooms of the house. He splashed it on the dinner table, across James and Dorothy's bed, up the stairway to the loft, over all the furniture, and through the boys' room. He stepped outside and poured the liquid across the steps and porch, and threw it against the wall. The cabin that had welcomed guests with the aroma of ham and fried okra now reeked with the odor of fuel oil.

Hiram threw a wad of burning corn shucks through the open front door. The house erupted into a blaze. The fire darted through the house like a hungry fox. It leaped onto the tables and across the cupboard. It dashed up the steps in a glowing streak as it chased the oily path to every part of the house.

Mounted on his horse, Hiram watched with great satisfaction. The sight of the flames exhilarated him, and he relished his moment of revenge.

A soldier, in a pang of remorse, looked at Dorothy and said, "I'm gonna untie the woman."

"I don't care what you do with her. She ain't no threat to me," Hiram barked. Then from the lane, he called out his final order, "Everybody get the hell outa here!"

Finding new fuel in the aged timber of the cabin, the fire raged. Black, ugly smoke billowed into the afternoon sky. Shingles on the roof cracked apart as flames gnawed away at the cabin's vitals. With a roar, the roof opened up and a tower of fire shot skyward. Columns of smoke from the barn, the shed, the smoke house, and even the outhouse joined the symphony of death. The destruction was total and complete.

Midnight passed, and embers still snapped and burned red in the charred remains of the home. The chimney, now only a mound with its hearth buried under an avalanche of ashes, stood blistering hot above the bed of coals.

Dorothy stared at the ruins, without feeling. The house no longer mattered. Even as she looked upon the body stretched silently beside her, there were no more tears. She reached out and touched the patch of scraped skin on his neck. Somehow, it was not James.

Her attention was drawn toward a cluster of palms where the crickets had suddenly stopped chirping. Someone, or something, was approaching. Dorothy closed her eyes in resignation. There was no fight left in her. There was nothing she could do—or would do—to defend herself.

Dorothy sat still and waited. She did not move or resist when a rough hand grasped her wrist.

"Miss Dorothy, it's me," a familiar voice whispered.

"Jethro!"

"Yes, Ma'am. I hope I didn't scare you," he whispered apologetically, "but I just had to come back! I just couldn't stand it! Knowing you were here all alone with Mister Jim."

"God bless you, Jethro."

"I brought a shovel, Miss Dorothy," he said, helping her to her feet.

"Jethro," she asked, "how did you get away?"

He paused for a moment, trying to find the right way to answer. "I killed Hiram Jr."

"Jethro! Oh, Jethro!" she groaned and put here arms around him.

"Don't worry about that now, Miss Dorothy," Jethro consoled her. "God knows I never wanted to kill anybody. I just did what I had to do."

Minutes passed with neither of them speaking. There were no answers, no explanations for this awful day that had forever changed their lives.

Jethro reached for the shovel. "If you'll show me where, Miss Dorothy, I'll do it."

Dorothy moved in the direction of the garden. "James always said the best land on this farm was in the garden, in the okra patch. That's where I want him. In his favorite spot."

A hundred yards from the house, in the light of the moon, Jethro pressed the shovel point into the soil. "About here?"

"About there," she answered, and turned away at the first sound of the shovel.

When the ground was ready, Jethro collected pine boughs from the swamp. He carefully lined the grave with the soft green limbs.

Dorothy and Jethro—the two people in his life, joined to him not by birth but by love and God's design—laid James to rest. They grieved silently, standing arm in arm. They would have liked to memorialize him and recite special memories of his life. But they could not have gotten through this night if they had allowed themselves to consider how great was this loss.

Dorothy broke the silence. Sweetly and tenderly, she began, "The Lord is my Shepherd . . . ", and through sheer determination, she somehow managed to recite the entire twenty-third Psalm.

Then Jethro sang softly,

Jesus, I my cross have taken, all to leave and follow Thee.
Destitute, despised, forsaken, Thou from hence my all shall be.
Perish every fond ambition, all I've sought or hoped or known.
Yet how rich is my condition! God and Heaven are still mine own.

Let the world despise and leave me, they have left my Savior, too.
Human hearts and looks deceive me; Thou art not, like them, untrue.
And while Thou shalt smile upon me, God of wisdom, love and might,
Foes may hate and friends disown me, show Thy face and all is bright.

"How I loved him, Miss Dorothy!" Jethro sobbed. "There never was a better man, Miss Dorothy."

Dorothy embraced him, and they both cried. "Jethro, just once . . . after all these years . . . after all this," she whispered, "couldn't you call me 'Mama'?"

"Mama," Jethro's body trembled with sobbing as he laid his head on her shoulder, "Mama Dorothy . . . Mama Dorothy . . . ."

Jethro stepped back and held Dorothy at arm's length. "The Lord gave me a Word today, Miss . . . Mama Dorothy. You're the one who told me God would speak to me personally, and today He did."

Dorothy looked up into his eyes, "Tell me, Jethro. Tell me."

"Someday, there's gonna be a new house right here, Mama Dorothy. We're gonna be a family again. Together we're gonna finish the work God began," Jethro pulled her back into his arms and hugged her warmly. "We gotta hang onto that, Mama Dorothy. We gotta hang on by faith, no matter what else happens."

"I love you, Jethro," Dorothy said through tears.

"I love you, too, Mama; but I gotta go," Jethro said as he kissed her on the cheek.

"Where will you go?"

"I'll hide in the swamp. I camped out enough with my brothers to know my way around in there," Jethro told her.

"Maybe you can make it to Elder Sheffield's place. He lives away from town, and I know he'll help you hide," Dorothy told him.

"I gotta go now," Jethro said.

"I love you, Jethro," Dorothy said again.

As he ran toward the thicket, Jethro stopped and looked back towards her, "By faith, we're gonna be together again. We're gonna 'fight the good fight of faith.'"

At daybreak the next morning, Dorothy began walking. She pulled her bonnet low over her face, wrapped her shawl about her, and spoke to no one. Elizabeth's house in Quitman was forty miles away. There was no other place to go. She had to get away from Madison, away from Florida, away from anyone who might question her about Jethro's whereabouts.

Along the Bellamy Trail, Dorothy accepted short rides from strangers who were fleeing federal troops on the east coast. Like Dorothy, they were grieving for lost loved ones and understood her silence.

Her last ride dropped her off in Madison. From there, she walked north. Two hours later, in the distance, she recognized the sullen house sitting back in the trees on the west side of the road.

She was directly in front of it when Hiram rushed onto the porch. "Your nigger killed my boy!" he screamed, "And you ain't getting away this time! Do you hear?"

Hiram grabbed the collar of his ferocious dog, trained to attack and fight to the death. He jerked the animal's head upwards, until its front paws clawed the air. Hiram pointed directly at Dorothy as he let go of the collar and screamed a one-word command, "Kill!"

Growling and snarling, the dog bounded toward Dorothy. As it leaped the fence, a gun blast sounded from the porch; and the animal fell straddling the pickets.

Carolyn stood a few feet from Hiram, holding her multi-firing pistol, smoke still spilling from its muzzle. Without a word, she turned toward Hiram and pulled the trigger again.

A look of bewilderment gripped Hiram's face as he clutched his chest and slumped downward. Unseen by and unknown to Carolyn or Dorothy, Hiram's fall did not end when his body came to rest on the front porch.

In a dimension hidden from human eyes, Hiram was dropping into deep, thick darkness. He was immediately surrounded by grotesque beings, mocking and ridiculing him. In unison, they chanted spitefully, "You rejected Him! You rejected Him!" They could not utter the Name, but Hiram fully understood Whom he had denied.

"Aha! Aha!" they screeched. "It's forever! It's forever!" Again, he needed no explanation. He was consumed by the horrific knowledge that there would be no end to this. Along with the loathsome beings who taunted him, he was eternally damned.

Hiram wanted to call on the Name. He wanted to beg, to plead for mercy. But he could no longer speak the Name of Jesus. His last chance for repentance had been left behind in another realm. At the speed of light, Hiram was descending into the place of never-ending agony and perpetual regret.

Still pointing the gun in the direction of Hiram's limp and motionless body, Carolyn lingered in the total silence that swooped down upon the place with the second gunshot. Stunned by her own actions, she was unable to feel remorse for what she had done or relief at finally being free of her tormentor.

Dorothy started running. If Dorothy could get to the Georgia line, she would never come back to Florida! Never!

How she got there, she could not remember; but two days later, Dorothy arrived at the Okapilco Creek south of Quitman. A boy, fishing on the far side of the bridge looked up when her steps sounded on the planking.

As she neared, he studied her, "You going into Quitman?"

"Yes," she answered, "I hope to find a friend."

He studied her appearance, "You must've come a long way, Ma'am."

"From Madison. Danbury is my name."

He sprang to his feet. "You must be kin to Mr. Danbury who got hanged!"

"Yes," she answered, "but how did you know?"

"Everybody in Quitman knows! They ain't talked about nothing else since it happened! I wanted to go, but my papa wouldn't let me."

"Go?" She rushed to him, "What are you talking about? Who are you talking about?"

"I'm talking about Mr. George Danbury. The one Miss Elizabeth was gonna marry," the boy gave her a puzzled look.

"George . . ." Dorothy slumped to the bridge.

Four days after leaving home, on the west bank of the St. Johns River, Franklin and Edward watched the flickering lights of Picolata two miles across the water. It was a tranquil scene, and for the moment, softened the terror of war.

"It's kind of like crossing the Jordan," Franklin philosophized, looking at the wide expanse of water before them. Late the next afternoon, they stood outside the stone walls of the ancient Castillo de San Marco in St. Augustine. For the first time since the war had begun, the American flag flew above them. They stopped their horses long enough to stare lovingly at it.

"It gives you a good feeling, doesn't it?" Franklin asked. "It's kind of like coming home—seeing Old Glory flying again."

Edward agreed. Riding forward once more, they crossed the moat and were stopped by the guard outside the walls.

"We would like to volunteer for the Union Army," Franklin announced. "We have left the Confederacy."

"You want to see Commander Rodgers," the soldier answered, eyeing them curiously, "His office is on the left of the court yard. Ask the guard at the end of the hall for a pass. Dismount your horses here and walk them through to the stables on the inside right."

Commander Rogers received them warmly. The next day when the U.S. Independence pulled away from the coast of Florida, the brothers stood at the rail with their hearts pounding as they watched the beach line disappear. Fear and homesickness, unlike anything they had ever known, gnawed at their gut. Franklin, moved a few feet away, dropped his head on the rail, and closed his eyes. Nothing in his childhood had prepared him for this moment.

At Baltimore, the brothers stood in line with scores of other men, awaiting orders at an aged, surrey barn that had been hurriedly converted into an Adjutant's Office. When their turn came, Franklin presented the papers from Commander Rogers in St. Augustine.

"Welcome to the North," The officer spoke compassionately. "I wish to God that everybody in Florida had the same sense you've got! Our hope is in ending the war as much as in winning it." He shook hands with each of them. "You will board the train leaving in two hours for Philadelphia. I hope you're warm. There are no uniforms to issue until you arrive there."

Franklin and Edward were crowded with hundreds of others into eight, over-packed cars while they all waited for the train to leave. Besides themselves, only a few were without uniforms; and they attracted much attention. A young soldier standing in the aisle was astonished they had traveled all the way from Florida to join the Union Army. He spoke with a heavy European accent. "You should have stayed in Florida rather than come all this way just to fight for the North."

"But you're fighting for the North!"

"Yes, but I've got nothing else to do. I have no job and no family. I am fighting only because I will be paid. If I had a home, I would be fighting to protect it!"

"But we are fighting for our home," Franklin defended, "We are fighting for what we believe is right."

"You will make good soldiers then," the man replied. "Men who fight from the heart fight better than those who fight only with their hands."

"Actually we won't fight at all. We're going into the Medical Corps."

"My God!" he exclaimed. "That is the hardest job of all! Anybody can shoot a man and then look away so he won't see him die. But to take a knife and cut off the arm of someone while you are looking at him, that takes courage!" He looked admiringly at the brothers. "God knows, I hope I never need you! But I am glad to know that somebody is willing to do your kind of work!"

After a delay of two hours at the Susquehanna River, waiting for another military train to pass, they moved on. Every hour as the train made its way north, the men standing in the aisle exchanged places with those who were seated. The train wound through the snow covered hills of northern Delaware under a bright, full moon. Edward was fascinated by the scenery. When it was Franklin's turn to be seated and his to stand, Edward pressed his face against a window and watched the changing countryside slide past. War seemed remote and unreal in a surrounding of white fields on a moonlit night.

The snow was pure and white; and he wished the train would stop long enough for him to get out into it. After midnight, his opportunity came. Edward felt the train slow down. He saw a scattering of farmhouses on both sides of the track. A few minutes later, city buildings and the long shed of a railroad station appeared. He pressed against the glass in time to see the name, "Wilmington, Delaware," painted on the end of the building.

When the guard opened the vestibule gate, Edward followed him outside and stood in the snow. "We'll be here until they load all that mail," the guard informed Edward. "Get on board as soon as they're finished."

Edward walked with him to the loading platform. The air was cold and very still. Edward's breath made a cloud of steam. It was the first time he had ever touched snow.

When the last cart was emptied and the whistle sounded, the guard jumped back on board. Edward hurried to catch up with him.

"Halt!" An elderly guard stepped from inside the building and blocked Edward's way as the train began to move. "You can't get on that train! That's a troop train!"

"But you don't understand!" Edward yelled, "My brother's on that train. I'm going to Philadelphia with him!" The man grabbed his arm and held firmly as the cars slipped by. "You don't understand! I'm supposed to be on that train!"

"When you get a uniform, you can ride with the troops!" the old guard shouted, "but not until then!"

Edward made a desperate lunge, pushed the old man from him, and broke away as the last car sped past. "Wait!" Edward screamed, running down the tracks and waving his arms, "Wait! Stop! Franklin, stop the train! Stop!"

Edward kept running, stumbling on the crossties, yelling his brother's name, until the train disappeared in the distance. And he fell headlong in the snow.

Chapter Twenty-four

The town of Madison faded like an October flower. All able-bodied males, teenagers to grandfathers, were shipped out to protect Confederate interests in Tennessee and Georgia. Women left behind could not hold back the jungle of weeds and wild growth that rapidly reclaimed the land. Where well-tended farms once spread across the fields, briars and thistles now grew in abundance. In the period from 1861 to 1864, much of Florida's acreage returned to its wild state.

Food and basic necessities were scarce. Fat cattle and hogs, flocks of chicken and geese, all vanished; they were either slaughtered to feed the starving or stolen. Many women died of privation, and orphaned children became a burden to struggling relatives who were hard pressed to care for their own.

Dr. Thad reluctantly butchered his milk cow and hung her in his smoke house. Three days later, while the doctor was delivering a baby, robbers broke in and carried off the bony carcass. Throughout the state, the story was much the same. Refugees who had fled the enemy's occupation along the coast and crowded into the interior, now struggled to protect their meager belongings from thieves.

Even so, as the war continued to hammer them, they persevered with a determination defying logic.

The federal plan was to bring its final blow to the Confederacy by attacking Georgia, from the north and from the south, simultaneously. On Georgia's northern boundary, General William T. Sherman set his sights on Atlanta, and prepared for his infamous march to the sea. In North Florida, seven thousand Union troops under command of Brigadier General Truman Seymour, prepared to enter Georgia at its southern mid-section and split Georgia like a piece of firewood. Only two thousand infantrymen and several hundred cavalrymen were available to oppose the federal forces. To make matters worse, among the Union troops were some two thousand black soldiers, many of them escaped slaves, who were fighting with the same passion as those who—nearly one hundred years earlier—had signed the Declaration of Independence.

It was a cold February morning in 1864, and the wind whipped Carolyn's bonnet and dress as she stood by the track of the Pensacola-Georgia Railroad in Madison, waiting for an eastbound train loaded with soldiers. The crowd around her was in near panic. A new invasion of Union troops was pushing toward them from the Atlantic; and the trainload of Confederates, already exhausted and bone weary, were on their way to Lake City to stop them. When the train, blowing steam and scattering ashes, finally arrived from Tallahassee, Carolyn hurried from car to car, handing baked sweet potatoes through the windows to the hungry men. They snatched them eagerly.

"God bless you, boy!" she spoke with each touch of their hands, "God bless you!"

"Ma'am! Ma'am!" A young soldier called from a window. As she turned back, he thrust a crumpled envelope toward her. "Would you mail this for me? Please, Ma'am, this is for my mama."

"Of course!" she smiled. "I'll be happy to!"

"I don't have no money or postage," he added apologetically, "I hate to ask you to do that for me, too."

"I'll be glad to!" she assured him, and stuffed the envelope into her apron pocket.

As she stepped back from the window, Odessa Mallory nudged Carolyn's attention toward the loading ramp. Odessa was now a widow, having lost her husband to a long illness. Odessa wondered if it might have been Tuberculosis, but Dr. Thad was never able to give a definite diagnosis. Odessa was pointing at a small, black and white cow being prodded into a freight car. "There goes my last heifer. Them soldiers need it more 'an me."

"You're a good woman, Odessa," Carolyn replied softly.

"If my Gilbert was still alive, I'd want somebody to give him food." She turned toward Carolyn, "but look who's talking! I'll bet you don't have enough potatoes left for supper tonight."

"I'll get by. If these soldiers can manage on such a meager diet, a skinny old lady like me surely can."

As the cars pulled away from the crossing, the two women moved towards Dr. Thad's wagon. A fifteen-year-old Confederate solider lay on a straw pallet in the back of the doctor's wagon.

"He came in on the train, and I've got to get him to the infirmary." Dr. Thad spoke to Carolyn, "Would you ride along and help me get him settled?"

The two women climbed into the wagon. Carolyn nudged Odessa into the middle seat, between herself and Dr. Thad.

"His name's Theodore Lacey," Dr. Thad said as the wagon rattled over the tracks.

Carolyn reached back and laid her hand on the boy's forehead. It was apparent he was running a fever, and she patted him affectionately on the cheek. "Theodore, if there's anything special I can do for you," she said with a smile, "let me know. I'll be glad to do what I can."

He didn't answer. Instead, he reached up and caught her hand. With moist eyes, he held it close to his face.

"I'll check on you often at the Infirmary," she assured him in a loving voice, "My name is Carolyn McKay, and I visit the men there nearly every day."

The boy nodded his head slightly. He closed his eyes tightly, in a futile effort to conceal his tears.

The wagon bumped over ruts in the square as they made their way to the makeshift infirmary. Carolyn looked despairingly at emergency shelters crowded under the oaks. Tents, lean-to's, and covered wagons had become home to women, children, and men too old to be of use to the military.

Dr. Thad directed his wagon toward the buggy company where a large, adjoining shed had been converted into an Infirmary. The shed and the courthouse provided hospital space where the old doctor administered his mission of mercy, spending countless hours among invalids, wounded, homeless, and undernourished refugees.

As he stepped down from the wagon, Carolyn looked appreciatively at him. Dr. Thad was thin, bald, and in frail health. She appreciated him for all the good he did, and for the friendship he had so freely extended to her and to John when they first arrived in Madison thirty years earlier. Carolyn felt great admiration for this man, but she did not want the love he so desired to share with her.

Dr. Thad's helper, a young black man, rushed toward them as they reached the buggy company. Caduceus, like most of the residents of Madison, was thin and scrawny from a poor diet and overwork.

"Caduceus," the doctor called, "I've got another one. Help me get him in!"

With Dr. Thad and Caduceus on either side, and a little help from Carolyn and Odessa, the soldier was carried through the large open door and into the dark interior of the barn.

Harlow Bentley, holding an official-looking bulletin in his hand, hurried from the post office and followed them inside. He waited for Dr. Thad to find a place for the soldier before he spoke.

"You may lose that darkey of yours, Thad," he warned. "The Confederate Congress has just called for the draft of twenty thousand Negroes into the Army."

"When did they do that?" Dr. Thad felt anger well up inside him.

"Two days ago. February seventeenth."

"How in the devil do they think we can survive? Negro workers are all we've got left!"

"Blacks or no blacks, ain't gonna make any difference to us," Harlow answered, "if them federals don't get stopped!"

Carolyn turned quickly toward him. "How close are they?"

"Don't know for sure, somewhere this side of Baldwin. Just got word from the telegraph office at Live Oak. Our soldiers are going to try to hold them back at Olustee."

Dr. Thad shook his head. He looked about the large, makeshift infirmary, already crowded with patients. "And I thought I had trouble now!" He shook his head and turned to the two women. "You two better go on over to Mrs. Blanton's and get busy making bandages. There won't be enough bed sheets to wrap up all the wounded. As soon as fighting breaks out in Lake City, you're going to see the woods swarming with refugees."

At noon the next day, ten miles east of Lake City, the yellow pine forest at Olustee exploded with a roar of cannon and rifle fire. Bark splattered, tree tops were blasted away, and men charged each other through a veil of blue and white smoke. They fought hand-to-hand, bayoneting each other, and firing at close range. Where the railroad passed between two small lakes, the Confederates barricaded themselves in and waited for the arrival of their enemy.

Here, under tall pines, nearly nine thousand men bombarded each other. By nightfall the Union troops were in full retreat. Hundreds of men lay dead, hundreds more were wounded; and there were no locomotive engines to move freight cars of injured soldiers back to the safety of the Atlantic coast. The survivors hurriedly piled the wounded and dying into railcars and, with ropes tied to their bodies, pulled them back to the safety of Union lines. Florida's beleaguered little army had successfully repelled the Union forces, and in so doing, had extended the war.

At noon the next day, Dr. Thad's worst fear became a stark reality. A westbound troop train steamed into Madison with its whistle screaming. It came to a halt, and bystanders stared unbelievingly as scores of wounded men stumbled down its steps. They came with blood dried in their hair and on their clothing. Some were so weak, they collapsed into the dirt. Corpses of those who had died en route were laid on the side of the track. Dr. Thad, Carolyn, Odessa, and every willing townsperson came running to their aid. Union soldiers were among the gravely injured.

"My God! My God!" Dr. Thad yelled. "Where can we put them? The courthouse and barn are full!"

"Bring them to my house!" A man replied as he pushed his way through the crowd, "I have room, lots of room."

"You, Marshall? Your house?"

"Yes! Use every bed I've got! When those are full, lay them on the floor!"

Carolyn rushed to him. Marshall Cason owned the most beautiful mansion in Madison. More than any other place in the county, it had the beauty and elegance of a Virginia home. Still new and perfectly furnished, it was hard for Carolyn to imagine its linens and carpets stained with blood of the wounded and dying.

"Mr. Cason," she whispered, "thank you! God bless you!"

Wagons seemed to appear from everywhere as townspeople came to help. Within minutes the Cason Mansion, with its beautiful formal gardens and stately columns, was transformed into a ghetto of dying men, many of them screaming in agony. The kitchen table became Dr. Thad's operating table, and the gardens became graveyards.

The scene was to be repeated across the South. In July, news reached Madison that Atlanta had fallen. All of the city's beautiful homes, its hospitals, churches, businesses, and barns had gone up in Yankee smoke.

In Lake City, long rows of Confederate graves from the Battle at Olustee memorialized Florida's commitment to the cause. But the sacrifice of the fallen had now been negated, and the Union was virtually assured of victory in Georgia. Even so, hynotized by the frenzy of war, the South fought on. By autumn, the Florida Legislature was debating the use of ten-year-old boys as soldiers.

Odessa and Carolyn were heating water for tea in the living quarters they shared. The two of them now made their home in Elder Blanton's barn, so they could be within walking distance of the infirmary.

As they poured their tea, Dr. Thad stepped through the barn door. "I don't have but a minute," he said between coughs, "I've come to ask a favor."

"Yes?"

"It's about that boy, the fifteen-year-old we took off the Olustee train before the fighting. You offered to help him," he looked at Carolyn. "It's a big request. The Yankees burned his home at Cedar Key, he lost both his parents, and nothing I do seems to bring him out of depression." Carolyn waited. "His only aunt lives in Marianna, and he's asking if you'll take him there on the train."

"Of course, I will!"

"I knew you would," Dr. Thad smiled, "and though I need you badly right here, I think I can get by for the few days you'll be gone." Then he added appreciatively, "If we can help some of these youngsters survive the war, God will be pleased."

"When do we leave?"

"You can take tomorrow's train to Tallahassee, and then the stage coach from there." Dr. Thad stopped again in thought, "Are you sure you can manage?"

"Yes! Yes! I'll be fine!"

The next day, bundled against the chilling northwest wind, Dr. Thad, Carolyn, and Theodore, waited in a buggy at the crossing of Moseley Hall Road and the railroad. Half a mile away, the train rounded a curve and rattled over the trestle. When they climbed down from the buggy, Dr. Thad let his hand rest on Carolyn's waist, "Remember that we need you here, so don't forget to come back to Madison," he said flirtatiously

Carolyn laughed, "Thad! I could never forget to come back to Madison!"

"Carolyn! Carolyn!" his voice took on a serious, pleading tone, "You and I are getting old. There's no virtue in loving the dead. We need to give our love to the living. My wife is gone. Your husband is gone. We need each other." The expression in his eyes almost touched Carolyn's heart.

She steeled herself. "I'll be back, Thad," she answered kindly, but unemotionally, "and I'll go on helping you at the infirmary. Things will always be the same between us."

"But I don't want them to be the same, Carolyn! I want . . . ." His words were drowned out by the screeching of wheels on the rails.

"I'll be back within a week," she shouted above the noise. "Stay out of the wind as much as you can, and take care of that cough! If it doesn't clear up in a few days, you better see a doctor," she teased.

Carolyn and Theodore boarded the train. As it pulled away from the crossing, she and the young soldier waved. Dr. Thad threw a kiss.

Carolyn turned to Theodore, "By this time tomorrow, you'll be in bed at your Aunt Esther's house. She'll be as glad to see you as you are to see her!"

"But what if she doesn't want me? Maybe she don't have room . . . ."

Carolyn smiled and patted him on the shoulder, "Theodore, you can imagine more problems than any other fifteen-year-old I've ever seen!"

"That weren't imagining when the Yankees burned our house at Cedar Key, Mrs. McKay, and killed my mama! That was for real!"

"What about your papa?"

"They took him with 'em."

"The Yankees took him with them?" she asked in surprise. "You never told Dr. Thad that."

"No, Ma'am, I ain't wanted to talk about it."

"Are you sure they caught him?"

"I seen them when it happened, Mrs. McKay. My papa and several other men were the watch guards on our island."

"Tell me."

"Some of us escaped because the guards seen the Yankees coming and put us kids in row boats so we could get off the island. There weren't time for anybody else. When the Yankees burned Cedar Key, it looked like the whole world was on fire."

"Is that when your mama got killed?"

"Yes, Ma'am. Lots 'a folks got killed then, too. Never had a chance. Some folks escaped during the fight because they had rowboats. But Papa and the other guards, they only had a raft and poles. They didn't have a dinghy with oars. When they got into the channel, it was too deep for their poles . . . they drifted right out to the Federals!"

"Did the Yankees shoot them?"

"No, Ma'am, at least they didn't then. They took 'em onto the big ship. But there was a bunch of folks who were shot."

Carolyn put her arm around him, "Why don't you think of it this way, Theodore," She said, "You've already had your share of trouble. Let's believe that's all behind you, and things are going to get better from here on."

"That's what I was trying to tell myself back before the Federals got us at Cedar Key, Mrs. Mckay. I was saying 'it ain't gonna happen here', but it did!"

"And you survived!" she reminded him.

"Partly, I did. But my mama didn't, and I ain't sure about my papa. That's what bothers me now." He closed his eyes and spoke softly, as though confessing something dark and shameful, "I didn't even try to swim out and help my papa. I didn't even try! Next time, it'll be different! If I ever get a chance to kill a Union man, I'll do it, Mrs. McKay. I swear to God, I will!"

Carolyn fell silent. For the rest of the trip, they did not talk about war. In Tallahassee, they went directly from the train station to the stagecoach. They waited in a crowded room through the rest of the night and left early the next morning. On September twenty-third, after a wearying trip, they arrived in Marianna.

When they passed the post office, Carolyn suggested, "We can ask there about your Aunt Esther. Certainly someone there will know where she lives."

The horses slowed their pace, and the stage was about to stop when Carolyn and Theodore heard gunshots and yelling. Horses, headed in the opposite direction, galloped past them. People in the streets were running and screaming.

Carolyn and Theodore stuck their faces out the window in time to see men racing wildly past on horseback yelling, "Federals! The Federals are coming!"

Carolyn threw the door open and yelled up to the driver, "What will we do? Help us! What will we do?"

Without a word, the driver hurried the stage to a hotel. He sprang to the ground and dashed inside. Carolyn jumped to the running board and yelled, "Come back! Don't leave us here!"

Passengers leaped from the coach and ran screaming in all directions. Carolyn and Theodore started to the hotel when Carolyn spun around. She grabbed Theodore's arm, and ran back toward the coach. "Get aboard!" she ordered him. "We're getting out of here! Hurry!"

The two scrambled into the driver's seat, and Carolyn sent the horses into a galloping turn in the middle of the street. As they straightened in the road and started eastward again, Theodore leaped to the running board. "I ain't going, Mrs. McKay! I'm staying right here to fight the Yankees! I'm staying!"

The coach was racing, missing people by inches, as Carolyn held the reins and grabbed for the boy. "No! Theodore!" she yelled. "Don't leave me! We've got to get out of here! Both of us!"

The boy pulled from her grasp and sprang to the ground. Carolyn glanced backward only long enough to see him darting around horses and racing into the crowd. As she turned the coach at the next corner, a group of women screamed for her to stop. "Take us with you! Help us!"

As Carolyn pulled hard on the hand brake and reins, the women fought each other to get aboard. Hardly giving the last one time to grab the handrail, she raced forward again. At the Tallahassee Road she turned right, and a company of Confederate soldiers confronted her. "Stop that coach! Get out of it!" they yelled. "We need it!"

"This is a coach of women and children," Carolyn shouted, "Let us pass! Let us pass!" The horses jostled into each other as the company collided with the coach.

"We've got to have that coach to block the west pike! You'll have to find another way out!" The men yelled, climbing aboard, and fighting with Carolyn for the reins. "We've got to barricade the roads! Get out!"

"You'll not have it!" Carolyn shouted, holding firmly to the reins. "There are women on this coach! Get out of the way!"

Soldiers sprang onto the stagecoach from both sides and grabbed the reins from Carolyn's hands. They snatched the doors open and pulled the screaming women onto the street.

"We got no choice!" they shouted. "We've got to block the roads! Get inside the buildings and hide!"

Carolyn was thrown to the ground and barely avoided being trampled. Behind her, a woman yelled, "The church! Let's get in the church!"

The women ran together towards a steeple a short distance away. As Carolyn reached the church doors, she heard the roar of gunfire. Fighting her way through the crowd, she dove inside, fell onto the church floor, and rolled under a pew. From beneath the next pew, a woman was crying loudly, "God have mercy! God save us!"

A dozen bullets hit the stained glass windows and splattered slivers across the sanctuary. An oil lamp suspended over the altar swung back and forth from the impact of a bullet. As more gunfire exploded from the cemetery, Carolyn was struck by the realization she had chosen the worst possible place to hide. Confederates were entrenched behind gravestones on one side of the church, firing at Union soldiers positioned on the opposite side of the building. More windows shattered with an explosion of gunpowder. Women screamed, "God help us! Oh, God help us!"

Suddenly the church filled with smoke. Carolyn crawled along the floor under the pews, toward the altar and the door beside it. As she reached the front pew, the building shook with a loud booming noise, and the main window fell inward, breaking into pieces across the altar. Carolyn covered her eyes and threw herself against the door. It swung open into a short corridor leading to the outside. With rifle bullets digging into the stone wall, she dropped from the steps to the ground and scurried on her knees toward a timeworn tombstone. While the church blazed, Carolyn lay motionless in the sunken ground behind the gravestone. From her hiding place, she heard the roof of the building collapse in upon the pews.

Like the roof of the church, Marianna had fallen to the Yankee invasion. By nightfall, all was hauntingly quiet again, except for the wailing of mourners. The Union invaders carried off nearly a hundred prisoners from Marianna's already depleted ranks of men. Also confiscated were two hundred horses, four hundred cows, and six hundred black slaves.

Madison quickly learned of the Union attack on Marianna. Dr. Thad and Odessa anxiously awaited word from Carolyn, wondering whether she was dead or alive. There was no way they could have known that on the second day after the Marianna attack, Carolyn had been evacuated to the interior of Alabama. At word that the northern half of Florida from the Gulf to the Atlantic, including Madison had been invaded and pillaged by Union Troops, women hurried out of the state. Though the falsehood was soon exposed, many women, including Carolyn, were already gone. At Luverne, Alabama, in the care of an impoverished and illiterate family, Carolyn fell ill and lay stranded.

Dr. Thad grew weaker, and his coughing became steadily worse over the next few months. On the evening of February 2, 1865, Dr. Thad waited with Caduceus at the Madison railroad stop for the westbound train. He carried little with him. Caduceus sat beside him in the buggy as they watched the distant curve for the lights and whistle. This was the same spot where he stood the day he put Carolyn and Theodore on the car for Marianna. For a while, neither man spoke.

Then Caduceus broke the silence. "How long you gonna' be gone, Dr. Thad'us?"

"I don't really know, Caduceus. If the sunshine and salt air helps me, maybe it won't be too long."

"Ain't you afraid o' dem Yankees down there at Saint Marks?"

"No more than I'm afraid of dying here." The doctor looked at the spots on his handkerchief and shoved it back into his pocket, "It's a good time for me to go. The hospital has nothing but old injuries, nothing that won't get well by itself."

"If Mis' Caroline comes while you'ze gone, what you want me to tell her?"

Dr. Thad stuffed a wad of money in Caduceus' pocket, "She won't be coming back."

"You think dem Yankees done killed her?"

"I don't know how she died. I only know she would have written . . . if she were still alive . . . ."

In the distance the train whistle sounded and the old man climbed down from the buggy. When Caduceus jumped out and stood beside him, Dr. Thad hugged him firmly. "Take good care of the house, and keep the hospital swept out. Whatever Miss Odessa tells you, you do it."

The black man's eyes were wet with tears, "What if sump'in happens and you can't get back?"

"If I don't make it back, everything I own belongs to you, Caduceus. I've already arranged it all at the courthouse. Ask Miss Sally in the clerk's office. She'll tell you."

"But you gots a daughter? Ain't you leavin' it all to her?"

"No, Caduceus, she's never coming back to Madison. When she left, I knew she'd never be back. She has no use for Florida." He turned his face away. "Caduceus, you're all I have, and everything I have is yours."

"But I'm wantin' you here, Dr. Thad'us. That ole house don't mean nuttin' if you ain't in it. I needs you, Dr. Thad'us!"

"Caduceus, you'll never know just which day you'll hear me at the door. And when I come, I want you to be here waiting for me. Understand? If I'm gone a month—or a year—I want to find you right here in Madison!"

Caduceus nodded, and Dr. Thad hugged him again. "When you came to live with me, I gave you the name `Caduceus'. That means something special to a doctor. It's the symbol of healing, a staff he leans on; and that's what you've been to me all these years. I've depended on you, and you've never disappointed me."

The train stopped at the crossing, and Dr. Thaddeus got into the rear car. Caduceus carried his black medical bag and a small suitcase. He pushed them under Dr. Thad's seat.

Before Caduceus stepped off the train, the old man hugged him again. "Take good care of yourself and our little farm."

"I gonna' be waiting right here in Madison. When you gets back, I gonna' be right here!"

Chapter Twenty-five

C aduceus watched the train heading westward into the sunset. Faint puffs of smoke against a golden twilight somehow made it all seem final. Even after the train was completely out of sight, he stared at the spot on the horizon where it had disappeared. Dr. Thad'us will be back, he told himself.

Passengers were crowded into every available spot on the train. In the forward part of the car, a dozen Confederate soldiers lay collapsed against each other in exhausted sleep. To Dr. Thad, the sight of wounded soldiers had become as common as the brass cuspidors on the floor.

When darkness came and the passengers were quiet, Dr. Thad found solace in the rhythmic sound of the wheels against the track and the tannic smell of the swamp. Occasionally, through breaks in the trees, he saw stars. In the moonlight, he checked the faces of the other passengers. Convinced they were all asleep, he reached under his seat and removed the black bag. For a moment, it rested on his lap.

Then, rising silently, he walked to the vestibule at the end of the car and stepped outside. With the wind whipping his clothes and the smell of engine smoke burning his nose, he held onto the rail. For a while, he stood there. He looked fondly, yet remorsefully, in the direction of Madison. He would never go back.

He raised his black bag and opened it. One last time, he admired the gleam of the polished metal instruments. Then he dumped them onto the track. When the last glimmer was lost from sight, he dropped the bag. He watched it bounce on the cross ties and vanish into the dark.

After an overnight stay in Tallahassee, Dr. Thad caught the morning train to St. Marks. He had ridden it many times. He knew every curve the train would encounter between the Wakulla River and the St. Marks River along its way to the Gulf. On past trips when the engineer stopped to cut wood for the burner, Dr. Thad enthusiastically offered his assistance. On this trip, he felt like an engine with no firewood left to burn. His health and his stamina were gone, and there would be no rekindling of the fire of his life.

Dr. Thad stayed in a home on the town's only street, a narrow, shell-rock road that led to the three-hundred-year-old ruins of the Spanish Fort. He walked to the site daily, talked with Confederate soldiers who had fortified it against possible Union attack, and rested in the sunshine. He spent most of his time on the west side of town where the Wakulla River emptied into the Gulf. He watched schools of fish swimming in its crystal water. In these tranquil surroundings, the war seemed distant and unreal.

For the first three weeks of his visit, the weather was mild and clear. But on March 3, 1865, Dr. Thad awoke to find the town wrapped in a heavy fog. It smothered the fort, the rivers, and the tidal flats around St. Marks.

Under the cover of fog, launches from the federal ship Magnolia came ashore just out of sight of the village. The Union troops landed without resistance and swarmed the area while St. Marks slept. Residents awoke to the terrifying news. They rapidly crowded onto the train and into wagons. While the townspeople made desperate efforts to escape, Dr. Thad lingered. In the chaos, no one noticed.

He dressed himself in his dark raincoat and walked in the direction of the landing. He carried an oil lantern with a windproof shield around it, to conceal the light. Two thousand men had come ashore. They were camped on the edge of the beach, awaiting daylight. With his face covered and the sounds of his movements obscured by the pounding of high waves against the shore, Dr. Thad slipped into close range, undetected.

He was within a hundred yards of the Union troops on a small peninsula of oaks and palms when he turned his back toward them and removed the shield from the lamp. He quickly swung around, exposing himself in the light of the lantern. Instantaneously, several shots rang out in the dark. Dr. Thad dropped the lamp, clutched his side, and fell backward at the base of a palm.

For several minutes he lay unmoving as the ground beneath him turned red with blood. Slowly, very slowly, he righted himself and leaned back against the tree. He took deep, gasping breaths. For nearly an hour, he waited in the underbrush for death to come. But the blood stopped, the lantern went out; and, in the east, dawn began to break. The pain was intensifying, and his breathing was becoming more labored. As a doctor, he recognized the symptoms of slow blood loss.

The fog began to lift, revealing a grey-white sky. In the morning light, Dr. Thad reached inside his coat pocket and removed his wallet. He tossed several Confederate five-dollar bills into the wind. From the black leather pouch, he pulled out his collection of photographs. He looked at the faded picture of his son-in-law, a handsome young man with friendly eyes who had died in the Seminole War. He lovingly remembered his daughter, his only child. He knew she would have a good life in Pennsylvania with her wealthy aunt. His wife Margaret had been dead so many years he couldn't remember what it was like to be married. He remembered that he had loved her, but he could no longer recall the feelings he once had for her. Caduceus, faithful, loyal Caduceus. He hoped he had done enough to prepare Caduceus for life on his own.

These four pictures, he laid on the ground beside him.

There was one more he held lovingly with both hands. His hands trembled as he stared at the picture of Carolyn and John. She was so young, with a lace-trimmed high collar. Her pose was dignified, and her hair perfectly arranged. She was a Virginian, as regal and refined as any woman in the nation. He remembered the day he took the photo from her house, many years ago. He was there to repair damage done by Seminoles who would have taken Carolyn's life, had she not been in the barn, tending to her ailing cow. He almost smiled as he realized—Carolyn had gone to the barn that night to administer the special potion he made for her cow. He had told her it was his "All Purpose Remedy"; but, in truth, it was a unique formula, made with extra care, just for Carolyn's cow. For the first time, he realized, that potion had saved her life.

Still holding the photo, he leaned back against the tree and closed his eyes. A moment later, the wind took the pictures of his wife, his daughter, his son-in-law, and Caduceus. The breeze scattered them along the beach.

There on the sand at St. Marks, in a very private spot, Dr. Thad turned loose of his long career and his long life. He died on his own terms. He did not endure the slow death Odessa's husband had endured. Odessa would never know that it was tuberculosis that had made her a widow. She had already suffered the loss of her only son; and he had spared her the grief of living the rest of her life, wondering if she, too, would go through the same, agonizing death as her husband. He never told Odessa he knew the cause of her husband's death.

Odessa, he thought for the first time, she would have married him. She would have been a good and faithful wife. She could never have thrilled him as even the very thought of Carolyn still did, but she would have brought joy into his life. Perhaps he should have been wise enough to see that long ago. It was too late now.

Dr. Thad did not die of slow-killing tuberculosis but from a fast-moving bullet. His deepest desire was symbolically fulfilled—he died with Carolyn in his arms.

A short distance away, Union troops moved their cannons and big artillery into position for their long march to Florida's Capitol in Tallahassee. The route of their slow caravan would take them across the St. Marks River at a rock formation called Natural Bridge. There was no other way, and they knew the Confederates would be waiting for them there.

When the train from St. Marks arrived in Tallahassee Saturday night, March 4, 1865, it raced at top speed with its whistle screaming every mile of the way. It screeched to a stop near the state Capitol. As people rushed in curiosity from their homes, they were shouted the news of two thousand Yankee soldiers, already ashore and marching toward the city. But there were no troops to meet them. Panic spread like a tidal surge.

At best, Florida had fewer than a thousand men to defend its own capital. In desperation, Governor Milton ordered the cadets of the West Florida Seminary to defend the town. Sleepy-eyed boys were pulled from their beds, and guns were thrust into their hands. They were sent to Natural Bridge to stop the invaders.

As the Union soldiers approached the bridge before dawn, the woods suddenly exploded in a thunderstorm of howitzer shells and rifle fire. A volley of bullets stopped every attempt of Union forces to cross the rock span over the St. Marks. The battle lasted all day, and there was no surrendering of ground by the Florida boys. Of the entire Civil War, this was the only battle fought and won to the accompaniment of shrill voices of children. In the late afternoon, the Union bugle called for retreat; and as the sound echoed through the woods, youngsters charged over the stone bridge after the enemy. Escaping to their ship and blocking the rebels' rear attack by felling trees in the path behind them, the federal Army abandoned its assault on Florida's capital city.

Though the federal troops were moving steadily toward victory, Floridians had shown their stubbornness and invincibility. Florida's capital was the only Confederate capital east of the Mississippi River to remain unconquered through the entire Civil War.

One month after the battle at Natural Bridge, on April 9, 1865, a message was telegraphed across the land: "Appomattox, Virginia. General Lee surrenders. War over."

Caduceus watched silently as the men outside the courthouse stared in unbelief at each other. He listened as they repeated the words slowly.

Without waiting, Caduceus raced into Madison Square, screaming at the top of his lungs, "The war is over! Oh, thank you Jesus! The war is over! I'ze free!"

From across the square a group of elderly women raced toward him. One woman pleaded, "Caduceus, what are you saying? What are you saying?"

Caduceus seemed not to hear her. He shouted and sang, "The war is over! Oh, thank you, Jesus! I'ze free! The war is over!"

Odessa Mallory ran from the Infirmary and grabbed his overall strap. "Where did you hear that, Caduceus! How do you know?" He paid her no attention but kept shouting.

The next moment, several men rushed out of the telegraph office.

"Is it true?" Odessa yelled. "Is the war over?"

"It is," they answered somberly. "We lost. General Lee surrendered."

Caduceus was still dancing and waving his arms. "Bless the Name of Jesus! There ain't gonna' be no mo' war! Everybody's gonna' come home! Hallelujah! Dr. Thad'us is comin' home! An' Mis' Caroline! Jethro! Franklin, Edward, an' all the Danbury's! Everybody's gonna' be back in Madison! I'ze free! I'ze free!"

Odessa clapped her hands and joined him as a mob filled the square. Patients from the infirmary filed out into the street. Men from the post office rushed into the crowd weeping, "But we lost, Odessa!" one of them yelled at her. "Don't you understand? We lost!"

"Can losing be any worse than warring?" Odessa replied. Then she grabbed Caduceus around the neck and rejoiced with him, "Thank God, Caduceus! Thank God! The war is over!"

Raising her hands over her head and clapping in a frenzy, she shouted the words of a hymn, "Tell it all ye nations; hear it all ye dead! The war is over! The war is over!"

Chapter Twenty-six

That same morning, when Dr. Thad sneaked through the marsh of St. Marks and chose the place where he would die, Franklin disembarked from the Magnolia with the Union troops. Franklin was back after three years. He dropped to his knees, scooped up Florida beach sand in his hands, and kissed it.

During the Battle at Natural Bridge, Franklin's medical team remained one mile behind the line of fire, rescuing as many men as possible. Franklin treated an old soldier from Illinois, a man Franklin had met on the Magnolia and with whom he shared his dread of returning to Florida as an invader. The soldier's lung was punctured, through and through, by a Confederate bullet.

In a palmetto thicket where he lay dying, the old man offered Franklin some fatherly advice. "Son," he said, laboring to breathe, "this war is only hours from ending, and you're home. Don't get back on that ship. God has kept you unharmed this long, and He is able to keep you safe a few more hours until the war is over." With his final breath, he pleaded, "Don't get back on that ship, boy. Stay right here in Florida."

When the Magnolia pulled away from Florida's coast, Franklin was not on board. He stood alone in the jungle of trees close to the beach, surrounded by scattered bodies of the dead. St. Marks had been evacuated hastily. Frightened residents had abandoned their homes, some leaving their clothing, hanging on lines. It was from these, Franklin dressed himself in civilian wear.

Traveling mostly at night, he went as far as Wacissa where an elderly couple welcomed him into their shanty home in the woods.

He was with the couple when the news came of General Lee's surrender. For several weeks, Franklin waited, afraid to venture out. Not everyone in Florida accepted General Lee's decision.

It was not until May that Franklin stood at the entrance to the family lane on the Bellamy Trail. His heart was pounding out of his chest. At this very spot, he and Edward told George goodbye, a lifetime ago. The whole world had gone crazy that day. Finally, he was home again.

The trees overhung the road as they always had. Across the trail, he saw a pile of timber on George's homestead, now almost hidden by an overgrowth of weeds. The lane looked unused; but, other than that, everything was as he remembered it. A Confederate prisoner told Franklin he had seen his family, that all of them were well. Giving no further thought to the unkempt path, Franklin ran.

Familiar trees, stones, fallen logs flashed past. Little things he had forgotten were waiting for him, welcoming him. As he rounded the bend in the lane and the field opened up before him, he shouted, "Mama! Papa! Jethro! I'm home! I'm home!"

Suddenly, he halted. There was no house. The barn was gone. The smokehouse had vanished. "No! God! No!" he screamed, "God, No!" He yelled at the top of his lungs, "Papa! Mama! Jethro!"

This couldn't be so! The prisoner at Chickmauga had seen them. He had talked with them! Somehow this must be the wrong place. He ran toward Carolyn's house. At the edge of the clearing where the woods and pasture met, he saw the fields overgrown and abandoned; and he knew immediately Carolyn's house was empty.

Like a hundred thousand others across the South, his home had been washed away by a tidal wave of fire. Every hope that had sustained Franklin through the war was now gone. Madison was gone. And he had no place to go.

All the pain of the Chancellorsville and Gettysburg, battlefields rolled in upon him at one time. He had awakened from a bad dream to find himself in a worse reality. What a fool he had been to believe the good, the pure, the love in men would prevail. Fool that he was! Fools that all men were! What had his family done to deserve this? Who had the right to drive families from their homes and hunt them down like animals?

Franklin stood for a time, his eyes red and his cheeks wet with tears, silently staring and remembering. Then he started walking. He walked all the way to Brother Blanton's house in Madison, several times refusing the offer of a ride.

When he stepped into the parlor, the old man reached for his cane and rose from his chair. He rejoiced at the sight of Franklin as he would have at the appearance of an angel.

"Franklin!" His voice was frail with age but melodious with gladness. "It's you! It really is you!"

Franklin grabbed him, hugged him warmly, and wept on his neck. "I've already been home . . . I didn't know . . . I didn't know . . . ."

Elder Blanton sat down on the divan and pulled Franklin beside him. "All the other tragedies in my life," he spoke slowly, "even losing my own son Jeremiah during the Seminole War, did not bring me as much grief as what happened to your parents and their home."

"Tell me about it," Franklin said softly.

"Your father and your brother George were both hanged, and the house was burned. Apparently it all happened right after you and Edward left for the North."

Had the soldier at Chickamauga lied to him, or had he just confused his family with somebody else's family? Franklin could not think about that now. "Mama? What about Mama?" So many questions rushed through his mind. "And where is Papa buried?"

"The last time your mama was seen, it was on the Cherry Lake Road. Carolyn McKay saw her there. She was headed north. I don't know anything about your papa's burial."

"So no one knows what happened to Mama? She could still be alive?"

"We don't know, son, we just don't know." The old man rested his head on the top of his cane. "She may still be alive. I hope and pray she is, but no one really knows."

"Brother Blanton, if she is alive," Franklin assured, "I'm going to find her. And if she isn't, I'm gonna know it."

"Your mama disappeared right after Hiram Crowley was killed."

"Hiram was killed? How did that happen?"

"Carolyn did it. That dismal house on Cherry Lake Road, that's where Hiram and Francina were living. Carolyn was at that house when your papa was hanged and your home was burned. Carolyn never said why she was there, and you know Miss Carolyn. When she doesn't want to talk, you can't make her." Franklin listened intently to every detail. "Hiram turned his dog loose on your mama, and Carolyn killed both of them. Shot the dog first . . . then Hiram. That's the last anybody saw of your mama."

Brother Blanton looked wistfully out the window. "Carolyn brought Francina, Hiram's wife, back here to Dr. Thad. The doctor did everything he could for that poor woman, but she died a few days later. I visited her, prayed for her; but she never said a word to me. Strange."

"What about Carolyn?" Franklin asked.

"Carolyn stayed here. She and Odessa lived in my barn and helped Dr. Thad with the wounded soldiers. Then she just disappeared when the Yankees invaded Marianna. She went there to help a young soldier find his aunt, and nobody has heard from her since."

"I'm afraid to ask about Jethro . . . but tell me. Where is he? What do you know about him?"

"He was captured by those raiders when they burned the house and hanged your papa. Jethro escaped by killing Hiram Jr. Then like your mama, he disappeared."

Franklin bent over sobbing. "I'm going to look for Mama and Jethro until I find out where they are or what happened to them."

As he stood up, Elder Blanton rose with him and embraced him. He kissed him on the cheek and prayed for him.

"My prayers are with you, son," the pastor said as they parted. "And when you find your mama and Jethro, bring them home to Madison."

"With God as my witness, Brother Blanton, I swear I will."

From the Blanton home, Franklin walked to the military post at Moseley Hall and spent the night. The next morning on a government wagon, he rode to Tallahassee. He went first to the newspaper office where he placed an ad requesting information about his mother and Jethro. The he looked for a boarding house.

That afternoon, Franklin sat on the porch of a large, rambling house on the Wakulla Springs Road. It was owned by a widow,

Mrs. Pansy Gadsen. Mrs. Gadsen showed him his new quarters and described his roommate.

She led him to a converted pantry adjoining the kitchen. There was one large window and a wide four-poster bed nearly as big as the room. "Arnold is a young feller, and he's quieter than a mole. He's from Olustee. Been here about a month."

The following week, Franklin worked three days at the sawmill and spent the rest of his time searching for his mother. Over the next few weeks, Arnold went with him as far west of Tallahassee as China Hill, Concord, and Midway.

With not even a word about his mother or Jethro, Franklin decided it was time to move on.

Chapter Twenty-seven

Franklin left Tallahassee and headed north. Thomasville, Georgia, was forty miles away. It was new territory, and it was the western terminus of the Atlantic and Gulf Railroad. If he did not find his mother in the Thomasville area, he could take the train to Savannah.

He started walking. As he traveled over unfamiliar road, loneliness came upon him with a power he had never known. In the isolation of the long walk, he realized he could never again build a true friendship as long as he pretended to be something he was not. In Tallahassee, he had hidden his identity as a Union soldier. He resolved he would never again do that.

At times during the night, Franklin stopped, rested for a while, and then resumed his slow pace into Georgia. Two days later, he entered Thomasville. For the first time, he saw its red clay streets, wooden boardwalks, and scattering of brick buildings. And he saw that, like Madison, the town square was shaded by massive live oaks with moss dangling from their limbs. At the corner of Jackson Street and Main Street, he crossed hurriedly to get out of the way of a wagon hauling cotton bales. Another pedestrian retreated to the boardwalk along with him.

"There's as much cotton here as in Tallahassee," Franklin spoke to the stranger.

"That's something I wouldn't know about," the man replied, "I'm a sawmiller myself."

"Really? That's the kind of work I do. Do you work here in Thomasville?"

"I got my own sawmill in Quitman," the man answered, "about twenty miles from here."

"Quitman!" Franklin spoke eagerly. "Do you know Elizabeth Darnell and her Aunt Bessie Hackett?"

"Why, of course! Elizabeth's Aunt Clarabelle owns the biggest house in town. Everybody knows that family." He studied Franklin for a moment, "Where are you from?"

"Madison. Florida."

"Don't suppose you know an old preacher down there by the name of `Blanton'?"

"Elder Benjamin Blanton? He's our pastor at Blue Springs Church."

"What's your papa's name?"

"Danbury. James Danbury."

The man stuck out his hand. "Hancock's my name. Washington Hancock."

Franklin took his hand and smiled. "I'm Franklin Danbury."

Mr. Hancock turned and pointed at a gang of children running toward him from the rail yards. "You need to meet the rest of my famous family. Me and my wife had so many children, we had to get names out of the Bible and history books. She died when our fifteenth, Washington Lafayette, was born." He frowned at the memory. "Elder Blanton preached her funeral at old Zion Church."

"He baptized all my family," Franklin said.

Mr. Hancock grabbed Franklin's hand again. "Son, if that old man baptized you, that tells me more than if you'd talked for a month about yourself. The old man couldn't be fooled!"

"Mr. Hancock, I was a Union soldier."

Mr. Hancock's eyes narrowed, he folded his arms for a moment, and studied Franklin. "You don't sound like you're bragging. So why are you telling me?"

"I want you to know the truth."

"That is exactly what I meant when I said the old man couldn't be fooled! It's honesty that made you tell me that. Old man Blanton wouldn't baptize anybody he thought wasn't solid as a rock." He looked Franklin squarely in the face. "I'm a true-blue Confederate, but I'd rather have an honest Union man working for me than a cheating, lying rebel. Come to Quitman with me. I need another sawmiller."

"Do you mean that?"

"Never meant anything more in my whole life. Come on! You can't stay at my house unless you're ready to go stark raving mad. With fifteen children and no wife, I don't recommend my place to nobody; but there's plenty of other places in Quitman where you can stay."

Mr. Hancock's wagon, pulled by a team of oxen, left for Quitman in the afternoon; and Franklin shared the front seat with him and two of the boys, Taylor and Washington. The other thirteen in the back took turns standing on a syrup barrel and leaping from the tailgate to the road.

"I don't know why God wasted all that energy on young'uns," Mr. Hancock groaned. "If my sawmillers had half that energy, we'd already have cut down every tree in the county!"

When darkness fell, the wagon pulled to a stop twelve miles west of Quitman. The children scrambled from the wagon at the home of Maggie Caruthers, Mr. Hancock's sister.

"Children," he yelled as they ran toward the house, "be sure to hug Aunt Maggie's neck and tell her how glad you are to see her! Tell her a couple of times." He turned to Franklin. "If I was Maggie, I'd get out that back door fast as I could and run to the woods."

"Aunt Maggie! It's us! All of us are here to spend the night!"

Franklin lingered behind as the children took turns hugging their aunt. When they had finished, he stepped up and extended his hand, "I'm Franklin Danbury," he said. "I'm riding with Mr. Hancock to Quitman. I'm going to work for him."

"Riding with that bunch?" the woman stared at him. "You must be a brave man! A very brave man!"

At daybreak the next morning, Mr. Hancock waited in the wagon as the children finished devouring their breakfast of biscuits, cane syrup, and grits. "Hurry up!" he yelled, "We've still got a long ways to go!"

As the last ones came out the door, he slapped the oxen with the whip. Taylor and Washington ran to catch up.

Several hours later when they arrived at the edge of Quitman, Franklin studied the homes. George had described Aunt Clarabelle's house to him, and he was sure he would know it when he saw it. A short distance ahead, he recognized the elegant old building. "There it is! That big one with the columns! That must be the one!"

"It's the only one in Quitman like it," Mr. Hancock replied. "There's no mistaking that house. It's rundown now, like everything else in town, but it was mighty fine in its day."

As the wagon pulled into the gate, an elderly woman appeared in the slight opening of the doorway and stared. Her face was attractive and surrounded by neatly-combed hair. There was an air of refinement about her, even though her dress was faded and torn. When Franklin got down from the wagon and started up the walk, she smiled at him across the veranda.

"Are you Mrs. Williams, Elizabeth Darnell's Aunt Clarabelle?" he asked.

"Yes, I am," she answered politely.

"Ma'am, I'm Franklin Danbury."

"From Madison?"

"That's right. I'm George's brother."

Aunt Clarabelle raced down the steps toward him, "George's brother! I am so happy to see you! So happy!" She threw her arms around him weeping, "You're George's brother! How wonderful! Let me look at you, Franklin! George told me all about you!"

Franklin returned the hug as though she were someone he had loved all his life. It was almost like hugging his mother.

"Aunt Clarabelle," Franklin spoke with a tone of sudden caution in his voice, "I was a Union man. Some folks around here wouldn't appreciate your hugging me."

"That is their problem," she answered, still holding his arm, "We've had enough hate to last forever! If you are George's brother, that's enough for me!"

Mr. Hancock waved to Clarabelle, and called to Franklin, "Come on down to my house for the night! Miz' Williams can tell you how to get there."

"Franklin is going to stay right here with me," Aunt Clarabelle called to Mr. Hancock as he nudged one of the oxen on the rump and moved slowly from the yard. Several children had already run ahead of him toward the sawmill.

Franklin and Aunt Clarabelle entered the house with its spacious hallway, curving staircase, and once elegant interior. Aunt Clarabelle explained apologetically, "There isn't much left, Franklin, but I'm thankful for what I have. Some folks lost everything. At least I still have a roof over my head." Leading him into the parlor, she said, "There is so much that I want to ask, Franklin. I know very little of what happened to your family."

"I probably know less than you. I found out from my pastor that Papa and George were both hanged, the house burned, and Mama disappeared."

"I was not here in Quitman when George was hanged; but it was a horrible, horrible day!" She pointed toward the east, "It was right over there on that big oak in the square. And poor Elizabeth, that precious girl!" Mrs. Williams began weeping. "Forgive me, Franklin, for my display of emotion. It's just that with your being George's brother, it all comes back more powerfully." Franklin consoled her, and she continued. "Elizabeth left the same day as the hanging and never returned. She went to Savannah. She was there when Sherman took the city and was still there when I last heard from her."

"Where did they capture George? Did the Confederates hang him?"

"He was caught at Columbia Church by a mob of vagrants. They were scoundrels, Franklin, not soldiers! They roamed these woods pretending to protect us! We are still plagued by their kind. Some of them were from Madison."

"Do you remember anything about the name, `Crowley'?"

"Oh, yes! The Crowley's were the worst of those criminals; and, believe me, your father and George weren't the only ones those villains hanged."

"Do you know anything about my mother?"

"No! No! How I wish I did! And I wish I had been here. Perhaps I could have done something!" Mrs. Williams' grief was evident as she continued, "All I know, Franklin, is that your mother was found by a boy on the bridge. At the Okipilco Creek. And she was unconscious."

"Mama came to Quitman? When? How long was she here?"

"She got here three days after George was hanged."

"Mama walked all the way from Madison?" Franklin was overwhelmed with heartache for his mother. He covered his face with his hands as he leaned forward sobbing.

Aunt Clarabelle slipped her arm around him. "Yes, son, she came looking for Elizabeth. But Elizabeth was gone before she got here." Mrs. Williams hesitated before she went on, "You never knew my sister Bessie did you, Franklin?"

"No, Ma'am, I never met her."

Aunt Clarabelle paused, "She was my only sister, Franklin, but in all my life I have never known a more unloving human being. Even as a child, she was peculiar. I never once saw her hold a kitten or play with a doll. She did not know how to love. The day of her funeral I cried only for the selfishness of her life, not for her death!"

"What does that have to do with Mama?"

"The day your mother collapsed on the bridge, the boy who found her took her to Bessie's house." Aunt Clarabelle agonized for Franklin as she told him what happened next. "After everybody else left the house, my sister put your mother in the buggy and drove her back to the Florida line."

"Oh, God! Oh, Dear God! Miss Hackett did that?"

"Franklin, she was capable of being a very wicked person."

"Has anyone heard anything since?"

"There was never a trace of your mother after that. It was during a time when the area was infested with roguish men. Even women in town were not safe."

Franklin turned toward Mrs. Williams. His eyes were red and wet. "So you think she was probably killed?"

"It . . . it seems, Franklin . . . if she were alive . . . someone . . . somewhere . . . would know something . . . but nobody does." Franklin bent over again sobbing, and Aunt Clarabelle cried with him.

"I've done nothing else but search for her since the war ended," Franklin said between sobs. "There's not a place between Lake City and Marianna that I haven't written or published requests for information about her."

"That's why I have to think she's gone." Clarabelle rose again and walked across the room to the window. "If I had been in Quitman, things might have been different. But I was at the mineral springs on the coast." Mrs. Williams wiped her eyes. "Bessie died just a week after Elizabeth left. It was as if she lived only long enough to wreck the girl's life, and then she departed. I have wondered a thousand times, Franklin, why God let her live! Everybody would have been so much better off if she had died years ago! Years ago!

"Elizabeth loved George in a way few girls ever experience. She truly loved him. She wrote poems about George, she sang about him, she sat for hours in this room and talked with me about him. I think it only made Bessie hate him more. It made her more determined to destroy what she had never been able to have for herself."

Franklin's upstairs room was large, at the corner of the building. It looked down on the southeast portion of the yard and the Quitman Square. It would have felt more comfortable had Mrs. Williams not told him where his brother died. The tree glared at him like an ugly gallows only a short distance away.

Early the next morning, Franklin arrived at the sawmill for his first day of work. Franklin was cautiously friendly with all the men but did not try to join their conversations. He quickly learned that one of the men, J.W., did not like working with a Union man. In the several weeks that followed, Franklin sat with the men in the shed at lunchtime; but he stayed out of their discussions. When he could, he helped them with their work; and several times assisted J.W. without being asked.

On weekends Franklin traveled to nearby towns, posting notices and making inquiries about his mother. It seemed Dorothy had disappeared. Aunt Bessie, the person who had last seen her and might have had some information, was dead. It was as if his mother had vanished without a trace.

Autumn passed into winter, and the months of January and February were painfully cold. The skies were gray, the work was difficult, and the long weeks depressing. When April came, it was like a resurrection. Redbuds, dogwood, and wild azaleas filled the woods; and trees, turned green again with a soft, furlike covering of leaves.

The first Friday in April, the sawmill crew lined up to receive their wages from Mr. Hancock. While he had them all together, Mr. Hancock made a plea. "None of us has any extra money; I know that. But I hear the Findley sisters who live near Denmark Lake were hit hard by the winter, and they're in bad need of help." He took a fifty-cent coin from his pocket, "I wonder if some of you men can help with food, and one of you would take it to them."

The men looked sheepishly at each other and then at the ground. Franklin spoke up, "I will, Mr. Hancock. I'm the only one here who doesn't have a family to look after. If you'll tell me how to find the place, I'll get out there first thing in the morning."

"Thank you, Franklin," he answered. "It may not be easy to find. I've never been there, but I'll tell you what I know."

The next morning Franklin saddled his horse, slung a sack of food on either side, and rode out of town. He carried dried beans, cheese, flour, a small slab of bacon, and a bag of rice. Following a map on a scrap of paper, Franklin took a road on the west side of Bailey's Creek for about four miles. In the thick woods, he found the small pond Mr. Hancock had described. He went around it and looked for a trail on the east side. A short distance beyond, he found the cabin.

An hour after he left town, Franklin rode up to the shack. He noticed a patch of collard plants with stalks stripped of leaves. Except for a trace of smoke from a stovepipe, there were no other signs of life.

As Franklin dismounted from his horse, a tiny form of a woman appeared in the doorway. She stared at Franklin cautiously from the shadows.

"Are you Mrs. Findley?" he asked.

"Yes," she replied somewhat less fearful at the sight of the bundles of food strapped to the horse. Franklin smiled at her and began untying the bags.

"Mr. Hancock at the sawmill told me about you. I brought you a few groceries." As he took down the packages, she ran eagerly to the horse, her ragged and soiled black dress sweeping the ground behind her. Franklin placed the lightest sack in her arms and carried the others inside.

The woman darted ahead, calling to the other woman who was still inside the shack. "We have food! We have food, Dorothy!"

Franklin froze. It couldn't be! For a frantic second, he dared not hope. Then he bolted into the cabin and stood transfixed at what he saw. In the dim light of the room, his mother raised up in the bed before him.

"Mama! Mama!" he shouted, dropping the food to the floor. "I found you! I found you!"

"I knew you'd come, Franklin!" she cried, waving her arms toward him. "God told me you'd come! He told me!"

Franklin fell across the bed, shouting and rejoicing. He hugged and kissed his mother. He laughed, and he cried. Dorothy gripped him with all the strength she could muster, shouting his name and praising the Lord. Franklin lifted her from the bed and cradled her lovingly in his arms.

"I knew you'd come, Franklin! God told me you would! He told me you'd come!" She raised her hand into the air, "Thank You, Lord! Thank You, Lord! You told me You would 'restore the years that the locust hath eaten'! You said You would once more make me 'a joyful mother of children'!" Her frail voice suddenly became charged with ecstasy and power. "And You have, Lord! You have been faithful to Your Word!"

Franklin spent the night in the cabin. He prepared the evening meal and shared with the two women everything that had happened since he and Edward left home. In grief, he listened as his mother told of the destruction of their home, of the deaths of George and his father, of Jethro's capture and escape, of Carolyn's shooting Hiram Crowley, and of Dorothy's own rescue by Mrs. Findley.

The three of them slept in short spurts that night. Several times, Dorothy got out of bed to make certain Franklin was really there, that his arrival had not been just a dream. Franklin slept on the floor at the foot of his mother's bed. He was awakened frequently by the touch of her hand and the sound of her rejoicing, "He's really here! Thank you, Jesus! He's really here!"

Three weeks later, after his mother and Mrs. Findley had recuperated at Aunt Clarabelle's house in town, Franklin and Dorothy prepared to return to Madison. Mrs. Findley would stay permanently with Aunt Clarabelle at the big house in Quitman.

The morning of their departure, the townspeople gathered along the roadside to wave goodbye as they passed. Mr. Hancock and two of the men from the mill were there, and even J.W. sent word he was glad Franklin had found his mother.

Franklin and Dorothy were still delighting in the wonder of God's amazing reunion as they reached the state line. When they approached the rock pile marking the division between the two states, Dorothy asked Franklin to stop. She stepped down from the wagon. While he watched, she reverently crossed the boundary on foot.

"I remember that awful day, Franklin," she said, "when I passed this spot heading north. My whole life was in ruins behind me, or so I thought. But by God's grace we have both come home. Franklin, we shall complete everything God has planned for us! His grace does not fail us, and we will not fail His grace!"

They passed the site of Hiram's house and found it burned to the ground. Even the trees were scorched. Nothing remained but a charred place in the earth. Dorothy tried not to look at the spot where Hiram's body had fallen.

A short time later, they entered Madison and rode to the Blanton house. Another family now lived there. Elder and Mrs. Blanton had both passed away. Mrs. Blanton had preceded him by only a few months.

"How everything has changed, Franklin!" Dorothy said as they rode out of town and took the Bellamy Trail to their lane. "I wonder if we'll ever find Carolyn again."

As they neared their homestead, Franklin broke into song.

"Where did you learn that song, Franklin?" Dorothy asked him.

"God gave it to me, Mama. During the War—and all the time that I was looking for you—it kept me going."

At the entrance to their lane, he stopped the wagon. With no one but his mother, Heaven, and the trees to hear, he stood up and shouted the words from his soul.

"Come back, rebuild your island in the sun,
Reclaim the prize, the power of love has won,
Renew the hope that violence tore apart,
Restore the vision in your heart!"

Franklin remained standing there in the wagon long after the song was finished. His mother, taking his hand firmly in hers, wept. No longer was she crying tears of remorse or defeat; these were tears of joy.

A few minutes later the wagon stopped where there had once been a cattle gap. All that remained was a recess in the earth with rotting timbers projecting above the debris of leaves. On either side, the split-rail fence was covered with vines; and sections had fallen in. The site of the house was now a mound of blackberry briars. Nothing else could be recognized. Even the palm trees on the south side of the yard were wrapped in a thick tangle of poison ivy vines.

Franklin dropped down from the wagon and walked across the yard. A field of sage grass and pine saplings bowed before him in the wind where their pasture had been.

Dorothy followed him, "It looked like this thirty-three years ago, Franklin, when your papa and I first arrived and began clearing the land. It looked much like it does today."

"No matter how hard it is, Mama, it's got to go on being our lives."

"But it will never be the same, Franklin . . . ."

"And we won't pretend it is. But the memory of a beautiful past deserves the best we can give it for the future."

While Franklin walked around the mound where the house had been, Dorothy stared silently at the tree where James had died. Together they pushed their way through the waist-high weeds filling the area between the house and the edge of the garden. The site of the well house was hardly visible.

Franklin took her hand, "Mama, do you think you can find the grave?"

"It will take some searching," she said, looking across the field. "Jethro and I buried him at night."

Franklin went back to the wagon and returned with the scythe. "Step back, Mama," he said, as he began swinging at the briars.

Dorothy's gaze fell on a spot in the distance. "It's somewhere near that patch of fennels," She pointed toward the southwest. "That's where the okra patch was."

Dorothy pushed around Franklin and made her way through the weeds. "That's it!" she shouted. "That's it! That's where the grave is!"

Fighting through blackberry vines and briars that tore at their clothing, they broke through a cluster of fennels. "Franklin!" Dorothy exclaimed, staring at the grave in astonishment. "Who could have done this?"

The area around the grave was clean and free of weeds. The dirt had been carefully mounded, and a neatly-made wooden cross stood at the head. A bouquet of wilted daisies lay at the foot of the grave.

"Franklin!" Her eyes widened as she looked back to him. "Who, Franklin? Who?"

They did not have to wait long for an answer. A loud shout came from the backside of the field.

"Mama Dorothy! Mama Dorothy!" Jethro raced frantically in their direction. "You're home! You're home! Praise the Lord! Mama Dorothy! Franklin! You're both home!"

They hugged, they wept, they shouted, and they all praised the Lord.

"God is good! God is good!" Jethro shouted. "Mama Dorothy, Franklin, Miss Carolyn, and me all back home!"

"Carolyn! Carolyn!" Dorothy screamed. "Carolyn is home?"

"Oh, yes! Yes! Praise the Lord! God brought all of you back to me." Jethro cried as he told them Carolyn was living in her house again. He told them of the loft bed he had built in Carolyn's barn where he now lived. He told them how he helped Carolyn restore her garden; and how, near the swamp, he had cleared a portion of land and was growing vegetables.

"Miss Carolyn will be so happy to see you, Mama Dorothy," he said. "She will be so happy! She was afraid that none of you was ever coming back to Madison. But she sure didn't quit praying! That woman has learned how to pray!" In a joyful but serious tone, he added, "She ain't the same as she used to be. Miss Carolyn knows the Lord like she never knew Him before."

Jethro, Franklin, and Dorothy spent a few moments at the grave. "Papa," Franklin spoke softly toward the mound, "I'm back, and Mama and Jethro are with me. We promise you, we won't quit. You taught us how to love, and we've come home to prove that love wins!" Franklin broke into hard, racking sobs. "We will rebuild, Papa," he wept. "But we will build more than a farm. We will build a monument to God's grace! Papa, we'll prove that 'where truth once lived, its promise never ends.' We've come back to start again."

The three of them piled into the wagon, overjoyed with anticipation. Dorothy trembled with excitement. "I haven't seen Carolyn since the day she shot Hiram!"

"Miss Carolyn shot Hiram!" Jethro asked in shocked amazement. "She never told you?"

"No, Ma'am!" Jethro hung his head and quietly added, "And I never told her that I'm the one who killed Hiram, Jr. God knows I didn't want to kill anybody," Jethro cried softly.

Dorothy put her arm around him. "Tell us about it, Jethro. You never really explained to me how it happened."

"After he killed Mister Jim, Junior took me to the log jail," Jethro began. "They locked me up, and everybody left. Then Junior came back later with a whip."

Jethro leaned forward and held his head in his hands. "He came in that room to whip me, and something just came over me. I was faster and stronger than Junior. Somehow I got hold of his throat, and I didn't turn loose until . . . he was . . . dead . . . ."

"Jethro," Dorothy consoled him, "you did what you had to do to get through the war. War makes people do things they never wanted to do, never even imagined they could do. God knows your heart, Jethro."

Then it occurred to Dorothy, "Jethro, you took an awful chance coming back like you did that night."

"Yes, Ma'am, I knew I should've run out of the county as soon as I killed Junior, but I just couldn't stand thinking of you here with Mister Jim . . . and nobody to bury him right . . . ." Jethro paused. "I stole that shovel . . . just like I stole them violin strings . . . ."

"Violin strings?" Dorothy wrinkled her forehead in bewilderment.

Franklin and Jethro looked at each other. Even in the midst of recounting the horrors of war, the mention of those strings made them both chuckle. "We'll explain it all later, Mama," Franklin said. "Finish telling us how you got away and what you did all through the war, Jethro."

"After I left that night, I didn't go to Elder Sheffield's, like you told me to, Mama Dorothy. I knew what would happen to him if he got caught hiding me," Jethro explained. "Instead, I walked to the Suwanee River and followed it all the way to the Gulf. Then I got put in jail. They thought I was a runaway slave, and a man from Cedar Key, Mr. Wheeler, showed up and said I belonged to him."

Jethro shook his head. "I couldn't tell 'em Mr. Wheeler was lying. If I told 'em who I really was, and they found out I just killed a white man, it would've been way worse for me! So Mr. Wheeler took me to Cedar Key and made me work in his turpentine warehouse."

"Is that where you spent the war?" Franklin asked.

"No, I wasn't there very long at all. The Yankees burned Cedar Key. I never saw so much fire. Folks were running and screaming like it was Judgment Day!"

"So how did you get away from Cedar Key?"

"I was hiding in an empty barrel in Mr. Wheeler's warehouse, but when I heard all that screaming and hollering and smelled smoke, I decided I'd best not stay in that barrel! Just then the Yankee soldiers came in with axes and started chopping the turpentine barrels and setting 'em on fire."

"What did the Yankees do when they found you?" Dorothy asked.

"They asked me if I wanted to stay there or go to Key West. So I went to Key West and stayed there with the Yankees until the War was over."

"And how did you get back to Madison?" Dorothy asked.

"When the War ended, they put me on a boat to St. Marks. And I walked home from there."

Franklin smiled in amazement. "Jethro," he said, "God brought us both home the same way. I got off a Union ship at St. Marks and walked from there."

For a few minutes, the only sound was of the wagon splashing through the creek, as the three sat silently. Each of them quietly contemplating God's wonderful orchestration and provision, even in the seemingly insignificant details of their lives.

As they emerged from the shadows of the lane with Carolyn's field and house coming into view, Dorothy was flooded with joy. It was as beautiful as she had ever seen it. Flowers bloomed in the yard, the shrubbery was trimmed, and it almost seemed a halo hovered over the place. The clouds and blue sky framed it with a touch of glory.

"Thank You, Lord!" Dorothy prayed aloud, "Oh, thank you! Bless you, Lord! It looks just like it used to! Carolyn never gives up! She never gives up!"

As they approached the cabin, Carolyn raced out of the door. "Carolyn! Carolyn!" Dorothy shouted, "Darling! I'm home!"

"Franklin! Dorothy!" Carolyn shouted back. "I prayed night and day for this moment! I never quit believing! I knew you would return!"

A celebration—one that has been surpassed only by the celebration of a saint entering into glory—broke out in Carolyn's front yard. There was shouting and rejoicing, hugging and praising, dancing and singing, laughing and crying. In that glorious scene, even Carolyn's flowers seemed to turn their faces toward heaven in adoration.

Over the weeping and worshipping, Carolyn shouted ecstatically, "God is not finished, Dorothy! There is more to be done! 'He who has begun a good work in us will perform it.' He said it, Dorothy; and He will do it!"

That afternoon Jethro trapped a young turkey in the woods, and Carolyn roasted it. She made stuffing with wild hickory nuts, and seasoned it with rosemary from her yard. As a side dish, she stewed cattail roots from her pond; and she baked an eggplant pie for dessert.

Dorothy was thrilled to see Carolyn's gilt-edged China had survived the war. Carolyn chuckled, "I buried it in the mud between the pond and the barn."

As Carolyn poured the hot sassafras and lemon grass tea into the China cups, they all marveled at the exquisite homecoming banquet. "Oh, Lord, we thank You," Jethro prayed over the meal. "You have truly prepared a table before us . . . in spite of every enemy. Surely goodness and mercy shall follow us all the days of our lives. In the Name of Jesus! Amen!"

That night they talked themselves to exhaustion, sharing their tragedies and their triumphs, the fears that nearly devoured them during the years of separation, and now, most of all, the excitement of being home. The two men slept in Jethro's room in the barn, and the women, in the house.

As they drifted off to sleep, a glorious peacefulness settled upon the place. A holy calm spread over the woods and washed the weary pilgrims in assurance. For the first time in many years, there was a complete freedom from fear. And, even more than that, there was wonderful anticipation; they knew they were on the edge of God's great climax.

Franklin was the last to fall asleep. The words of his father's favorite hymn filled his mind. He had heard it with his ears a thousand times at Blue Springs Church; but tonight, for the first time, he understood it with his heart.

There shall I bathe my weary soul
In seas of heavenly rest,
And not a wave of trouble roll
Across my peaceful breast.

Chapter Twenty-eight

Daybreak came, golden and beautiful, announced by a thousand chattering birds in the woods around them. Franklin and Jethro filled the wagon with tools. Then they rode to the Danbury homestead and began clearing the land in preparation for the new home.

Franklin and Jethro worked from sunup to sundown. Friends from Blue Springs Church and from Madison came to help. Even some, who had once been their bitter foes, offered their assistance.

Dorothy and Carolyn made daily trips to the Danbury farm, bringing lunch to the men and inspecting the progress. During one of those noontime visits as Dorothy prowled about the cabin site, her foot struck a dark piece of metal, protruding from the soil. With tears filling her eyes, she lifted a long iron bar from the charred dirt.

"Franklin! The fire poker! The wedding gift from my brother Tom!" she shouted, gripping it like a lost treasure. "Look! It's as strong as it was on my wedding day, just like the Bible verse Tom gave me along with it!" She wept joyously as she kissed the rusted end, "'May the Lord watch between me and thee while we are absent one from the other.' God even watched over a fire poker while we were apart. How much more has He watched over each of us!"

In the joy of their new beginning, one thing still troubled Dorothy. As much as she and Carolyn loved each other, Carolyn still kept her past behind a veil of secrecy. One morning over a cup of tea, the veil was lifted.

Carolyn and Dorothy sat at the kitchen table after Jethro and Franklin had headed off to the work site. "In all our years together, I've never told you the story of my family . . . my father . . . my sister . . . especially about Hiram . . . and the whole ugly account." Carolyn confessed, "it was pride that kept me from being open and honest with you."

Dorothy interrupted her, "Carolyn, you don't have to tell me anything! I love you regardless!"

"I know that, Dorothy, but I have been unfair to you, not telling you the whole truth from the start." Carolyn began to sob, "Junior was not Francina's son. He was my son, my only child."

"Your son?"

"Yes. Yes, I was his mother. He died without ever knowing."

"Hiram Junior was your son!" Dorothy was incredulous.

"There's so much to explain, Dorothy. You will find this difficult to believe; but Hiram was once a wonderful, exciting man. He was a brilliant young attorney with a promising career. My father hired him to work in his law firm."

"Carolyn! That doesn't seem possible!"

"But it's true. Everyone in Washington loved him, including me. We were engaged to be married, and our wedding was going to be the big event in Washington society."

Dorothy took another sip of tea as she tried to absorb the remarkable story unfolding before her.

"I never told you about my father. Dorothy, he was a magnificent man! I don't think Virginia ever produced a finer judge and statesman." She looked at Dorothy with sorrow in her eyes. "My father was a good man, and he suffered terribly."

"But what did that have to do with Hiram?" Dorothy asked.

"Hiram seemed so charming and intelligent. None of us knew there were two different people living inside of him. Soon after our engagement, he became violent and raped me."

"Oh, Carolyn! Carolyn!" Dorothy reached across the table and took Carolyn's hand.

"I found out I was pregnant, Dorothy, but I refused to marry him. I did not want to spend my life under the control of a violent rapist! But Francina wouldn't believe me. Francina and I had always been so close, but she wouldn't believe anything I said about Hiram. I desperately tried to convince Francina and my parents, but no one would listen to me," Carolyn gripped Dorothy's hand, as if trying to draw strength to go on.

"Francina accused me of having the baby by another man who had once courted me. It was horrible, Dorothy, horrible. Francina was totally deceived by Hiram. By the time she realized what he was, they were already married!

"Hiram finally admitted to her that he was my baby's father. And too late, my father saw through him. Dorothy, I didn't want to put my parents through the humiliation of a daughter raising an illegitimate child." Carolyn dropped her head to the table and sobbed. Her body trembled as she told her friend, "I went away to have my baby . . . and then I gave my baby to Hiram and Francina to raise . . . the worst mistake I ever made . . . Oh, God, the worst mistake of my entire life!"

Dorothy put her arms around Carolyn, and Carolyn wept on her shoulder. "I so regretted giving up my baby! I desperately wanted to be with my son, Dorothy. That's the only reason I endured Hiram in my house. I just wanted to be close to my son!"

"Carolyn! Carolyn!" Dorothy wept along with her. "You poor dear! You've suffered so much pain, with no one to support you!"

Carolyn wiped the tears from her eyes. "Hiram destroyed everything! Francina withdrew into a shell, and she never came out. She was a talented, skilled musician; but she never again touched a piano. Hiram destroyed her, and he destroyed my father."

Carolyn paused for a moment to calm herself. Then she continued, "You may recall there was enormous chaos in Washington between the administrations of President John Quincy Adams and President Andrew Jackson."

"Vaguely," Dorothy replied, "only vaguely. I wasn't really following politics in those days."

Carolyn poured another cup of tea. "In 1828, very near the end of President Adams' term, Supreme Court Justice Trimble died. President Adams announced he intended to appoint my father to replace Justice Trimble as soon as the election was over. Dorothy, my father was above reproach. He would have been a wonderful Justice, but Hiram saw to it he didn't get the appointment."

"How in the world could Hiram do that?"

"Mrs. Jackson suffered an awful character assassination during the campaign. Rachel Jackson was a divorcee, and questions about her morals and the legality of her marriage to Jackson came up during the campaign. As you know Jackson defeated Adams, but only a matter of weeks after the election, Mrs. Jackson died. Jackson blamed his wife's death on the stress of the brutal personal assaults against her. Rachel Jackson was buried on Christmas Eve, in the dress she had planned to wear to the inaugural ball."

"Oh, how tragic! But what did all this have to do with your father?" Dorothy asked.

"Hiram convinced President Jackson my father was the source of the personal attacks on Rachel." Carolyn shook her head.

"There was tremendous bitterness between the two Presidents, and my father got caught in the middle. Mr. Adams and my father both supported the Anti-Masonic Party, a one-issue party devoted to ridding the country of Free Masonry. Before he became President, Mr. Jackson was the Grand Master of the Tennessee Free Masons. So that was another source of contention between Mr. Adams and Mr. Jackson, and one more blow against my father."

"Oh, my," Dorothy said. "I had no idea there was so much strife in Washington, D.C.!"

"Hiram used that strife and contention to destroy my father's career, and he did everything he could to destroy my father personally. He even went so far as to tell President Jackson that I had given birth to an illegitimate child. Of course, Hiram didn't tell the President he was the father of that child! He made himself look like a hero in the President's eyes for protecting the family name by raising the child of his wayward sister-in-law!"

"Oh, Carolyn, what a burden of grief you've carried!"

"Dorothy, Hiram ruined my father's reputation and his career! He destroyed my sister's life!" Carolyn wept bitterly as she poured out her heart. "And it was my fault! It was all my fault! If only I had never fallen in love with Hiram, none of this would have happened!"

"Carolyn, Carolyn," Dorothy comforted her. "It's not your fault. It's not your fault! No matter what mistakes you made, Hiram raped you! You didn't cause Hiram to rape you! It was the evil in Hiram that brought so much suffering to you and your family!"

"I haven't told you everything yet, Dorothy. There's more I want you to know about me, and about Francina." Carolyn took a deep breath and continued, "Francina and I weren't just sisters, Dorothy; we were identical twins. We looked and acted so much alike, people had difficulty telling us apart. When we looked at each other, it was like looking into a mirror," Carolyn smiled. "We used to joke with each other. I'd tell her how beautiful she was, and she'd tell me how beautiful I was."

Dorothy said, "Carolyn, if Francina looked just like you, then she truly was beautiful!"

Carolyn continued her revelation. "A few years after Hiram and Francina married, he went totally berserk and had to be committed to an asylum. John and I married during that time and left Virginia. We knew if Hiram ever got out of the asylum, someday he would come looking for me. John thought, if there was any place we could escape from Hiram, it would be the wilderness of Florida."

Carolyn turned her face away, "For over fifteen years, I thought I had escaped Hiram. But he found me. He probably got the information by charming someone in the Land Office."

Looking again toward Dorothy, Carolyn said, "You have no idea how I welcomed our escape to Florida. The day John and I met you and James in Madison, you were such a wonderful relief from the awful scandal we tried to leave behind us.

"I'm so glad I told you, Dorothy," Carolyn looked lovingly at her dearest friend. "It's out in the open now, and it's out of my life. I am free of its control. In spite of the war and all the torments we've been through, I absolutely know that the rest of my life is going to be good! Dorothy, I finally have the inner happiness Elder Blanton preached about. I have 'the peace of God which passeth all understanding', and I will not let it go!"

Four months from the day Dorothy and Franklin returned, a new house and a new barn stood majestically on the sites of the first cabin and barn. This house was much larger than the original cabin. It was a two-story home, with an upper and lower porch across the front, fireplaces at both ends, and an entrance hall. The high ceiling, large rooms, and openness welcomed all who entered. But this was not just a bigger building. The first cabin had been the seed; this was the full-grown stalk. Dorothy and James had built a cabin with an unknown future; now she gazed at a beautiful, new home with a triumphant past. The first cabin ended in disaster, crisis, and failure. This house testified to success, victory, and accomplishment.

As they prepared to light a fire in the fireplace, Dorothy recalled a night, thirty-three years earlier when James built a fire, and they ate their first meal together in the cabin. That first puff of smoke from the cabin's chimney marked the beginning of their life together. Now as the first puff of smoke went up from this new chimney, it boldly declared the truth of one of Dorothy's favorite Scriptures. Franklin etched it on a board and nailed it above the fireplace.

A wise man . . . built his house upon a rock:
And the rains descended, and the floods came,
And the winds blew, and beat upon that house;
And it fell not: for it was founded upon a rock.

On Friday morning, October 5, 1866, while Franklin and Jethro burned piles of rubbish in the field, Dorothy walked to the new cattle gap and leaned against a fence post. The fresh bite of autumn was in the air, and the fire-red leaves of sumac and dogwood blazed in patches along the lane.

For nearly thirty years, the lane witnessed the good and the bad that had come into their lives. Sunlight filtered through limbs overhead exactly as it had the wonderful day she and James stood under the oak and Elder Blanton pronounced them husband and wife. Dorothy could still picture the sun shining on her mother's pink taffeta bonnet. That afternoon, as Mama, Papa, and Tom waved goodbye from the lane, none of them knew they would not meet again until eternity. Elder Blanton had come down this lane with the news of the Fort King massacre, and later with Jethro, dripping wet in his arms.

Of all the children, Edward loved the lane the most. When she could not find Edward, she always called in that direction. His boyish voice had answered so many times in reply that she could imagine hearing it now. At the bend, she envisioned him coming toward her, his blonde hair shining in patches of light and his young frame bouncing with every step.

Between the shadows and splashes of sunlight, she caught sight of something moving in her direction. She strained to look. Was her imagination playing a game? It was not the frame of a boy but of a man that limped toward her.

"Mama!" a loud and robust voice called. "Mama!"

Rushing toward her as fast as his crippled leg would allow, Edward raced up the lane.

"Edward? Edward!" she shrieked, raising her hands as she ran to meet him. "Is it you, Edward? Is it really you?"

He grabbed her with all his strength, buried his face in her hair, and sobbed.

"You're home! You're home!" she shouted, "Edward, you're home!" Lifting her eyes heavenward, she let out a shout of absolute praise, "Oh, Lord! Oh, Lord! You brought him home! Thank you Jesus, You brought my boy home!"

They darted across the yard, under the oak, past the house, and into the field. "Edward's home!" Her voice echoed across the farm, "Franklin! Jethro! He's home! Edward's back!"

There was a moment of utter silence. Then from the backside of the pasture, a shout of triumph and joy, of happiness and fulfillment, arose. It went higher than the column of smoke that spiraled into the bright Florida sky.

Franklin and Jethro ran. Edward and Dorothy ran. They shouted, leaped, and yelled. The earth rang with the sound of their rejoicing.

Overhead another cry was heard. A Red-shouldered Hawk, gliding in hourglass patterns, dipped low over the field to proclaim her welcome. The ones below were not invaders; they were restorers. Near a cross-marked mound of earth, she watched them collide into a long-belated embrace.

The End.

Come back and hear,
The song of peace is sung.
Lift high your voice,
And cast aside your gun.
Its music pours
Through every open door.
Come back,
The War is o'er!

Come back, Come back!
To home fire's hope and trust,
The victory of love
Cannot be crushed,
Where truth once lived,
Its promise never ends,
Come back and start again!

Come back, Come back,
Come back to Madison.
Reclaim the prize
The power of love has won,
Renew the hope
That violence tore apart.
Restore again
The vision in your heart.

Epilogue

"And we know that all things work together for good, to them that love God, to them that are the called, according to His purpose." Romans 8:28

On her 85th birthday, Dorothy sat in the familiar pew at Blue Springs Church, the one she and James had shared so many Sunday mornings. These days her family filled several benches near the middle of the church. Under the ministry of Pastor Sheffield, none of her family sat outside under the arbors during services.

Today was not a Sunday. It was a Thursday in September of 1899, and the building was empty. For Dorothy, this sanctuary was a storehouse of memories. Her joys and sorrows, triumphs and trials, all seemed to be recorded in its timbers. In the solitude, she reflected on milestones of her life—her marriage to James and the loss of her parents and brother, the births of her children and the untimely deaths of three of them, her widowhood and years of separation from everyone and everything she loved, and the blessed restoration of three sons and her dearest friend.

Dorothy shared the large home, built on the site of the original cabin, with Edward, his wife, and two children. Across the way on George's homestead, Franklin lived with his wife and four children. Jethro and his family lived in a spacious home, expanded from John and Carolyn's cabin.

For many years, Jethro had held onto the hope that his natural parents might still be alive. He never found them; but in his search of Seminole villages, he found himself a wife. Carolyn, at the age of eighty-eight, had gone home to her heavenly inauguration. She left all her earthly possessions, including her China tea set, to Jethro, his Seminole wife, and five children. No child had ever grown up calling Carolyn, "Mama"; but Carolyn lived the final decades of her life in a family where five children grew up calling her, "Grandma."

Dorothy had experienced life in two realms. She had answered "The Call" to live whole-heartedly in the natural world yet fully in a higher reality. She had lived victoriously. Her feet solidly planted on the earth, but never entangled in the world. Her heart firmly fixed on "things above."

A reunion even more spectacular than her restoration to Franklin, Jethro, Edward, and Carolyn, anticipated her arrival. While she waited for that "Final Call", Dorothy rejoiced over her eleven grandchildren, all raised in the "nurture and admonition of the Lord." God had restored to her "the years the locust hath eaten;" and once again, made her the "joyful mother of children."

Ten miles outside of Madison along the Bellamy Trail, the Florida of Dorothy's dreams had become a reality. A family of Floridians—red, black, and white—lived in peace, together enjoying the blessing of the Lord.

It was "exceedingly abundantly above all" Dorothy had thought or asked.

LaVergne, TN USA
10 October 2010
200287LV00004B/3/P